A TWIST OF FATE

A
TWIST
OF
FATE

A NOVEL

SE-AH JANG

TRANSLATED BY S. L. PARK

BANTAM
NEW YORK

Bantam Books
An imprint of Random House
A division of Penguin Random House LLC
1745 Broadway, New York, NY 10019
randomhousebooks.com
penguinrandomhouse.com

Originally published in Korean by Aphros Media Seoul, South Korea, in 2023.
Hardcover ISBN 978-0-593-87514-8
Ebook ISBN 978-0-593-87515-5
Printed in the United States of America on acid-free paper

1st Printing

FIRST US EDITION

BOOK TEAM
PRODUCTION EDITOR: *Jocelyn Kiker*
MANAGING EDITOR: *Saige Francis*
PRODUCTION MANAGER: *Jane Sankner*
COPY EDITOR: *Jacob Reynold Jones*
PROOFREADERS: *Debbie Anderson, Michael Burke, Lara Kennedy*

Book design by Edwin Vazquez

The authorized representative in the EU for product safety
and compliance is Penguin Random House Ireland,
Morrison Chambers, 32 Nassau Street,
Dublin D02 YH68, Ireland.
https://eu-contact.penguin.ie

To my mother,

In-ho Kim,

My affliction and my remedy

Poor whims of fancy, tender and un-harsh. They are the enemy to bitterness and regret, and sweeten this exile we have brought upon ourselves.

—From *Rebecca* by Daphne du Maurier

PART

·1·

CHAPTER

· 1 ·

Can I reset my life? Can I hit delete and start over from a perfect clean slate?

These are the only thoughts drilling into my mind as I sit on a train that's picking up speed and leaving the station. On this foggy Sunday morning, my compartment's thankfully empty but for me. No breathing bodies nearby. Not a single soul apart from myself.

Earlier, shivering all over, I'd taken shelter in a dark corner of the station and waited for the first train to arrive, and when it finally did, my knees almost buckled from the surge of relief. No, I can't think about the price I had to pay for this escape route yet. Later, much later, when I'm alone and feel more like myself. When all this has blown over and I have cleared my head.

I'm leaning back in my chair, with my legs outstretched in front of me, when the door to the car flings open. My heart drops to my stomach. I quickly duck under the backrest of the seat in front and steal a cautious peek from behind it.

A woman has just walked in. A young mother, hair tied up in a bun and a baby in her arms. The large bag on her shoulder seems to be dragging her down with its weight. As she saunters her way through the aisle and closer to my seat, the young mother finds me and beams, eyes lighting up. What a twist of fate—finding a woman my age in an empty car this early in the morning.

The young mother seems unmistakably relieved at the sight of a fellow female passenger her age, despite my obvious discomfort. She stops at her seat just across the aisle and struggles to stash her bag into the small overhead compartment. I want to keep as low a profile as possible, but I cannot bear the sight of her fumbling around alone. I spring to my feet and help her tuck the bag overhead.

She returns a grateful smile. "How kind of you! My arms were about to fall off. You won't believe how heavy this little baby can be!"

But her smile evaporates faster than it appears. I feel the woman's eyes on my arm and scramble to pull my sleeve down. The sleeve hiked up when I lifted the luggage, showing the bruises on my wrist that had already begun to turn a horrible purple. I hurry back to my seat after exchanging an awkward, silent smile.

A quick glance tells me her baby is fast asleep and won't be crying loudly during my trip. I still have no idea where my destination will be or how far I'll be going, so that's one less thing to worry about.

There's no turning back now. The hard part's over, so no need to fret over a complete stranger who happened to spot some bruises on my wrist. Let's not act suspicious and let's just go back to avoiding eye contact, hiding behind the backrest and acting like a typical unfriendly passenger.

But the young mother, who now seems more relaxed and completely unaware of my wish, retrieves a formula bottle from a pocket in her luggage and says to me, "I had to hurry out today, but the formula cooled down just right."

She drizzles droplets of milk on the inside of her wrist to check the temperature and nods with satisfaction. What's with all this unguarded cheeriness and friendliness? I'm actually starting to worry that she won't leave me alone, acting all bubbly and nosey.

"Oh, you should see how this chubby one eats," she continues. "I always have to feed him on time, otherwise he becomes a little wailing devil."

The woman carefully holds the bottle to her baby's lips, feeling for the temperature again, but he's lost to the world. He's cute, with pinkish new skin, cherubic cheeks, and doe-like eyelashes.

I ask, out of politeness more than anything, "How old is he?"

Even before the words leave my mouth, I have a feeling I might get myself into trouble, but I can't help myself. What if she starts to chat and pry?

"He's three months now. He was born on December 12, so it's easy to remember."

There's something disarming about the woman's smile, and I'm smiling back despite myself. Without a trace of makeup, her face betrays the fatigue of a young mother looking after her infant child day and night, but she is a beautiful woman. She's fair-skinned with luxuriant hair and big dark eyes that turn light brown in the sun. She's about the same height and weight as me, but our similarity ends there. She is the kind of person who lights up everyone around her with her contagious smile. Had I walked a different path, made different decisions in the past, could I have become someone like her? Maybe I could have been a bubbly young mother, too.

"We've been running around since dawn to catch the first train, so this little prince is just not having it. I give up."

Shaking her head, the young mother wraps the bottle back up and puts it away.

"Spring must be coming late this year. It's still so chilly in the morning," says the woman, wrapping her baby tighter in a blanket. I get the feeling she's not going to leave me alone. But getting up out of nowhere just to move to another compartment, where there might be other nosy passengers, seems too much of a risk. Better stay here and engage halfheartedly. Who knows? Maybe she'll be my alibi. Unless she's going to be a witness? What should I do? As all these thoughts run through my mind, the woman asks, "How far are you going? Seoul?"

"No, um, I don't think so."

"I'm going to Juyoung-si, you know, the new city near Seoul?"

Juyoung-si? I haven't considered it an option. "What is it like?"

"My in-laws live there." The woman lowers her head with a hint of hesitation and smiles lightly.

I can't think of anything else to say, but it's unnecessary as she continues without pause. "Actually, we've never met before, but I'm just betting on the proverb that blood's thicker than water. I have no plan whatsoever."

"Oh, could you mean . . . ?"

"Yeah, they haven't even seen the kid yet, because I—we—got married even though they didn't approve."

For the first time, I make out a sign of agony on her face.

"Can I ask what happened with the baby's dad?"

She hangs her head and strokes the baby's right foot, which is sticking out of the swaddle. "He ran off with another woman. I thought he got into an accident when I couldn't get hold of him, but it turns out, he just wanted to move in with his mistress. I wish him dead, you know."

I cannot find words to respond, as my chest is getting tight. My breath catches in my throat. I force air in, out, in, out, nervous sweats making my arms slick. I can't lose my cool over mere words, can I? I've still got a long way to go.

The young mother in front of me is in her late twenties at most, and can't be far from my age. But she has already married a man whose family didn't accept her, started a family of her own, and even gotten dumped by her husband. There are people of all stripes and from all walks of life, for sure, and everyone comes with a fair share of trouble. You never know what someone passing you on the street, or on the train, is going through. I was probably too quick to judge her by her seemingly bright smile.

"I was all about how the only thing that counts is that we're together, but now that things have turned out the way they have, I have no one to turn to. My parents died when I was little, and I don't have any family or relatives. I've thought about raising a child on my own, but I don't know how."

The woman lets out a deep sigh.

"I don't know what my in-laws will say if I just show up out of nowhere. Maybe they'll just take my son away. I mean, my husband comes from money. You know, the kind of rich people so conservative and judgmental that they pay you to keep your mouth shut just because they don't want to hear your voice? My husband is the eldest son, too."

"So you've never met his parents before?"

"Yeah, they probably don't even know what my name is or what I look like. My husband was already living away from home when he met me, and he said he hadn't spoken to his family in a while, so I figured there was no way they'd approve of us getting married. You know how these people are—heartless, never cutting you any slack."

She shakes her head in disbelief. "I can't imagine how you could just cut off your son! I can't ever stay away from my son, and I'll forgive him no matter what, no matter whom he chooses to marry. But I guess not all parents are the same."

This morning, when I'd fled my house at dusk and hidden myself at the train station, I surely didn't imagine an encounter like this waiting ahead. But here I am, lending this woman an ear as she vents about her secrets.

"I know I'm such a coward—I didn't pay his parents any mind when I was so in love with my husband, but now I'm crawling back for scraps when I have my back against the wall. But I can't raise my son as a single mom. Not in this economy."

"I feel you."

"There's just so much I want to do for my son that I can't afford."

She almost looks like she's about to break down.

"I don't mean fancy clothes or shoes. I just want the best for my child. He has such a wealthy grandfather, and why should my son live in poverty and not see a dime from him when the old man can't possibly spend all that money on his own before he dies?"

The woman stares down at her infant.

"What's my pride, anyway? I'll kneel before my father-in-law and beg for his forgiveness if I need to. Don't you think this cute baby will melt their cold hearts? He's their blood, after all. Life is so short. Anyone can drop dead at any moment, so why hold grudges and shun your family?"

I don't know why, but the look she throws gives me chills, her bright chestnut-colored eyes boring into the depths of my soul. But her words ring true. Any one of us can drop dead, any moment.

CHAPTER

· 2 ·

When the young mother hands me a carton of soy milk, I realize I'm famished. Since I ran out with a wallet and nothing else on me this morning, I haven't eaten anything.

As the announcement of our imminent arrival at the first station rings through the aisle, we look across at each other and exchange brief smiles. Since listening to her vent about her life and in-laws, I've started to feel a secret sense of solidarity with the young mother, although, of course, given my situation, that's a stretch.

The car will start to get packed with more passengers from the next station onward, and this fragile feeling of peace will quickly wane. Our conversation will die down, and we'll be safely back to being two complete strangers again, before finally going our separate ways. I'll never see her again.

"It's still a while before Juyoung-si, isn't it?" I ask.

"Yeah, probably another hour or so."

I excuse myself before the young mother has a chance to say more. "I have to go to the restroom before it gets too packed in here."

When I throw a quick look behind, I find the mother gently rocking her sleeping baby. His soft skin and full eyelashes are a perfect mirror image of her, no need for a DNA test.

As I step out into the corridor, I feel a rush of relief. The train restroom proves to be in much better condition than I expected, with all kinds of amenities. To be fair, I have never traveled by train, unable to afford the fare.

He promised me countless times that he would take me to a nice place, that we would go on a trip together, but he always came up empty. Still, I like to believe he meant it. Sweet words that made you want to believe—he was good at that.

"Jae-Young, what do you think about Seoul?" he asked.

"Seoul? Really? I've never been there!"

"Then maybe we should go together sometime."

"When? Can't it be this weekend?"

"That's great, but don't you think we should have a talk first? You can't go on a trip with someone you don't trust."

"Someone you don't trust?"

That's when something crept into his voice. "Don't you have anything to say to me?"

"What do you mean?"

Whenever something like this happened, what I needed to do couldn't have been simpler. He had already made up his mind and reached a conclusion, and I just needed to act according to his script. But no matter how hard I tried each time, I could never figure out just what his script was about. After everything that we had gone through, I should have been able to read his mind, but I could never get it right, not once.

"You know, someone called you while you were in the shower."

"Who?"

"Your boss."

"Oh, I see."

"Don't you have anything else to say?"

"Do you mean the staff picnic? Everyone's so into the idea. I mean, we never really even got to planning, but this time, Soo-Jung is quitting soon, so we decided to go for real."

"A picnic? I wasn't talking about that."

"Oh?"

I could feel a sense of dread creeping into my abdomen. I was falling for his trap again.

"I was talking about how you're taking a day off next week. Your boss called to ask if he could swap you with someone else. Some scheduling conflict."

His good-looking face hardened with each word, threatening enough to make it hard for me to breathe. I hadn't gotten it right this time, either. As usual, he had set me up and hoped for some sort of confession from me, hoped that I would reveal something he could twist—that would give him an excuse to explode.

"So, a day off? How come you never mentioned it?"

"Huh?"

"Did you swallow your tongue?"

He took a step forward, and I took a step backward. The half-basement rental we lived in was so damn small that it only took one step to literally have my back against the wall, but I pressed myself there as if my life depended on it.

"Hee-Jung asked me to tag along while she picks out her wedding dress, that's it."

"I don't believe you."

"It's true! Call the boutique! Or Hee-Jung. She set a date. That's all there is to it!"

"So when were you going to tell me?"

He moved closer. Over six feet tall with broad shoulders and long legs, he always towered over me with his overwhelming presence. Handsome, with a baritone that won women over, and he even smelled good. A perfect stud. But whenever he zeroed in on me like this, all the hairs on my forearms stood on end.

"I was going to take a day off next week, so I was going to tell you this weekend, or even later today!"

"What about the picnic? When were you going to tell me about that?"

He grabbed my wrist. Gently at first, then with increasing force. I looked down at my wrist clenched tightly in his large hand.

When we first started dating, it all just added to the butterflies in my stomach—how different we were. He was large while I was dainty. Standing next to him, I always felt waifish and feminine, like some doted-on only daughter from an aristocratic family. It never failed to astound me how his large hand completely enveloped mine, and we'd even joke we were Beauty and the Beast.

But his large hand was also good at breaking my fragile wrist with the slightest pressure. And the wrist would break with a clear popping sound, like a pencil tip snapping off. Like the sound of your knees popping when you stand up after hours of sitting down. And then I'd be unable to work, with my arm in a cast.

Everyone at the barbecue place where I worked was really nice about it and let me manage the counter until I fully recovered, and, genuinely worried, told me to be careful not to slip in the bathroom again. No one thought that my "princely" boyfriend had anything to do with it. They would say things like:

"When I was getting off work, I saw Jae-Young's boyfriend holding her by the waist and smooching her like this, huh?"

"Wow, like in *Gone with the Wind*?"

"Yeah, yeah! Love wasn't just in the air but reeking all over!"

"Oh, the honeymoon phase! I could use a little love myself. My babe is getting old and can't even aim very well in the bathroom these days."

"Ew! Sis! Nasty!"

And then we would all close the store giggling uncontrollably and walk out into the dark night together. All the while, I would laugh along. I'd never had a family in my life, but I finally had someone passionately in love with me and showering me with attention. I didn't tell anyone how that passionate lover was giving me bruises where people couldn't see, and how, at night, whenever I rolled over, a terrible pain knocked air straight out of my lungs, or that I now censored every word before it came out of my mouth.

"I haven't even decided if I'm going to the picnic yet. Let go of me!"

"So you don't talk to me before you make a decision like that?"

"Well, I was going to . . . Ouch! Let go!"

"Are you ordering me around now?"

"That's not what I meant!"

Just one look at his face, and I could tell we were back in the same place. Back to one of those moments when he would turn into someone I hardly recognized. Once he did, the situation would quickly get out of hand. And nothing could stop him. No amount of rationalizing. Then, soon, there would be nothing but a gripping hand and so much pain that my eyes would roll back in my skull and I would see white.

CHAPTER

· 3 ·

I catch a glimpse of how pale I look in the bathroom mirror and splash water on my face, trying to bring back some hint of life.

There's no time to wallow right now. I have to figure out my next step. I can always reminisce later. Later, once everything's in the clear and I'm sure I'm safe. Where to go? I have no one in this world, which means I can go anywhere, but I also can't really hide forever since I won't have any support.

This train heads for Seoul. In such a large and sprawling city, it would be easy to blend in, but how would I make a living—how would I survive in a place like that? A lump at the back of my throat seems to be growing and growing as I ponder these questions.

Just then, there is a frenzied knock at the door. The train has apparently stopped at the first station, because I can hear people talking outside. I quickly wipe my wet hands on a paper towel and open the door. An elderly woman is in such a hurry that she shoves me aside and runs into the restroom before I even manage to let myself out. The corridor between the cars is packed with people who have just boarded the train.

The day is now in full swing, sunlight flooding the train. I hear a baby wailing somewhere. Keeping my head down, I make my way through the crowd and step into my car. A few people have entered through the door on the other side and are storing their luggage on the shelves at the far end.

As soon as I walk in, one of the passengers looks over and waves her hand. "Oh my God, you're back. Mama, you can't just leave your baby here and go off somewhere! I thought the poor thing was abandoned! Hurry along, your child needs you! He almost looks like he's choking!"

What?

I stagger back to my seat as the train starts moving. *And look here—* the train has become just like a game of hidden objects. Same seats, different pictures. The young mother is nowhere to be found.

The sun has snuck in and is now making large patterns on my seat. Across the aisle, where the woman was sitting, is now only her baby, curled up and wrapped in a tiny blanket. As if he hadn't been sleeping like an angel, he's now heaving with a full-blown wail, furious, his face getting red. I look on the shelf and see the mother's luggage is still there. I try to explain that I'm not the mom, and maybe she just went to the bathroom.

But they're already settling in and chattering away among themselves. An old man loudly complains a few seats away. "Thought I was going to have a quiet ride, but no luck today."

I scoop up the crying baby and look around. This side of the car is still largely empty, the only passengers being us and an old couple who have just stepped in. The rest is a sparse cluster of solo passengers here and there, all of whom do not amount to more than a handful of people.

Did she need to use the restroom so badly that she couldn't wait for me to return? Why on earth did she leave her child alone like this?

I'm nearly deafened by the sound of the baby screaming in my ear. I think he's hungry, but I have no idea what to do. I clumsily pick him up and rock him gently, just as I've seen on TV. When his eyes were closed, he looked like a doll, but now it's as if I'm holding a hot iron ball.

The train suddenly jolts and almost knocks me over with the baby in my arms. Growing more impatient by the second, I walk over to the far end of the car where the old couple is sitting and ask them, "Hi, did you see by any chance the other woman who was with the baby—the one with a bun?"

"What? We haven't seen her. By the way, the baby's been crying since we got here. You can't just leave your baby with a babysitter. It's not like the old days! And please do something, would you? Maybe you should change his diaper. He's crying his eyes out!"

An old lady glances over, shooting daggers with her eyes, so I back off quickly. What choice do I have? I'm tempted to tell this old couple that the baby's mother has suddenly disappeared and ask them to help me alert the authorities, but I can't be put on the spot in my current situation. It's too dangerous to draw attention. No one will forget the young woman who refused to comfort a wailing child. I wouldn't forget a suspicious woman who was fidgeting with an infant baby in her arms, would I?

I can very well imagine how this old couple will excitedly tell the police, "The baby was crying so loud we couldn't help but look over and notice the woman was somewhat out of sorts. She seemed distraught, and she went on to claim that it wasn't even her kid!"

No, no more attention. Back at my seat, I gently put down the riotous baby and reach for the woman's luggage on the shelf. Inside the heavy bag are diapers, the bottle I saw earlier, and other items for the baby like his clothes and bibs. The formula bottle feels lukewarm to the touch now. I cautiously lift it to the baby's lips, just as the young mother did. He whimpers like a puppy and stubbornly keeps his mouth shut at first, resisting the bottle. But when I rub a few droplets on the corner of his mouth, he licks his lips and soon starts sucking vigorously.

With the baby not wailing anymore, I feel my shirt sticking to my sweaty back. The old couple glances my way now and again, and I stoop to hide myself behind the seats in front. The baby sucks hard on the cooled formula. His dark eyes and soft skin and pink hands clutch the bottle tightly, like a lifeline.

I let the baby wrestle with the bottle for now and carefully look around again. The scenery outside the train window is rushing by, and if the woman didn't get off at that station earlier, she's probably still on this train somewhere.

But the elderly woman from earlier is just coming out of the restroom on this side of the car, huffing and puffing, and from the one on the other side emerges a middle-aged man with a cell phone in hand. That means the young mother isn't in the restroom at either end. Even if she'd been in a hurry, would she leave her infant child to go to the restroom in the next car? I've never had a baby or raised a child, but even I know that's ridiculous.

Was she planning on leaving him on the train from the very beginning? Had everything she'd said been a lie? Clearly it was all so farfetched, like a soap opera, but she'd acted like a decent person. She'd seemed nice and sweet and good-natured. I could see the apparent love in her eyes. But what, beneath it all, was she plotting?

Yes, I know now people don't show their true colors right away. Just like there are people who whisper sweet words in your ear one moment and turn into monsters ready to beat you to death the very next. Love is a dangerous, unpredictable emotion that will uproot your life in a heartbeat. I know this for a fact, so I'm sure there are also some people out there who will do everything in their power for their children and yet be overwhelmed by the gravity of feeling too much love all at once.

As the baby furiously gulps down the formula, I sit fighting this unshakable feeling that I'm not going to find the young mother anywhere on the train. I've barely calmed the baby down, but he's starting to cry again now that the bottle's almost empty. My anxious eyes spot a diaper sticking out of the woman's bag. I've never had to change a diaper in my life, but at first glance it doesn't look too different from a sanitary pad. At this point, I am prepared to do almost anything to keep the baby from causing more of a ruckus. As I carefully unwrap the blanket, praying it's not time to change his diaper, my fingers stumble upon a small folded note.

CHAPTER

· 4 ·

I'm so sorry to spring this on you. I know we've only just met, but I beg you, please take my child to my in-laws in my place. I didn't mean to do this, I really didn't, but you looked like such a good person. The truth is, I don't have the courage to go to my in-laws without my baby's father.

I never even got a marriage license—I got dumped for another woman before I could, but you know, I really loved him, and I have no idea how to go on living like this on my own. I've thought some terrible thoughts, too, but whenever I look into my son's eyes, I just can't do it. An irresponsible mom like me had better disappear. Please take care of my son.

You have the address of my in-laws below. Just ask anyone about "Chairman Jung's house," and you'll have no problem finding it because everyone in Juyoung-si knows the Jung family. My son's name is Seung-Joon Jung. We haven't gotten the birth certificate yet, but he's up-to-date on all the vaccines. He's just been weaned, so you can feed him formula, and he sleeps like a log because we've done a good job of sleep training. If he cries, just rock him gently. He's a very amenable baby who will go right back to sleep if you do. He's got atopy on his legs, so if he seems uncomfortable from the itch, please apply the lotion that's in the bag.

Please tell my in-laws that I'm a coward if you need to, just so you won't get in any trouble. I know this is a big favor to ask. God bless you!

I'm about to lose my mind. What a rash decision! Look how she's scribbled all this down in such a short time. I didn't think she'd be the kind of person who would entrust her infant child to a complete stranger, but obviously I was dead wrong. Hadn't she looked very calm and collected, with a bright smile? And so eloquent. She must have been going through a lot since her husband left her.

And what had she said about me—that I looked like such a good person?

She'd misjudged me completely. Nor did she have an inkling of what I'm capable of. *What have I gotten myself into?*

We were both way off in our first impressions of each other. I debate my options, looking between the baby, who's fast asleep, and his mother's note. What should I do with him, just leave him on the train? Have a breakdown right here and cry myself to death on the spot? I can just get off at the next stop if I want to. He's just some girl's baby, after all, and I can't be held responsible for someone else's child when I've got my own nose to the grindstone.

Then it dawns on me.

When you're running away from something, you can't act predictably. At times like this, you shouldn't do what makes sense, what anyone expects you to do. In a movie, when you're being chased, you go around in circles and throw the chaser off your tracks, go to the places they'd least expect. To places you've never been to and that no one associates with you, where you'd be unrecognizable. No, you don't run toward a big city full of people, because your sanctuary will be somewhere unexpected and unfamiliar.

I glance down at the address scribbled in an obvious hurry and pocket it. Maybe, just maybe, this baby will be my lifeline instead of my undoing.

CHAPTER

· 5 ·

"Well, this is the place, I'm telling you!" the taxi driver yells at me for the third time.

"Sir, I don't think this is it. This doesn't look like someone's house at all."

"I just followed the navigation, and this is the correct address!"

It was a short drive out of town, past a housing development of luxury townhouses, and now we're here in the middle of nowhere, no other houses in the vicinity.

The taxi driver has dropped us off on a dead-end street leading to a wide, uphill path at whose far end stands a massive iron gate. A long, high wall flanks the heavy gate, and what's behind the gate is completely hidden by overgrown shrubbery and overhanging branches. It looks more like the gate to a huge national park than to a family home. The driver must have brought us to the wrong place. There's no way this is the right address.

"If you gave me the correct address, this must be the place, so just take a look around and see if there's a doorbell, would you? I don't know what you were expecting, but this must be a grand place."

The driver ushers me out, turns the car around, and drives away, mumbling how it's well past his shift thanks to me.

I'm left standing alone on the verge of panic, a sleeping baby in my arms, a diaper bag at my feet.

This morning, the only thing I had to my name in this world was a thin wallet, and now I'm carrying all this around like a pack mule. And I've arrived at a destination where I have no idea what to expect.

The baby thankfully has stayed asleep through all this, but my arms are getting exhausted. I haven't eaten anything except for the soy milk the young mother gave me on the train, so I'm now feeling sick to my stomach after having gone through a series of unbelievable events. I'm beginning to doubt I made the right decision. I can't believe I'm on a stranger's doorstep to drop off someone else's child, when *my* life's a big mess and I'm on the run.

As I step closer, it looks all green behind the gate—lush shrubs and long hanging plants form great walls like in *The Secret Garden,* obscuring whatever lies beyond. All around me is deafening silence. I grab the iron gate and give it a few good shakes. After a few minutes, when no one comes, I debate making a scene to get someone's attention. Maybe there's an intercom or some kind of doorbell I have yet to find?

I'm practically pressing my nose against the gate, peeking through the bars, when there's a violent movement in the tall grass. The green leaves swaying a few feet away part to reveal the sun-kissed face of a man, startling me.

"Dear God!" I take a step back, lose my footing, and almost fall to the ground with the baby in my arms. I quickly grab the gate with one hand and steady myself.

"What are you up to?" the man asks coarsely, out of breath and glass-eyed. His voice comes out raspy, like the sound of fingernails scratching a chalkboard, and as he speaks with a hint of impatience, I catch a glimpse of jagged teeth between his purple lips.

"Well, I am here because . . ." I can't seem to find my voice, too stressed out and startled. "I've come here because . . ."

"No solicitors welcome here. You should count yourself lucky that I'm in the middle of something right now. Go home!"

After spitting on the ground, he starts to turn away in quick strides and shoves his way back through the leaves.

"No, it's not like that!" I burst out, stepping forward. If I miss this chance, I don't know where I would go with this child. "Wait a minute!

Is this Chairman Jung's house? If so, I've brought someone he should meet! Look here!"

A moment of silence. It falls so quiet that I can hear my own heartbeat. I swallow hard. Footsteps on dry grass and twigs. The man reappears from behind the bushes.

"What's that?"

A waft of sweat hits me in the face.

"Who the hell are you, and what kind of craziness is all this?"

"I was on the train, and you know, it's just . . ."

It's only then that I realize I don't know what to say, and I have come to make this outrageous claim with just a small infant in my arms, no proof, no idea of his mother's name or her husband's name, for that matter. Even if the house indeed belongs to this Chairman Jung, I don't even know if he is in fact the young mother's father-in-law.

"I've brought Chairman's grandson, his own blood. His name is Seung-Joon. He's the child of Chairman's eldest son."

I thrust the baby toward the gate to give the man a better look. For a while, he studies the baby with his sallow eyes, giving me and the child a hard look, and then he disappears again without uttering another word. As if he were never here, and the lush greenery just sucked him right back into some wormhole.

Now I'm completely drained. I knew this was all nonsense. I should have just left the baby on the train. Someone would have found the note and gotten the baby the help he needed. Why did I get involved with a woman I didn't even know? Why did I go out of my way to come here in the first place?

Should I just leave the baby on the doorstep and run away? But what if this is actually the wrong place? What if I made a mistake? I can't be on the run with a baby attached to my hip, can I?

A loud buzz takes me out of my agonizing thoughts, and the gate in front of me clicks unlocked. For a moment, I stand glaring into the green world beyond the gate before decidedly pushing through. A few steps in, I hear the gate lock again with a loud clang.

CHAPTER

· 6 ·

Behind the iron gate lies another world.

After a short walk along the trail through the lush shrubbery, I round a corner to an unbelievable view. The dense vegetation, I realize, is there to protect and conceal all this.

I had no idea there was such a paradise in South Korea, especially in a small town like Juyoung-si.

Before my eyes stretches a large expanse of lawn with what must be an Olympic-sized pool and a few lazy chairs with umbrellas around its edges. Centered around the pool are well-manicured plants that sprawl in every direction. Besides the pool, the lowest level of the terraced garden is decorated by a large freshly mowed lawn, with a pretty wooden bench on one side of a tall staircase wrapped in foliage. A few steps up the staircase, a grassy stone path winds up the second terrace to the house, which sits high up overlooking everything.

The house itself boasts large windows, spacious verandas, and ivy climbing up the sturdy stone walls. It's an impressive, grand Western-style mansion straight out of a foreign film. It looks more like a small hotel or resort than a family home.

I stomp across the grass, past the pool, and put more distance between myself and the iron gate. When I reach where the stone staircase begins, I crane my neck and look up at the massive mansion. I've never seen anything like it before. It's as if I've been dropped in an entirely different world. How could I have known an old mansion like this would be hidden behind a jungle?

Standing here, sweaty, my bare feet dragging my worn-down slippers with every step, I become painfully aware of how out of place I must look in this surreal environment. The baby in my arms is as heavy as a stone, and the bag on my shoulder threatens to separate my arm from the rest of my body.

Still, I can't help gawking at the house, and I hardly notice when someone sneaks up on me. I freeze on the spot, a scream catching in my throat. A sudden movement like this has always been triggering for me, since it usually leads to so much violence and pain.

I turn around, breathing heavily, to find the man from earlier. He seems well into his fifties, but too young to be elderly—a web of fine lines and scars runs across his face, and from his shabby shirt and many-pocketed work pants, I can tell he's probably one of the house staff.

"I didn't catch your name?" He approaches me, but I take a step back without answering him. The man looks disgruntled by my silence. I explain, raising my voice and clutching the baby to my chest: "I'm here to see the Jung family."

"They're not home right now."

The man spits again, and labors out a gurgling, hoarse voice, as if there's a pitchfork scraping his throat. "The chairman went to the hospital. And this isn't a place for strangers to barge in."

"But you invited me in, didn't you?" I've already made it halfway; I'm not about to turn back now.

The man limps a few steps closer. I quickly start climbing the stairs. The man yells in a threatening voice that makes the hairs on my back stand up. "Hey!"

"I'll wait inside until everyone gets here, then. Don't you think they should see the child at least?"

I don't know where the courage has come from. Part of me knows I have nowhere else to go if I get kicked out, but in truth, I also want to see more of this wonderful house.

"Well then—" As the man opens his mouth to say something more, we hear the sound of a door opening.

"What's going on?"

I turn around to see an elderly woman in an apron standing at the door of the mansion. I hurry up some more stairs. The baby and the bag are slowing me down, but I'm feeling newly energized. All I can think is how this is my last stand.

"I'm here to see Chairman Jung. I've brought his grandson." I shove the baby in front of the woman, whose eyes grow big as saucers.

"Oh my God, what's all this?" She takes one look at me and looks at a loss for words. "Mister, you can't just let anyone in!"

She shoots the man an annoyed warning as I try to explain: "I'll wait until everyone's back. I need to show them the kid."

"That's not up to us. No one's in a position to invite you in, miss. The chairman's not here right now, so come back later."

"You never know," the man blurts out in his squeaky voice behind her as the woman keeps shaking her head. "Think about the trouble we'll get into if by any chance that's really his grandson. You know how long he's been waiting."

At this, the woman glances nervously at me, then the baby, then the man standing behind her. For a while, with the woman trying to decide what to do, I stand in complete silence, waiting, and suddenly realize I haven't heard birdsong, not a chirp, since I set foot in this garden. It's dead silent here.

"They'll be back in about twenty minutes," the woman says, "so I guess you can wait and talk to them yourself." Finally, the woman makes up her mind. "The chairman doesn't tolerate any nonsense, so if you're not who you claim to be, you'd better leave now."

Am I completely mistaken to sense genuine concern in her hasty words?

Maybe this wasn't a good idea. Maybe I should turn around and get out of here before it's too late.

But right now, I have no other choice. I have nowhere else to go, no one to help me. If not yet, pretty soon, someone will find out what I've done. I'll be looked for. I'll probably have to pay for what I did.

But not yet . . .

"Okay, I'll wait, then."

I subtly raise my head a little higher and remind myself I'm the one who brought this family's grandson all the way here. A poor little baby abandoned by his parents, both of whom ran away like the irresponsible shits they are. But me, I've come here with good intentions, and there's no reason to back out now. If I get paid for this, it may even help me stay in hiding for a good while.

The woman reluctantly opens the door to the house and holds the door for me to enter. As I turn around in the doorway, the man's bloodshot eyes stare back at me.

He almost seems to make sure I'm really getting into the house. Or even that I will be safely stored away inside and won't have a chance to run away. I know it's irrational, but I'm momentarily possessed by this thought.

I shake the thought out of my mind and follow the woman into the house.

Behind me, the door creaks before shutting with a definitive clang.

CHAPTER

· 7 ·

For a moment, I can see nothing but complete darkness.

Once my eyes adjust to the dark, I can make out an enormous stairwell that stands before me, curving elegantly upward from floor to ceiling, out of sight. The ceiling soars absurdly high, the old parquet flooring groans with each step, and all the windows have heavy curtains draping over them. The slightest sound echoes through the entire body of this house that is also otherworldly cold. The moment the front door closes behind me, the warmth of the sun outside disappears. It's dark inside, the air stale. Could it be that once the air gets trapped here, it can never escape?

I follow the woman into a large room to the right of the stairwell. It's bigger than my past two cramped studios combined. A couch made of soft velvet, chairs of all sizes, and a small table occupy the room without cluttering it. The cabinets and the small table tell me this must be a living room of some sort. It's also graced by a floor-to-ceiling window, but even in broad daylight, the room is dark, with the thick curtains drawn to block out light.

The woman tells me to sit down and quietly leaves the room after a glance at the sleeping baby. It's bizarre how little sound she makes in this noisy old house, but maybe her slippers are some sort of magical device.

Once I'm left alone, I finally have a moment to catch my breath. I set my bag down on the floor and carefully look around the room, cradling the baby in my arms. The thick, fluffy rug and the chairs that come in all imaginable patterns and shapes have been put together to create an exquisite impression of harmony, and in the heavy-duty vases are fresh flowers that I've never seen before.

Taking in all this with awe, I rest my hip on the couch, which sucks me right into its soft swaths of fabric. I scramble to steady myself, but the baby hasn't even batted an eyelid, so I guess the mother was right; he's an easy baby.

As I'm trying to settle into the upholstered couch, the door opens to let in another woman much younger than the one who ushered me in. She sets a tray with teacups on the table and keeps stealing glimpses at me and the baby. She's probably in her thirties, with a light mouth and heavyset hips, but her uniform makes it hard to gauge her age. Aren't house aides all a bit older nowadays? But it's probably great pay with a reasonable workload, considering it's just dressing up nicely and managing a beautiful mansion. It's probably better than most grueling work out there. I don't know what the Jung family is like, but people are unpleasant everywhere, so dealing with all that in a better setting, within four safe walls, might be a much better bet.

When the woman leaves with the empty tray, but only after having a good look at us, I pick up a teacup and take a sip. I'm no tea connoisseur, but I do know that the teacup alone would have cost a small fortune. I down it in one gulp and turn it over to see "Made in England" emblazoned on the bottom.

When I first heard the phrase "wealthy in-laws," I didn't think much of it. I just assumed they were a bunch of stuck-up elderly people who lived in a nice, spacious condo and drove to church every Sunday in a foreign car.

But this is another story. This doesn't fall into the range of simply "well-off." This is generational wealth you don't even fantasize about. A level that defies common sense. Even a commoner like me can tell. A mini mansion with a pool and a labyrinthine garden, with a stretch of walking path from the front gate to the house sitting afar? We're talking about floor-to-ceiling stairwells the height of five meters. A house guarded by a mysterious man—I can't even tell if he's a gardener, handyman, or gatekeeper—with at least two maids ready to greet guests at all times.

This is the kind of place I would never have set foot in my whole life. It's a place of untold riches that the likes of me could never get their hands on, even if we tried our hardest.

What would it be like to live in a house like this and be served by people waiting on you hand and foot every day? I wouldn't have to lift a finger. I wouldn't need to worry about next month's rent. I can't imagine the kind of life where I don't have to cower in fear of my live-in boyfriend and dread when a fist is going to fly, where I don't have to always be on guard, figuring out how to respond the right way.

The boy's mother must have known, even marginally, about the wealth her husband came from. So why would she give up a chance at this? No one, not even the fabulously wealthy—like this family—can take all their riches to the grave. All of their worldly possessions will inevitably be passed down to the next generation.

She would have needed to put up with a bit of humiliation, sure, but just until the in-laws died, which eventually they would. Was it such a grim outlook that she had to give up her son, entrust him to a complete stranger, and run away? Even if her husband abandoned her, the aging in-laws surely wouldn't have deserted her. No, maybe they would have even doted on the grandson instead of the runaway son and provided for him and his mother. Either way, it was something to contend with, so why didn't she bet on that very likely possibility?

The vague expression from her letter flashes before my eyes: "An irresponsible mom like me had better disappear."

What could she have possibly meant? Did it just mean that she'd stay out of her child's life and never show her face again, or maybe something else? What kind of love is so desperate that you're willing to leave your child behind?

I stare down at the bruises on my wrist.

I know love doesn't last forever. That sounds like a cheesy commercial, even if it's true, but there is something that outlasts love—

That's when I hear the front door open, followed by the creaking of old floorboards and the sound of people talking.

The family must have finally returned. My heart starts pounding against my chest, my fingertips growing numb. It's finally time for me to explain myself. I stumbled through it unprepared earlier, but now I have to get it right. I only have one shot to do a good job of explaining how this baby came to be in my care.

I hear someone running briskly, closer and closer. Before I have a chance to straighten up, the door swings open.

"You're my brother's wife, aren't you?"

CHAPTER
· 8 ·

First impression: very put-together. Sharply cut pants, an expensive belt, a crisp shirt tucked in, a nice jacket to finish the look—an ensemble to flatter a flat stomach.

Above the torso sits the kind of face that brightens a room when he walks in. A wide grin that seems to have no cares in the world. It's a stranger, but one who looks oddly familiar.

I spring to my feet.

"Oh, I could not believe it when they told me, but . . ." The man rushes over and stands right next to me to look at the baby in my arms. I can tell how tall he is—at least a full head taller than me—but his face makes him look like an innocent boy, much younger than he probably is. "Is this him?"

"Oh, I mean . . ."

"Wow, this little guy really has my brother's eyes!" the man exclaims, then looks at me. "Oh no, I scared you." He takes a step back, holding out his hands, and smiles wryly. "When I got the call, I couldn't believe it—I ran over right away." Then he takes a quick look around the room and his welcoming smile slowly fades. "But I guess you came alone, right? Of course, I expected as much."

That's when I hear a commotion in the doorway. The man throws a glance back and warns me in a low voice, "Look, please don't talk about my brother. I don't think there's much hope for him, but my dad still hasn't given up."

I have no idea what he's talking about, but I hold my tongue.

I feel like I'm caught in a whirlwind, everything unfurling so fast, so frantically that I can't keep up.

"Take your time, take your time."

A gray-haired man in a wheelchair appears in the doorway with a man by his side urging him to take it slow. His body's strangely contorted, his wrinkled face distorted, but his eyes shine with discerning intelligence. One corner of his mouth, twisted and slightly upturned, gives the illusion of a permanent sneer.

A burly man follows the wheelchair close behind. Based on his short haircut, simple clothes, and comfortable sneakers, not to mention his forearms toned from physical work, I can tell he's a physical therapist or attendant, not a member of the family.

"Father!" The young man turns around and exclaims, "Look, it's my nephew! My sister-in-law brought him here! He looks just like my brother!"

"Oh, well . . ."

He shouldn't just start calling me "sister-in-law," now, should he?

I'm not exactly trying to defend myself, but it's not as if I'm just going to let things get out of hand. I try to explain myself, but my feeble protest is lost in the shuffle. The sudden commotion even entices a few house staffers into the room, and they're all now surrounding me, looking curious.

"I had such a weird dream last night, and look at what's happened!" I can see the corners of the young man's eyes getting slightly wet, his eyes growing red.

I raise my voice to finally explain who I am and why I'm here. "Would you please let me speak?"

But the words barely leave my lips when the room suddenly goes silent. The old man's motorized wheelchair has pushed through the small crowd and makes a beeline for me. Instantly, alarm bells go off in my head. The kind that tell me to watch out right before a fist is suddenly thrown or an argument starts. It's that gut feeling letting me know something's going very wrong.

It's not too late. Just hand over the baby, say goodbye, and walk away—after, yes, maybe getting paid for all my trouble—because that's been the plan all along. I'm sure they'll pay me off well, and I can just take the money and run off to hide somewhere.

As I stand, the old man grunts and twists his body as if to stretch out his arms. His aide quickly comes over and pulls his arms out of the blanket covering his lap. The old man winds his neck to look me in the eye, and gives me a piercing gaze that makes me tremble with fear inside. All the people in the room hold their breath. After a moment's hesitation, I carefully place the baby in his arms. The aide quickly slides in a cushion to support the baby.

The moment the old man twists his neck again to look down at the baby, the baby opens his eyes. What perfect timing. Everyone gasps—me, the young man, the aide, and all the staffers. The baby's big, black eyes take in the image of us, a makeshift family who's come together under the strangest circumstance. But the baby doesn't break into a wail as earlier. Instead, his face brightens up with a big smile. The pure kind that makes you sigh. And it seems to captivate the old man. The old man writhes, letting out an odd sound that resembles a mumbled question. He looks up at me, his eyes filled with tears. I don't know what to say, so I nod.

"It's your grandson."

He nods back, tears now streaming down his face and drooling out of control. A soft moan escapes his distorted mouth, which is covered in spit.

"Father, why are you crying? This is a happy day. It's like my brother's returned!"

The young man grabs and shakes his father's arms, smiling. This is my last chance to come clean. Everyone's happy and smiling, so this is it.

But for some reason, I can't do it. I mean, where would I go? Some people are probably searching for me already.

"I'll get out of your hair, then."

I force myself to make for the foyer, but something stops me: the old man's hand clutching the end of my threadbare hoodie. And suddenly, the young man's standing close to me again: "You're not just leaving like this, are you? We've got a lot of catching up to do, don't you think? We've just met each other!"

"I can't possibly."

"Don't you have something to tell us? Isn't that why you're here?" The young man looks at me intently. I feel like I'm about to be sucked into his big jet-black eyes. "It doesn't feel right to let you leave like this. Please?" The man smiles slightly. "Just one meal, yes?" His tone is coaxing, almost pleading.

I fidget, looking around the room. Everyone's looking my way now. Anticipating. And I can't seem to bring myself to reject all these people and make an exit.

Maybe I'm safe here, in this impenetrable mansion, among strangers. No one knows I'm here except for the young mother. And didn't she say, after all, that an irresponsible mom like her had better disappear? And if I'm right, she's probably gone, in the worst sense of the word.

The old man mumbles.

"See? That's what my dad wants, too, so why don't you tell us your story when we sit down and eat?"

I look around once more. The old man's body may be emaciated and his face contorted, but his clothes shimmer like silk, and on the young man's wrist shines an expensive wristwatch.

I look down at my old hoodie stained with the baby's drool, then at the bruises on my wrists peeking out of the tattered sleeves. The bruises that have turned purple, as it turns out, become the dealmaker.

This is a safe haven no one knows about.

Yes, I will have to leave here someday, but not today. Not right now. The rest is so easy, once I realize the dire situation I'm in, and the right words to say at this moment.

"Of course I will, Father," I say, smiling at the old man in the wheelchair.

CHAPTER

· 9 ·

"For such a big old house, it's totally unprepared for guests, so I'm afraid this will have to do. But this room comes with a separate bathroom. You'll be comfortable here with the kid."

Despite what the young man says, my room is not just adequate.

It's twice the size of my place, and heavenly compared to my cramped half-basement, which always has bitter wind blowing in through warped windows, and whose only perks are a toilet, no hot water, and a shabby kitchen.

On the other hand, my room here in this mansion is almost eerily large. It has dark hardwood floors and a spacious bed in the middle. A wide-open window looks out onto the sprawling garden, half hidden by laurel trees and branches.

"I've stocked the cabinets with towels, but if you need more, look under the sink. It's usually warm here, so this comforter should be enough for the night."

The older woman who first showed me in and the younger one who brought me tea earlier have both followed me in and soon busy themselves rearranging the room. They lay out fresh, clean bedding and bring in some beautiful cushions and pillows. It already looks impeccable to me, but they fuss over every little detail, worrying it's not up to standard after having been unoccupied for so long, and they keep dusting, vacuuming, and mopping while I stand there with the baby in my arms, feeling uncomfortable and singled out.

I leave them to the fuss, and I sneak off to the en suite bathroom. There's a huge bathtub, a mirror, a sink, and a separate shower stall. How many rooms like this are there in this house?

The young man—the younger brother to the dad of this baby—has accompanied me and notices the look on my face. He tells me, "Since my dad fell ill, he's been a little sensitive, and we've rarely had any guests. But this room used to be my brother's, so we've been diligent with the upkeep." His voice quivers ever so slightly.

I doggedly avoid his eyes, pretending to coo at the baby. Somehow I've gotten caught in the middle of all this drama, but I can't keep it up for long. If this baby's real father, or the young mother, shows up on the doorstep, it's all over for me. So it's best to stay here until I figure out what to do next and then just take off.

"But I waited and waited and waited, hoping that maybe someday he would come back. But he didn't show up, not even once. All these years. I don't know about my dad, but honestly, I've given up." The young man sweeps locks of his hair out of his face and looks up, sighing. Our eyes meet, and my heart skips a beat. "So where is my brother now? Are you two in touch at all?"

I shake my head no. For now, I'll just have to go with the flow and think on my feet. Thankfully, he doesn't seem to know what his actual sister-in-law looks like, so the young mother at least didn't lie about the estrangement. The only thing this young man seems to know is that his brother and the young mother were living together before he had a change of heart and abandoned her, but I can't let this guy keep nosing around and asking too many questions.

I steal a glimpse at my left ring finger. It's a good thing I'm wearing a ring, even if a plain, cheap, unadorned one. A rich man's son, after leaving home penniless to earn his own living, would never have been able to buy the young mother a fancy ring. Try as I may, I can't remember what kind of ring the young mother had on.

"Can't say I'm surprised." The brother turns to the open window with a bitter smile. "My brother's always been that way, even before he left home. Moody, selfish. He's changed so much since the incident. But I think it's just an excuse."

The incident? What could he mean?

"He must be out of control again," he continues. "I thought he'd change after marriage. Seeing that you've come all this way without my brother, though . . . Oh my, I didn't mean to offend."

"Oh, I mean—speaking of marriage, we haven't had a chance to register our marriage yet." For now, I'll just have to parrot what the young mother said: "I thought he'd change once we had a kid, too."

"Change? My brother?" The brother lets out a laugh and shakes his head. Partly knowing, partly bitter, partly mocking, even slightly condescending in the face of my naivety. "He always disappoints you, doesn't he? No matter how many times you give him the benefit of the doubt."

He continues, sounding somewhat wistful, "I used to think the same, and placed trust in my brother even when no one else did. I thought, each time, that things would turn out differently. I don't know how many years I wasted thinking that and hoping for the best. Sister, I hope you don't get your hopes high. He's not one to change easily."

Our eyes meet again as he raises his head and looks me straight in the eye. Maybe I'm mistaken, but for the shortest second, his wet eyes shine with a flash of what looks like anger, though it's gone in the next second. He bites his lip slightly and looks down at the baby again.

"I want to think it has to do with the baby," he says, stroking the sleeping baby's cheek with his fingertips. "Fatherhood can be overwhelming, so of course he was tempted to run away, feeling he doesn't want to get tied down. He doesn't know how to love. He's always been like that. I've tried to help him, but it wasn't easy. Did he ever tell you that he'd been in therapy?"

I shake my head again. It wouldn't be too suspicious that a young wife who basically eloped and married hastily out of love doesn't know such a private thing about her husband.

When I first arrived here, I was trembling to the bone, but the more I talk to this guy, the more I seem to get the hang of it. I'm figuring out how to behave properly in this household, and talking to the younger son of the family does help me gather some important clues and bits of information I can use to my advantage.

"My brother was anxious, depressed, and had anger issues. He wasn't always like that, but I think people do change after a big trauma. I think the incident—"

We hear a polite tap on the door, which is already wide open.

When I turn around, the younger maid's lingering behind us, hesitant and apologetic.

"Sir, the meal is ready, and Chairman will be expecting you downstairs soon."

"Ah! Ms. Heesun, I'll be right down, thank you."

His serious expression quickly brightens.

"Well, that was a bit of a ramble, but the bottom line is, welcome! Don't feel pressured at all; you and this little guy really belong here, and we're all very happy to have you! You must have been through a lot."

The man leans toward me and adds in a whisper, "Don't be intimidated, just eat and tell us all how you've been doing. My dad always had a weak spot for my brother, and he's been waiting for him, even though he acts as if he doesn't care and is still mad at him. Inside, he's really happy to see you and his grandson, so this is your chance to get what you want, remember."

Just then, the elderly maid appears with a heap of clothes in her arms. "I've found some clothes for you to change into, but I don't know if they're your size."

The brother says, "Please take your time getting ready before you come down. I'll let my dad know it will take some time. Don't worry about it. We've waited all these years, so what's an hour or two more?"

The maid carefully transfers the baby to her arms, reassuring me, "I'll take care of him while you get ready and have dinner. Please enjoy yourself."

Staring down at the baby, she adds nonchalantly, "How many months old is he? Should I get him some baby food?"

My heart drops, but I keep my cool. "He's three months old."

I recall the young mother's clear, cheerful voice: *He's three months now. He was born on December 12, so it's easy to remember.*

I quickly add, "He was born on December 12."

"Ah, so it's a little early for baby food," the maid says. "Have you weaned him?"

"Yeah, he's just been weaned, he's on formula, he's up to date on his vaccinations, he's healthy except for a little bit of atopy on his legs."

It all comes out too fast, maybe too naturally, but all in all, I'd say I've nailed it.

The brother has been smiling beside me as I talked. "Mrs. Suwon is a veteran with babies, so no worries!"

The older maid nods, smiling. "My daughter got married early, so I already have a grandchild his age."

"Well then, I'll wait for you downstairs," the brother says. But before he leaves the room like a gust of wind, he throws a quick look over his shoulder. "By the way, I'm so happy you're here, sister!"

I can't help but smile at the warmth in his voice. I leave the baby in Mrs. Suwon's care and walk into the marble bathroom.

And I think, *This is for the best. At least I'm safe tonight. This is my refuge.*

CHAPTER

·10·

This long, winding stairwell is so exquisite and grand that it feels like a well-crafted stage. The perfect stage for me to play someone else. I try to move slowly and gracefully as Cinderella would in her glass shoes, but as I descend, somehow my mind drifts to another fairy tale I read as a child: *Bluebeard,* whose many wives disappeared not long after marriage, and who owned a sinister mansion. And his poor bride who peeked in a locked chamber and walked in on his horrifying secret.

The old wooden stairs creak ominously underneath as I make my way down, lost in thought.

"This way, sister!" comes a cheerful voice. "I'm here to escort you in case you get lost."

I feel a little relieved to see a smiling face waiting at the bottom of the stairs.

"Your clothes fit well? We were worried we might not have any spare clothes for you."

"They're a little baggy, yes, but really comfy."

"You look great. You seemed a little tired earlier—are you feeling okay?"

"I'm feeling much better, thanks for checking."

Upstairs, I'd taken my time washing my hair and enjoying a long, scalding shower in the spacious bathroom. A luxury I couldn't even have dreamed of in my half-basement rental. The towels, stacked by size, were fluffy as if they'd never been used, every single one of them embroidered with the initial of the family's last name, *J*. I stepped out of the bathroom in a fluffy robe, also with *J* embroidered on the chest, and rummaged through the pile of delicate clothes left on the bed. Each one was tasteful and thoughtfully designed; even the plain white T-shirt was a textile masterpiece. They were all a little big on me and I could tell were not brand-new, but they had been well kept. I wondered whom they belonged to: the mother-in-law or maybe a sister-in-law?

After much deliberation, I picked out a long tan linen dress with a belt at the waist. I had no idea what would be appropriate for dinner in a house like this, but I thought I couldn't fail too badly with something classy yet casual.

The brother urges me: "Not to rush you, by the way, but my dad's been waiting for a while. He's very excited and he doesn't put up with tardiness."

"Oh, of course, of course."

I hurry after him to the back of the house. We walk through the large living room and into the dining room, the entirety of which is filled with a dining table that can easily seat twenty people. The abundance of flowers on the table and the fancy lighting overhead lend the room the ambience of a fancy restaurant I could never afford.

At the head of the table sits the elderly man in the wheelchair, with the aide sitting right by and holding a napkin in front of his chest. To his right is the young man who just became my brother-in-law, and across from him is what I assume to be my seat, but I don't see any other family members.

A bowl of porridge is placed in front of the old man, along with side dishes that look like typical Korean fare. The dozen or so sides and the grilled fish are plated on expensive-looking china as if in a fine-dining restaurant. But watching the aide carefully spoon a dollop of the porridge, with a small piece of fish flesh balancing atop it, into the man's mouth, I realize this feast is probably of little use to him in his condition. I murmur an apology, "I'm sorry it took me so long," and find my seat.

For me and the brother, they have prepared a hearty steak and some salad, and my mouth waters the moment my eyes set upon them. Since this morning's single carton of soy milk, I've been running around on an empty stomach. The brother steps in to lighten the mood: "Don't be; you sure needed some rest. Is my nephew asleep, by the way? What was his name, Seung-Joon?"

He adds, "I'm going to have to get used to that name. How does that little guy sleep so well away from home? I bet he's a good boy, sister."

"Yeah, I've done sleep training, so he's got no problem sleeping through the night," I quickly chime in.

"Mrs. Suwon will take good care of him, so please eat in peace."

"Ah, yes."

"Gahhhh . . . daaau . . . ha . . ."

The old man sticks out his skinny hand and starts to mumble something. His mouth comes slack and hangs half open, his voice quite loud. But nothing that comes out of his mouth is intelligible.

"Excuse me?"

"Haaaaaaaaan . . . aaaaaaah oohh yeeeet?"

Clueless, I uncomfortably shift in my seat, looking for help, and lock eyes with the brother sitting across from me. But he looks just as puzzled. We quickly drop our gazes to our plates, sharing a brief moment of the same discomfort.

As the old man waves his hands in frustration, the aide next to him pulls a notebook out of his pocket and lowers his head to bring his ear close to the man's mouth. He jots down notes and has the old man verify the information as he drools and spews out words that are halfway between a scream and a shriek.

The brother gestures toward the aide: "By the way, this is Mr. Choi. He comes here six days a week to take care of my dad, rehabilitate him, and run some chores for him. Sometimes he sleeps over, and I can say he scratches Dad's itch far better than anyone in this household."

Mr. Choi flashes a quick, polite smile, nodding to acknowledge this, and I nod back. He double-checks some of what he's written in his notebook a few times with the old man before turning to me. It's like cryptography. How on earth do you communicate if even your own son can barely understand you? No matter how rich you are, that's no way to live.

Mr. Choi goes on to interpret for the old man: "He's saying that if you move in, he wants you to commit to raising the child full-time."

Momentarily lost in my own thoughts, I snap out of them. Did he just say move in?

"Father—could you possibly mean . . . ?" The brother almost springs to his feet but quickly finds his composure.

The old man spits out another unintelligible groan. Mr. Choi listens intently, but realizing he needs help, he gestures toward the brother for some aid. The two men kneel down next to the old man, head-to-head, and listen intensely and discuss among themselves for a while.

What a strange sight—an old man in a wheelchair with a half-squashed body, and two young men in their primes kneeling obediently by his side, stooping over to cater to his needs, with the light of a crystal chandelier swaying overhead! None of this feels real; it's like something out of a play. On the dining room table sits the feast of fluffy white steamed rice, tantalizing side dishes, and juicy steaks, all getting cold. There's a loud war going on in my stomach, but my mouth feels parched.

I can't help but hold my breath, not knowing what my fate will be. Is this man going to ask me to leave with the baby, or is he going to ask me something about the baby's father? I'm terrified that he will yell at me any moment, "You're not her, you imposter!" I'm scared to death that if I get kicked out right now, I'll be completely lost in the dark streets outside. Even worse, what if they decide to call the police?

I don't know why I'm so worried about getting kicked out all of a sudden, when just a few moments ago I couldn't wait to extricate myself from all this.

Finally, the brother returns to his seat. He's smiling nervously, but I can't decide if it's a good sign.

He lowers his head and starts to speak, toying with his cup as he treads carefully to find the right words. "My dad has a lot to say, for sure. He wants you to know that he hasn't forgiven my brother. He won't look for him anymore. But the kid, Seung-Joon, needs to grow up here with the rest of the family."

"What?"

"In short, he won't oppose if you and Seung-Joon want to move in."

I throw a quick glance toward the old man and am met with that piercing gaze again, the corner of his mouth twisted up like a sneer.

"He says he'll take care of you two as long as you stay out of trouble, raise the kid well, and listen to him."

Mr. Choi reads off his notes and confirms what the brother says. The old man tilts his head and whispers something in his ear.

Mr. Choi adds, "And Chairman also wants you to know that you shouldn't expect his help if you decide to move out and live on your own."

The old man lets out an uncomfortable, chortled laugh.

"And he also warns, if you're going to move in, you should brace yourself, for sure, although things will be much better for the kid."

Brace for what? Complete obedience and dutifully following through with the child-rearing clause of this verbal contract?

I look up and around slowly: the sharp-eyed old man, Mr. Choi seemingly getting very uncomfortable, the young man with a twinkle in his eye.

Is it this easy?

They haven't even checked my ID. They haven't asked me where I'm from, what I've been doing for a living, or who I am. They haven't even asked for any proof that I've been living with the eldest son or have anything to do with him. Why? Do they just blindly assume that the baby is enough evidence?

Or maybe he doesn't really care about my identity to begin with. I'm the undeserving commoner chosen by the wayward son, so when I show up with the grandson bearing their family name, they have no problem taking me in for the time being, only to kick me out when it's time and keep me separated from the kid.

Whatever these people are up to, it doesn't matter right now. I'm not going to be here long anyway, and here it is, a golden gate leading to the temporary peace I desperately need.

So I guess, after all, I'm a Cinderella who's just descended the grand stairwell to stumble upon this serendipity.

And what fate! Going overnight from living in a half-basement rental with no hot water, with nowhere to go and no one to turn to, to being the daughter-in-law taken under the wing of the super-rich. A wealthy father-in-law, cute brother-in-law, and all the help in the world anyone could hope for raising a child? I'm talking about the kind of family that won't let you wear a T-shirt if it's not designer. The kind of family that will keep you from harm, behind the strongest castle walls you can find.

You never know when a precariously built sandcastle like this will crumble and everything blow up in your face, but for now, there's no reason to refuse the only hand that's offering help. More than anything, I don't want to. The things I'm running from are so dark, so dreary, so frightening . . . I'd do anything to be able to stay in the light these rich people seem to be pouring into my pit of despair—a pit I was sure I'd be left in. There's no time to think, nor any reason I should.

"I mean—"

"If you need a little more time to think about it, you can."

"No!"

Everyone turns to look at me—at the determination in my voice.

"We're staying here! We'll do as you say. Thank you, thank you!" And then I quickly add, "Father."

I can feel the room's air change instantly, tension ebbing and everyone relieved. A smile creeps up on the brother's face, and on the old man's as well. "Then we're all on the same page."

The brother lets out a pleased laugh, picks up his fork, and looks down at his plate, startled. "This won't do anymore. Ms. Heesun!"

His call's immediately answered by the younger maid from earlier.

"These are all cold now. Please bring us new plates, would you? Please bring my sister-in-law her food as well. Nice and warm. Speaking of which, sister, why don't you let her know what kind of food you like later? Now that you're part of the family, she should make note of your preferences as well."

"What? Ah, yes, of course."

The maid looks back and forth between me and the brother in bewilderment, then gathers my plate. The juice and blood from the steak have formed small swirls on the china. They bring to my mind what I'm running from—a body that has probably been getting cold for some time, lying in a pool of blood even right this second.

But my disturbing thoughts are interrupted by the voice of Mr. Choi: "Oh, and Chairman said the sooner the better for paternity testing."

CHAPTER

·11·

I barely remember how I got back to my room. Throughout dinner, I replied mechanically to Mrs. Suwon's praise for the baby's incredible gentleness and wonderful sleep habits, then hurried out and slammed my bedroom's door behind me as soon as I could. Now here I am, pacing around my room, chewing on my nails.

Of course, it was too good to be true, an unbelievable stroke of luck! Things never go that way for me. How utterly foolish of me to assume that a family of this status would believe the claims of a strange woman and accept a child she's brought to them without question? And a woman in shabby clothes with bruises on her wrists, for that matter?

I glance over at the baby sleeping soundly in his crib.

I shouldn't have believed the young mother so blindly. She could have been unstable; I met her on the road after all. Who knows if she was really in a relationship with the eldest son of this family?

If it turns out that the child is not this family's blood relative, that's the end of the story. I'm sure a report of fraud will only be the beginning. There's going to be a thorough background check, and it's all going to come out. They'll find out what I'm running from.

I vividly recall the clang of the frying pan in my hand as it struck his head, and the feel of it bouncing off my wrist. I can still see the red streaks of blood splattered across the floor. Sure, I panicked and ran away, but I didn't think for a second I could stay on the run forever. I'd just wanted to buy some time. It had all happened so suddenly that I hadn't been able to think straight. But now, with the way things are going, I'm afraid I'm going to lose more time by sticking around here.

Why not just leave the kid behind? He's got a house full of money, so things can't go terribly wrong for him. For me, it's now or never.

As I'm about to bolt out of the room, the door swings open so I almost bump into the person who walks in.

"Whoa! Are you okay?"

Damn! The brother catches me off-balance, flailing my arms.

"I just wanted to see if you enjoyed your meal, how you're settling in, and if you need anything at all."

With my heart racing, I need to take a moment to think of what to say. Then, "Oh, he's already sleeping like an angel. He's a good boy, just like you said!"

The brother glances over at the baby on the bed and turns my way with what resembles a smirk on his face. "I was worried you might get the wrong idea because of what my dad said earlier."

Hands thrust in his pockets, he looks as agitated as I must have looked just now pacing around the room. "I hope you know he didn't mean anything by it. It's not that I don't trust you."

I'm at a loss for words. I'm not sure if it's even safe to say anything in response just yet.

"My dad's just making sure everything's in the clear," he continues, "because he hasn't seen my brother in a long time. And he cares a lot about what people think. We've got hired help and prying eyes, and he needs to convince all those people more than himself. But you know, one look at my nephew's face, and what more is there to say?"

When I see him smile out of the corner of my eye, I feel a bit relieved. I glance back at the baby in the crib. With his smooth skin and unusually long eyelashes, he looks just like the man standing in front of me. So far, everything the young mother's told me has checked out. The brother has been acting friendly, and I haven't sensed any major red flags, so why not stay on his good side?

"Hey, now that you mention it—when and how should we go about paternity testing?"

"Oh, I think we're likely to ask someone we know, maybe Dr. Kwon. He's a psychiatrist, but he can probably refer us to a lab or somewhere they do these tests. If we go through my brother's stuff in the storage room, there's probably a comb, and we can use that for testing."

He pulls up a chair next to me and sits down, motioning me over. I plop down heavily on the bed. The room is dark. On the bedside table is a lamp that Mrs. Suwon left on, its light bathing everything in a golden glow and making me feel warm and cozy inside. Even in these moments of anxiety and fear, this place feels like a paradise that will shield me from the rest of the world.

"Just think of it as a formality, and if you need anything, just let me know. I'm totally on your side." He hangs his head for a moment, then chuckles to himself. "I know I made a big fuss the first time you saw me, and I'm sure that made you a little uncomfortable, now that I think about it."

"No, not at all." I hold out my hand.

I'm pretty sure the brother's actually younger than me, but by how many years? He's definitely in his mid-twenties, and judging by his cheerful demeanor and lack of wrinkles, my guess is he's been a pampered youngest child his whole life.

"I guess I was just so thirsty for any news of my brother that I couldn't contain myself. I felt like I'd known you for a very long time even the moment I first saw you."

"You don't say?"

He nods.

"Yes, something like telepathy. I felt an instant connection." He chuckles again. "I mean, my brother and I had this incredible bond, like we had one mind, so it's no surprise I felt that way with you."

"Really?"

If he and his brother got along so well, why didn't he introduce his live-in girlfriend? Did the father of this baby leave home because of his overbearing parents? But where's their mother? Could she be living in a different house?

"Even after he moved out, we still kept in touch for a while. We're not anymore, but I'd still hear some news now and again. It's been almost seven or eight years since he left home. I mean, as a little kid, I used to follow him around a lot, and I don't know why he seemed so grown-up when I was younger, even though we're actually only six years apart. Sometimes I even think he ran away because I was too clingy or something. Oh, come to think of it, he did mention me to you, right?"

"Oh, of course! I mean, he told me that you've got such energy—"

He burst into laughter at my fumbling attempt. "Oh, I'm sure he told you something like, *Soohyun, that kid is such a weirdo!*" But then he lowers his voice. "Anyways, I'm so glad you're here. I know you've been through a lot with my brother, but don't hate him too much. He wasn't always like that. Going through such a big incident at a young age can change a person, you know?"

For a moment, he seems to be staring off into the distance, beyond the light of the lamp, as if reaching into his mind for some bygone memories. "So wherever he is now, maybe he'll come to his senses one day, maybe he'll come back for you and Seung-Joon. Until then, you can stay here as long as you need to. My dad's happy to see you, and you have no idea how happy I am you're here. You know, living at home without anyone my age, after my brother ran away, hasn't been much fun, to be honest. And it's not like I can exactly talk to my dad. It's been a really hard few years, for sure, but now that you're here, I feel like I can finally breathe a little," he says, standing up. "If you find yourself struggling with anything, I'll help you as much as I can, so don't you worry. Young people stick together!"

The brother grins and holds out a hand. I reach out my own sweaty hand and take his, which turns out to be warm and strong.

CHAPTER

·12·

"This house may look enormous, but it doesn't have a lot of rooms. My parents preferred to have a spacious living room and garden. As you can see, by the front door on the first floor, there's a parlor, across from which there's a study. Then, past the stairwell, farther in, the living room, and then beyond that the dining room and kitchen. And behind where I was sitting yesterday is my dad's room and his aide's. It used to be one big master suite. But after my brother's mom passed away, we completely remodeled it for my dad's use. And when my dad fell ill, we renovated it again so it'd be like a functioning hospital room."

My brother-in-law, Soohyun, as it turns out, is the epitome of friendliness. He's three years younger than me, but much taller, with childlike innocence and cheerfulness. Perhaps owing to his life as the youngest in a rich family, he's got certain pure, boyish looks about him that make everyone instantly warm up to him. His presence is definitely a ray of sunshine in the somber atmosphere of this enormous old mansion occupied by a wheelchair-bound old man who can barely speak.

"There are a few more rooms in the back that we don't use much these days. Those rooms are for the rare occasions when we do have guests over. Apart from those, there's a room attached to the kitchen that the helpers use, because they all commute, but they still need a place to rest, and when it's busy, like during the holidays, they often sleep over. No one but me and my brother has ever used the second floor, actually. Even before my dad fell ill. The room they put you in used to be my brother's, and the one next to it used to be mine."

He smiles slightly before quickly adding, "Oh, but don't you feel uncomfortable. I'm in a different room now, just across the hall from yours."

"Oh, not at all."

I throw up my hands and smile, but my mind's elsewhere.

His brother's mom? I mean, even though I joined this family as a sort of daughter-in-law, there are a lot of things I can sidestep since the young mother and this family had been so estranged. But I still have no idea how much I should pretend not to know, and how many questions I can ask safely. I'm just proud of myself for having survived three days now in this unbelievable household full of twists.

I still don't have the courage to leave my room by myself, except to follow Soohyun around, but the idea of eating three meals a day and not having to worry about cleaning or laundry is a dream. Not to mention that it's pure bliss not to have any fists flying at me. And I was able to text my coworker at the barbecue place to let her know I'm doing okay, so that's one more thing off my checklist. Now I can relax a bit.

My boyfriend's parents are very sick. It seems they haven't got much time left. So I'm visiting them with my boyfriend. They're living in another province, so I don't know when I'll be back. I don't think I'll be able to make it to work for a while, or promise when I can return, so I've decided to hand in my resignation. I'll text the boss as well. Say hello to Hee-Jung, Yoo-Jung, and the other girls for me. I'll let them know when I get back. Once I'm back, I'll treat you all to some nice dinner! I'm so sorry!

What a cold-hearted bitch! I didn't even get to say goodbye, how could you! But it's all good. I guess you're walking down the aisle soon? Come back with a diamond ring on your finger, girl!

I chuckle to myself when I read the text. A diamond ring is out of the question, but I did somehow end up with in-laws and a kid, so I guess she's not entirely off the mark after all. And they aren't regular in-laws, for that matter. What would my coworkers say if they saw me right now? They'd be completely speechless, I'm sure, at how my life has changed overnight, and how my day is now entirely different from the moment I open my eyes.

Every morning, I now revel in the comfort of my bed for a while, savoring the fragrant silkiness of my bedding. I love how the sheets cling to my bare feet. And I remember how, curled up on that old futon in my half-basement apartment, I couldn't fall asleep without my socks on until late spring. The linoleum floor sent the damp chill right up through my thin blankets and threatened to frost everything within reach. Absolutely everything.

Which is to say, the body might hold. It might take a while for it to begin to smell. How long? How long for it to get really, really bad?

When I think about it too much, I feel chills down my spine, and I jump up. At that moment, there's a knock on the door, and Heesun enters. The young maid I had noticed before, Heesun is in her mid-thirties, was hired from a staffing agency, and works here six days a week. At first, I couldn't understand why a young, healthy woman would work as a domestic helper in a house like this, but after watching her for a few days, I can't imagine a better job for her. Although she sometimes finishes late, she is relatively on time, and the working environment is very comfortable. There is always a shortage of workers because it's such a big house, but no one in the family throws a tantrum like those rich people who sometimes make news, and the old man has his own aide, so she can get her job done in peace.

In truth, I would sell my soul to work in a place like this. To be fair, I don't know what everyone thinks of the sudden addition of another family member to take care of in a previously quiet house. But everyone here has been perfectly professional so far. If anyone was doubtful or uncomfortable, certainly no one showed it. Not one person questioned having to call a strange young woman "ma'am" all of a sudden.

"I've heated the milk, ma'am."

When Heesun approaches with the bottle, the baby giggles, wiggling his arms and legs. Just as the young mother said, Seung-Joon is an incredibly gentle baby. He never cries as long as his diaper is dry and formula gets served on time. Most of the time, he's either smiling or sleeping peacefully. He rarely ever wakes up in the middle of the night wailing.

It's actually me who keeps startling awake. Every night, I pass out and drift to a deathly, dreamless sleep, but for some reason, I always wake up drenched in a cold sweat in the dead of the night. Sometimes I might even scream, but I can't be sure. Could Soohyun hear me in the room across the hall? For a few nights, I try sleeping with my phone's recording app on, but my own grunts and moans scared me even more, so I no longer do.

Still, once I set my head on the pillow at night, I'm asleep only seconds after. This is because I am constantly on edge during the day. All kinds of thoughts plague my mind. Do I have to greet the house staff, or wait for them to acknowledge me first? Should I check on the old man or wait for him to ask for me? Should I help in the kitchen in the morning, or can I just lounge around until breakfast's ready? There's no manual on how to behave. I would have a nervous breakdown if I had a mother-in-law to cater to on top of all this. But I've been told that she passed away before her time.

Oddly enough, though, I don't need to pretend to be someone else here, as I did with him. It's not like they have any idea about what Seung-Joon's mother was like, so I can just be as awkward and out of fashion as I actually am.

Playing the role of the "abandoned woman who lived with the eldest son" proves to be a lot easier than I feared. No one ventures to ask me any probing questions. No one asks me how I fell in love with the son, how I'd been doing before I suddenly appeared on the doorstep of this house. Whenever a conversation steers to that kind of subject, everyone is quick to smooth it over and change topics. And those are all very telling signs. I can definitely tell the eldest son was quite the troublemaker, something everyone in this household avoids at all costs. He must have been the black sheep that always manages to be born in this kind of family, as if that's a must-have for the super-rich. One night, I overhear gossip among the kitchen staff:

"He wasn't just your typical dick, either. He really was impossible, I heard."

"Wow, that bad? What did he do? Did he kill someone?"

"Oh, I don't think so. But I heard it wasn't too far off. No surprise that he had to go to therapy and get on meds. The chairman was going to send him abroad, but something went wrong and he couldn't go. I heard he got even worse after. I mean, I personally think it's for the best that he didn't get to travel. Can you imagine—a troublemaker like that living unsupervised? When things got really bad, he would completely lose his temper and no one could even go near him."

"Do you think it was because of his mother?"

"I don't know, that seems like an excuse. Not everyone without a mom gets so screwed up."

"You've never met him, either, have you?"

"He's been out of the house for about eight years, and I've only heard stories. I came to work here around the same time you did, and all the people who used to work around that time are gone."

"Of course, that new staff member hasn't met the oldest son, has he?"

"Mr. Kim? Of course not, he's been here only for a few months!"

"Do you think they'll ask Mr. Kim to leave when his two years are up? This place changes staff over those two years."

"Well, you never know. He's a gardener, handyman, fixes cars, fixes plumbing, eats and sleeps in an outbuilding, does all sorts of odd jobs, so maybe he's an exception. It's nice to have someone like that. Where are you going to find another one? For a housekeeper, you can get a staffing agency to replace them every two years with no problem, but how easy is it to find someone like that, who's got no one and nowhere to call home?"

"Ugh, but I still get creeped out every time I see him. That face, that vibe, he looks so sinister."

"But he keeps his mouth shut, does his own thing, and doesn't cause any trouble, so he's an asset."

"No home? No family?"

"Apparently, once upon a time, there was a big accident that broke the family apart. And he got really sick after."

"What kind of accident? How bad do you think it was? Do you think he could have served time?"

"Hey, careful! I don't know the exact story, but this family doesn't just hire anyone, you know. And after how impossible the oldest son was, they probably don't expect much from people anymore."

"That's a shame. I wish I got to meet the eldest son!"

"Do you really think you could work with someone that intimidating hanging around here all the time?"

"I'm curious, though. I've never met anyone so notorious before."

"Wow, you sound really clueless."

"Well he is Soohyun's brother, after all. So they must have something in common, right? Wouldn't the eldest be handsome, at least? Then maybe . . . haha."

"Handsome or not, he was a troublemaker all the same. Why do you think a family like this cut off the eldest son? There must be a good reason, don't you think? You know how some people these days do unspeakable things to their families. So it's good that he's gone."

As I give up on my midnight snack and trudge back to my room barefoot, I, too, wonder how this family could so completely erase the existence of the eldest son.

I mean, there's no trace of him in this entire house—not a single photograph, not a single object belonging to him. All that's left is a room so plainly furnished that I can't imagine what the original owner was like. A large bed, a chest full of drawers, a wardrobe, a nightstand, and an ordinary landscape painting on the wall. The next room, which used to be Soohyun's, is empty of furniture. Now the easternmost of those twin rooms is occupied by me and Seung-Joon.

Why had he left such a big, fancy house—and a spacious room with a bathroom? What kind of mess did he make, in order for the entire family to just give up and not look for him? How much did the young mother know about all this? How did the two even meet in the first place? I mean, the young mother was friendly and feminine, but she was no femme fatale, certainly not the kind that could have captured the attention of the son of such a wealthy family.

I've been lost in thought for a while, holding the bottle for the baby.

"New towels and a new robe, all stocked up," Heesun says cheerfully as she comes out of the bathroom.

"Oh, thanks, but all the towels were used once, so I can dry and use them again."

"We don't do that in this house. Once a towel is used, it stinks, even when dried."

This is how the rich live, I guess.

"Oh, and by the way, it's grocery day, so I'll be ordering a few things. Do you need anything? What kind of baby formula should I get? Is there anything in particular you've been feeding him?"

Formula? My heart sinks.

Who am I to know? Are there particular formulas he doesn't like? A million thoughts race through my head. I duck my head and pretend to wipe the corner of Seung-Joon's mouth, hoping not to give anything away.

"Oh, well, the formula . . ."

Just then, my knight in shining armor appears in the doorway.

"Do you have a moment?"

"Ah! Soohyun!"

My excited voice sounds awkward even to my own ears. Heesun bows slightly and quickly leaves the room.

Soohyun doesn't acknowledge her at all. From what I've seen, he's a nice man, but not overly friendly with the hired help. It's as if he's aware that they're necessary pieces to keep everything working but he doesn't see them as much more. If I were still that woman living in the half-basement rental, he'd treat me pretty much the same. But right now, he's acknowledging and smiling at me, and he speaks only to me. Because now I am one of them, a member of this family.

"The results are in, I just wanted to let you know."

"Results?"

"The paternity test." Soohyun waves an envelope and lowers his voice a pitch down.

"Ah!"

Yes, I've completely forgotten—how could I? It had been on my mind for fleeting moments, but part of me was so willing to forget about it that I kept tucking it away into the far corner where my dark secrets and worst fears reside. I've wanted to mindlessly bask in the glow of this new, comfortable life for as long as I could.

"We got the results so quickly thanks to Dr. Kwon. My dad was the first to see it, and he told me to break the news to you myself."

"Then . . ."

My heart thuds in my chest.

"I think my dad was too embarrassed to deliver the news himself. He probably regretted suggesting the test in the first place." He smiles broadly as he hands me the manila envelope. "Anyway, this makes it official! Welcome to the family, sister!"

CHAPTER

·13·

The foreign car with upholstered seats, which even *smells* fantastic, seems to promise a paradise-like ride from the very moment I get in.

Soohyun merrily announces: "Alright, fasten your seatbelts, we're off!"

This is the one out of five foreign cars sitting in the garage that I picked out without thinking, just like someone would choose which socks to put on in the morning.

Ten days ago, the morning breeze was still chilly, but today is warm. Spring has arrived while I've been hiding inside the walls of the mansion. The sunlight streaming through the car window feels warm on my skin, and the air smells completely different, springy and refreshing.

My life, at long last, has also fallen into a peaceful routine as spring has slowly taken over outside. I no longer obsess over news, and my cell phone, which I keep on vibrate just in case, has remained quiet. So when I'm asked to go out with Soohyun, I barely hesitate. Ten days has been long enough. I deserve a brief outing after such an imprisonment, don't I? It'll be just an hour or two, after all.

I must have gotten used to the world behind the Jung family's walls, because when I step outside, I feel uneasy and awkward—and exposed. The paternity testing may have removed one important hurdle, but that doesn't mean I can relax just yet.

"Have you figured out what you need? Check everything off the list while you're out, because you're going to need to buy a lot of stuff. Don't worry about the budget. We've got my dad's card!" Soohyun pats his pocket.

"I can't think of anything right now."

Compared to Soohyun, who expertly drives with only one hand on the wheel, I must surely look conspicuous to anyone who cares to watch, with my upright, nervous presence in the passenger seat, both my hands clasped in my lap.

"Uh, that's not good," Soohyun says, laughter in his voice. "Well, tomorrow's another day. We can always come back for more stuff later. That'd be a good excuse for us to escape and have some fun outside, no? You must feel cooped up staying home all day long."

"Oh, I can't possibly bother you so often."

"It's no bother! It's nice to go to the department store once in a while. I haven't been in one of those since my dad got sick. I've been holed up in the house."

"So, he's been . . ."

"It's been a little over seven years? He collapsed not long after my brother left, and I'm sure even my brother knows he's to blame."

Not knowing what to say, I keep looking straight ahead.

"At least I have a job," he says, "so I have some breathing room."

"Oh, you have a job? What do you do?"

"I just have a title at my dad's building management company. There are the actual experts who take care of the whole management, and I just come in a few days a week and take care of some stuff. It's almost embarrassingly cushy. But without this job, I've got no reason to go out at all, so a day like this is a cause for celebration."

Soohyun chuckles as he deftly turns the wheel. "By the way, my favorite Italian place, Bellini's, is in the back of the department store. They have abalone pasta and gelato that's to die for. Let's go get that after our shopping spree; what do you think?"

"Would that be okay? Should I call the staff?"

"Oh, no worries, I'll make the call and tell Mrs. Suwon that we won't eat at home today. This is going to be fun! I haven't eaten there in a long time."

He smiles, tapping the steering wheel in amusement.

"But don't you go out on dates or anything? You're so young, aren't you giving up too much because of your father?"

It's a bit presumptuous, but since I'm both older and his sister-in-law, this is probably not out of line.

I've spent the last ten days shadowing and observing Soohyun around the house, and he seems to be living the life of a late-blooming rich kid. Now I know that he does have some kind of office job, but he still spends most of his days lazing around, occasionally going out if he feels like it. He wakes up late, works out in the home gym by the garage, goes out for a bit, and then comes back in for an early dinner. He usually doesn't spend the entire day at home, but he is always around when I need him, occasionally stopping by my room to give Seung-Joon a hug or inviting me out to the garden for a stroll and chat.

This whole time, I had been wondering if he had a girlfriend or even any friends, and what he was up to all day long. I've definitely found solace in the fact that he doesn't go out all day long. His presence has proved to be comforting, which I very much prefer to being left alone in a large, unfamiliar house.

"A date?" He responds with his own kind of odd laughter.

"Are you seeing anyone right now?" I ask.

"Not right now. Well, how do I explain?" He lifts his free hand to ruffle the locks of hair on the back of his head. "I mean, there are girls I can casually call up and have a drink or two with. But it's hard to find someone who's willing to take the time to get to know you, really open up and talk. You know, someone to be in a committed relationship with? It's rare to come by. I'm always in awe of people who just seem to find their matches."

"Aww, but you must be popular. I bet girls vie for your attention."

"Me?"

"Sure. You look like a K-pop idol, you're such a gentleman, and well, you're like royalty."

He laughs in a big way. "All of which amounts to 'no substance.' I do have a lot of female friends. A lot of girls who confide in me. I guess

I'm not intimidating and can be easy to talk to. But it's not like I can date everyone who seems even slightly interested. I want to be careful and take things slow. You know, like my brother."

"Like your brother?"

"Yeah, you know, he's super picky. The second I saw you, I knew why he would have been into you."

"Really?"

Based on what? When we first met, I was dressed in an old hoodie and rumpled cargo pants. Needless to say, the young mother wasn't exactly my twin sister.

"It's hard to put into words, but you have that *thing* my brother loves, that subtle vibe. That's why I had no doubts even when my dad asked for the paternity test. At first sight, I could tell you were exactly my brother's type."

"I have no idea what you mean." I press him, feigning nonchalance.

"You felt authentic and approachable. My brother can't stand games or tricks."

"Yeah?"

"You know, all those games girls play to get a guy's attention? Batting eyelashes, being cute. Most guys fall for those tricks. But my brother sees right through them. When someone's being fake, he picks it up right away. Quite a few girls got their hearts broken because my brother was that way. He hates ploys of all kinds. But you're the opposite."

"I am?"

"Yeah. You're, like, transparent." He smirks, as if he's said something deeply ironic. "You're the type whose face always betrays her feelings, a real open book. I bet you're a terrible liar."

If he only knew what lies I've been telling to his face all this time.

"He was lucky to have found someone like you. I bet he doesn't even have a death wish now."

Soohyun stays silent for a moment, drumming his fingers on the steering wheel, ruminating on something. "But, I don't know, I'm not so blessed."

I turn my head to study his expression. His brows are slightly furrowed as he concentrates on the road ahead, and he looks a little for-lorn.

"I think it has to do with my attachment issues," he continues. "I went to a counselor once, and Dr. Kwon said it's probably because I parted with my mom too young."

"Oh, then when did . . . ?"

"My mom died when I was ten, and that's when I came to live here."

What does that mean?

"Oh, didn't my brother tell you? We have different mothers. I am, so to speak, a bastard son."

A quick glance at my dumbfounded expression, and Soohyun bursts out laughing.

"Oh, you had no idea?"

"None at all." I shake my head. This isn't one of those things I should pretend to have known.

"I lived with my mom in a different house until I was ten, and my dad would come over once in a while, and then my mom died in an accident. After that, I came here to live with my dad and his family."

"Oh?"

"My father married late, so he had my brother when he was almost forty-five. I'm six years younger than my brother, so I was a real surprise. I remember going to kindergarten for the first time and being shocked at how young the other dads were."

Not sure how to react, I try to read his face, but Soohyun rambles on nonchalantly as if none of this has left any lasting scars.

"When I first came to live with my dad, I was a nervous wreck. But my brother took me by the hand and showed me around. How cool he looked! You know—he's so tall and handsome. He looked like the kind of man I'd always wanted as my dad. Now that I think about it, he couldn't have been super happy with a younger brother that his dad had with another woman, but he looked after me anyway. He was always kind. He was on my side. I even wanted to be like him when I grew up."

As he deftly turns the wheel and pulls into the department store's parking lot, Soohyun casts a quick glance at me and smiles. His eyes seem tinged with red, and I feel a twinge of sympathy.

"In a way, it's my brother who set the bar so high. For women I'd like to date, and the kind of person I'd like to be. Although, he became such a different person in the years before he left. I wish you'd gotten to see how he used to be, because he was such a great person back then, before the incident."

"The incident?"

"Oh, his mom's accident. That really changed him. By the way, we're here now!"

He pulls the car into an empty spot in the parking lot, turns off the engine, and looks back at me. A smile spreads across his face.

CHAPTER
·14·

When was the last time I had fun shopping?

I don't remember ever having fun buying anything in my life, except for those days when I'd just left the orphanage and went shopping for clothes and school supplies with my foster mom in our new neighborhood. Or when my boyfriend got a big bonus and took me shopping, urging me to pick anything. The only form of shopping I ever knew, apart from those rare moments, was worrying about how much was left in my thin wallet and then picking only what I absolutely couldn't do without. Very occasionally, when things were really bad and the clerk seemed to be in the dark, I would sneak out with the items I needed stashed under my arm.

But this time, everything's different.

"I feel like a fool—I haven't shopped at a place like this in a long time."

Soohyun leads me to "one of his favorite shops," which I realize is an Italian import luxury store. It brims with all sorts of luxurious colors that look like money, from cream and taupe to muted gray and a shade of soft red bean paste. I squint at a thin T-shirt on a rack near the entrance with a price tag that has six zeros on it.

"Oh, Mr. Soohyun, you're here. It's been a while, how's Chairman?"

The manager greets us with an overly enthusiastic voice.

"Oh, this is your sister-in-law? Then she's the wife of your brother who's been living abroad?"

"Yeah, yeah. Since my nephew was born, my sister-in-law came to South Korea first. My dad wanted to do something really nice for her, he's so happy to have a grandson. He basically forced his credit card on us. She hasn't shopped in Korea in a long time, so please take good care of her."

Soohyun looks over and flashes a wink. I laugh, and the tension seems to ease a bit. When I meet the manager's eyes again, her facial expression has completely transformed, hospitable and eager to please.

What happens next is actually a bit of a blur. Like a film on fast-forward. A few more clerks show up out of nowhere, and I'm soon left alone in the dressing room. One by one, I put on the dozens of clothes that are handed to me from outside, and each time, I come out to look in the mirror, only to go back in to repeat the whole process. Soohyun proves to be the best shopping partner. Parked on the couch in the middle of the store, he never seems to get bored, and whenever I emerge from the dressing room, he gives me honest feedback like "That's perfect!" or "Oh, that's not a keeper." After a while, I feel more relaxed, and it starts to feel like a fun game. The best part is that I don't have to think about anything while trying on clothes. Who I'm supposed to be, what I should and shouldn't know, none of the usual complexity that's my life as an imposter.

"Well, you definitely look good in this style, with legs for days. And what a perfect fit! You don't look like you've just had a baby at all," the manager says with a look of satisfaction as she smooths my pants.

"I know!" the clerk next to me exclaims. "You look so good in that. How many months old did you say your baby was?"

"Three months, and he's already talking," Soohyun brags with pride.

"No, he's not," I said. "Soohyun, you're being too nice."

"Uh, no, you just missed it. Yesterday, when I gave him a little shake—like this—he just laughed and went, 'Da, Da!' Maybe he was trying to say 'daddy.'"

"You're really enjoying watching your nephew, Mr. Soohyun." The manager chuckles. "Everyone is getting married late these days, so uncles and aunts love their nieces and nephews even more. That's why baby gifts sell so well."

The clerk standing by chimes in. "You should come back with the baby sometime. I'd love to meet him, now that I've heard all the good words from Mr. Soohyun. But really, you're in fantastic shape for a mother of a three-month-old."

"You know what? I was just thinking the same thing," the manager says. "I mean, how did you lose all that pregnancy weight so quickly? I think I rolled around like a snowball for like three years after I had my baby."

"Yikes! Young moms these days don't even gain much weight, just a big belly."

"Yeah, I guess so. But you must have been born with a great body, because your stomach is so flat. I stole a glimpse in the dressing room earlier, and you don't have any stretch marks, either. Oh my God, I'm way out of line. I'm so sorry!"

"Oh, it's just that the pregnancy was so hard on me that I lost my appetite completely. My morning sickness was really bad. So I was really on an involuntary diet all the time," I explain, stumbling back into the dressing room, a pile of clothes in the cradle of my arms. I can feel Soohyun's gaze flicking this way.

I quickly close the dressing room door and remove the silk blouse I have on. The mirror reflects my stomach, smooth and flat, without the slightest trace of a pregnancy line. My heart starts beating fast again. I feel claustrophobic.

What the hell am I doing? Can I keep this up? Was this really the right choice? I have no idea. Maybe I'm in so deep now that all these doubts are meaningless.

I glare at the closed door.

No—maybe there's still a chance.

Why don't I just walk out that door right now with the new clothes on, say I need to use the restroom, walk down a few blocks, run into a random café, change back into my old clothes, leave the kid in the house, and disappear? Sneak a couple of the outfits with me, maybe? They won't be able to locate me just using CCTV footage if I disappear right now. The kid's actually their blood, so they'll raise him well, and I won't have to feel guilty about stealing someone else's identity. I won't have nightmares about the young mother rolling over in her grave and coming after me, either.

I won't have to pretend I know what I'm talking about, I won't have to figure out what questions to ask, and I won't have to get bogged down in this family's history of extramarital affairs, "the incident," or other complicated matters. Of course, right now, being the daughter-in-law of a rich family may seem like a wonderful position, but how long will it last? Am I going to spend the rest of my life in that big house, pretending to be their daughter-in-law and raising someone else's kid? After all, it seems the richer a man is, the longer he holds on to life. So I'm probably going to grow old and die unmarried and single, without a chance of having a real relationship, let alone a second marriage, as long as the old man keeps on living. What if the kid grows up and starts calling me "mommy"? How would I feel about everything then? What if the eldest son, the troublemaker, comes to his senses and suddenly comes back home?

And I have to think about what I did before coming to this house. I can't just sweep it under the rug and pretend it didn't happen. It's only a matter of time before someone finds out, as the days get hotter and the small house starts to reek of death.

Is it really safe to stay in that mansion? Wouldn't it be better to walk away while I still can?

A million voices chatter in my head. I stand there, staring at the door.

This is probably my last chance to walk out that door and forget about what's happened so far and leave everything behind.

If I leave for Seoul right now, I'll probably manage to get a part-time job at a restaurant or a convenience store. I'll probably make it, even if just barely.

Just then, there is a knock at the door.

"Ma'am, how do you feel about the dress? Do you need a different size? I brought you a pair of sandals that I think will go great with that dress. I left them at the door. Try them on."

"Sister, what do you say you try on that dress and then we come back after eating something? I got a table at Bellini's!"

These unfamiliar designations—ma'am, sister—not to mention a fancy Italian restaurant, a new pair of sandals.

This life as the daughter-in-law of a family with money and power, shopping in broad daylight in a department store with my father-in-law's black card and having a brother-in-law who escorts me to all these fancy places.

Is it wise to throw this away? Would I trade this for freedom?

No, who am I kidding—I wouldn't be free, even if I left all this behind right this second.

I'd be lucky to get out of here without getting caught, but I'd still be miserable.

I work for the next ten, no, twenty years and I still wouldn't be close to being able to afford any of this, even this fine Italian silk blouse in my hand. A traditional market vendor might occasionally call me "ma'am," but only with a snotty, sniffling little boy on my back as I count and recount the pennies in my purse, hesitating dozens of times, barely able to afford a bag of fruit. When I get home, I may have a husband waiting for me, just so he can grab me by the hair and yell because I'm late for dinner, or because the house is dirty, or because I bought fruit that he doesn't want. Next to me, my child will be scream-ing and wailing like crazy, and that child will grow up to do the same thing as his father in a vicious cycle, and he'll meet a woman just like me. And who knows, maybe one more swing of the frying pan in the heat of the moment, and the next thing I know, someone will be rot-ting in jail.

I grab the doorknob, take a deep breath, and stick my face through the door, smiling. "Give me a minute. I'll get dressed, and we can get out of here!"

With a quick slip of my hand, I grab the sandals on the doorstep. They are high-heeled, gold-plated, and made of green crocodile skin. After shutting the dressing room door behind me, I lift them up to my face and inhale the scent of the fragrant leather.

That pretty much seals the deal. Yes, this is it: my whole new life.

CHAPTER

·15·

An exotic aroma wafts through the restaurant decorated in gold and green just like my new pair of crocodile-skin sandals. It's a weekday, well past lunchtime, and a wave of relief washes over me as I sit in the quiet among relaxed diners.

A server leads us to a sunny window seat and pulls out a chair for me to sit in. Our table is set with a bunch of flowers, and the napkins are embroidered with the restaurant's name in gold thread. Soohyun takes a look at the menu, explains the dishes to me, and asks for the wine list.

"Oh, in the afternoon?"

"Don't you worry. It's not for me, since I'll be driving. But this is the real deal, and I want to make sure you get a taste."

Everything goes wonderfully. The food is heavenly and the wine so flavorful that the cheap wine I used to buy at the grocery store was like vinegar in comparison.

As we dine, Soohyun tells me funny stories and makes me laugh. What a guy—handsome, clean-shaven, well-built, well-dressed, and even witty. Just a few weeks ago, I had no idea that a man like this— whom I never would have met under different circumstances—would be sitting across from me, staring at me fondly and making me laugh.

I can tell that I'm blending in seamlessly with the people around me. No one glances my way questioningly. Even as I ask where the restroom is and excuse myself, I feel like my spine is straighter and my gait is different, walking away. The pretty woman coming out of the restroom with fresh makeup smiles warmly when our eyes meet, before sneaking envious glances at my sandals.

Everything feels so natural: washing my hands in the marble-lined sink, drying them on a real towel instead of a tissue, nonchalantly tossing the wet towel into a basket, as if I'd done it this way my whole life. I realize that this is *the* life. The kind of life I would never have known had I just walked out of the dressing room earlier and disappeared. So I don't regret my choice one bit.

"Have some more," Soohyun offers.

"Ouch, I'm full, no room for more—really."

"My brother likes his women waifish and thin, doesn't he?" Soohyun picks up the water bottle and pours himself a glass, nudging me in passing. "He's very, you know, particular. I think you would have been always stressed out, trying to tailor yourself to his liking."

He apologetically smiles, avoiding my eyes. "It would have been hard enough to raise a child, but on top of managing another—"

"What? Oh, no, it's not like that. I didn't go on an extreme diet or anything. What I said at the store earlier was just . . . It's not like I've been skimping or starving myself. I've never been a big eater, and I got a bad case of morning sickness when I was pregnant with Seung-Joon."

"Oh, don't worry, I didn't mean anything by it. I was just wondering if you felt pressured or anything. Because my brother's always been into lean women, and I know how he can be."

He glances at my wrist and quickly looks away. The bruise is now yellow. The last ten days of eating good food and taking it easy have fleshed me out nicely, but when Soohyun first saw me, I probably looked like a starving bobcat.

"Well," he says, "I've heard that raising kids is so hard that you lose weight. One of my married friends talks about it every time we hang out."

"Yeah, that's part of it, too; especially when you're breastfeeding, you really lose weight." I parrot what my coworkers have said in the locker room at work, but I stop myself as I catch his cheeks turning slightly red. Suddenly, I feel like a shameless old lady.

In the following moment of awkward silence, Soohyun quickly asks for dessert, and we quietly spoon gelato from our bowls.

The rest of the afternoon is filled with more shopping. With Soohyun standing next to me, urging me on, I buy what feels like an entire boutique. From clothes of all shapes and textures to fabulous homewares that will "make me comfortable at home"; dozens of pairs of shoes, from sneakers to heels and rain boots; and the high-end lingerie I pick out while he's purposely away.

On the advice of the store manager, I request the services of a personal shopper at the department store, and a wonderful world opens up. Without lifting a finger, I sit in the VIP lounge, and clothes, shoes, bags, and jewelry arrive one after another. When I see a pair of silky panties, woven with delicate lace, that costs over $100, I stop looking at the price tags altogether. With everything I've picked up so far, I've already gone way over the rent on my old half-basement.

When I finally don't have an ounce of strength left in my body, Soohyun asks to have my picks from today delivered straight home, and he hands the store manager a plain black card. On the way home, he smiles cheerfully at me as I sit stretched out in the passenger seat, exhausted.

"The women I know say they never get tired of shopping, but you're not one of them."

"Well, I didn't think I'd ever get tired of it, either, but I've been doing this all day long, so I'm probably good for a whole year."

"Anyway, that's a relief," Soohyun says, one hand on the steering wheel, his eyes on the road ahead.

"What is it?"

"I feel like you're really part of the family now. Before today, I was . . ."

I straighten my back and throw him a look.

"I was a little nervous," he finishes.

"Yeah?"

"I thought you might disappear at any moment." Soohyun laughs nervously as our eyes briefly meet.

"You've made a big commitment. I thought maybe you'd be so pressured that you could just leave Seung-Joon behind and disappear."

"Did you?"

"Yeah, my house, uh, doesn't feel that inviting. There's a lot going on, and people gossip, and all the rumors."

Rumors?

"I was raised in that house, and it's never felt like home to me, either. I'm sure you've heard some of the stories from my brother, so when my dad was going through the whole paternity test thing, I was a little nervous. Worried that I'd wake up in the morning and find out you got mad and ran away the night before. But now that we have all that behind us, and now that your things are piling up in the house, it's like, oh, she's really settling in and becoming one of us."

Why is this man so happy to have me here? Why doesn't he seem suspicious in the least, just accepting that a strange woman is his sister-in-law?

"Guess I've been lonely, living in a big house with no one to turn to." As if he's read my mind, Soohyun smiles apologetically. "Or maybe it's because I still can't give up on my brother, you know? Now that you and Seung-Joon are living with us, I feel he'll probably come back someday. I know it's unlikely, but there's still hope."

Is it really that unlikely? If so, why?

The thought sends a chill down my spine. Judging by her vague note, the young mother didn't have the courage to show up here alone. But what about the baby's father? Would the eldest son ever show his face here again?

Even a runaway tramp is bound to come back home when he runs out of money, and what if he finds out that the wife and child he abandoned are here? What if he brings a new girl home with him? What if he comes home one day and finds his kid with a complete stranger?

As I fiddle with my hair, anxious, my hand touches my earlobe and finds the hard stone resting there. Soohyun and I had quite the tussle over this:

"Hey, I don't think I need these. They're too much."

"Wow, but they look great on you."

"I was about to plug the holes in my ears anyways so I won't have to wear earrings anymore."

"Why not, ma'am?" asked the store clerk. "You look so good."

Soohyun nodded. "Are you sure you don't want them? You're beaming, sister. These are diamond, aren't they?"

"Yeah, these are called sesame diamonds, and they're really classy, aren't they? Same design or not, the diamond's always a different sparkle than a zircon."

I wonder if I would have ever worn a pair of diamond earrings in my life if not for Soohyun. Thank goodness I won't need to deal with a boyfriend who would have yelled, "Who are you wearing earrings for?" when I got home. I don't have to be afraid that someone is going to rip my earlobe trying to yank them off.

I should focus on here and now. Who would have thought I'd be sitting in a fancy foreign car? If the baby's father ever shows up, I can sneak out of the house. I'll leave the kid behind and escape through the bathroom window. Everyone will be so caught up in the prodigal son returning that no one will even notice I'm gone until it's too late, so there'd be no harm done. They'd be afraid of embarrassment, so they wouldn't report me if I left all these fancy gifts behind. They wouldn't have lost anything. If I run away with a few small expensive items like these earrings, I'd even have enough money to last me for a while.

Having planned out my escape route like this, I feel a little better. I push all the complicated, frightening thoughts to the back of my mind. I can't undo what I've done. I just have to move forward.

And yes, I realize that if I'm going to move forward, I need to make sure I do everything right from now on.

Perhaps Soohyun was nervous about my leaving because I haven't been fully invested in the role of his sister-in-law. He must have sensed my doubt and anxiety. Now that I've made up my mind to stay with this family for the time being, I need to make sure I blend in. Secrets are dangerous. So I have to get rid of any evidence that I'm keeping them.

When I get home, the sullen man mowing the lawn—the one who let me into the house upon my arrival—sees me and bows his head.

Everyone calls him Mr. Kim. I still cringe every time I see him because he seems so out of place in this house. I try not to let it show.

"Ma'am, you're back!" Heesun, just coming down from the second floor with a bundle of towels, greets me.

"Yes, where's Seung-Joon?"

"Mrs. Suwon just fed him formula and made him burp."

I scurry upstairs to greet my new life: a nicely cleaned room with the baby lying on the bed, smiling into empty space, full and in a good mood. Clearly, he's been having as great a day as I was. His complexion is definitely better than when I first saw him, his cheeks plumper.

After washing my hands, I give the baby a quick hug and sit down next to him. I pull out my phone to do something I should have done a long time ago. The truth is, I've been reveling in the comfort of this charade, too focused on living a comfortable life to fully commit to being someone else. I haven't had to present a fake ID or to change my personality, my tastes, or my face. Really, I've just been myself. I've only had to lie about giving birth to this baby and to do the job of raising him, which hasn't been all that hard. After all, I'm playing a young mom who's new to parenting.

So it hasn't occurred to me until just now: It's okay to be myself, but I need to thoroughly disguise my past. Now that the paternity issue has been resolved and I've been taken in as the daughter-in-law, it's important that I have my stories straight. I need to be able to explain how I met the eldest son, what my time with him has been like, and so on. To do this well, I need to erase my real past. I don't want any surprises.

Just as I'm about to scroll through my phone for photos of him, I hear a knock on the door.

"Sister, dinner's ready! I don't know about you, but I'm still a little full. Why don't you come downstairs with me and see what we're having, though?"

"Yes, I'm coming!"

I quickly shove my phone under my pillow.

CHAPTER

· 1 6 ·

A breeze gently brushing my hair, crickets chirping far away. The smell of freshly cut grass. The stars scattered like shards of glass in the jet-black sky.

The night sky from a rich man's garden looks a thousand times more beautiful than I ever knew.

It's a view completely different from another I once absorbed in a dark alley after work, on my way home after 11 P.M., chatting with my coworkers.

Back then, the night sky had a slender bloodred crescent rising through dusty gray clouds without the faintest lick of a breeze. I had to trudge through the stifling air, my legs as heavy as soaked cotton.

On nights like these, I'd catch a glimmer of light at the end of the alley—a small cigarette burning red—and my heart would sink.

"Jae-Young, your hubby's here!"

"Gosh, young people these days don't get married that fast, sis. You gotta enjoy dating for a while, have fun before you seal the deal. She's practically a kid."

"Good evening, ladies."

"Hi, handsome! You really are like a movie star, aren't you? Why are you here hanging out with us? You should be in a film!"

"By the way, aren't you being overprotective? Jae-Young can find her way home on her own! She's not eight years old."

"Oh no! Yoo-Jung is getting jealous again. If you're jealous, tell your boyfriend to come pick you up, too!"

"He's glued to the computer screen! He's always gaming, staying up until two A.M., and he can't be bothered to pick me up. I should find myself a better man."

"Yeah, do it already, won't you? I'd rather help you get a new boy-friend than hear you whine about it all the time. Oh, you know that handsome guy who said hi to you and Jae-Young at the barbecue place? What about him? If he ever comes back, you should definitely go for him!"

"Anyways," I said, breaking the tension before it escalated. "Later, guys. We're going this way."

"Alright, alright. Jae-Young, you did a good job today. Have a nice night!"

As the commotion died down and the alleyway quieted, he dropped the cigarette to the ground, stubbed it with his foot, and took my hand in his. His hand was cold, as if he'd been standing there for a long time.

"You shouldn't have waited so long," I said. "Did you have dinner? Aren't you hungry?"

"Oh, it's okay, I ate. Come here."

He released his grip and pulled me in with one arm, hugging me tightly. Half-trapped in his much larger arms, I felt crushed, but at the same time, protected. Everything was like that when I was with him. His affection seemed to engulf me in breathtaking flames but also gave me a strange strength. I couldn't help but hold on to him because I didn't think I could survive without him. His affection was all I had. I didn't know how to live in a world without it, nor did I want to.

We walked shoulder to shoulder through the dark night, side by side. We must have looked like a comical circus duo, with our height difference and staggered gait.

"By the way, who was that?"

"Huh?"

Not again.

"That guy who said hello?"

Instead of the caring, handsome boyfriend who always picked me up late, his inner monster was coming out. At first, the monster only made brief appearances at predictable times, but more and more often, the monster took over. It would replace my sweet, handsome boyfriend without warning and refuse to leave.

I shifted uncomfortably. "Oh, one of the guests was interested in Yoo-Jung. I was just, uh, standing by."

"So what did he say? Will he come back?"

"Oh, I don't think so. You know how guys like them are. They don't really follow through. Let's go inside, it's so cold out!"

"So did you fool around with him? All of you girls?"

"Don't be ridiculous, I was just being polite. He was just a diner."

"Isn't Yoo-Jung the slutty one?"

"You shouldn't call her that. She's just got a big personality."

"She flirts with everyone, doesn't she? No good can come from being around someone like that."

"What do you mean? Are you telling me I can't even hang out with girls now?"

Oh, shit. I'd blurted it out. I should have just left it alone. When I forgot to bite my tongue, I would blunder into these moments. I revealed my true feelings.

"What?"

"Nothing."

"No, no, no, you just said something, say it again."

"It's cold, honey, okay? Let's not do this here, let's go home."

"So you're fine hanging out with a slutty girl? Are you going to take every man's dick that comes your way, too?"

"Absolutely not. And we did none of what you're insinuating. Let's not do this; I'm so tired."

"It's always about you."

"I have an early shift tomorrow and have to get up early. I don't have time for this."

"It's all about your schedule and your mood, just like it's always been."

"I never said that, cut it out."

"How *dare* you?"

I was sick and tired of it. Tired of repeating the same conversation every single time a man showed up to flirt with my friends, tired of feeling like talking to a wall.

"I'm giving you so much, what else do you want me to do? I've changed where I work three times! I've deleted all the contacts of the boys I know, the ones I used to work with, the bosses I used to work for, the ones who used to set me up with jobs! How am I supposed to fit in? I keep telling you there's nothing you should worry about, but you never listen to me!"

Then came a flash of fire in my eyes and a searing pain in the back of my head. In the next instant, he grabbed my head and shoved it against the wall behind me. My head slammed into the hard concrete, and overwhelming pain hit me.

"Please! Let's just talk!"

Then he grabbed me by the hair and dragged me down the alleyway. The stench of sewage and garbage from the shops was nauseating. As he shook me, my scalp burned. There was no way I could fight off this man, over six feet tall, 80 kilograms of chiseled body with broad shoulders and a broad chest.

"Say it again, bitch. Look at me and tell me again with a straight face. You think you're doing so much for me? Huh, so much?" I could hear the sneer in his voice. "If you're doing so much for me, well, let's see if you can get it right," he whispered, blowing hot breath into my ear as I writhed in pain. "Why don't you get down on all fours and beg?"

The memory of that day—when I crawled on my knees in that narrow, dirty alleyway, crying and begging, "I'll never spend time with that bitch again." The memory of that miserable woman with her tear-stained face screaming, "Baby, I'm sorry, I love you," is tucked away in the back of my mind like it's not mine. I've never really dug it out, but when I do, it's only as real as a movie scene.

I lie in the darkness, both feet stretched out in front of me. It's the perfect weather for a little outing.

It's become a habit of mine to sneak out into the garden for some alone time for a few minutes after I put Seung-Joon to bed. In the mansion's front lawn, a small bench is tucked into a recess; it's become my sanctuary. This is where I can let myself decompress, away from people's prying eyes. Three or four grassy steps lead from the bench down to the pool. I haven't gotten a chance to take a dip yet, but it feels good just looking at it. It feels like a place where I can erase the memories of my dark past.

Heesun and Mrs. Suwon have gone home from work, and it's quiet everywhere. I take out my phone and flip through the photos. The couple there looks so happy. That's what photographs are: embodiments of false memories. You think you've captured the truth of the moment, but it's really just a glorified illusion.

Hi, honey.

Sorry, but not sorry.

One by one, I erase his faces: in the park where he confessed his feelings to me not long after we met, on his birthday when I was gleefully smearing cake on his face, and in the cramped half-basement room where he was kissing my cheek, laughing happily.

To make this new life truly mine, I need to leave my past behind. Looking at these pictures makes me realize that I deserve to be happy. Mine has been a hard and torturous life, a struggle that I can't expect anyone to understand. Now I'm ready to let go of who I used to be.

"What are you doing?"

"Dear God!"

My phone falls to the ground with a loud clatter.

"Oh! I'm sorry, sister. Did I startle you? I thought you heard me."

"Ah, Soohyun."

"Are you okay?"

"Yeah, yeah, I'm fine, I just needed some alone time."

I bend over in a panic and grope under the bench. I hope my phone is shattered or the screen's blown out. How long has he been standing behind me? How much did he see?

My heart keeps pounding so hard that it threatens to jump out of my mouth.

"Oh no, it's not broken, is it?"

He bends down and begins to rummage around under the bench, too.

"No, leave it, I've got it," I mumble, and even drop to my knees, fumbling around in the dark grass.

"Ah! I found it! It's here!"

I hurriedly reach out, but it's too late.

Soohyun turns around and holds out my cell phone with its brightly lit screen. A picture of my boyfriend with his arm around my shoulder, smiling broadly, is clearly visible on the screen. My breath catches in my throat. A million thoughts race through my head.

If I turn and dive in, would I hit my head on the bottom of that pool and die? Would that put me out of my misery instantly? *No, I'll just say I used to know this guy and dated him only briefly.* Or maybe I could tell him he was my cousin, or maybe he was a friend, or maybe he was a stalker who used to bully me.

That's when Soohyun waves my cell phone at me as if to say, "Here it is."

"Sorry." He smiles. "I didn't mean to pry."

His chuckling voice follows as I hold out a trembling hand and take the phone.

"But damn, my brother always looks so great in photos, right?"

CHAPTER

·17·

The excruciating pain, the flashes of light in my eyes, the loud and clear pop, and the red streaks spreading on the floor.

These are the memories of that day in my head.

"I haven't even decided whether I should go to the picnic, so let go of me!"

"Oh, now you just get to decide everything on your own?"

"I mean, I mean . . . Can't we just talk?"

"Are you ordering me around?"

"You know I'm not!"

The moment I saw his face, the moment I realized that instead of my handsome and loving boyfriend, I was facing a monster again, I became sick of it all.

Everything that was about to happen replays in my head like a movie I can watch over and over again. I let out a laugh because it's so obvious how it will end.

As he tugged at my wrist and tried to grab my hair with his other hand, I ducked low and reached under his shoulder. I grabbed the handle of an old frying pan from the sink behind him. It was gnarled and lightly greased from years of use. It was a hefty, heavy thing, but I knew I only had one shot, so I lifted it as high as I could with all my might and then slammed it down on the back of his head.

Clang!

There was a heavy clang, as if a New Year's bell had been struck.

The frying pan hit his hard, round head, then bounced back and dropped to the floor. The blow itself might have been unremarkable, but it was enough to set off a chain reaction like a series of dominoes.

He staggered back, off-center from the blow. I quickly stepped away, dodging his hands as they flailed to grab something. He slipped, the side of his head hitting the corner of the old sink hard. Then came a sound similar to an eggshell cracking. One of his hands landed on top of my foot. I tried to take a step back, but I had my back against the wall, cornered.

I stood against the wall, shivering and looking down at him. I felt like at any moment he would rise to his feet, his face red with rage, and strangle me.

"Hey . . . honey? Are you okay? I didn't mean to . . ."

A strangled sound came out of my mouth. It was so unfamiliar that it sounded like someone else's voice. It was as if my lips were moving of their own accord, spitting out random words.

"Baby? I'm sorry. Please?"

But he didn't stir. His fingers on my bare foot didn't move, either.

I knew I had to get away, but unable to move, I just stood there, clueless, until I caught my first glimpse of the red stain: a single, sticky streak of vivid red slowly crawling and spreading across the worn and tattered vinyl flooring. I squatted down and stuck out two fingers to give his shoulder a nudge. My hand shook so violently that it looked like I was having a seizure.

"Are you okay?"

The red streak grew. I barely remember what happened after that; the memory is in fragments. I do remember muttering incessantly that I needed to get out of there.

"I have to get out. I've got to get out. Get out, get out!"

I was about to walk out the front door, slippers on, when I remembered my wallet. I frantically searched my pockets, but it was nowhere to be seen. I realized that I would have to climb over his immobile body to get into the bedroom where it might be, but I couldn't bring myself to do it.

I think that's when the tears started. The moment I turned around,

I felt like a hand was going to reach out and grab my ankle like in a horror movie. I would rather bite my tongue and die. I even thought I'd take out a knife from a kitchen drawer and defend myself if my boyfriend came to and I had to face his full-blown rage.

That's when I noticed my wallet, sitting haphazardly on the corner of my shoe rack's top shelf. Drained after work last night, I must have left it there while taking off my shoes. I quickly shoved it into the back pocket of my pants and headed out the door.

It was well past midnight, but I could hear dogs barking and people talking and laughing in the alleyways near my apartment. My neighborhood stayed awake, restless, until dawn. There was always drinking, fighting, and chatting. Even the sound of our arguments would have been lost in the general noise of life there. I stumbled out of the alley, wiping my face—which was covered in tears, snot, and sweat—with the back of my hand.

A bloodred crescent moon hung in the sky. Like the single distorted eye of a god smiling and winking at me. Oh, how I wanted to spit on it! God had never blessed me, had dealt me one horrible hand after another for all these years. And now this? The more I thought about it, the calmer I grew, the trembling in my hands slowing. Blood rushed back into my cold body, and my dazed mind seemed to slowly wake up.

I got myself out of the alley, crossed the street, and started walking in the direction opposite my usual commute. At every fork in the road, I continued to turn in the opposite direction. I'll admit that the train station was not a great choice. But I had no other option. The bus I would have taken was canceled, and I couldn't take a taxi without a clear destination. Plus, all I had in my wallet was a debit card and some cash. The credit card in my name had been cut up earlier in the year in a mutual effort to save money, and my boyfriend said that due to his bad credit, he couldn't get another one for a while. He said he'd been paying off his late father's debts and his credit was in trouble. But he was working, and he brought home a decent amount of money every once in a while. On special occasions, he would buy me gifts. So I didn't think much of it.

I never doubted the stories he'd told me about himself.

His family had once been well off, he'd said, but his father squandered the fortune that had been his grandfather's, and there was nothing left. His mother had died when he was a little kid, and while he had a half-brother, they were no longer in touch. He and his family grew apart, and they told him to never come back. He said he was basically an orphan now. He told me that he was alone in the whole world and that no one cared about him. I told him that I understood what he meant and that I would be his family. Yes, that's what we'd promised each other. That we, the two of us, could be a family.

How I'd clung to those words. When I'd first met him, I was lonely, having grown up in the system. I did end up with a foster family, but eventually they sent me back, and I'd been living alone ever since. I'd always been hungry for a family. Someone I could trust, someone who was really on my side. But I guess I'd ended up alone again.

I hid at the station until it was time for the first train. As the day slowly dawned, I became more clearheaded.

I had time to get in the clear. I lived in the half-basement of a dilapidated two-story building at the end of a cul-de-sac. The rooftop room was occupied by a truck driver who was away half the time, and the second floor had been empty for over a year. The landlady was a single woman in her forties who lived in Vietnam, so we rarely saw each other face-to-face. My deposit was enough to cover a year's worth of rent, so no one would be coming to collect. He was between jobs, and I could message my coworkers at the store that something came up and I could no longer work there. So no one would be looking for us for some time.

I know—what a cute little darling I was, so clueless as to think I could commit a perfect crime and get away with it just like that. But I didn't exactly have a plan.

I'd just wanted to buy myself some time. After a while, once I got my shit together, I might have even gone back to my place. I could have owned up to what I had done and made amends; I could have gone to the police and come clean. The police could have run some tests and proven to me that the frying pan I swung didn't kill him, that hitting his head on the sink had. And after all, hadn't what I'd done been self-defense? Isn't that the truth? I wasn't the bad guy. What had happened was bound to happen. The bruises all over my body would have proved it. So I wasn't trying to be some kind of a mastermind on the run. I just wanted to figure out what to do next.

But I also never planned to learn the true identity of the man I killed in this way.

CHAPTER
·18·

"Are you okay?"

I look up to see Soohyun looking genuinely worried.

"What's wrong? Oh, the phone's fine. It's not cracked or broken."

I can't think of anything to say back.

His brother is my dead boyfriend, the very man in this picture? The young mother's husband, the baby's father? Then this is his house?

I am not in the wrong place after all. I'm not in a stranger's house, filling in for a woman I met on the train who had nothing to do with me. No, technically, I *am* the undeserving woman the eldest son chose. He never asked me to marry him, but we had been living together for over a year and a half anyway.

I stare blankly at Soohyun, who stands in front of me with an awkward smile on his face.

I mean, this is actually my boyfriend's home, and these people are his flesh and blood. The home of the man who made me happy and hurt me, who made me cry, laugh, and scream for countless days over the last few years. The man who made me tremble in terror, and whose blood was on my hands.

I remember him telling me: "At home, I always went by my nickname, Hyunni. So I've never used my full name much. It almost feels like someone else's name!"

Lies, all lies. Who the hell was the man I believed I loved? The man who promised to have my back, who taught me what it was like to have a family, who taught me what it felt like to love and be loved, who taught me what pain was like, what fear was like, what true terror was like? Who the hell was he?

"But we both know we shouldn't be fooled by his looks, right? My brother in these photos . . . he's always pretending to be a cool guy, faking a smile like that. Putting on a show."

Soohyun laughs and points with his chin to the cell phone in my hand. I can't bring myself to laugh along with him. I'd thought I'd gotten used to masking my emotions well, but I'm failing miserably this time.

"I guess you're still missing him a lot."

He studies my expression and turns away, pretending to look at the mountains in the distance. Of course, he has every reason to think I'm missing his brother. After all, I came out here in the middle of the night to sneak a peek at these photos alone, didn't I?

"That's the kind of person he is. He can be so sweet and make you fall head over heels for him one moment, and then suddenly he's gone. You seem to be in a lot of pain."

I stare up at Soohyun's face in the light. Why haven't I noticed it before? His face—yes, different, but also eerily and unmistakably similar to my boyfriend's. That's why I instantly felt so at ease with Soohyun, a complete stranger. Or am I just making all this up after the fact?

"Those bruises"—he gestures to my wrist—"I actually saw them the first day you got here. I knew then that you must be my brother's wife. He was the same way when he was living with us. He could never control his emotions."

"He was the same here?"

"Oh." Soohyun looks back at me and lowers his eyes slightly. He seems regretful, seeing the horrified look on my face. "It wasn't always like that, you know. He's a sweet person by nature, and although we're six years apart, he was more than just a brother to me. His mom was strict, so he's the only one I could lean on. When he suddenly told me he was going to study abroad, I cried day and night. I felt so lost because I was going to be alone in this big house. I feel guilty saying this, but when things didn't work out and he had to stay here, I even se-cretly sighed with relief. But after the incident, everything changed."

"How did he change?"

"I don't know. He started having nightmares. He'd wake up in the middle of the night, screaming."

"Nightmares?"

"It didn't happen every day, but quite often. And whenever it did, the next morning, he'd come down to the dining room with bags under his eyes. He'd go sleepless for days on end, wandering around the house at night. I think he was trying not to fall asleep, afraid of the nightmares. He would down cup after cup of strong coffee to stay awake. Once, I took a sip of my brother's coffee and I thought I was going to drop dead. It tasted like poison."

Strong coffee and nightmares. Yes, sounds like the guy I lived with.

Two or three times a month, usually on nights when we got into a fight, he would wake up screaming and shaking with fright, his whole body drenched in sweat, and he would cling to me like a little child.

He said it was because he was so sorry for what he'd done to me. He swore he'd never lay a finger on me again, and that he was dis-gusted with himself. Then he'd ask me to hold him.

"I'll never do that again, honey. I'm sorry. I can't help myself. I'm going crazy," he would mumble with his arms around my waist, his lips in the nape of my neck.

Whenever I asked him what the hell one of his dreams was about, he never answered, just held me tighter.

"Was he upset that he couldn't go live abroad?"

"I guess so. He was in no condition to go anywhere with the injury, so that must have been frustrating."

"How did he get injured?"

"Oh, my brother's ankle. He fell down the stairs in the house and broke it. That's why he stopped playing ice hockey and everything."

I knew he had a bad ankle. But he told me it was because he'd got-ten hurt on his first construction job. He would complain about how it throbbed on a rainy day. But ice hockey? I'd never heard of him playing. There are quite a few things I've learned about my live-in boyfriend today.

"I personally think it wouldn't have been any different had he gotten to go abroad, though. I don't think he was genuinely interested in ice hockey; he was just trying to run away."

"Why? What was he running away from?"

Soohyun shrugs.

Shaded by branches overlooking the pool, we sit side by side on the cozy bench, water rippling gently in the night breeze.

"I'm sure he wanted to get away from the memory of the incident. And being in this house was a constant reminder of what had happened."

"You mean what happened to his mom?"

Soohyun nods in silence.

"What happened?"

"Um, did my brother tell you anything?"

"He just told me that she died in an accident when he was young, but he didn't go into detail."

That much is true.

This is what he told me: After his mother died in an accident, his father remarried, and he didn't get along with his stepmother, which is why, after his father died, he ran away from home and worked odd jobs. In hindsight, there were so many things left out of his story. I never once imagined him growing up in this kind of family, even though all my friends thought of him as a "princely boyfriend."

"But that can happen to anyone. Losing a parent in an accident doesn't mess people up that badly."

Soohyun hesitates, looking down at his toes. "Uh, I think it's because it wasn't a simple accident."

"How so?"

"She died in this house."

"In this house?"

"Yes, it was sort of a substance accident."

"Oh my!"

"She had a pre-existing condition."

"Then you were both at home?"

"Yes, we were home."

"Gosh. That must have really traumatized you guys. You two were at such sensitive ages, no?"

"Well, that's not the only thing."

"What do you mean?"

Soohyun shrugs and smiles bitterly. "I guess . . . he never believed it was an accident."

CHAPTER

·19·

What are the odds that two women in a relationship with the same man would run into each other on the first train at dawn?

I met a woman I didn't know on the train and was asked to take her kid to her in-laws' house, which, when I got there, turned out to be my boyfriend's house. What are the odds?

There's no other explanation. This was a setup from the beginning. What a bitch! What had she said?

"I don't know what my in-laws will say if I just show up out of nowhere. Maybe they'll just take my son away. I mean, my husband comes from money. You know, the kind of rich people so conservative and judgmental that they pay you to keep your mouth shut just because they don't want to hear your voice? My husband is the eldest son, too."

"So you've never met his parents before?"

"Yeah, they probably don't even know what my name is or what I look like. My husband was already living away from home when he met me, and he said he hadn't spoken to his family in a while."

I gaze at Seung-Joon's sleeping face and gently brush back the fluffy hair that has fallen over his round forehead. I take in his flawless skin and long-set eyes, and there's no doubt in my mind, even without a paternity test, that this is his son. The woman gave birth to my boyfriend's child just three months earlier. Based on the length of her pregnancy, they had been together for at least a year. Unless they had a one-night stand, they must have known each other for a long time before that.

In two months, we'll have been together for two years. And just a month after we started dating, we moved in together. He was probably already in a relationship with her when we started going out, or he started seeing her right after I moved in with him.

How long had he been cheating? He must have known about the child. In the end, ours wasn't a great love—it wasn't even love at all. I was beaten, cheated on, and deceived. How could I have been such an idiot?

A handsome young man with no major handicaps, with a clear show of intelligence, but he still wasn't able to hold down a normal job. He'd explained that he had gotten very sick in high school and had to take a few years off from school, a setback that made him fall behind, so he couldn't get into university. He'd said he had been struggling ever since he left home. He couldn't find an office job, so he worked as a manual laborer, and his situation gradually improved when he got a forklift operator's certificate. Sometimes he would be away from home for weeks at a time when he was assigned a job at a construction site, but he always came back with a lot of money.

At first, I hated how frequently he had to go away. But when he started to show his true colors, I was thankful for all the time he spent away from home. Now I realize that while he was away, he must have been *having fun* somewhere else. How great that must have been, considering that he'd even fathered a kid without my knowing.

If I had him in front of me, I wouldn't hesitate to hit him with the frying pan one more time. And this time, I'd make sure to knock his head off.

I want to yell, *Why didn't you just leave, you son of a bitch!*

Why didn't you just leave me alone and go live with your other woman and your child!

Then I wouldn't have gotten blood on my hands. I had endured all that suspicion, control, and violence because I thought he was "too in love," only to realize that I was being taken advantage of by a cheating scumbag.

I think of the face of the woman on the train again.

Soft, plump cheeks, flawless skin, a look of innocence. A pair of brown eyes.

She'd looked like a happy new mom—nothing like me, a woman bruised and battered, jumpy as a starving bobcat, startled by the slightest sound. She'd looked almost cuddly, sweet, like a fluff of cotton candy. It's obvious that she had never been beaten. Unlike me, she had been treated with love and kindness. That's for sure. And she knew him better than I did—she'd told me all about her husband's—my boyfriend's—family history.

No wonder I kept thinking that she hadn't seemed like someone who would leave her child behind. She must have thought out a foolproof plan. By no means was she impulsive enough to give her baby to a random woman she'd just met on a train. Clearly, this was all an elaborate scheme, and I was a carefully chosen prop.

What the hell really happened that day?

I replay the events after my flight from the apartment in my mind. In a panic, I'd gone straight to the train station and waited for the first train, afraid that my boyfriend would wake up and chase me, blood dripping from his head. Luckily, the station was full of people coming and going, so I was able to blend in with the crowd. I got a coffee from the vending machine and waited, shivering, near the women's restroom until the train pulled in and I jumped on.

I was sitting with my back to the window, staring anxiously at the passersby, when the woman came in. I was sitting in the very back and the car was empty. But she didn't even bother to walk farther, just crossed the aisle and stood next to me and started to put her luggage up. Sure, it might have been the seat she'd bought, but who wants to sit next to another person in an empty car? And with a baby in tow?

She was obviously targeting me. She must have been following me the entire day. The more I thought about it, the more clearly I could see how things had unfolded. She was definitely aware of who I was. She probably noticed that there was something off about her husband.

In her eyes, I must have been the other woman. So she'd kept tabs on us—me. She had always been watching.

I have no idea which one of us he started dating first, me or her. He might have already been her lover the first day I met him, when he'd rescued me from some drunk at the convenience store where I'd worked.

"I swear I paid five thousand won! This bitch is trying to cheat me!"

"Sir, you paid one thousand won. I counted it out and showed it to you."

"You think you're going to get away with this? You're going to cheat and take my money because I look drunk? You twat!"

That's when my boyfriend had grabbed the drunk's wrist like a prince on a white horse.

"I was watching it all, and you're the liar. Why don't you just go on your merry way, or do you want me to call the police and check the surveillance camera?"

His low, threatening voice was so sexy, it was love at first sight.

As the drunk walked away, I quickly grabbed a cold can of beer from the store fridge and handed it to him.

"I'm on a bit of a beer hiatus right now, so how about a coffee tomorrow instead? I'll be off work around three, so I'll be free; can I come pick you up?"

I'd never been asked out so politely. It almost felt strange. I fell in love with the nonchalant way he threw words around, the bass of his voice, and the twinkle in his eye.

But even then, he was probably already seeing her. He must have been going back and forth between the two of us, showering her with love and rewarding me with all his dark, violent tempers. To one of us, he had been honest, revealing his family history in detail, but to me, everything he'd said had been a lie.

He must have needed a side piece to fulfill his darkest desires, to escape from his mundane, domestic life with a bright and cheerful wife, from his child growing in her belly. He wanted to have both worlds. It would have been easy to keep the two of us clueless with a job that required him to be gone for days at a time, traveling from place to place in search of construction sites. When he told me he'd be away on a job, he must have gone home to her, and they would have had a happy time together as a family. Then, when his libido wasn't satisfied by his pregnant wife, or when he was tired of playing family, he must have come back to me and vented his anger whenever he felt like it.

The young mother might have been blissfully unaware of her husband's violent side, but as it went on, she must have begun to sense something was off. One day, she must have followed him and found our home, and I bet she was furious. She might not have been able to accuse him of being a cheater, not having officialized their marriage yet, but discovering the existence of another woman when she was about to have his child?

And this is what terrifies me: Instead of attacking me directly, pulling my hair and yelling, she'd chosen to ambush me with her bright smile, to leave me with her child. Instead of entering her fabulously wealthy in-laws' home herself, she'd chosen to send the person she wanted to punish most.

I realize there must be something dangerous about this house. But what?

There is not a single picture of my boyfriend here, and his family has never mentioned his name. They say he left home for one reason or another, they don't expect him to come back, and they're not even waiting for him. They don't bother to report him missing. Even though he's the "eldest son."

It's definitely my fault that I was so focused on roleplaying that I didn't think to look into why. But I hadn't realized I was going to stay here for this long, and I certainly had no idea how I was connected to all this.

The mother must have known about this bizarre situation—not only about the family's wealth, but also my boyfriend's trauma, his mother's death, and something about this house that she wanted to avoid.

Why the hell would she let her kid into such a strange situation? Just to get a fresh start?

The woman had no intention of coming here on her own. She'd wanted a courier to bring her child here safely and a scapegoat to take her place if things went wrong. The child, a blood relative of the family, would be safe, but she'd decided that this was a dangerous place for herself.

That means this was not a blessing in disguise, but her chance at revenge. I'd walked right into her trap.

Coming to this house was a huge mistake. It was all my fault— getting caught up in the luxury clothes, the pool, the cute brother-in-law, the illusion of being the daughter-in-law of a rich family, not to mention failing to recognize or outright ignoring all the red flags.

I jump to my feet and pace around my room.

Things have been okay so far, but what's going to happen next? How much risk am I putting myself in by staying?

Then, another thought: If she'd followed me onto the train, where and when did she start trailing me?

From the house?

How much had she seen? All of it?

She might have. Our terrible fight. How it started . . . and how it ended.

CHAPTER

· 2 0 ·

When I stagger down the stairs, the air is potent with lemon-scented furniture polish. The doors to each room on the first floor are left wide open, and I can hear the hum of a vacuum cleaner.

Speaking of which, is today Wednesday of the second week—the cleaning day? It must be. A big house like this requires the entire staff to stick around all day for a thorough cleaning, to get into every nook and cranny. A loud buzzing sound comes from the garden. Mr. Kim must be using a leaf blower.

"Good morning!" Heesun greets me as she comes out of the parlor, dragging a heavy bundle of curtains that she must have just pulled down. Everyone's in the middle of a busy workday. I don't feel comfortable having slept in, being greeted when I don't look the least bit presentable.

"Sorry, I didn't get much sleep last night."

"Oh, because of the baby?"

"Not exactly. Just a lot going on . . ."

"Oh, Seung-Joon's awake, isn't he? Mrs. Suwon is cleaning the kitchen. I'll just drop this off and take over so she can go look after Seung-Joon."

"Oh, everyone's so busy. If you just hand me the bottle, I can feed him."

"Oh, no, you've got your breakfast in the dining room, ma'am. You go ahead and eat. We'll take care of Seung-Joon."

Heesun doesn't waste any time talking but walks breathlessly toward the kitchen.

As I pass through the empty living room, bright sunlight pours through the open front door. I can see dust floating in the air, the scratches on the old furniture and floorboards, and the dents in the staircase handrail. Everything familiar has taken on a new feeling of freshness now. This is no longer a home I'm disconnected from; this is the house my boyfriend spent his childhood in, the place that showed up sometimes in the stories he'd told me.

"It was just a house, nothing special."

"This? It's a very old scar. I tripped and fell down the stairs when I was a kid."

"I hate old furniture. I don't like vintage or antique or anything like that. Isn't it all junk?"

There was nothing in his memories that brought a smile to my lips. No cozy reminiscences about his parents or family, no pleasant family anecdotes that a normal person would have shared. I chalked it up to a mother who passed away when he was young, a half-brother to take care of, and a loveless upbringing. Just like me, who didn't have any good childhood memories to share because I'd grown up in an orphanage and always had to fend for myself. But obviously I'd been wrong. Had I grown up in such a grand and impressive house, I would have had plenty of memories worth sharing. See? A rich brat always whines the loudest.

Isn't it funny, honey, that I'm cuddling up with your child in this fancy house you couldn't wait another second to get the fuck out of? The child you've been hiding from me, you son of a bitch.

I also notice that the doors to the aide's room, my father-in-law's room, and the basement are wide open. I tiptoe quickly past the father's room. I wish I could be the cheery daughter-in-law who stops by and says good morning, but I don't have the energy. Not yet.

The past few nights have been sleepless, and my head is foggy, with growing bags under my eyes.

"Ouch!"

"Oh no!"

A bowl hits the floor with a clang and shatters. Just stepping into the dining room, I've collided head-on with Mrs. Suwon carrying some soup out on a tray. This has resulted in a mess all over the antique floor tiles, my clothes, and Mrs. Suwon's apron.

"Oh, I'm sorry, what have I done?"

"No, I'm to blame. The soup got cold, and I was trying to heat it up for you."

Heesun, who's heard the commotion and realizes what's going on, quickly grabs a rag and cleaning solution. I watch in a daze as the two women frantically clean the stains, then I quickly bend down to help.

"Give it to me," I say. "I'll do it myself."

"No, no need, ma'am."

"Please, leave it to me," I insist. "I'll take care of it. By the way, Seung-Joon is awake, could you go upstairs and take a look at him?"

Mrs. Suwon gets to her feet and leaves the dining room, glancing behind uncertainly. In the meantime, Heesun snatches the rag from my hand.

"No, Ms. Heesun. This was my fault."

"It's okay, it's my turn to clean the dining room anyway. I'll take care of it."

"But . . ."

"Please, go eat your breakfast. I'll just put this away and bring the soup back." Heesun smiles wryly, clutching the rag, and begins to wipe away the stains in a frenzied manner.

It's hard to believe that I, who used to wipe down dirty grills every day, should now leave such a small task to someone else.

Heesun looks up at me as I linger around. "These are marble tiles, so you have to be careful or you'll leave marks," she mutters in between spraying and mopping the floor with the cleaning liquid. "This is my specialty. I panicked when I first got here, but now I'm an expert. I can do this blindfolded. It's sad, though—now that I've gotten the hang of it, I've reached the end of my two years here."

I stop in my tracks. "Oh, come to think of it—"

Heesun looks up.

"So you're both really leaving at the end of two years?" I ask in a deliberately vague tone, as if I've known this all along.

"Well . . ." Heesun laughs uncomfortably. "That's what we were told when we first signed on."

"How long do you have left?"

"Me and Mrs. Suwon, we both have about five months left," Heesun says wistfully as she continues to mop.

"That's a shame. It would be nice to have some familiar faces stick around," I mutter to myself as I walk toward the dining room, only to stop and throw a look back.

"By the way, what's with that two-year rule—?"

"Sister!"

I've barely opened my mouth when Soohyun suddenly appears.

"Have you eaten? It's such a beautiful day! If you haven't already, how about brunch outside?"

Before I realize, I'm swept up in the wind of his momentum, grabbed by the arm and dragged out of the dining room.

I glance back and see Heesun look in my direction and quickly turn her head away.

CHAPTER

· 21 ·

"I feel bad for leaving like this; they've prepared breakfast for us."

"Oh, well, I'm sure they'll understand, I do this all the time. I'm quite impulsive, you know."

This man with the big smile is no stranger to me now: his flawless skin and lanky limbs, a slight dimple that pops up when he smiles, slender eyes—all reminiscent of my boyfriend but also so different. It's no wonder I didn't compare them at first. Despite all the glaring similarities, they contrast like night and day. The younger brother, who was born out of wedlock, is a cheerful person, so why did my boyfriend turn into such a monster?

"What do you want for dessert? Fig pie or crème brûlée?"

"Anything sweet sounds good!"

"You have a sweet tooth like me! It's settled, let's have some crème brûlée!" The corners of his eyes crinkle into a smile as he folds the menu and sets it aside. The look Soohyun has on his face right now is actually pretty familiar. Come to think of it, all three of the men in this family, including Seung-Joon, smile with their eyes just like that.

"I got up early for work today and walked out into such a beautiful day. So I thought I'd bring you out. It's cleaning day, and with all the mess, I need to apologize for leaving you alone all morning. I wouldn't know what to do if I stayed home on cleaning day."

"You saved me, for sure, but I don't know if I should be doing this. I feel a bit guilty that I didn't tell Father I was going out."

"My dad doesn't like to be disturbed when he's resting, so I'm sure he'll understand. We can get everyone some snacks on our way back. What do you think?"

I nod.

"I'm glad I have a sister now. I haven't always been very considerate. I usually just come and go as I like. The staff are all nice people, but I'm much younger than them, so they can get a little bit cliquey, too."

"Well, you hire new staff every two years, so that can't really help." I throw a glance at him. As the daughter-in-law of this family, I'm not out of line to mention something like this in passing. Still, it doesn't feel right to impose.

"I guess so."

"Isn't a house as big as yours better left to people who've been around for a while and are used to things? Training new staff can be a lot of work, I imagine."

"I'm not used to this yet, either."

"Is it because of that incident you mentioned? Is that why there's a two-year cycle?" I ask as nonchalantly as I can, folding my napkin.

Soohyun's expression darkens ever so subtly. "Well, sort of."

"You said it was an accident." I don't say the rest out loud: *although your brother thinks otherwise.*

Soohyun lowers his voice. "Yes, but it happened in the house, and everyone thought it was a 'preventable' accident."

"Preventable?"

"It was a food allergy–related accident, so that's what I think, too. My brother's mom had a severe nut allergy."

"Oh, so it was something she ate."

Soohyun nods. His face has turned serious, his smile evaporated. "It wasn't just a mild allergy. Something like that can be life-threatening."

"You must have had some kind of medicine at home."

"Of course we did, shots and pills and everything. It's weird that an accident happened at all in the first place. All of the house staff back then had been working for us for four to six years, and they knew everything, like what's okay to put in the food, what's not, all that kind of stuff, but it still happened."

Our dessert arrives.

We stop talking for a moment and watch the plates being set at our cozy window-seat table. The smooth surface of the crème brûlée glistens golden in the sunlight that's streaming through the glass.

"I couldn't believe what was happening right before my eyes. She took one spoonful, and all of a sudden her hands and feet went limp and her neck and face puffed up. That was the first time I realized that a person's face could turn purple like that."

"No. . . . So you were there, too?"

Soohyun nods. "My brother and I were in the garden. We heard people shouting, so we ran home, only to find her lying on the dining room floor."

"How old were you then?"

"My brother was eighteen and I was twelve."

"Oh my!"

I try to imagine a woman collapsing on the floor of the dining room where I spilled the soup earlier today. A well-dressed rich lady gurgling with a purple face, holding her swollen neck in pain. A handsome high schooler and his skinny brother watching it all, helpless.

"Someone ran into the master bedroom and grabbed the first aid kit, because we always had epinephrine pills and shots on hand, but the box turned out to be . . ."

"Empty," I offer, to which Soohyun nods.

"The allergy attack was really quick, and we lost valuable time trying to find her meds. By the time the paramedics arrived, it was too late."

"You watched all of that?"

"Not on purpose. My brother covered my eyes and tried to drag me away, but I still saw because everything happened so fast." Soohyun looks away from me, pensive.

Neither of us has touched the crème brûlée.

"So he thought someone on the staff did it intentionally."

"Well, they were in charge of everything from food to cleaning. If they'd wanted to, they definitely could have. Of course, the police investigation didn't turn up anything concrete."

"But why would anyone want to do that? I'm sure it was an accident. I can't see why someone would try and kill her."

"Um . . ." Soohyun hesitates for a moment, as if he's embarrassed, then explains, "Actually, not too long before the accident, one of the staff was let go and we parted ways on bad terms."

"One of the helpers?"

"Yeah, one of the female staff got caught trying to steal a piece of jewelry, and everyone went ballistic."

"Oh my God."

"She'd been with us for a long time, and she'd had some money problems in the past. She said her husband got into an accident, and she'd been borrowing money from us here and there. Not exactly ideal for someone working the kind of job she was. So we fired her, but we were shorthanded with the holidays right around the corner, and it's not like we could hire people on such short notice, so we had an agreement that she'd work through the end of the week, and then on Saturday, the accident happened."

"So, he thought it was the helper."

"Well, we didn't have any hard evidence, but we didn't have any counterproof, either."

"So that's why your family doesn't trust people."

"Yes, that's when things started changing. Ever since, we've only hired everyone, even aides and caregivers, on a two-year term."

I nod.

"And that's when my brother changed."

Anyone who witnessed such a horrific event firsthand is bound to be traumatized. But why is it that an eighteen-year-old high school student was more shocked and disturbed than a twelve-year-old junior high school student? Is it because one person was more resilient and the other wasn't as able to withstand the shock? If not that—

"He must have loved his mother so much."

"I think it was the other way around."

"What?" I lift my head and look at Soohyun, but he doesn't meet my eyes. He seems to be looking somewhere far away, beyond my grasp.

"She was the kind of person who wouldn't leave anyone alone. Very neurotic and sensitive. She drove everyone crazy. She was especially obsessed with my brother. She was extremely strict about everything, whether it was grades or behavior. So my brother probably—"

Soohyun stares into the distance with a dreamy expression on his face and mutters: "Maybe he wanted his mother to die."

CHAPTER

·22·

When I open the door in the morning, there's a bouquet of flowers waiting.

Going out early today. Have a good trip to the doctor's office.
It's a beautiful day, so have a nice cup of coffee and enjoy yourself.
And call me if you need me!

The sweet note makes my day.

When I wake up these days, things are so good I feel like I'm floating in the clouds.

Didn't someone say that heaven and hell are both in the mind? I've decided not to think about the complicated, headache-inducing thoughts that pestered me when I got here.

I'm living in the home of the man who beat me and cheated on me. The woman who bore his child sent me here. So what?

All in all, my decision to stay here is mine. I doubt Seung-Joon's mother would have predicted this. If I had just handed the baby over to his family and gone on my way, the outcome would have been completely different.

Besides, maybe this was all just a weird coincidence, and the young mother was simply on her way to her in-laws on the day I met her, just like she told me. Maybe she was fed up with her child's father because he stayed away too often and never came home. Maybe she'd decided to throw it all away and start over. She'd just happened to meet me that day, and thanks to me, her son was able to come here safely. So in the end, everything turned out fine, and there's nothing stopping me from enjoying this life.

Outside, the world is still quiet. As far as I know, nothing has changed, and no one is looking for me. Maybe I can stay here forever. Maybe this isn't a trap; it's a stroke of luck.

A life where cleaning, laundry, and meals are done without lifting a finger. The luxury of shopping at will with my father-in-law's black card. Nightly bubble baths in a sprawling mansion with a pool. And a sweet, adorable brother-in-law who leaves a bunch of fresh flowers outside my room in the morning.

After breakfast, which is prepared to my taste as always, I go up to my room and come back down carrying Seung-Joon and a bag that Suwon has prepared for me. Mr. Choi is pushing the chairman's wheelchair out, so I greet him, showing the child to the old man.

"Oh, are you going to the doctor now?" asks Mr. Choi, who's become quite friendly with me over the past few weeks. The old man barely turns his twisted head to look at the baby and tries to form something that resembles a smile.

"Yes, I'll be back soon, Father."

I no longer mind this unfamiliar designation. Somehow, knowing exactly who the eldest son of this family is gives me confidence. *After all, I've been beaten and deceived by your son, so I deserve this, right?*

When I walk outside, Mr. Park, the driver, waves at me in the garden. When I climb into the black foreign car parked in front of the gate, it drives away smoothly and without a sound.

The shiny twelve-story building, which houses both maternity and pediatric wards, is owned by the old man. He has two more buildings downtown and several more scattered throughout other cities. And the hospital staff, as it turns out, are eager to take special care of the child, in spite of the fact that I have no birth certificate for him, let alone a marriage license. After all, I am the daughter-in-law of the building owner, and this child is his first grandchild.

Soohyun accompanied me to my first appointment, and he took care of all the paperwork for me the first time around so that I got to see a doctor right away. When they asked him about Seung-Joon's lack of a birth certificate, he probably explained it away as an inheritance issue.

Now that I'm the daughter-in-law of this family, it seems general rules don't apply to me. But how did the young mother manage to vaccinate a child whose birth wasn't even registered? Did my boyfriend pull some strings at the time? Did he maintain some connections even after he left home? I still have a lot of questions, but there's no way to find any answers right now.

I'm sure there's much gossip and tongue wagging behind the scenes, but the staff are friendly to my face. I'm always given priority, escorted to the VIP room, and never have to pay for my appointments.

"How did you get such a handsome baby?" is the standard greeting. They don't hesitate to give silly compliments like "He's got all the good qualities of his mom and dad, and his mouth is just like yours" or "He's got his uncle's eyes!" which makes Soohyun laugh out loud.

"While you're here, why don't you have a gynecological checkup," one of the nurses suggests today. I decline with a vague smile and walk out, leaving the polite staff behind. I feel envious stares from mothers in the waiting room. This is my life now.

I wait in front of the elevator, one hand searching in my luxury bag for my sunglasses. I decide to have a cup of coffee at the open-air café on the first floor before contacting Mr. Park. As Soohyun wrote, the weather's too good to waste. I have nothing to fear. My life is so sweet right now that I'm able to forget all my worries and fears, so I might as well enjoy this paradise a little longer.

As I fumble around for my sunglasses, the elevator doors open. It's packed with people who have already gotten on, and I smile nonchalantly, taking a step back.

When the door slowly starts to close again, I see something unnerving from the corner of my eye. The chestnut-colored hair tied up in a bun. The unusually flawless and dewy skin. The pale pink floral dress. I don't know what caught my attention first, or if I really saw anything at all. I haven't even made eye contact with her or gotten a good look at her face, but I know in that moment. It's undeniable. There she is, amidst all those people, in the corner of the back row: the woman, the young mother.

"Wait! Wait!"

I frantically press the elevator button, but the doors have already closed. I scoop up Seung-Joon and run for the emergency exit. This is the ninth floor, so maybe, just maybe, if I hurry up a little, I can catch up with the people getting off at the first floor.

But when you're carrying a seven-kilogram baby boy and a diaper bag, it's hard to keep up. The staircase turns out to be a long way down. By the time I reach the first floor, I'm dripping with sweat. A throng of people is piling into the elevator, the people from earlier already long gone.

I dart out of the building, but there's no sign of the young mother in the passing crowd. I stand dumbfounded in the middle of the sidewalk, looking everywhere. What have I just seen? Did I really see her in that elevator, in that crowd of people, or could I be mistaken?

Out of breath, I look up at the building. From the tenth to the twelfth floor, there are hair salons, nail salons, a caregiver academy, a tax accountant academy, an aesthetic academy, a dentist, a psychiatric clinic, and a pharmacy. There's no way I can walk through all of them asking if any of them has seen a girl whose name I don't even know.

That's when my cell phone jangles in my purse. "Hello?" I answer the phone, my eyes unfocused. My sweaty hands keep shaking, and I feel like I might drop the phone.

"Sister? Are you done with your appointment? What are you up to? Taking a coffee break? Enjoying your freedom?"

Even at his cheerful voice, I can't smile as I usually would.

"No, just going straight home. I'm not feeling well."

I don't have time to enjoy my freedom anymore.

I'm chilled to the bone.

CHAPTER

· 2 3 ·

My fingertips are slick with sweat as I grope through the vines for the keypad hidden by the gate. My first day here, I stood dumbfounded, staring up at the high fence, but now, even with my trembling hands, I have no problem punching in the numbers.

I hurry through the wall of drooping green plants and into my familiar paradise, Seung-Joon in my arms. Mr. Kim, who's in the middle of trimming branches, nods his head to acknowledge me. I take a brief pause and try to slow my racing breath. The pool water, sparkling gold in the afternoon sun, seems to calm down my pounding heart. The peace exuding from the garden, which is a sanctuary behind the property's high walls, quiets down my blood. If that woman is out there, there's no way she could just barge in and disturb this tranquility. No one can force me out of this place.

After taking a deep breath, I walk past the pool and up the steep flight of stone steps, at the end of which I see a shiny silver wheelchair parked next to a bench. The old man's sitting alone. It looks like he's out for some fresh air. As much as I'm dying to go up to my room and have some time on my own, I can't bring myself to just breeze past him.

"I'm back, Father."

The old man's dull eyes come alive as he twists his head toward my voice. I sit down gingerly on the bench, holding Seung-Joon up so he can see him better.

"He weighs 7.5 kilograms—a pretty good weight. And he's healthy as a horse. We just need to keep up the good work, the doctor said."

An expression that vaguely resembles a smile appears on the old man's twisted face as he looks down at the sleeping child. Saliva drips from the corners of his shriveled mouth.

"Are you getting some air here? Mr. Choi must have gone away for a moment?"

"Uh-uh-uh-uh."

Obviously, there's no way I can decipher that and answer. But with my overwhelming thoughts, silence is actually better for me. We sit side by side for a while without saying a word, enjoying the view and looking down at the pool. The sounds of Mr. Kim's pruning shears mingle with the occasional chirps of a bird from above, and a warm, fragrant spring breeze glides through our hair. A perfect moment of peace. Everything here seems to be so far away from the noise of the outside world.

The man sitting right next to me has created and built the paradise in front of me. He is the ruler of this house, and even if he's handicapped and shriveled, there are still sparks of intelligence in his eyes. And now I belong in this house, in his family, and this baby I'm holding in my arms is his grandson. We're under the wing of this cranky old man. This thought alone makes me feel as if everything's going to be alright, as long as he's here to protect us.

I'm suddenly embarrassed for having freaked out. It's ridiculous I got scared shitless. There's no reason Seung-Joon's mother would have been in the building after abandoning her child and running away so shamelessly. If she wanted to claim her rights, she would have shown up here a long time ago. It makes no sense. I probably imagined it all because I've learned to expect the worst.

I let out a sigh of relief and stretch my legs. Just as I'm beginning to feel my eyelids grow heavy, I notice a little stream of water across the stone beneath my feet. What is this? Was Mr. Kim watering the garden, or did he leave the hose running? As my eyes follow the trail, they find a faint yellow pool under the wheelchair. Holy shit!

I scramble to my feet. The old man's ink-colored pants are soaked through. Either the aide forgot to put in a urinal or something's gone wrong. I can see the faintest tremor in the old man's arm resting on the armrest. Our eyes meet. The old man's sunken eyes dart from side to side in panic, his lips trembling, tears pooling. In an instant, tens of thousands of thoughts flash through my mind. Should I run up to the house and call Mr. Choi? Should I call Mrs. Suwon? They must be used to this kind of situation. This must have happened before. The old man won't want me to help him get undressed and change into new clothes. Even though I'm supposed to be his daughter-in-law, I'm still a woman after all.

However I look at it, this is a huge blow to the old man's pride. We stare at the stream of yellow liquid for a moment, speechless, spending a few unbearably long seconds not knowing what to do. Finally, I carefully lay Seung-Joon down on the bench. He's fast asleep, exhausted after our time outside. I quickly remove the blanket from the back of the wheelchair and drape it over the old man's lap. All the while, I don't say a word. I just send him a brief look and flash a reassuring smile.

"I'll help you inside, Father. Don't you worry. I've got strong arms."

After smoothing out the blanket wrapped around the old man's lower half, I begin to push the wheelchair toward the mansion. He proves to be quite heavy for someone so thin. I struggle a bit to get up the little hill beside the stairs, but I make it.

When I open the front door, Mrs. Suwon comes running. "Oh, Chairman, are you uncomfortable? Mr. Choi told me not to disturb you for a while so you could get some air."

"Oh, no problem at all," I say. "He was just getting a little tired."

Mrs. Suwon attempts to take over the wheelchair, but I decline help. "I'll handle this, but could you please go get my bag and Seung-Joon from the bench outside? He's asleep."

"Oh, yes, yes."

Mrs. Suwon throws me a curious look, probably wondering why I'd choose my father-in-law over my infant baby, but she runs out right away. Meanwhile, I push the wheelchair into Chairman Jung's room. It smells faintly of disinfectant in here, and it's dark with all the blinds drawn. I manage to maneuver the heavy wheelchair into the attached restroom. The spacious, wheelchair-friendly bathroom is equipped with a toilet, incontinence diapers, and a holder for IV fluids.

"Just a moment, Father."

I leave the wheelchair in the bathroom and rush back into the bedroom. Where's a change of clothes? Undergarments? Am I allowed to go through the cabinets in here?

"Hang in there a minute. I'll find everything, I'll find it!"

I try to reassure the old man, chattering away as I open the closet next to the bed.

On one side is a pile of thick blankets and bedding. I quickly slam the door shut and open the next one. It's filled with the kind of outerwear a man his age would wear when he goes out, including high-end brand hiking suits and jackets. I nervously slam the door shut again and open the next one—a chest of drawers.

"I'm sorry, I should have come in here more often and learned where you keep everything. But don't worry too much, Father. I was pretty good at scavenger hunts when I was in school."

I mumble to him as I search, trying to comfort him. Finally, I open the top drawer of the dresser and find the old man's underwear. I quickly grab a pair and take a deep breath. It's okay, I can do this. He's just an old man. I have to do this. I have to do this.

I slam the dresser door and run back into the bathroom. I carefully take off the blanket and begin removing the old man's wet socks while I talk gibberish. I want to reassure the old man and not shame him.

"The doctor said that Seung-Joon is growing very fast compared to other kids his age. Maybe it's because he's a boy, but he's definitely growing faster than most."

"Huh? Chairman?" comes a voice from behind me. I've just put the wet socks in the sink when Mr. Choi walks in.

"Ma'am?"

"Ah, Mr. Choi!"

"Is everything alright?"

"Father must have been in the garden a bit too long, so I brought him in." I quickly smile at the dumbfounded Mr. Choi.

"Ah." He takes one look at the large wet spot on the old man's pants and realizes what happened. "Oh, allow me to take over." He smiles and holds out his hand.

"I could take care of this—"

"It's okay. It's my job."

I shut up at that point and pull my hands back, carefully handing over the old man's new underwear.

"Father, Mr. Choi is here. I'll get going now."

I smile as gently as I can, as if to signal that everything's okay. There are still tears in the old man's eyes. As I tiptoe out of the room, I hear Mr. Choi talk to the old man behind the closed bathroom door.

"I'm so sorry I'm late. The call got on a bit too long, but you've done a good job with your daughter-in-law, sir. Young women these days don't dare to do hard work. If I hadn't made it in time, she would have taken care of it herself. She's definitely more gutsy than she looks. And thoughtful—considering she didn't ask Mrs. Suwon to take over."

I quietly close the door to his room and walk out. My armpits and back are drenched in sweat.

What would have happened had Mr. Choi been a little late? Even then, I would have just gone ahead and changed him into new clothes myself. I would have taken the old man's pants off and stripped him of his wet underwear. I would have looked the old man in the eye and dutifully smiled, doing it all without a word, like the filial daughter-in-law I'm supposed to be. I would have done more than that.

Because he's my lifeline. Because there's nothing I won't do to keep my place here.

CHAPTER

·24·

When we've just finished eating and put down our cutlery, Mrs. Suwon comes over and sets up wineglasses.

"Huh? What is it? Are we opening this today?" Looking over at the bottle of wine in front of me, Soohyun glances back and forth between Mrs. Suwon, me, and the old man, who sits at the head of the table.

"Well, Chairman specifically asked me to bring this out." Mrs. Suwon smiles meaningfully before leaving the dining room.

The old man's eyes meet mine. Until now, it's been hard to read his expression, but this time, I can sense the subtle difference. Now I can clearly see that the corners of the old man's eyes have softened. He seems to be smiling at me in secret. Mr. Choi, who's been assisting the old man right by his side, also smiles at me.

"Hey, this isn't the usual fare," Soohyun says. "Is today a special day I don't know about? This is a bottle of vintage from the year when my brother was born, and my dad loves it."

"Oh," I say, "I had no idea this was such a special wine. I guess he's giving me extra credit for having a nice little chat with him this afternoon."

After throwing a glance back at the old man, I shrug at Soohyun.

"What? Really? That's all it took? Wow, Dad, you were never so soft with me!" Soohyun chirps playfully.

But the old man doesn't look in his son's direction and instead lifts his head ever so slightly to look at me in between gulps of liquid food. Now I don't feel as uncomfortable or afraid to meet his eyes, although I still can't quite figure out how to read their complex emotions.

Even as I raise my wineglass for a toast, those eyes remain fixed on me.

"You must have gotten really close with my dad. I'm so happy," Soohyun says after dinner as we stroll together in the garden.

"I should try harder. I feel I've been neglecting him with all these excuses—that I'm trying to settle in, too busy looking after Seung-Joon—"

"Well, you don't have to push yourself too hard."

"No, I'm going to check in on him more and keep him company."

"Well, I don't know if you should." Soohyun lets out a short laugh and scratches the back of his head. The six lights illuminating the pool and garden bathe his delicate face and smiling eyes in a golden glow.

"Oh, why, is there something wrong?"

"Well, my dad might misread that kind of gesture as 'sympathy,' though I'm sure he's rewarding you for showing some effort today."

"Do you think so?"

Soohyun nods. "Before he fell ill, my dad had this horrible temper. Everybody was scared of him, save for my brother's mother. She actually had my dad under her thumb."

"The two of them must have been lovebirds."

"Not at all." Soohyun smirks before continuing. "It's only because my brother's mother was the source of all his wealth. And of course, there was me—who made my dad a sinner in her eyes."

"All of this came from her?"

"My dad's a self-made man who used to work in a small town where he owned a machine parts factory. That's how he got started. He became pretty successful, but if not for my stepmom, who was the daughter of a very rich man, he wouldn't have gone much further."

"So all of this—"

"Yeah, all the buildings, land, this wealth all started with the money my brother's mother had. Of course, my dad doubled and tripled it, but he must have felt insecure about it his whole life. Since he fell ill, he's been acting even more insecure."

"I see."

"Now that we've gotten the heavy stuff out of the way—how was your day at the hospital?"

Soohyun smiles, and I smile back. As I survey his thoughtful eyes, his head tilted as he listens, I feel all the fear and anxiety from earlier today dissipate.

As we stand under a dark sky with black clouds, a cool, gentle breeze sends the pool water softly rippling. Again there is the familiar sound of insects, the fragrance of spring. How I enjoyed the delicacies and the wine my father-in-law brought out for me; how I now enjoy the face so intensely focused on me. Suddenly, everything feels unrealistically blissful.

"I'm done with work for the week, by the way," Soohyun says affectionately as we walk up the garden stairs side by side. "I've had enough of the nine-to-five routine. If you want to go anywhere, I'll be your designated driver. Just ask and I'll give you a ride."

Soon, we're back inside the house. We've made it a habit to walk around the garden after dinner, chatting about this and that, and then to go upstairs to call it a night. I've gotten used to our nightly routine.

"Are you sure? I'll think about the offer."

"Yeah, think about it and let me know. And try not to get crushed under your big, fast-growing baby at night."

On the second floor, I giggle at his joke, wave, and close the door to my bedroom.

Soon, I'm sprawled out on my bed in my dimly lit room, with only the nightstand light on. After running my fingers lightly over Seung-Joon's plump cheeks, I begin to undress. That's when the darkened

room slightly lights up with a purring sound—the cell phone inform-
ing me there's a new text message. I nearly fall over, startled with my
pants halfway down my legs. I quickly check my phone, which glows
brightly in the darkness on my bedside table. Three simple words flash
across the screen.

How's it going?

CHAPTER

·25·

Through a door held ajar, I listen.

From the sound of it, the house staff seems busy making breakfast.

It's not even seven o'clock yet. I can't go downstairs; it's unusual for me to be up this early, so it would arouse suspicion. I haven't slept a wink all night, and it feels like I've been locked in my room for a decade, but I need to wait so everything looks normal; I can't risk doing anything out of the ordinary.

> How's it going?

Time screeched to a halt the moment I processed that text. The blood in my veins ran cold, and I stood frozen, staring down at my phone screen. Then, as if a spell had been broken, I jumped up and locked my bedroom door. I locked all the window latches, looked behind the shower curtain, in the closet, and under the bed. With all the lights on in my room and the bathroom, I sat curled up in bed and stayed up all night. I would have jumped out of the window and left if not for Seung-Joon's comforting presence.

I had nowhere to hide. I wanted to run away. I was scared to death.

I didn't dare touch my phone again. I threw it away into a corner and stared at it, chewing my fingernails.

How's it going?

There were no more messages all night long.

The sender had an unfamiliar number with an area code from Juyoung-si. There's a chance it was a misdirected message. Or maybe a phishing scam. It could be one of those things where the money is deducted if you call the number back. But I couldn't just brush it off like that. How could I sleep in peace, knowing full well that there was *someone* out there on the other side of the walls wondering "how it's going" here.

My first thought was to call a cab as soon as the sun came up. But I couldn't just leave Seung-Joon behind and take off before any of the staff woke up. It would be totally out of character. And it would mean giving up everything I had here and running away for good, and I couldn't possibly do that after everything I've been through.

So I scrapped that plan pretty fast. Instead, I'd decided to follow my regular morning routine, then go out by myself to figure things out.

I'd get dressed, go downstairs at a reasonable hour, and come up with a believable excuse: "I need to do some shopping today. I'm going into town to get some baby stuff and get my hair done. I need you to watch Seung-Joon."

It's not like I'm a prisoner here, so I can plan out my own day, right?

I hold out for as long as I can. When Seung-Joon starts to whine, I finally force myself to head downstairs. Heesun, who's been setting the table, is surprised to see me all dressed up.

"You're up early, aren't you?"

"Oh, a busy day ahead. I'm going to get my hair done and do some shopping."

"Great! I was going to ask you what your schedule looks like today."

As I hand Seung-Joon over to Mrs. Suwon, I'm surprised to hear a cheerful voice from behind me.

"Morning, sister!"

Cheerful voice, cheerful expression, as always. As if he's just stepped out of the shower, Soohyun's hair is damp. He's the definition of lively.

"You're up early too, huh?"

"Yeah, I've been working out for a while." He smiles as he runs a hand through his wet hair, then looks at me with his eyebrows furrowed. "Are you feeling okay?"

"Ugh." I laugh with a grunt and avoid his eyes. "I didn't get much sleep. Seung-Joon gave me a hard time."

"Oh no!" Soohyun's expression turns serious. "Does that happen often?"

"What do you mean?"

"Not getting enough sleep. Whether it's because of Seung-Joon or for some other reason."

"Oh, nothing serious. Just once in a while, maybe once or twice since I've been here?"

"That's good. I just wanted to recommend some sleep aids if you needed some."

"Like sleeping pills?"

"Well, it's not really a sleeping pill. It's more like a sedative. I take it when I'm on edge, and it calms me down and helps me sleep. It's not bad for you."

"Don't you have to get a prescription?"

"It's not a prescribed drug, so there's no need." Soohyun smiles sheepishly. "Since there are so many sensitive people in the family, we make sure to keep them in the house. Dr. Kwon—who helped us with the paternity test before—he's been doing counseling for us and prescribing things like this since forever. He also helped a lot when my brother was in a bad place. My father hasn't been feeling quite like himself since he fell ill, so he often takes them, too. What about this: I'll give you some just in case, and you can take them when you're having a bad night?"

"Do I look anxious?"

I wonder if it's obvious despite my best efforts.

"Oh, I was just taking a wild guess." Soohyun waves his hand, flashing his teeth. "This might not be the most comfortable place for you, and I know it's not the easiest place to live in. I'm just trying to make things easier for you. I know you're worried about a lot of things—about my brother. We have no idea where he is or if he's ever going to come back. I'm even thinking about reporting him missing."

"No, that's enough—all of it!"

I must have shouted too loudly. Heesun, passing by, flinches and looks at us.

"No, I mean, you've been so much help. I can't possibly ask for more." I smile as I grab Soohyun's arm and nudge him to the dining room. "It's not that I'm unstable. It's just sleeping with an infant by my side catches up with me now and again. But feel free to give me those pills. I'll try them tonight. One good night's sleep and I'll be fine. Oh well, since I'm up so early, I think I'll have breakfast and go shopping."

Soohyun's face, which has been looking quite serious listening to me ramble, lights up at the last word. "Do you want me to tag along?"

"No, no, that's not necessary. I can just take a cab by myself."

"Nonsense. At least take a car."

"What? A car?" I stare at him, and his eyes sparkle with a hint of mischief.

"Yeah, pick one. Good thing you're going out today. It helps me with my mission."

"Mission?"

"Oh, it's my dad. He wants to give you a really nice gift. I mean, what the hell did you do yesterday that he'd feel like giving you a gift, when I've never gotten a single present from him?"

"Oh, I just . . ." I stammer, not knowing what to say.

"He told me to get you a car—or so said Mr. Choi."

"A car?"

My head spins. I've heard of people giving them out as gifts, sure.

But why shouldn't I get one? I did a great job with him yesterday, didn't I? All this just in return for turning a blind eye to the old man's human moment, for a sweet gesture, and for thinking on my feet. My efforts have all paid off, I guess. But I have something more important to think about right now. This isn't the time to bask in small victories. Not yet.

"Do you have a favorite car?—Oh, before that, do you have a driver's license?"

"I have a license, but I've never had a car. I didn't get to drive a lot."

My boyfriend and I had owned a cheap used car for a while, but we had to get rid of it before long since it broke down so often. Other than that, when we went out for a picnic or something once in a while, I'd driven a car owned by a store I worked at.

"It's great you have a license. Once you get a car, you can drive yourself whenever you feel like going out."

"That's too much, though. There are already a lot of cars in the garage. I can just . . ."

"Oh, come on. Take the offer while my dad's feeling generous. He rarely ever gets like this."

"Yeah?"

"He doesn't do anything for free. He only bestows gifts and favors upon those who deserve it, so claim your prize."

A car. A car of my own.

"How long would it take—to get a new car?"

"Well, it depends on which model you choose, but I'm going to say in a month or two, if I pull all the strings I can."

"A month or two."

That's absolutely too long. My blood might dry up in the meantime. And what I have to do can't be put off. It has to be today. Now.

"Well, let me sleep on that."

"Start with the ones we have in the garage and drive them one by one to see how you like them. Then you can pick a brand you like, or you can look into something else entirely when you feel ready." Soohyun's eyes sparkle. "That's why I asked if I could tag along. Pick one out today and take it for a test drive. Why don't I go with you?"

"Oh, really, it's okay. I need to start doing things on my own. You've done enough."

"Oh no—I was going to use the excuse of helping you so I could go out, but I guess I got caught. I respect that you want to do things on your own sometimes, so I'll just go to the garage and help you find the key."

He flashes a sweet, boyish smile, and my chilled blood begins to run warm again.

He's a ray of sunlight that makes me forget everything. That alone gives me strength. I feel like I can do anything.

So I fine-tune my trembling voice and hide my chewed-down fingernails behind my back. I should face this head-on, I think. I've gotten here by jumping over one hurdle after another, so maybe I can get over this one. Yes, I can do this.

"Do you have an idea of where you're going? Are you sure you'll be okay on your own?" He looks worried.

"Don't worry, I've got this." I smile at Soohyun. "There's someplace I need to visit."

CHAPTER

·26·

The expensive car I pick for the day moves silently and smoothly, but there's no time to enjoy the ride. My hands keep shaking on the steering wheel and my heart pounds as I drive down an unfamiliar road. At this point, I don't know if I should keep going, or what would be the right decision. Too late to change course, I keep driving forward.

After about thirty minutes, I find myself in a familiar neighborhood. A river flowing behind the train station, a stretch of roads running alongside, a scattering of buildings large and small. My heart pounds hard. I twist the wheel and drive past the station. I remember running up those stairs like a cat on fire.

After passing a few bus stops, I head farther into a neighborhood of project apartments, shops, and shabby villas. A car like this has probably never been in this neighborhood. When I stop the car in front of a store along the main street and get out, a group of young men who've just come out of the building gawk, wide-eyed, in my direction.

Wringing my trembling hands, I wait for them to pass and duck into an alley behind the convenience store. Nothing's changed. In a neighborhood like this, life flows like stagnant water, unchanging. The only thing that *has* changed in a month is me. I've driven back here in a fancy foreign car, wrapped in luxury goods from head to toe, to clean up the ugly mess I left behind.

I should be in a hurry, but I deliberately wander up and down a few alleys. Like an elementary school student procrastinating on her least favorite assignment, only to cram at the last minute. I'm buying time so my pounding heart can calm down a bit.

When I'm calmer than I was this morning, I stand in a familiar alleyway, in front of a gate I know like the back of my hand. I feel ready to face whatever awaits me when I climb down the stairs and open the door.

Maybe. Just maybe.

CHAPTER

·27·

I look up and see that my building also hasn't changed, right down to its cracked windows.

No sign of people moving inside. The garbage bags piled up at the mouth of the alley and the filthy dirt on the ground make it look as if not a thing has happened in my monthlong absence.

I open the gate and stand at the top of the staircase leading down to the basement for a while. In April, the basement's usually filled with a chill that would call for a heater, but lately it's been so much warmer.

I inhale, trying to detect the sickening odor of death, which I know from preparing meats at the barbecue place. That dank, musty stench. But this is a place where all sorts of foul odors converge. I can't smell anything out of the ordinary.

Eventually, I take cautious steps down the stairs. I hadn't had the mind to lock the door the day I left, so it must be open. All I need to do is turn the doorknob. Yes, turn the doorknob—

"Sister?"

"Gah!" I bounce up like a spring in the doorway, my head hitting the low ceiling. Tears well up in my eyes from the pain. "Soohyun? Why are you here?"

"Sister, what are you doing here?" Soohyun descends the stairs carefully, step by step, a worried expression on his face. His neat, stylish outfit feels out of place in this dreary building.

"I worried you might have trouble with the car you borrowed, so I decided to follow you to see how you were doing, but . . . you got on the highway right away! I couldn't find the right time to turn around, so I just kept following you, and now I'm here. I'm sorry. But where the hell am I, and what are you doing all the way out here?"

"I just wanted to . . ."

Do I tell him I got lost while driving, or do I just tell him it's my friend's house?

Can he handle what he'll see when he opens this door? The sight of his brother lying in a pool of blood, deteriorating and rotting? What if I tell him I don't know what's going on, that there's been a robbery, and I insist that we call the police?

What if I let him lead the way to get in first, and hit him on the head from behind?

Could I pull that off twice?

"So, this must be it." As I run hundreds of scenarios in my head, Soohyun has made his way over and now stands next to me.

"This is where you lived with my brother, isn't it?"

"I just wanted to come back, one last time. You know, maybe . . ."

"Maybe what? You think my brother might be back?"

"It's nothing like that."

"Or are you looking for something else?"

"You know—this was a mistake. We should go back, and now that I think about it, I don't think I brought my key."

"It looks like it's open?" Soohyun grabs the doorknob and jerks it back.

The door swings open, and he steps in without a second thought. I turn toward the stairs and wait for the right moment to flee. If I hear a scream, I'm going to run.

But nothing comes except silence. What's going on? Did Soohyun faint at the horrible sight?

I yank the door open. Soohyun's back stands tall in front of me and blocks my view. I follow in hastily, without taking my shoes off. We're here. So there's no way to hide what I've done now. Maybe it's time for a confession. So let's just . . .

But when I look down at the floor, there's nothing. Nothing.

Not even a speck of dust on the old linoleum floor, which has been mopped and swept clean.

What the hell happened?

Has my brain shut down, are my eyes playing tricks? The last thing I saw here was a man lying face-down in a pool of sticky blood. But now there's not a single trace of blood.

I hurry through the whole place.

I go back and forth and look in every room, but there's not a thing! Only a faint scent of dust in the air, as if the house has been sitting empty for a long time. But there's no sign of blood, no trace of a body.

I quickly go into the bedroom and check the closet to find it empty. The shabby old quilt and the few articles of clothing are all gone. Household items are still in the cupboards, but the dishwasher, utility room, and bathroom are spotless. I remember the house being a complete mess, with used cups and dishes all over the place, but none of those are here now.

Someone has cleaned everything and wiped away every trace of what happened that day. No sign of the body, and I start to wonder if there ever was one. If not, there's only one possibility. The man I thought had dropped dead after that blow to his head woke up, came to his senses, cleaned up the mess with his own hands, and left.

When I stagger out, I find Soohyun standing in the same spot, clearly in shock, staring at the moldy sink. "You guys lived here?"

Soohyun's standing exactly where my boyfriend lay bleeding that day. Where he teetered and briefly leaned against the sink after being struck in the head. Where he lost his balance and slid to the floor, hitting his head on the corner of the sink.

"In this cramped place?"

I nod. My head is so completely blank that no words come out at first.

"This doesn't look like a place where people can live."

"It isn't as bad as you think."

"But two people with a baby?"

"Everybody lives like this, more or less." I swallow the next phrase, "Ordinary people, at least." Right now, I can't afford to teach a well-bred young man the ways of ordinary life.

What the hell happened here after I left? Someone hauled a six-foot-tall burly man away from here, and then cleaned up the whole mess? No freaking way.

It makes more sense that he didn't die that day but survived the blow, even with all the bleeding. That one blow must not have been enough to end his life.

I look around the cramped living room while Soohyun stands there, completely at a loss for words. I keep looking here and there, hoping to find some trace of my boyfriend somewhere, some tiny clue.

Let's say someone was hit in the head and fell unconscious, bleeding, and woke up. Then why on earth would the person clean up the scene of the crime? To help his attacker? No way. I'm sure he would want to end me for good. To take matters into his own hands instead of calling the police. To punish me himself.

How's it going?

Hadn't that simple text been such a loaded question? That's it—he must have been watching me. So, after all, I can never escape his grasp. He will come for me. My hands start to shake uncontrollably. I cannot breathe. Suddenly, the walls of this small half-basement seem to close in on me.

"Is there anything you're looking for, sister? It looks like there's nothing left here."

Soohyun turns around. His hard, frowning face looks like a stranger's.

"No, nothing. I just want to—"

"Let's go."

He grabs my wrist roughly, his hand as cold as mine.

"What?"

"Let's get out of here."

Soohyun looks straight at me now. It's a look I've never seen before.

"From the looks of it, there's not much left here. It looks like someone just cleaned up and left. If you were looking for something, just forget about it."

"Soohyun."

"I don't know how you lived here with my brother, but this is not your home anymore. Let's go back home."

It's the most determined look I've ever seen on his face.

"If you need anything, clothes, household items, or anything else, I'll buy you new ones. Just forget about this place. My brother—"

He stands still for a moment, unable to speak. I can see the muscles in his jaw tense from him clenching his teeth. His grip on my wrist is so tight that it hurts.

"Yeah, I don't think he's coming back."

He's probably too shocked that anyone could live in such a shabby place, and even more shocked that his brother ever lived here. He stares at one of the sinks, which is littered with dead cockroaches.

Soohyun guides me out of my darkened half-basement and into bright daylight. It feels like waking up from a terrible nightmare, only to realize you're in another dream.

My boyfriend will never leave me alone. He'll find and punish me for how I fought back, how I ran away to his family and violated his home, how I've become the guardian of his child.

Soohyun and I don't exchange a word, each lost in our own thoughts, as we walk out like sleepwalkers. Soohyun whisks us back through the alleyway, still holding my wrist the whole time. His grip feels like a lifeline.

I feel like no one can hurt me while I'm in his hands. I will never let go. After all, I have no idea what's going to happen next.

CHAPTER

·28·

My eyes pop open.

It's dark and quiet all around. I lie in bed for a while, dazed. Only after I hear Seung-Joon's raspy breathing do I finally come to my senses and reach over to turn on the nightstand lamp. A golden glow spreads through the dark room. That's when I hear it again.

Tap tap.

Knocks? Someone stomping their feet? What is it? I hold my breath and listen. For a moment, it's dead silent. I roll onto my side and try to relax, but there it goes again.

Tap tap tap.

I jump up like I'm on fire. My heart's thumping.

What the hell? What is it?

By the window directly across from my bed, I can see the long, floor-to-ceiling curtains swaying slightly. So long and thick, in fact, that a full-grown man could easily hide himself there if he wanted to.

Tap tap tap tap.

The same sound again. Cautiously, I slide off the bed. I can quietly reach the door and run out. Soohyun is sleeping just across the hall. I can go knock on his door and ask for help. He'll protect me!

But as I reach for the doorknob, I catch a glimpse of the baby's feet twitching, toes wiggling. I'm scared to death, but I can't leave him alone. I change my mind at the last minute. I grab a water glass from the bedside table, and with the glass in my hand I move toward the curtain.

One step, then another.

Tap tap tap tap.

I grab the curtain's hem with my left hand, holding the glass firmly in my right. I count to three in my mind and then yank the curtain open.

Tap tap tap.

Raindrops are hitting the window in diagonal, dotted streaks. I stagger back, trip over my own feet, and fall to the ground. A sharp pain shoots through my tailbone, and I'm out of breath for a moment. I just lie there, panting, sprawled out on the floor. The room seems to spin around me, my throat dry and strangled. The walls around me are closing in, and I feel like I'm going to pass out.

Every day has been like this since visiting my old place. I wake up in the middle of the night disoriented, drenched in sweat from head to toe. I jump at the slightest shadow on the window's curtains. In the dining room, I get surprised by Mrs. Suwon's touch when she serves me a plate of food from over my shoulder. Once, I jumped up, sending the food flying everywhere.

The usually reticent Mrs. Suwon even said something the other day: "Ma'am, why have you lost so much weight? Is the food not to your taste? Is there anything you'd rather eat?"

Bags grew under my eyes, and my hair matted on my head. When I did manage to fall asleep, I'd always have a nightmare where I'd run like crazy to get away from someone. I would run, run, run, and run, and then I would fall off a cliff.

I wish Soohyun and I *had* walked in on a rotting corpse that day, because then at least I would know for sure that he was gone—he can't come back from the dead to stalk me.

But now I don't even know what or whom I'm dealing with, or just how many people out there know I'm here in the mansion. What they want from me, what they're plotting.

All this uncertainty drives me crazy, even though every day's gone peacefully, without any strange texts or calls since my visit to my old place. Not knowing where this story ends is making me lose my mind. Because there's much left to my story, because he can't just text me and taunt me for fun and then be done with me.

I feel like I'm trapped in an endless stretch of dark tunnel, unable to go backward or forward. Will there ever be an end to this? Maybe when one of us disappears. And chances are, it'll be me.

Since I've gotten back, I've been scanning every inch of this house. Overnight, I transformed from a shy visitor quietly hiding out of sight to a full-blown investigator. I had to know how many doors there were, how many rooms there were, all the entrances and exits, every single window in the house. I even snuck down to the basement that serves as an extra storage space and looked into the empty room adjacent to my bedroom. That room, which used to be Soohyun's, now looks like a massive threat. Anyone could hide in there. I got the key and made sure to lock all its windows and doors, but I still don't feel remotely safe.

I lie back down on the floor, spread-eagle, and try taking deep breaths. I read somewhere about this breathing technique—slowly inhaling for four counts, holding my breath for a count of seven, and then slowly exhaling for eight counts to release tension in my body. My hands still shaking, I try to focus for a little longer, but I give up and spring to my feet again.

There are things that you just can't manage on your own. You need to get the right kind of help. I rush to the bathroom and open the mirrored closet. With trembling hands, I rummage through the cabinet, sending the contents tumbling into the sink.

I manage to find a small bottle, still half full. When I first got it from Soohyun, it seemed like overkill for my anxiety, but now it might be the easiest way out. I take out a pill, pop it in my mouth. Will it be enough? I swallow another pill. I cup the tap water in my hands and drink some, then sit down on the bathroom floor with my legs stretched out and take a breather.

I can't go on like this forever. It's only a matter of time before I go insane. But I don't have any other options right now. Do I leave this house right now? What should I do then? Turn myself in? But what should I say, how would I explain myself?

My abusive boyfriend beat me up, and I was trying to defend myself, but I didn't mean to hurt him?

I freaked out, ran away, and then I took a stranger's child to his in-laws' house?

I got greedy for money, so I lied that I was the mom, and now I have the real mother and my boyfriend somewhere out there, waiting to catch me off guard?

The image of Soohyun's smiling face flashes through my mind, and I wonder if I could ever go through all this without his warm, reassuring presence. Has there ever been anyone in my life who has so firmly held my hand and said, "Let's go back home"? Has there ever been anyone who has been so affectionate, so gentle, so supportive?

The tension leaves my legs, the meds starting to work.

Before I came to live in this house, my life had been a daily battle. I had to choose every word that came out of my mouth wisely. Every time I left work, I always dreaded that my boyfriend would be watching me from afar just to find anything he could use against me. At home, I was never sure if he was going to turn around and punch me at any moment. So things are actually better than they've ever been. The worst is yet to come. The world is not over yet.

I feel my body slowly tilt to one side. A moment ago, the world felt like a spiked ball of anxiety, but now it's starting to whirl, going in circles around me.

The next morning, Mrs. Suwon finds me on the bathroom floor.

CHAPTER

·29·

I walk down the stairs to find the front door hanging wide open.

I've overslept again, as I have for the past few days. My mind is foggier than actual fog. On my slow way to the dining room, I stop dead in my tracks. What's that?

A new frying pan sits on a table in the parlor. The instruction manual and plastic wrap are stacked nearby. My blood turns cold. A sleek black handle and a body of shining silver. It's clearly the pan I struck my boyfriend's head with. The only difference is that this one's brand-new and not dented.

"Heesun! Heesun!" I bellow. The tearing, sharp voice sounds as if it belongs to someone else. "Get over here right now! Come on, get over here!"

I scream and scream and scream. There's a short ruckus in the kitchen, and shortly I hear footsteps.

"Yes? What's going on?"

Startled, Heesun appears at the door, followed by Mrs. Suwon and then Mr. Choi.

"What is this? Who sent this? When did it arrive?" I stutter, out of breath.

"Oh, just this morning."

"This morning? Where's the box?"

"I threw it away, ma'am."

"Threw it away? What do you mean you threw it away? Who the hell throws away something like that?"

I run out of the parlor screaming at the top of my lungs.

"Ma'am?"

Mrs. Suwon hurries out to follow me. Mr. Choi stands in the doorway, staring at me with his mouth agape.

"Where did you put the box?"

"Out in the alley—the garbage truck came by this morning, so if you let me know what's going on, maybe I could help."

"Who sent that to you, who sent that to you?"

"I placed an order with a department store last week and they said they were out of stock, so we had it shipped from the courier. I've checked everything to make sure it's okay," Heesun says in a shaky voice. "I'm ordering a new pan because the other one is getting old. We're supposed to order our own kitchen supplies and report back to you at the end of the month, so that's what I did. I'm sorry I didn't ask you first."

Mrs. Suwon wrings her hands, looking helpless.

"We usually handle all the orders for supplies without getting approval first," adds Mr. Choi, who's been listening from the sidelines. "I'll be sure to ask in the future. I'm sorry, ma'am, I didn't know you wanted to be informed in advance."

I stagger back into the parlor.

I pick up the frying pan and take a good look at it. It's a different pan. It isn't the cheap Chinese one I used. This one is a high-end imported brand I don't recognize, and much bigger. It's so heavy I can barely lift it with one hand.

My legs give out and a buzzing sound rings in my ears. I flop down on the couch in front of the table. Another pill before I'd left the room would have helped; then I wouldn't have caused such a commotion. I run my hand through my hair, my head throbbing, before hastily standing back up. I wobble for a moment. These past few days, I've been out of control without the meds.

"I'm sorry. I don't know what got into me. I read an article about some frying-pan brands using materials that are harmful to the human body. I guess I just got paranoid. I'm sorry for making a fuss about nothing."

I can see the two women exchanging glances. I'm sure they're thinking there's something wrong with me, bags under my eyes, sudden weight loss. Not to mention I'm falling asleep in the bathroom and getting startled at the slightest sound.

"From now on, I'll inform you in advance of the items I'm going to order, always."

"No, no, I've become too sensitive to health issues. I should really keep my mind off these things. Please do as you always have."

I gesture for the two women to leave, and I apologize to Mr. Choi for causing a scene.

"Oh, not at all," he says. "It happens. Especially when it's about your family's health." He laughs. "Anyways, since you're here, I'm glad I get to say goodbye before I leave."

"What?"

"Oh, well, it's my last day."

"Last day? Does that mean you've been around for two years already?"

"Oh, a little short of a year." Mr. Choi looks a little apologetic and embarrassed.

"Oh, but—I wasn't informed that anyone new was coming. Who's going to take care of my father-in-law in the meantime?"

"Mrs. Suwon will take over for a short while."

"Of course."

"I'm already booked up for the next year, so I can't stay with you until the new person gets here, I'm sorry."

"No, don't worry. By the way, is the next person someone you recommended? Or from a job posting or a staffing agency?"

"Well, I don't know, maybe Soohyun does? I got a referral myself because I know Chairman's chiropractor, so maybe they used connections like those. It's a nice house, the job pays well, so you won't have a problem finding my replacement. Don't worry about it too much."

—

But finding his replacement proves to be no easy task. Just five days after Mr. Choi's departure, everyone seems to be struggling.

One day Mrs. Suwon even comes to me and Soohyun with a very troubled look on her face and confesses: "I don't mind cleaning rooms or serving meals, but I can't do the bathing or anything else."

"Oh, don't worry, we'll use home-care service for stuff like that," Soohyun replies coolly, but I'm getting worried.

The task of caregiving normally falls on the eldest daughter-in-law, so it's only right that I step in for my father-in-law, who also happens to be the one with the money. And I won't resent it, either, because since that day in the garden, an invisible bond has developed between the old man and me. After all, he gifted me a nice shiny foreign car. When I get up in the morning and go to his room to say good morning, he offers me a crooked smile with a gaping mouth, and tries to point affectionately at Seung-Joon with his gnarled hand.

But something has to change. I don't get much sleep these days, I have to take the meds to get even the briefest shut-eye, and I have a hard time waking up in the morning. Even when I do, I'll be sitting absentmindedly well into the afternoon. If I stop taking my meds, my nerves will soon get the best of me, and I'll be irritable all the time. I haven't made a big mistake in front of the old man yet, but I'm also not supposed to lose my cool like I did with the frying pan.

"We're a little shorthanded at the moment, so we'll have to wait a bit."

Perhaps conscious of the unspoken disapproval from the female staffers, Soohyun excuses himself.

It is after ten days of relying on part-time home care that the problem is finally solved. Solved, but in the most unexpected way.

This morning, I wake up to a cloudless, sunny sky, feeling like I can finally make it through the day without my meds. As I change Seung-Joon's diaper and laze on the bed with him (he's now starting to turn over on his own), I hear someone calling my name from downstairs. There are no ominous signs that my life is about to fall apart.

Assuming that maybe it's one of those pleasant surprises from Soohyun, I trot lightly down the stairs, smiling, into the shimmering morning. Life may not be perfect, but at least everything's as normal as can be right now.

At the foot of the stairwell stands a young woman. Chestnut hair tied low at the nape of her neck, she has on a plain gray cardigan tucked into black pants. Her pale face and round chestnut eyes, from a distance, look oddly familiar.

"Sister, meet the new caregiver."

"Hello, my name is Hyojin Cha."

That woman. That face I'll never forget even in my dreams. The young mother beams at me.

PART

· 2 ·

CHAPTER

· 3 0 ·

HYOJIN

THEN

There they go again, hugging each other like the world's ending to-morrow. Once the sparks start flying in the air, they'll have to skip dinner again.

"Wait! Wait, honey, I'm almost done with the dough, just pour this on, I'm really hungry!"

She pulls herself from the man, who has his arms wrapped around her waist, and barely escapes his fumbling hands. Soon, the smell of cooking oil wafts through the open window.

My hiding spot behind a dumpster next to a large telephone pole is a perfect vantage point. From here, I can peer into the half-basement at the end of the alley. I can see the sordid sight of this couple giggling and fondling each other at the sink just below the window, thanks to the L-shaped layout of their kitchen.

Having stood outside too long, I'm breaking out in a cold sweat. Whenever I come here, I lose track of time. I stare at the world beyond the not-so-big window as if I'm watching a soap opera.

I think I should call it a day. Today, nothing much seems to have happened. For better or worse. Last time I was here, things were a bit different.

I'm about to turn around when I hear a man's loud voice behind me. "What?"

Of course—it's not going to be quiet today. They always seem to be at their happiest seconds before they lose their way and end up in a dark place.

"Myeongil restaurant?" he asks. "Isn't it far from here?"

"It's not too bad," she replies. "Only a twenty-minute bus ride from our store. Didn't I tell you? The chive pancake I had there was so good, that's why I'm making this today."

"You never told me." His voice has changed. It's not the same tickling voice that was whispering sweet words into her ear a moment ago. Every time he speaks in that voice, he feels like a complete stranger.

"No, think hard. Remember? Last time—" There's a quiver creeping into the woman's voice.

"I remember nothing. I always remember everything with absolute certainty. I remember exactly what you said, where we went, everything. You didn't mention the restaurant, not once."

"Does it matter? I'm telling you now. Oh my God, this is going to burn. Wait a minute, let me flip this, it's going to burn!"

"What does it matter? So when did you go there and with whom? I'm pretty sure you never went with me, right?"

"With my coworkers," she says.

"Oh, that's convenient, isn't it?" He bursts into laughter. The sexy way his Adam's apple moves when he throws his head back and laughs is just like I remember it. Except that now it seems somehow cruel and dangerous. "Every time something happens, you just blame it all on the girls at the store, and everything is good, right?"

"I'm not making this up, I'm serious! Who else do you think I went with? I don't have any other family or friends to hang out with."

"Maybe there's a guy friend I don't know about. Have you forgotten already? That skinny little bastard who came to our door the other day?"

"How many times do I have to tell you that's Hee-Jung's cousin? He came by to see her and then drove me home, and not just me, but all the girls, because he just happened to have a car."

"You think I'm an idiot, don't you?" His laugh is louder this time.

It's the crueler, more dangerous laugh that makes the hairs on the back of my neck stand on end, even from this safe distance.

Suddenly, there's a stabbing pain in my stomach. A kick in the gut. It sucks the breath right out of my lungs. I bend down and try to recall what I've read in books about how I can control breathing. I've heard that even a fetus can sense danger. I think the fetus also realizes that things are getting out of control.

I turn around. On top of my being in so much pain now, their routine is so obvious that there is nothing to see anymore. Clutching my stomach, I stagger out of the alley. Behind me, through the open window, there's the sound of something clattering and breaking. A frying pan filled with hot oil must have been knocked over, and he must have grabbed her by the hair.

As for the rest of their day, there will be a few fists thrown, some tears shed, and then some intense sex to make them forget all about it.

"Maybe they'll make you a little brother today," I murmur, stroking my belly.

> They're so in love, like a couple of doves. No one could drive a wedge between them.

With one hand trying to stroke my pain away, I take out my cell phone and type in a thorough report on what I've seen of them today. Because, after all, this is my job.

CHAPTER

·31·

Hiding behind the curtains of my room's window, I watch them, biting my fingernails.

Two people stroll on the lawn by the pool, basking in the sun. From what I can see, they speak at a respectful distance from each other, without any hint of either intimacy or discomfort. Just like earlier, when the three of us were face-to-face in the foyer downstairs.

"Ms. Hyojin used to work for my dad as a caregiver. I hired her back because I couldn't find anyone else. You know I was desperately looking for a replacement, then out of nowhere, she called me."

"Hello, my name is Hyojin Cha. It's been a long time since I saw you, Soohyun! And this here must be the sister-in-law. You said she's married to your older brother who moved out a few years ago?"

That sneaky wench!

The innocent look on her face sent goosebumps down my arms; in the foyer, she'd acted as if she had never laid eyes upon me before today. Her face didn't show a hint of makeup, just like the first time we met, and her hair was tied up in a ponytail. She was definitely neither casual nor bubbly today, though. Comfortable pants hitting at the ankle, a nondescript blouse, and a light cardigan lent her the impression of a stern, hardworking nurse. How many other faces could she be hiding?

———

Even through the open window of my room, I can hear Soohyun's laughter. I strain my ears as hard as I can, but I can't make out what they're chatting about. What would she be saying to Soohyun?

"You've seen Seung-Joon? I've done a good job raising him, no? I asked that woman to bring him here, but you said she's been staying here all this time? What did she tell you? Did she say she's the mom? What a crazy bitch!"

Could that be it?

"Let's report her to the police right now!"

Or would she burst into my room and accuse me of stealing her child?

"Did you think it was fun to fool around with someone else's husband? I've been watching you all this time, and I sent you here on purpose! The father of my child, who you thought you'd beaten to death, is alive and well. Are you scared? Well, you should be!"

But had any of those been her plan, she would have grabbed me by the hair the first moment she saw my face, so why is she acting like she has no idea who I am?

How's it going?

That text must have been from her. I'm sure she and Hyun-Wook, that bastard, are planning to fuck me over. So has she come here just to drive me insane?

As I keep biting my fingernails, I realize my hands are shaking. Ha! I'm going to lose my mind.

I take a pill from the vial on top of the dresser by the window and swallow it without water. The bitter aftertaste helps me regain my composure.

First, let's do some thinking. I need to figure out what's really going on. Of course, I could still drop everything and run away tonight, leaving a short note behind.

I'm sorry. It's all my fault. Please forgive me.

Three sentences would do, and since I've gotten the baby home safely and taken care of him all this time, maybe they'd let it slide.

At least I now know who this Hyojin is and her connection to this family, so I did learn something from her arrival.

She used to work here as a caregiver, but how long ago was that? Was it before my boyfriend ran away? Did they already have a thing going on back then, and she quit after finding out she was pregnant with his child? Or did she just serve for two years and leave like everyone else, only to run into him later on and get pregnant?

Anyway, judging by her shameless, daring reappearance, both the old man and Soohyun seem to know nothing about Hyojin being Seung-Joon's real mother. But why would Soohyun bring back his father's old caregiver? Why was it so hard to find another? He could have paid more to find someone who had never worked here. Hyojin must have pushed, trying to get back into the house, but why?

My brain, which was shocked into a brief shutdown earlier, is starting up again now that the meds have worked their way into my system. One thought follows another. I'm sure Hyojin's back for *me*. To get back at me for sleeping with her baby's dad! To make me pay the price for taking her place in this house!

That's the only explanation I can think of.

What got into me anyway, that I ended up playing this game? Stealing someone's identity was never going to be smooth sailing!

In hindsight, it was all for nothing. I want to rip my hair out as I have no one but myself to blame. It's my fault for losing my mind over this mansion, the glorified position of an eldest daughter-in-law I've never dreamed of, the gift of a foreign car, and luxury shopping sprees—not to mention being so blinded by that handsome younger brother-in-law that I didn't even know I was walking right into my own grave. Now I have to get myself out of the hole I've dug.

Every time *he* would grab me by the hair, I thought I might die at his hands, but I survived it all. In the end, he went down, not me. I mustn't forget the feeling of that frying pan, the way it bounced back with a resounding *thunk!* when I hit his head.

I pace the room like a wounded animal, trying to think through what's taken place so far. What the hell does Hyojin want? I get that she's back to mess with me, but if she's not going to call the police or alert the family, what is her end goal?

A loud cry startles me out of my thoughts. Seung-Joon's waking up.

"Okay, here we go, here we go. Shhh! Good boy, my baby."

I quickly scoop him up. Rocking him gently in a familiar rhythm, I gingerly walk back over to the window, and Soohyun and Hyojin look up at the sound of Seung-Joon's loud cry. I duck behind the curtains, but I'm one beat too late.

My eyes lock with those of the woman standing two stories down in the garden. My heart drops to my stomach. Soohyun also looks this way and waves. His smiling face, just like Seung-Joon's, is full of warmth.

That face, that smile, that look in his eyes. It's addictive.

Can I give up the consolation of someone who was so eager to help when I was at my lowest?

Even if I could give everything up—a beautiful house, luxurious clothes, a foreign car—I feel like I can't ever give up that smiling face.

I cradle Seung-Joon securely in one arm and hold up my other hand to wave back. The woman stands next to him, her face void of any emotion. Her white, masklike face stares up at me.

I quickly back away from the window and close the curtains.

My hands begin to shake harder.

CHAPTER

· 3 2 ·

My trembling hands no longer get in the way of changing the baby's diapers. Seung-Joon's piercing black eyes stare up at me when he stops crying, his baby smell wafts up, and his tiny hands reach to squeeze my fingers—and none of this unnerves me anymore. When I first got here, I didn't even know how to hold him, but now I'm no longer a clueless mother. But I still wonder why I didn't just leave him at the front door and run away that day. What am I to do now?

"Hey, little guy! You and Mom must be in a good mood today, huh?"

"Gosh!" I stumble back in surprise, wet diaper in hand.

Soohyun rushes over, grabs my hand, and pulls me up. "Oops, sorry, did I scare you?" He was standing in the garden just a moment ago, how the hell did he come up here so fast?

"My dad's been sensitive to sound ever since he got bedridden. I've developed a habit of going around quietly. Are you okay?"

He gently sits me down on the bed, then he takes care of dressing Seung-Joon and putting away the wet diaper for me.

"Dinner's ready a little earlier than usual, so I thought I'd let you know. I should have knocked even though the door was open." He looks apologetic.

"No, don't worry about it. I'm okay."

He places his warm hand in mine. "I doubt it for some reason."

This time, he leans over to take a closer look at my face, staring deep into my eyes. "You don't look so good. Did you take your meds last night? If you're not feeling well, consider taking them. A good sleep pattern, once disturbed—it's hard to get back in a good rhythm."

It's hard to tear my gaze from those eyes that show genuine concern, that look light brown in the afternoon sunlight streaming in through the window. Even as guilt and fear stab me in the chest, I can't look away.

What if I just get it off my chest, right here and now?

What if I tell him that I'm not his sister-in-law, and that the new caretaker is the real one? I've gotten over the one who caused me so much pain, so Soohyun and I would be just a man and a woman, nothing more, and maybe we could start over. I'd even go so far as to call Hyojin my sister-in-law if that means a chance with Soohyun.

If I explain that I was just trying to survive, that I didn't mean anyone harm, would he understand? I've never had anyone look at me like this, like they really care. So, Soohyun, show some faith in me, and I'll also give my life another chance and try to be a new person. Do I not deserve that much?

"Are you sure your stomach isn't upset? You're ready for dinner?"

"Yeah, yeah, I'm good, really."

I force a smile.

"Well, that's good. Thanks to Hyojin, Mrs. Suwon won't have to worry about taking care of my dad anymore. So she can look after Seung-Joon when you come downstairs."

Soohyun gives my hand a gentle stroke and turns away to leave.

"By the way, when did she—I mean, Hyojin—work here?" I ask.

He looks over his shoulder. "Sorry?"

"I mean, was it a long time ago? Um, did he ever know her?"

"My brother?" He thinks for a moment, his head tilted to one side. "No. She was here right before Mr. Choi, so I don't think it's been that long. A couple of years ago? She started working here long after he moved out."

"Oh, I see. She must have done a good job, seeing how you brought her back a second time."

"She did," he says. "She's not a physical therapist like Mr. Choi, but still a certified caregiver and nursing assistant. And she put up with my dad's crankiness better than most."

"So she'll be here for another two years?"

"Not sure." Soohyun gives me a puzzled look.

"The two-year clause has been put in place because of trust issues, and that was because of your mom's accident, right?"

Soohyun's smile fades. "Yeah, it's been a while. But I feel we should honor that principle. My dad always said people like us shouldn't trust anyone but our family, and in a way, I agree. This time, we were desperate, so I asked her to come back, just for two years. But you never know."

If only I could expertly hide my emotion behind a mask like Hyojin does. I don't want to show how I'm feeling on the inside. Apparently I've failed, because Soohyun studies my face, concerned.

"You're not offended, are you?"

"Oh, no, I'm not. Why would I be?" I wave my hands, instantly regretting the exaggerated gesticulation.

"Oh, you know," Soohyun says, "I hope you didn't get the wrong idea—because a young female caregiver used to work in this house."

I understand: His elaboration implies that there was nothing between him and her.

"As long as we can stay polite and professional," he continues, "like we did with Mr. Choi, there shouldn't be a problem. At least I'd like to believe so. After all, Hyojin will be spending most of her time here taking care of my dad. It's one less thing for us to worry about, and you can keep an eye on her and let me know if something seems off."

His gentle voice is always so calming, reassuring. Even though he's younger than me, he always finds a way to sound so mature and convincing at times like this. I was right before. How could I ever give him up?

"Well then, I'll see you downstairs." Before walking out, he momentarily stops at the door and looks back as if he's just remembered something. "Oh, by the way, I think you should also let her help you a bit. Maybe she can help out with Seung-Joon. She seems to really like babies. Hyojin said earlier that Seung-Joon looks just like you and that he's very cute."

CHAPTER

·33·

When I walk into the dining room, Soohyun sits alone at the large dining table, which is perfectly set under the bright lights. He looks up from his phone and flashes me a bright smile.

"Today's menu is thistle bibimbap. I love it—come sit!"

With a smile on my face, I sit down across from him, as Heesun comes over and pours me some water. It feels natural to have someone else fill my water glass at all times now.

"My dad's eating in bed today," Soohyun explains, catching me looking at the empty seat.

"Is he feeling unwell?"

Although we haven't had many meals with the old man present, we, including Mr. Choi, did get used to dining together. Usually, the three of us would make small talk, with the old man craning his neck to listen in silence. Sometimes, the old man drooled or stray pieces of food slipped from his mouth; Mr. Choi always caught it before the old man got uncomfortable, expertly wiping his chin while navigating the conversation. The routine became a natural part of my day. It has come to feel like proof of my security, that I really am part of the family.

On a day like today, though, I can't complain about eating alone with Soohyun, with so much on my mind. But a small part of me is worried about the old man. Although it's debatable if I'm really worried about him, or generally nervous about Hyojin whispering God knows what in his ear.

Sitting at this table, I'm not sure if I am the same old Jae-Young Yoon, or the daughter-in-law of this family, or Jae-Young Yoon pretending to be the daughter-in-law of this family, or someone else entirely. Even as this house now feels familiar to me, I feel so changed, not quite my old self. My life seems divided into two chapters now: before and after I entered this place. Perhaps the old me died the moment I swung the frying pan that day, and the one sitting here is the new me, born at that moment. Except that the new me is still a flimsy shell, not yet fully fleshed out, and will probably break before I reach full maturity.

I feel no appetite, but I force myself to pick up my chopsticks just as someone appears in the doorway. Startled, I drop my utensils on the floor. My heart also drops as I bend down to pick them up. Hyojin has walked over and is now standing behind Soohyun's chair, towering over him like the grim reaper.

"I was worried about Chairman's appetite, but he finished the whole bowl. I helped him brush his teeth and wash his face, so he's going to rest until it's time to take his meds."

She smiles, rolling down her sleeves. A fake smile.

"Oh, that's good," Soohyun says, pulling out the chair next to him and asking her to sit. "He must be feeling better."

"Yes, I think he's just a little tired."

She sinks into the chair all too casually. The way she looks between me and Soohyun betrays no hint of anxiety, and she doesn't even seem to be particularly avoiding me. How can she do that, just like a professional actress?

Soohyun hollers to the kitchen, and Heesun brings in some rice and bowls and sets them on the table.

"The previous lady, Mrs. Shinlim-Dong, made a great thistle bibimbap, you know? But the new lady must also be a great cook. Look at this!" Hyojin whispers at us. She begins to stuff rice and side dishes into her mouth.

The way she talks, even her voice, reveals nothing of the woman I met on the train. She doesn't act like the blushing young mother who spoke softly and nervously. Who is this woman with a straightforward, daring face, blunt words, and a commanding voice? Which one is real?

While Soohyun chats with her, I can't take my eyes off Hyojin. When her eyes meet mine, I look away, almost like a boy with a crush.

"And fresh kimchi! I've missed this flavor so much, do you still make your own here?"

"Sure. You know how much my dad loves it."

"The ladies here work so hard, can you believe it?"

The woman's stare pierces me like a dagger, making me unable to look away.

"I don't know how they manage to sweep, mop, and keep this big house sparkling clean. On top of all that, they cook and make kimchi every season. The staff here won't have time for anything else. There's much temptation when you work in a big, fancy house like this. If the owners come off a bit too careless or lenient, your staff might get the wrong ideas and start thinking bad thoughts. You know, there are all kinds of people in this world. Don't you think so, Mr. Soohyun?"

Suddenly, a glass of water spills and the table is flooded. "Ugh!"

Soohyun has knocked over his glass. I push my chair back and scramble to my feet.

"Oh, I'll get it," the woman says. "I know where the dishcloth is."

She whisks out of the dining room like the wind as Soohyun and I fumble around. I grab a fistful of napkins from the table and hand them to Soohyun so he can dry his pants. I can see the flush in his face, and I can hear the swear words coming out of his mouth. I've never seen him like that before. If he were a normal twenty-something guy, that kind of language would be nothing, but it doesn't suit the Soohyun I know at all. It's incongruous. I mean, look at his innocent face.

With the young mother gone, it's just the two of us left in the dining room, so he could have made some sort of excuse, but he keeps his mouth tightly shut and just wipes his wet pants. Maybe he's embarrassed to make a mistake in front of me. But if that's not the case—is he being so awkward because he's conscious of Hyojin?

"Here, I've brought plenty, don't worry." Hyojin returns with a bundle of clean dishcloths.

I pick up a few and awkwardly help her wipe the table.

"I'm sorry, I must have been talking too much, distracting you."

I look up, realizing the woman is talking to me. Dark, clear eyes look straight at me. I can't bring myself to say, "No, I'm fine," so I just keep my head down and keep wiping down the table.

"Soohyun, are you okay?" Seemingly indifferent to my silence, Hyojin turns her head in Soohyun's direction again.

Is she finding this situation amusing, or is she actually flirting?

"Ah, no, it's fine." When Soohyun looks up, a smile's back on his face. He's completely regained his composure, his voice calm again. "I'm just going to go change my pants, this is so embarrassing." Soohyun flashes a smile, pushes his chair back, and stands up.

"Oh, me, too!" As I scramble to my feet after him, both their eyes dart in my direction. "Ah, I just think I've heard Seung-Joon," I try to recover. "I'll head upstairs for a bit."

"Isn't Mrs. Suwon watching him?" Hyojin asks, feigning innocence.

"Yes, she is, but—"

"Why don't I take a look?" Her eyes coldly scan the room.

Soohyun looks back and forth between us, then down at his pants and the stain in its embarrassing place, and quickly disappears.

So, here we are, just the two of us left in the dining room. Time seems to stand still as we sit facing each other across the messy table. If she reaches out, she can get a good grasp of my hair.

I can almost hear her growling, "Yes, it feels good to take my place, I bet, everything that's mine, my husband and my child and my place in this family?" I hesitantly take a step back, thinking I need to get out of here. My room on the second floor is calling me to come back and hide.

But before I can, Hyojin suddenly sits back in her seat and picks up the spoon again as if nothing's happened. "Your baby's so cute, but you have a lot on your plate with such a young one, am I right?" she asks as I watch her nonchalantly move the spoon around.

I glare at her. What's your deal now? Why do you keep pretending you don't know me? What the hell do you want? Are you trying to drive me crazy?

I rub my hands over my thighs, clenching and unclenching my fists. Short of breath, I try to fight off my sudden craving for my meds. If I could just pop one, just one, right now.

"When's the kid's birthday?" she asks, picking up fried anchovies with her chopsticks without looking in my direction.

"He was born on December 12. Easy to remember, right?" It takes all my courage to force out a reply. I'm ready to play along now. But Hyojin's expression stays the same.

"They say it's better to give birth when it's cold." A wicked grin twitches her lips as she glances over, but without a trace of smile in her eyes. "I was born when it was cool. My mom used to say, had I been born in the summer, she would have died as she couldn't stand the heat. So I was a good daughter in that regard, if nothing else." She chuckles to herself.

What's so funny? All this is funny to you?

"I always thought my mom would look after me if I ever had kids," Hyojin mumbles to herself. "Life doesn't go according to plan, I guess. My mom died in such a ridiculous way that she didn't even get to see me get married, let alone meet my kid."

Hyojin keeps chewing and shoving the rice into her mouth, looking past me—still frozen to the spot like a totem pole—off into the distance.

"Your parents aren't available?" she asks. "Is that why you've moved in with your in-laws? You must be missing your husband a lot. He should have accompanied you. Honestly, no matter how rich your in-laws are, you still need someone who's really on your side, don't you? Ah! Have you already found a new advocate, maybe?"

Hyojin's been mumbling but suddenly looks up at me and holds me in a piercing gaze. For a moment, my breath catches in my throat. I feel as if her fingers are on my neck, strangling me. I cannot breathe.

No, I can't stand this. I need my meds. My meds!

I slowly back out of the dining room, then turn and run out. I can hear the sound of Hyojin boldly clanking her cutlery behind me.

CHAPTER
·34·

I'm just stepping into the living room when I almost bump into Soohyun, who has just come back after changing into a new pair of pants.

"Oops!"

Soohyun grabs my shaking shoulders with both arms.

"Sister, have you already eaten?"

"Oh, I'm feeling a little under the weather, actually. I thought I'd feel better after eating. But I'm not getting any better, so I'll just skip the meal."

I gently nudge his arm away, excuse myself, and make my way quickly through the living room and up the stairs.

"Let me know if you need some meds for indigestion!" shouts Soohyun from behind.

When I rush into my room, Mrs. Suwon is just putting Seung-Joon to bed.

"He's finished a whole bottle. Such a big appetite! I bet he'll get so tall!"

Mrs. Suwon throws me a smile before leaving the room, but I'm too tired to return the favor. I rummage through the bathroom cabinet, pop two pills at once, and wash them down with tap water cupped in my hands, before collapsing onto the bathroom floor in a heap.

One thought echoes through my mind: *Get out. I need to get out of here.*

This bitch can't be in her right mind. Why else would she not even remember she entrusted me with her child, or pretend to remember nothing? Or she's a sociopath ready to do anything, maybe even kill me, to get away with abandoning Seung-Joon? While I was so distracted by money, she must have entangled me in some malicious scheme of hers. I should just get out of here right now, leaving Seung-Joon behind. Hyojin and Soohyun must be busy eating, so this may well be my chance. I'll take some of the luxury goods and my jewelry, which I can sell for some cash so I can stay in hiding for a while.

My foggy head seems to clear all of a sudden, and I can breathe more easily. I slowly get up, splash some cold water onto my face, and step out of the bathroom much calmer. Seung-Joon is lying in his crib, flailing his arms and legs, giggling. I bend down and search under my bed, avoiding looking at his eyes and chubby cheeks. I find the bag of clothes I stashed there, but after a thought, I kick it back under the bed. No time for packing. And even the bag itself belongs to Hyojin. I rummage through the jewelry box, shove a few items into my pockets, and grab my phone and wallet from the bedside table.

I turn around to grab the doorknob when I hear a *ding*. With trembling hands, I check the text. I thought it could have been Soohyun, but it's from an unknown number. A video. The thumbnail is a blurry, dull gray image. Only idiots would tap on things like this these days, and I don't have a second to waste on this right now. I need to get out of here. I just turn off my phone screen and grab the doorknob again.

But—if I'm not wrong, I've just seen something?

About to turn around to leave the room, I stop dead in my tracks.

The shape that peeks through the dark gray of the still image lingers in the back of my mind. In the doorway, I play the video.

CHAPTER

·35·

The black-and-white video begins with someone's back to the screen.

It's a woman with her hair tied up in a tight bun and wearing a dark gray hoodie.

The camera is pointing down at an angle from the top of her back.

The woman with her back to the screen takes a step forward, and the figure standing opposite her begins to move.

A man. Broad-shouldered and tall.

The woman is busy doing something and the man comes up to talk to her.

They stop what they're doing and talk some more.

I turn up the volume, but there's no sound. As if the video was not recorded with sound in the first place.

The man is now leaning against an old sink and continues to say something.

The woman turns her head and starts to walk away, but the man grabs her wrist in his large hand. She tries to pull her arm away, but he doesn't budge.

Their conversation seems to get heated. You can't hear them, but you can tell just by looking.

He's too strong for her to fight off.

She tries to back away, straining, trying to break free somehow. It's almost too much to watch.

My wrist burns with pain. I'm sure the woman in the video is going to end up with a solid bruise.

After a moment, the man reaches over with his other hand and grabs her by the hair as firmly as he's clutching her wrist.

She has nowhere to go. She can't even move.

With her head down, she's groping with her free hand for the sink behind the man.

Unable to wiggle out of his tight grip, she moves her fingers desperately over the sink like some monstrous creature squirming to life.

Finally, the woman's hand finds the handle of a frying pan lying on the sink.

His hands on her wrist and her hair, he doesn't notice.

Her free hand flies high in the air.

The frying pan then makes a large semicircle and hits the man on the back of his head.

It's a silent video, but I almost hear a *thunk!* in the background.

The man staggers from the unexpected blow.

You can't see it on the screen, but he probably lost his balance as his sockless feet slipped on the linoleum underneath.

Had he quickly grabbed something and held on, he could have centered himself. But he releases his grip too late, not willing to let go of the woman.

He stumbles and slips, slamming the side of his head into the corner of the sink.

The frying pan, as it turns out, isn't the blow that ends his life. It's his own hands and feet that eventually bring the man down.

Now all I can see is the woman's back. She's on her knees, looking at the man who's fallen to the ground. But the man doesn't get back up.

The woman gets up and takes a step back. What an irony—her hair disheveled from the man's grasp, she looks like she's had one hell of a night in a lover's bed.

The woman stands motionless as a photograph for a while, then cautiously approaches the man again, bending down. She brings a startled hand to her mouth, as if to hold back vomit, and the next moment she's up and running around.

The video—which runs for six minutes and twelve seconds—ends with my face appearing as I rush out the door. Off I go, looking utterly stunned and terrified.

CHAPTER

·36·

I can't even lift a finger as the phone slips from my cold, shaking hands.

"I'm fucked!"

That's all I can think of. I don't even wonder who filmed this, how, and why they'd send it to me now.

From the angle, it looks like the camera is hanging from the ceiling near the front door. Maybe where our motion-sensitive light fixture sat. The half-basement is so cramped that there's only a ramshackle kitchen to the right, a shoe closet to the left, and a small room off to the side. When you walk in the front door, you can see everything.

But I had no idea there was a camera there.

Did the landlady put it up there? She could have put it up for safety when she was living alone, but I don't think so. We made a few shoddy repairs when we moved in—replaced old sensors that made the lights flicker—and my boyfriend would have noticed a surveillance camera right away. Short-fused, he would have complained about it, for sure, and maybe even gotten into a fight. For all I know, he could have run down the street screaming, "Sue me! I'll sue you right back!" So it can't have been the landlady.

So who the hell was it? It's definitely someone who wanted to watch our every move. Someone watching us . . . no, on second thought, maybe not "us."

"Who was that call just now?"

"I called the store and they said you left earlier. Why are you forty minutes late?"

"What have you been doing at home all day? I sent you a text earlier, but there was no response. Have you been out somewhere?"

I know who would have wanted to know my movements day in and day out, what I was up to every single moment. I pick up my phone with my shaking fingers and watch the video from start to finish again. Needless to say, the caller ID is unfamiliar.

But now I'm sure who it must be.

It must be the person who put up the camera to begin with.

Someone who was spying on me.

Someone lucky enough to have come back from death who's now gnashing his teeth, eager to take revenge.

Who else would have asked me, "How's it going?"

Probably one and the same person.

My mind's clear now, as if a veil of fog has lifted. In my head, a puzzle piece clicks into place.

Hyojin could not have pulled this off by herself. She couldn't curate all this without help. Tricking me into this house was no accident, nor one person's plan.

Everything starts to make sense.

This is definitely the work of more than one person—a team of two like-minded people, probably. The man I once loved, and the woman who carried his child.

The man I was sure I killed and the woman who is now downstairs munching on bibimbap, trying to make me lose my mind.

Those two must have teamed up and were plotting against me.

He must have come to after I ran out that day. He would have been unconscious for a while, but the blood loss didn't cost him his life. As soon as he came to, he must have called Hyojin. He must have told her to go after me right away, gritting his teeth. Vowing to never forgive me for slipping through his fingers and making my escape. And so they hatched a plan to finish me. Using their own child as bait.

My posing as Hyojin was probably not in their original plan. Now they were probably just buying time so they didn't lose track of me. Had I just run away with Seung-Joon, they would have used the video to charge me with attempted murder and abduction, and had I dropped Seung-Joon off and gone on my way, they would have been able to trace my location based on how I got here, starting with the neighborhood surveillance cameras.

But when I foolishly decided to stay in the house, I gift wrapped and delivered myself to those bastards. So they decided to drive me crazy little by little, one from inside the house and the other from outside.

I hop to my feet, my phone in hand.

I can't just sit and take all this. No one died, no one lost anything, and no one was harmed. It's wrong to steal someone's identity, but a woman who chose to abandon her child in the first place deserves it. If Hyojin wanted to be this family's daughter-in-law, she should have come here herself with her child. I took the place she gave up, so what's wrong with that? Why should I have to suffer?

But as my conviction grows stronger and my heart rate slows thanks to the meds, all my mental energy turns in one direction: self-preservation.

Who will protect me if not me?

I jump up and double-check my wallet, which I'd shoved into the back pocket of my pants. I glance over at the bed and see that Seung-Joon's still asleep. The full lashes of his closed eyes cast pretty shadows on his flawless skin, making my heart ache—just as when I'm holding him in my arms and feeling his growing weight, or laying him down next to me and cooing at him. For a moment I stand there, thinking of the smell of milk wafting from him.

I guess I've gotten attached to him, seeing how I cannot bring myself to say goodbye to him.

But his real mom is downstairs, so he'll be fine.

"I'm sorry," I whisper before quickly leaving the room.

Even though my heart aches, I refuse to look back, even as I feel like I'm being tugged from behind. The old staircase creaks as I quickly descend on my socked feet, afraid to make a sound. Halfway down, I realize I've forgotten to leave a note behind—words of apologies asking forgiveness—but there's no turning back now.

I tiptoe toward the front door, knowing it's going to take them a while to clean up after the meal. By the time they realize I'm gone, I'll be on an express bus or a train. I grab the doorknob, holding my breath.

"Where are you going?"

The world seems to spin right in front of my eyes.

The hairs on the back of my neck stand on end.

CHAPTER
·37·

HYOJIN

THEN

The life of a pregnant woman in her last trimester is not one of plea-
sure.

As Koreans say, monks can't cut their own hair, and accordingly,
even though I'm a professionally trained and practicing medical assistant and caregiver, it's hard to take care of myself as I get heavier.
Every day is a small or large struggle, whether it has to do with re-
membering to take my nutritional supplements, not slipping on the
way to the bathroom in the middle of the night, or dealing with an
upset stomach after eating something that doesn't agree with me. Why
is it so hard for me to take care of my own body when my life itself is
so simple and insignificant that I could disappear overnight and no
one would notice?

As I crawl around in my cramped apartment, preparing meals for
myself, tossing and turning at night with a heavy stomach, I wonder
what the hell I'm doing. I wonder why I'm not staying in that spacious,
cool, leisurely mansion, why I'm living here instead.

That isn't to say that a live-in caregiver is a cushy position by any
means, but my life in the mansion was far more comfortable. I had my
own small but cozy room, and I could have the swimming pool to
myself at night when everyone was asleep. I was willing to put up with
emptying the bedpan for the old man if it meant I could call that man-

sion home. For some reason, the house had always had male caregivers, but apparently their predecessors hadn't been able to meet the old man's standards.

I bet he couldn't tell them, "I'll pay you to be my hands and feet and run some sketchy errands for me in secret." Yes, the money he offered was a big sum, big enough that anyone would have been willing to bend over backward and do what they were told, but the old man didn't trust any of them.

He wanted me to find out the address of his eldest son who had run away from home, spy on him, and report back to him regularly. Ultimately, he wanted to make the son come back home by any means necessary.

This is what the old man demanded from me in exchange for his so-called activity fees. And I was to be paid a huge amount of money if I ever succeeded at the final mission. Not a life-changing amount, perhaps, but still a sum of money much larger than what I could see myself saving up until retirement.

"Keep . . . this . . . secret . . . from . . . Soo . . . hyun," the old man had said through his twisted lips.

I didn't need to ask why. The inheritance would be enough to set even the best of brothers at each other's throats, and the eldest son coming back home would mean a much smaller share for the one who stuck around all these years.

The old man must have been waiting quite long for someone trustworthy.

My careful personality had gained the old man's trust within two months of starting work there. One day after dinner, I put the old man to bed in his room and stepped out for my share of the meal. But I briefly went back into the room again for my phone and noticed something strange. A paper cup on the bedside table had moved a little. I could tell because there was a circular water mark under the spot where the cup had been before. When I glanced over, the old man was lying in bed with his eyes closed. His left hand, which I had tucked nicely under the covers, was poking out. But I kept silent, just grabbed my cell phone and left the room. Nor did I tell anyone about it afterward. Not even Soohyun.

I'm inclined to believe he didn't mean to test me, but I'm also sure he watched me more closely from then on. There were a few other minor slipups in subsequent days, all of which I shrugged off. That is, until the old man himself confessed that six years after the accident, he had begun to regain some feeling in his paralyzed left arm and part of his face.

He said he'd been training himself that way, little by little, without anyone noticing. Very carefully, so that no one would find out about his improving condition. Even his full-time aides didn't realize he was able to verbally communicate his wishes without too much difficulty now.

"Wouldn't Soohyun be happy to know? He worries so much about you."

The old man clenched his twisted mouth shut and shook his head.

He probably didn't want to get his son's hopes high—that's what I thought back then. I naively assumed they were a normal family.

So that's how the old man gave me, of all people, the mission.

Sometime after being tasked with this secret mission, I gave the old man the current address of his eldest son. I told him I'd hired a private investigator with the money he'd told me to take from his secret safe.

In truth, I didn't need an investigator to figure out where he lived. But I'd done exactly what the old man had asked me to do and had no intention of letting on that I hadn't just been hired by the old man alone.

With money coming in from both sides, I was living a fairly comfortable life for the first time. I was able to afford some quality designer clothes to keep in my room and could occasionally treat myself to a night out in those new clothes.

I might not have been exactly transparent about the "down payment" and where it went, but I did my job. I reported back to the old man and each time offered a detailed account of his son's life, spying on him and his girlfriend whenever they were out and about.

I provided all the details: his eldest son, handsome and tall, who used to be brilliant and the apple of his eye, and who was now leading a lowly life in a half-basement, living off the woman he was dating.

"This is the only picture I have, but it's a little shaky. I don't think I can take better photos. I don't want to risk getting caught. Don't you think it's better for me to just keep watching without doing anything rash?"

So the old man had only seen a blurry image of them in the distance, and had only heard about them through me: that they seemed to be in love, and that she seemed to be a good person after all. I kept everything filtered through a rose-colored glass, with the dark violence that tore my heart to shreds hidden.

So that the old man's love for his eldest son would not grow cold, I wanted him to stay oblivious to his son's despicable side and keep pining for him, hoping for his return. So that I could continue to do this job and earn a decent living. Because it was not yet time.

"They look pretty good together. They must really love each other. They look happy even though they don't have a lot going for them."

I didn't tell him that I'd known his eldest son for a long time, or that I used to be in love with him, and every time I saw them cuddling and kissing, I'd feel a surge of disgust that made me want to run in and knock it all over. I didn't tell him that whenever he grabbed the woman by her hair and threw his fist, I felt like bursting into tears, even though it felt so, so good at the same time. I told the old man only what he wanted to hear.

And in early July, when it was starting to get hot, I told the old man: "I'm not entirely sure, but I have news. I think she's pregnant. She doesn't show yet, but they're going to be parents."

The old man's eyes lit up.

CHAPTER

· 3 8 ·

For about a second, I consider ignoring it and walking away.

During the year and a half I spent with my boyfriend, my body became extremely sensitive to danger. Disregarding my gut feelings always ended badly. And that very instinct is urging me to ignore the person behind me and get the hell out of the house now. If the voice behind me had been someone else's, I would have obeyed my intuition and just pushed through with my plan.

Yet I can't help but let go of the doorknob and turn around. I don't want to disappoint the person I know is back there. I want to be the Jae-Young Yoon he knows.

"Oh, just going out to get some air," I say. "I'm feeling stuffy."

Soohyun approaches, frowning. "How's your stomach? Have you taken any digestive medication?"

"No—but I'll feel better after getting some air."

"You look pale. Let me see." He takes a step forward and carefully takes my hand, touching his other to my forehead. "Your hands are cold, and it seems you're breaking out in a cold sweat. You might actually be getting sick. Hold on, I'll go check if we have any—"

"Excuse me."

I hear a chilling voice from behind me, inside the house. And then I turn to see Hyojin's face floating against the background of the dark living room.

"Yes, Hyojin?" Still holding my hand, Soohyun turns slightly to acknowledge her, a hint of irritation in his voice.

"Are you free right now? Chairman wants to see Seung-Joon."

"Excuse me?" Soohyun lets go of my hand and turns around. This time, I feel an apparent thorn in his voice. Soohyun seems a bit strange tonight. He's not the sweet, smiling brother-in-law I know; something about him is strangely pointed and barbed.

"I don't mind taking him myself, but I thought it would be better if you could carry him," Hyojin says, with no hint of a flinch, without a care in the world. For a moment, there's a strange tension between us all. None of us dares to move.

Finally, Soohyun turns his head my way, smiling gently as usual. But it looks a bit forced. "My dad seems to have regained his strength. Sister, are you sure you're okay?"

"Yes. I'll go."

Unable to bring myself to look at Hyojin, I just stare past Soohyun's shoulder.

"I'll be in my room, then," he replies. "Just call me if you need me."

Hyojin turns to lead the way, her cell phone in her hand. I wonder if she sent me the video on that phone or if Hyun-Wook did. Or did he order her to do it? Just now?

Either way, I'm not going to make it out of here today.

The old man is my lifeline. Apparently, I can't just run away, so breathlessly afraid. For me, being the daughter-in-law of this family is the only protection I have left.

I give Soohyun's arm a little pat and trudge upstairs to get Seung-Joon. My gut's still warning me that it's too dangerous to stay here, but I decide to ignore it.

Timing's off right now.

CHAPTER

· 3 9 ·

The old man's room is silent and dark. A dim light from the bedside stand casts strange shadows on the walls. The smell of disinfectant mixed with his strange body odor is suffocating.

"Father?"

The meds thankfully have stopped the tremors in my hands. If not, I might have dropped Seung-Joon. Every time I blink, the image of me swinging the frying pan lingers before my eyes like an afterimage. Along with the way Hyun-Wook flailed as he staggered backward.

No, I can't dwell on that, not now!

I reach for the door behind my back and close it, before carefully stepping farther into the room.

The old man lies in bed with his eyes closed. He must have fallen asleep waiting for me, and I decide to give him a little time to recover and see if he wakes up. It's strangely reassuring to be alone with the old man in such a quiet, dark room, and I don't want to leave. I feel protected, as if in a fortress, where no one can hurt me. The old man's breathing grows louder and louder as he falls into a deep sleep. Seung-Joon asleep and slung over my shoulder, I stand hesitant. Who am I kidding—I am afraid that if I leave now, I will run into Hyojin.

As I walk by the old man's nightstand, I see a cluttered mess on the table. A few torn sheets of notepaper are scattered among the patient's essentials: medicine bags, cups, wipes, and an electronic thermometer. And a note, scrawled in cursive.

Se-Yool: Attorney Kim 010-3587-40xx /
Contact for document correction

It's scribbled with a ballpoint pen, but the old man couldn't have written it himself, arms skinny as skewers, always snuggled up in the quilt. I've never seen him move on his own in the entire time I've been here. It must have been written down by dictation, with Hyojin's help. That's my guess, at least.

I take out my cell phone and carefully snap a picture. The click makes the old man flinch. I quickly hide my hands, pretending to hug Seung-Joon tightly.

"Father?"

The old man opens his eyes and looks over. His face looks blank at first, but when he spots Seung-Joon, his face lights up.

"This—thi—"

A hand fumbles under the covers.

When I bring Seung-Joon closer, one corner of the old man's mouth turns up in a pout that I know is supposed to be a crooked smile.

"He's getting bigger by the day. Yesterday I weighed him, and he's already gained six hundred grams, so he's really going to be a big kid."

As I ramble on, my mood gets dark. When I see the old man stirring, I pull his arms out from under the covers.

"This . . . this." He seems to be trying to say something, but I can't make out his words.

"Yes? Can I help you?" Still holding Seung-Joon, I bend down toward the old man. "Father, would you like me to call your caregiver?"

It's the last thing I want to do, but I have no choice. Just then, the door to the next room swings open and Hyojin walks in, probably having eavesdropped the whole time.

"I'm here, Chairman. Anything you need?" Hyojin approaches us in exacting, confident strides. Bending over, she listens intently to the old man's mumblings, and after a moment she gestures to a drawer in the nightstand. "He wants you to open it."

Holding Seung-Joon in one arm, I step up to the nightstand, suddenly realizing that this is probably the first time I've seen her up close and personal since she moved into the house.

I glance over, but her eyes are emotionless, no hint of possessiveness or overwhelming maternal love, not even a hint of some general longing. She's just staring at me, expressionless. Clearly, she has no feelings for her own son. Or she's so consumed with her hatred for me that she couldn't care less about him.

Ignoring the chill down the nape of my neck, I open the drawer and find a pretty mint-colored box inside.

"Please open it now. He wants you to have what's inside—he's been so insistent."

Hyojin's voice comes out soft. The old man turns his stiff neck to look this way. His dull eyes come alive.

"I'll hold Seung-Joon. So you can open it yourself." Hyojin stretches out her hands.

"Ah! It's okay!" I quickly take a step back, not sure why. It's her child, after all. Maybe I should let her hold Seung-Joon once, to ease her anger, if nothing else.

And yet, I'm unable to let her hold him, afraid she's going to destroy everything she touches.

So I sling Seung-Joon over my shoulder and carefully untie the ribbon with both hands to open the mint-colored box. Inside is a hefty silver-colored bracelet with a heart-shaped pendant on it.

"You've given him a precious grandchild, so he wanted to give you a gift. I don't know when he bought it, but he's been saving it for occasions like this."

Hyojin smiles.

"Oh, this . . ."

I stand speechless, trying to find the right words.

"This is too much, Father . . . I can't possibly—"

"A mere thank you would do, ma'am. Isn't that right, Chairman? It's nothing for the mother of your precious grandson who's about to inherit a 130 billion won fortune."

Hyojin sees my face harden. "Oh no! That was way out of line, my apologies." She laughs and quickly covers her mouth.

What did she just say?

My vision blurs and the sound of Hyojin's giggling seems to come from far away.

CHAPTER

·40·

Even as I make my way through the dimly lit living room and up
the stairs, I still feel disoriented, a ringing in my ears. I wonder if
it's the pills I've swallowed in a hurry. The floor creaks as always, but
I can barely feel Seung-Joon's weight over my shoulder now. I've
forgotten how I was about to abandon him and sprint out the front
door.

130 billion? I mean, *130 billion*? Is that even humanly possible for
one person to have?

Of course, I knew full well that the old man wasn't just well-off.

A Western-style mansion, a garden with a swimming pool, exotic
cars in the garage, and tall buildings maintained by a twenty-something
son who never has to work for a living.

There's plenty of undeniable evidence pointing to his wealth. But
he's not even one of those famous celebrities or rich families anyone
would recognize. Until I set foot in this house, I had no idea there was
an old man living in a secret house on the outskirts of Seoul, hidden
from everyone, with 130 billion won to his name.

Of course, I don't expect it all to be cash. It can't be the exact sum
of 130 billion won stamped on his bank account. It must be in the
form of land, buildings, all the assets to be liquidated that amount to
that number in total.

But if those assets go up in price, they could be worth even more
than 130 billion won. What about the income generation that's feed-

ing into his account every single month? And the old man is nearing the end of his life. So variables abound from here on out.

After carefully setting Seung-Joon down on the mattress, I stand at the foot of the bed trying to calm my breath.

My braceleted wrist feels like hot coal. I'd tried to run away, thinking I'd be in handcuffs if I didn't, but instead, look at what I've got: a luxury sparkling platinum bracelet. I can't help but laugh, wondering if this is some comic strip I've stumbled into.

I worked ten hours a day for minimum wage, and now I just sit around and raise a baby to be rewarded with 130 billion won?

I try to clear my head, even though the meds are making me sweat profusely and my hands shake out of control. Of course, all that money won't be given directly to me; Seung-Joon will have a large share of the inheritance. All the family the old man has left in the whole world is his grandson and two sons, so of course he will.

That's when the video crosses my mind.

It's game over if Hyojin shows the video to the old man.

Worse yet, if she says she's the real mom and asks for a maternity test . . .

What is she waiting for, when she even knows the exact amount of the inheritance? She seems to know this family in and out, and of course she'd want her cut. However hard I try to figure out her motive, my foggy mind just won't work.

As I pace the room, biting my nails, I see a note on the floor that someone must have slipped under the door. I quickly pick it up to find a neatly written note.

Hope this helps you feel better soon.
I'm always on your side. Have a good night.

At the end is a smiley face. On the back is a digestive medicine stuck with a transparent piece of tape.

This is the kind of tenderness I've never been on the receiving end of. Had I walked out that door earlier, this would have been over. I don't know about the rest, but this I surely would have missed.

The sound of rushing water comes through the open window.

I grab the note and walk over to the window to look down—and there he is, Soohyun's slender form swimming from one end of the pool to the other.

What should I do? What am I *going* to do?

130 billion won and someone who promises to be on my side for the first time ever.

Isn't it worth fighting for? Worth a shot?

Wouldn't I cross the world for all this?

CHAPTER

· 4 1 ·

Grasshoppers and the rush of water—those are the only sounds echoing in the night garden.

The nighttime pool looks ten times more beautiful than in broad daylight.

Tall shrubbery surrounds the edges of the jet-black natural stone, blocking the outside world. The jade-colored tiles on the inside, where the water's splashing, give the pool an exotic look, but the top is made of dark, patterned terra-cotta tiles. On a breezy summer night, with the pool rippling under a dark sky illuminated by night-lights placed among lush trees, this feels just like a vacation spot in Spain or Morocco.

I take a deep breath. The short-mowed grass prickles the soles of my bare feet as I walk past the sunbed. The cool night air against my exposed skin awakens my senses.

Soohyun's still moving smoothly across the water from one side to the other, his movements precise and quick. When fully clothed, he always looks tidy and glossy, the picture-perfect youngest son of a rich family. But here, in the dark, splashing up a storm across the water, his lean, toned body is enough to take my breath away. I feel a whirl of strange desire in the pit of my stomach.

A pool all to yourself in the middle of the night. This is why the rich can't seem to give it up. They'll do anything to keep what they have. I stand on the edge of the pool for a while, watching him without saying anything.

After a couple of laps, Soohyun comes to the end and thrusts his head above the surface with a loud expulsion of breath. A spray of droplets mists through the air.

"Hmm?"

Soohyun rubs the water from his face and hair with both hands, before looking up.

"When did you come out? I thought you were asleep."

"The night wind just felt so good."

"I didn't wake you up, did I?"

"Oh, no! Not at all. I had a chat with Father, tucked Seung-Joon into bed, and was just barely catching my breath."

I wave my hands to assure him.

"Oh, thank goodness. I thought you were still having trouble falling asleep."

"I've been doing much better lately, thanks to the pills you gave me."

"Oh, good, good to hear. They worked, huh?"

"Yeah, they did. I feel so much better."

I grab the towel from the sunbed and hold it out for him.

"Ah! Thank you. I, uh, need a hand." Soohyun, still in the pool, reaches out for support.

I stumble slightly as I bend over and try pulling him to his feet. I let my foot slip, then wobble slightly as if I'm about to lose my balance, and splash into the water fully clothed.

"Oh God!" I sure can act.

"You slipped?" He stifles a laugh. "Look at you, sister!"

This side of the pool is just deep enough for me to stand up. I keep my head down, my hands covering my wet face, and find my footing in the water.

"What's wrong? I'm sorry for laughing. Did you hurt yourself?"

As Soohyun leans in, trying to get a better look, a loud water bomb rains down on him. I've caught him off guard and sent a cold splash of water his way.

"Oh!"

"What a scoundrel! How dare you laugh at me!" I say to Soohyun, who keeps his head away to avoid the shower of water raining down mercilessly on his face. I keep splashing in his direction without giving him a chance to breathe.

He smirks. "So this is how you want to play?"

I'm stunned for a moment as Soohyun begins to fight back.

Soon it's my turn to raise my hands in defense as he spins around like a swallow on water, sending water my way with both hands.

"Stop! Stop! I've lost! I surrender!"

"Shhh! Shhh!"

After screaming and taking turns sending water bombs flying, we finally come to our senses and look back toward the mansion, each gesturing for the other to be quiet, but we can't stop our giggles. I feel like a child.

"You're going to wake everyone up." Soohyun shakes his head disapprovingly.

"Look at me, look at the mess you made!" I open my arms wide.

I'm fully aware that the white T-shirt sticking to my body is revealing a navy bra trimmed with lace. Soohyun's eyes dart away for a moment, then back toward me, confused. The moment my eyes lock with his, I throw my arms around his neck and pull him in tight. We both lose our balance for a moment and slide underwater, but I refuse to let go.

Soohyun's eyes widen in surprise, and his head tilts as his eyes slowly close. His lost hands find and clutch my waist. And just like that, everything is submerged in the watery haze of a sweet early summer night.

With this kind of money, with this newly found love, nothing can scare me away.

I will not run away. I will sit tight and motionless like a rock until I can claim it all as mine, all mine.

CHAPTER

· 4 2 ·

I wake up to the sunlight streaming in.

It's been a long time since I've woken up feeling so clearheaded. Ever since I got here, I've always had a hard time sleeping at night because of all the worries plaguing my mind. For a moment, I cherish the feeling of my muscles being pulled in all directions as I stretch out on my bed.

I hadn't even needed my meds. I don't need them now. Last night, even without the pills, I'd felt drunk as if I'd downed a bottle of soju.

We'd giggled through the front door, leaving our drenched clothes outside, me in my navy blue lace panties with a towel tied around my waist, Soohyun in a robe he'd brought poolside. The stairs creaked the whole way up to the second floor, and through the dimly lit hall our wet footsteps left a distinct pattern on the old parquet. His hands secretly tickled the waist of my drenched T-shirt as I undid his to caress his firm bare skin. I basked in a giddy feeling, in long, moist kisses at my door. Droplets of water fell from his hair and landed near my eyes.

That was the moment the tight seal between us was broken.

We threw away all the platitudes like *you're my brother-in-law, we're family,* or *we're on the same side forever.*

"It's been so hard the whole time. I couldn't act on my feelings." As we groped each other in front of his door, Soohyun whispered in my ear. "I know now is not the time."

That's why we, having reached his bed, hands all over each other, suddenly stopped, both of us gasping for air.

"My brother meant so much to me," he said with a tremor in his voice. "I can't betray my brother, just in case—"

But I quickly covered his mouth with a kiss. "We don't have to think right now. Not now." I didn't dare look him in the eye as I buried my face in the nape of his neck and whispered.

"Although, he probably won't come back, maybe forever." Soohyun wrapped his arms around my waist, one hand stroking my back.

I asked, "Did you say 'forever'?"

"My brother, you know," he stammered. "I know he's changed; he's not the brother I used to know. He hurt so many people. I can't imagine how my brother can live with everything he's done. He will probably never show his face again, after what he did to you."

He hugged me a little tighter and muttered, "Sometimes I dream that my brother is dead."

It was a voice that could make your skin crawl—croaky, as if someone was strangling him.

"In this dream, he leaves me for good. And I follow him to hell, because I resent him for dying without my permission."

I pulled him into a hug without a word.

Perhaps he had still been stuck in a state of boyhood, unable to grow out of it since his trusted older brother left home. The first person he trusted and looked up to after losing his birth mother, and who stood by him when he came into the family as an illegitimate child. Considering how much Soohyun loved and missed his brother, if he ever found out his brother almost died at my hands, he would probably want to kill me. With these hands holding me so affectionately now, he might grab my neck and strangle me.

"I sometimes think my brother sent you my way," he murmured, burying his lips in the nape of my neck. He smelled faintly of grass and pool chlorine. "I felt like I'd known you forever even the first time

I saw you, and maybe that's why I don't want to let you go. But not today. Not yet. Do you understand?"

I nodded.

"My dad's gotten a lot weaker. He's been waiting for my brother, but he's probably lost hope by now. He knows my brother won't come back home. I think that's why he got so weak recently. After you and Seung-Joon moved in, he'd been feeling better for a while, but—"

I pressed my breasts against him through my wet T-shirt, arms around his neck, listening.

"I think he talked to Attorney Kim with his caregiver's help the other day, so maybe it was about you and Seung-Joon."

The note flashed before my eyes.

Se-Yool: Attorney Kim 010-3587-40xx / Contact for document correction

"He'll want to put you in his will instead of my brother."

"That's—"

I tried to pull away from his embrace, but he held me tighter, refusing to let go—so tight that I could barely breathe, and it hurt a little.

"I don't care, because my dad always loved my brother, not me. Had you not shown up in time, he would have donated everything he had, but now you're here, as is Seung-Joon. I'm sure he'll give you both the shares you deserve."

"I don't care about the money," I said, in a voice that made me hate myself, but that didn't matter anymore.

"That's for me to say, actually." Soohyun giggled, running his lips along the nape of my neck. "I just thought you should know—it's true that my family's wealthy, but it's not like I have a lot of my own. After my dad's passing, I won't be able to play rich boy like I do now, because I'm not on my dad's good side."

"No way, he had you so late, and you're the youngest son. You must be the apple of his eye."

"Quite the opposite." His tone was firm. "Maybe it's because I always fell short. I bet he'll leave everything to Seung-Joon. I'll probably just manage the buildings and collect some crumbs. But it doesn't matter. I just need you to understand my place in this family, before you make up your mind."

I pulled him closer without saying anything. We hugged each other tighter and tighter, as if our lives depended on it. I could feel his heart beating hard. In the end, we didn't cross the line, and we walked back to the door to my room, holding hands.

"There," Soohyun said with a sad look in his eyes. "Let's wait a little longer; we've already confirmed our feelings for each other, so let's leave it to the heavens to decide what happens next. Until then, promise me that you'll eat well, sleep well, and take care of yourself. Take your meds. That's all I want. Health is everything."

Before I slipped into my room, he joked, "If you're anxious, it makes me or Seung-Joon anxious, too," and gave me a feathery kiss.

So I slept through the night, safe and sound, without the meds.

I didn't feel anxious even when I thought about the video; I felt invincible. I knew that even though that video was a ticking time bomb, it couldn't destroy me. Soohyun's affection felt like the best insurance I could hope for. I finally understood what I had to do, and I was not going to let the video get to me.

Thinking about last night, I stare into the eyes of the smiling Seung-Joon and shower him with kisses. As I tiptoe to the bathroom, I feel beautiful and rejuvenated for the first time since I came to this house.

I've forgotten what that felt like for so long.

Since that first anonymous text, I've been having the worst time of my life, but I now know how to fight back, and I feel stronger than ever, like a soldier with all the weapons and ammunition I need, agile and ready to strike when it's the right moment.

I wash my hair, take a long shower, and slather myself in fragrant lotion. I scrutinize my face, pluck my eyebrows, get rid of peach fuzz here and there, and apply light makeup. I'm ready to go. Then I take out the medicine bottle that Soohyun gave me and pour all the pills down the toilet bowl and flush them.

Health is important, but I'm not going to take more of those. I'm going to make sure I eat well, sleep well, and stay healthy on my own.

I will survive. I'm going to get that fortune of 130 billion won and win over the man who's supported me through all this, because I deserve to put all my nightmares behind and be happy once and for all. I'll be safe with this family's son and grandson on my side.

The dickhead who came back from death and his foxy girlfriend? A freaky video?

Alright, let them go for it.

If Hyojin wants her place back, or the inheritance for herself, she'll have to do more than just hiding and pretending. She'll have to come out into the open and fight. But I won't make it easy. She'll have to pay the price for all her lies and deception, and she'll have to deal with the younger son of the family who's fallen for me head over heels.

Most of all, I'm not going to let her get away with trying to pin a murder that didn't happen on me.

But in order to handle her, I need to keep my head straight.

I can't be groggy on medication like last night.

Because I'm about to go ask that bitch face-to-face what the hell she wants.

CHAPTER

· 4 3 ·

I walk downstairs, a spring in my step, to crisp air blowing through windows and the front door, all of which are wide open as the house gets cleaned. I can hear the hum of the lawn mower outside in the garden. I glance out and see the sullen Mr. Kim working in silence, head down.

Suddenly, I think about last night with Soohyun in the pool. Were all the lights off in the outbuilding? Could that man have been lurking in the shadows, spying on us?

For a moment, I watch him at the open front door, only to turn away quickly as he suddenly looks up. Bloodshot eyes; a rough, scarred face; and white, unruly hair that covers his face. He looks strangely familiar, but I can't place just where I could have seen him before. His looks like the kind of face I've often seen at the construction site near my old place. There's nothing wrong with him, but he reminds me of my old life—that's probably why he unnerves me so much.

I tiptoe back into the house, almost waltzing. Anyway, now he's outside and I'm inside, a door dividing us. I decided to stay here in this safe haven last night instead of running away to live in the same world that he does.

"Ah, ma'am, you're up early," Mrs. Suwon greets me, a heap of quilts in her arms.

"The sun was in the middle of the sky, so I thought I overslept again."

"It's just nine o'clock. The days are getting longer."

"It's cleaning day today, so it's a bit of a mess. If you go wait in the dining room, I'll send in Heesun right away. Would you like an omelet? Everyone else had that. Or would you prefer Korean food?"

"Omelet sounds good, but 'everyone' already ate?"

"Yes, Mr. Soohyun and the new caregiver, they had an early meal and both left."

"Both of them?"

"Yes, Mr. Soohyun is going to work today, and Hyojin is going somewhere on an errand for Chairman."

"Oh, right."

I stride down, confidently, only to find no one here.

Instead of the large dining room table, I sit at a small round table by the window and eat the omelet and salad Heesun prepares for me. After a while, my hands are shaking and my vision gets blurry. I briefly regret dumping all my meds, but after three cups of strong coffee, I feel a little better.

Should I have kept a few pills just in case? No, there's no "just in case," because from here on out, I'm going to be at the ready.

With Seung-Joon in Mrs. Suwon's care, I feel a bit more relaxed. In a spacious house where everyone is busy at work, my time alone seems to pass slowly. This is the privilege of being the daughter-in-law of a rich family.

Sipping the last of the coffee in my cup, I stare at the door to the old man's room. The room next door is the caregiver's, connected to his. When Mr. Choi was here, it was just a break room. But now Hyojin has moved in and is living there.

I don't know if she has a place of her own, but she might have felt it'd be worth ditching whatever home she had to her name for the prize of 130 billion won. After all, that's the kind of money one would kill for.

So why didn't she just bring her own child here from the beginning? Because she misjudged and thought the old man would never forgive the romance between his precious eldest son and a lowly caregiver? No, that doesn't make sense. He even accepted a woman like me, a nobody, just because I brought him his grandchild.

So why the hell couldn't she come in here herself, instead of sending me on her behalf? Does she also have some mess to run from? Why couldn't she come in here and just flat out say she's Seung-Joon's mother?

Was I supposed to serve as a shield or a test subject, and now you're here to threaten me away? What is it that you want, money or revenge? What the hell is your plan? You seem to know me so well, yet I know nothing about you.

"You can't win a fight until you know your enemy."
   "What kind of bullshit is that?"
   "No bullshit. I'm going to teach you the art of fighting!"
   "Who would I have to fight, like, ever?"
   When he was in a good mood, Hyun-Wook would tickle me and crack this silly joke—but unless he was beating me to a pulp, who did I ever have to fight?
   "You never know, some dude could hurt you or bother you."
   "Forget it, no one cares enough to give me a second glance besides you."
   "You don't know that."
   Then there was that searching look in his eyes, surveying my expression. The way he doubted everything and tried to trap me.
   "Even if I were to fight a random guy, there's no way I'd win."
   "That's why you shouldn't just throw punches from the start, but take a good look at your enemy first. If you take a step back and watch him, you'll find his weaknesses. Like a limp, preference for the right hand, things like that. When you're fighting, you don't just go in blindly. Figure out what's what first."
   "So yeah, don't just jump in, but observe. I get it."

Don't just jump in, but observe first, right? I set my coffee cup down with a clatter and stand up. The whole staff are busy scrubbing every room and bathroom in this house. All the curtains and blinds are taken down, every inch of glass washed. The old man's room was probably the first, or maybe is the last on their list. I don't know when Hyojin will be back, but if she left early, I should have at least an hour or two to spare.

Now is the time to get to know my opponent.

After a careful glance around, I walk over to Hyojin's door and turn the knob. On cleaning day, doors are left unlocked, including hers. The longer I wait, the riskier it will be.

I let myself inside and shut the door behind me.

Soon, a darkness consumes me.

CHAPTER
·44·

HYOJIN

THEN

It was the end of July when I told the old man that I didn't think I could work anymore because of a family situation.

Although still five months away from my due date, it was just in the nick of time. I was starting to gain weight, making it harder to hide my pregnancy bump even in loose-fitting clothes. Of course, I told him not to worry because I would continue to watch his son and send him reports. I told him it was probably for the best that I could be his eyes and ears on the outside, even though I couldn't stay right by his side.

"I'm moving to a new place near where your son lives. I've got myself an apartment just a twenty-minute bus ride away, so don't you worry."

My apartment was brand-new, in fact, and had two rooms and one bathroom. The old man was satisfied, thinking it was his generous monthly payment that afforded me this new place. He gently asked me if I needed anything else and told me not to worry about any expenses that went into following his son. I spent hours and hours by his side patiently telling him about Hyun-Wook, and he was so eager to listen. The old man's trust in me by that point knew no limits, because I made sure to keep my mouth shut about his gradual recovery, even with his younger son.

He thought I was just a live-in caregiver who walked into his house one day. To this day, he still knows nothing of my history. He mistakenly believed that I had only just seen this old mansion, its spacious and fragrant gardens, and all the riches and beautiful things that come with overflowing wealth.

So he believed in the loyalty that his money could buy, in a purely contractual relationship without any self-interest or strings attached. That's why he spoke his mind freely and revealed to me his true feelings. If his eldest son did not return, he would give away all his wealth, but if I could return him back by any means necessary, Chairman Jung would divide everything equally between his two sons and give me a handsome reward.

Was it not a compelling proposition?

Even without all the selfishness secretly bubbling up inside of me, I would still have taken the bait.

Of course, my share of the bounty would pale in comparison to that of his sons, but if you consider the share of this child in my womb, wouldn't it be almost equal?

So I decided to keep the child after all. That was the moment I realized that something I had only considered a headache, after months of wondering if I should get rid of it, had become a lifeline. There was a time when I had gnashed my teeth, longing to destroy this family because all the gold in the world couldn't comfort my broken heart or save my broken life, but there it was—I had changed my mind.

I thought if the old man was going to give me a big lump sum, I might think twice about aborting the baby. If my child could be the future of his fine lineage and a significant nest egg for me, then maybe I could turn a blind eye to what his family had done to mine. Maybe I could forget how they had all trampled on my love and betrayed my trust.

But first, just a little bit of fun for me. Because, why not?

Money's good and all, but what's life without some devilish entertainment?

CHAPTER

· 4 5 ·

It's very dark in the room.

I lean against the door and wait for my eyes to adjust. The two small windows are both shut tight, the blinds down. I can barely make out any objects in the room in the feeble light that filters through.

Hyojin's room is small and simple, probably the most rustic in the house, furnished with a single bed and a built-in closet made entirely of wood. It's a tall closet with a wooden shutter-like door with slats. Then there is a small TV, a chair, and a table. On the bedside table sits a desk clock, a book about rehabilitation nursing, and a bell that looks connected to the old man's call button. In the corner of the room rests a set of heavy, hand-marked dumbbells, a yoga mat, and a foam roller, all of which I assume have been used by caregivers hired by the family. The plain, unadorned bedding is neatly arranged.

Careful not to make any noise, I head to the bathroom attached to the room. The old man might be awake, so I'll get in trouble if he thinks Hyojin has returned and calls her in. Her bathroom is spartan, with just a toilet, sink, and shower stall. The closet above the sink contains sanitary pads, cosmetics, toiletries, cotton swabs, and nail clippers.

I step out of the bathroom and look around the room again.

It feels like a cheap hotel room, devoid of character, nothing to show who lives here. Maybe Hyojin left it this way on purpose, to erase her presence entirely.

Kneeling on the floor, flat on my stomach, I look under the bed and reach around but find nothing except a puff of dust. I stand back up, listening in the middle of the room for a moment. Nothing but the faint hum of a vacuum cleaner somewhere in the distance.

Now there's only one place left to search.

The tall closet.

The door swings wide open, rattling a coatrack with a dozen outfits. Plain blouses, pants, shirts, and sweaters hang side by side. Underneath them lies a pair of fluffy slippers that she could use to muffle her footsteps. All of the items are so plain and neutral in design that they'd make her blend in anywhere. It's all utilitarian clothing, the kind a textbook would exemplify as "appropriate attire for a female live-in caregiver caring for an elderly man." No floral dresses or brightly colored hand-knit cardigans like one would expect for a chubby, fair-skinned new mother.

In one corner of the spacious closet lie a small suitcase and a duffel bag. I remember that Hyojin was dragging it along with her when she arrived. But when I pick up the suitcase, it feels weightless, so I don't even bother to open it. The duffel bag, though—a plain navy blue one that a guy might use as his gym bag—is heavy.

My hands tremble a little as they hastily unfasten the zipper. I wonder if a pill would have helped my unease, but I wipe my sweaty, slimy hands on my pants and open the bag. Inside is a bundle of clean underwear, a towel, a couple of T-shirts, and some socks.

No way—that's it?

With trembling hands, I sift through the pile of clothes and socks until my hand finds something hard inside: a wallet, a small camcorder, and an outdated cell phone.

Bingo!

I quickly open the wallet.

ID, credit cards, and a caregiver license, along with some cash.

The cards say "Hyojin Cha."

At least it's her real name.

The license proves she's a caregiver for real, too. She wouldn't fake documentation like this and carry it around, would she?

I don't know how old the photo is, but the woman on the ID looks very young, her hair down to her shoulders with bangs, with an air of meek gentleness about her. The younger version of Hyojin looks more like the young mom I met on the train.

As I'm about to close the wallet, I notice something poking out from behind the ten thousand won folded in half.

A photo? Who even carries a physical photo these days?

And not just any photo.

I tug on the corner and the photo slips out. It's a very old Polaroid with a tiny, crude heart scribbled in the bottom margin. The faces of the people in it are half blown out, almost masked. A corner of the photo has been cut off.

Two of the people I recognize. Familiar faces smile up at me.

He's wearing a sweatshirt in the photo, smiling out of the corner of his eye. He's still a child, I can tell. My boyfriend isn't that tall in this photo, but he's already well-built and attractive in a boyish way. So this is what he looked like when I didn't know him yet. The eldest son of a wealthy family, clean-cut with no rough edges. Perhaps this was a time when he had never even thought to grab a woman by her hair. His right arm is draped over someone's shoulder, but I can't tell who it is, because the photo is cropped right there.

The other person, half leaning against Hyun-Wook's left shoulder, is his brother, Soohyun. He was probably in middle school back then. He's thin and lanky, with a sensitive face that shows no smile. Leaning against his brother's shoulder, he even looks a bit nervous.

This photo is probably over a decade old.

How did Hyojin get her hands on this photo? Did she find it in this house when she was a caregiver? If not, why would my boyfriend give this woman an old photo of himself with his brother? When Hyojin was so close with him—so close, in fact, that they had a child together. There would be many photos of them together, so why is she carrying around this one, out of all of them, in her wallet? And who's the other person next to him, and why was the person cropped out?

I'm full of questions, but there's no time to waste. I pull out my cell phone and snap a quick picture before I slide the Polaroid back in, close the wallet, and put it away.

Now it's time to look at the old cell phone, but it's turned off. I try to turn it on, but it's out of juice. Damn it, I'm sure she sent me a video on this phone, and if I can just see if she sent me any threatening texts—no, if I can find a record of her and Hyun-Wook exchanging texts—it'd be game over!

Just then, I hear something outside.

I freeze and listen, fingertips cold and beads of sweat starting to roll down my back. I can hardly breathe. How does Hyojin stand living in such a small room?

Straining my ears, I can hear the distant hum of the vacuum cleaner. There are no signs of life at the door leading to the old man's room, so I decide I must have misheard. After all, it's still going to take a while to clean this big house.

I put the phone and wallet away and pull out the camcorder next. It's strange. Everyone has a smartphone these days. Who would be carrying around a camcorder anymore without a good reason? So she should have expected this. It's only natural that I feel a need to inspect this camcorder.

For a moment, I'm worried it will turn up nothing, like the cell phone, but the camcorder powers up just fine. I press play and stare at the tiny LCD screen.

I wasn't wrong at all. A video I recognize pops up. It starts with someone's back blocking the view. There it goes: I appear, my hair tied back in a simple ponytail. Then there's me and him talking, him grabbing my wrist, me trying to pull away, him not budging, me struggling, him grabbing my hair.

I watch the video, calm as still water. My hands are still shaking, but not out of fear. Maybe it's because I've watched it over and over again, but now I feel nothing even when I go through all those moments again, step by step. I've grown numb to the shock of what I've done, the way after picking at a wound over and over, a bumpy, rough callus forms over the fresh scar, and you get a thicker scab.

I'd been beaten all throughout my time with him, and I fought back just once. Is that so bad? If he wants to press charges, let him go for it! But I say it was self-defense. I'll say I didn't mean to kill him and I got so terrified that I ran away, and this video will be proof that the son of a bitch was harassing me. If he got up and walked away, it's not murder, and if he's dead and Hyojin cleaned up his body, she's an accomplice.

The more I think, the more energized I get. My plan looks fool-proof, doesn't it?

Before Hyojin can claim to be Seung-Joon's mother, she'll have to confess to the old man that she left his precious grandson in the hands of a complete stranger on a train. I could have kidnapped or abandoned him, but she didn't care. She took those risks. I deserve credit for getting him home safely. So technically, she and I are in the same boat. If she wants to bring me down, she'll go down with me, too.

That thought seems to bring life back into my body. If she came back for that 130 billion won, and she's harassing me out of greed, she'll have to get ready for the fight of her lifetime.

Nothing more to see here. I now know for sure that it was Hyojin who sent me that video, so I can sit her down and talk things out, all cards on the table.

Just then, the old floorboards creak outside the door. Footsteps. This time, I'm sure. A chill runs down my spine.

I jump to my feet, sending the bundle of socks in my lap to the floor. I scoop them up with one hand, toss them into the bag, and turn off the camcorder, but I notice something else.

The next part of the video is only supposed to show me freaking out and running away.

Six minutes and twelve seconds, that's the length of the video from the text message. It ends with an oblique downward shot of my face and head as I run away, and then it stops.

But the time at the top of the camcorder screen is still moving. He collapses, I bolt out the door, and the video continues to show the empty half-basement.

The footsteps approaching the room grow closer and closer, but I can't stop looking down at the screen. I need to know what the hell happened in that house after I left. Maybe this video will give me answers that will save my life.

I press the fast-forward button. The onscreen clock starts ticking rapidly.

Squeak.

Just outside the door, the floorboards creak again. This time too close.

No! Not yet!

"Hyojin?"

"Yes?"

Shit!

I hear Hyojin's voice from just beyond the door, and Mrs. Suwon says something to her as I press the stop button with a trembling hand.

But I've already seen something new. On the screen, another person has just walked into the half-basement. Exactly five minutes and thirteen seconds after I run out, the back of someone's head appears. The video cut off from there.

And I hear Hyojin turn the doorknob, laughing outside the room.

CHAPTER
·46·

Hyojin walks into her bedroom.

Standing in the closet and holding my breath, I watch her through the gap in the shutter-like wooden door. Thank goodness it's been getting so hot lately. If she had on a jacket, she would have to open the closet and hang up her clothes. I stand in the corner of the closet, clutching the duffel bag I haven't even got to zip all the way up, hands shaking and feeling like I might lose my grip. If I drop it, it would be the end of everything.

Once she walks into the room, Hyojin opens all the blinds, starting with the window. Then she goes straight to the bathroom and closes the door.

Should I leave now? No, it's too dangerous. What if I run into the maids, who seem to be downstairs at the moment?

Then it hits me. My house slippers, made of soft gray fabric, lie half hidden under the bed, just visible through the closet shutters. I left them there while I was crouched on the floor, rummaging.

The sweat that's begun to break out on my forehead trickles down my temples and into my eyes.

My stomach turns, and I feel like I'm going to throw up at any moment. Then I hear the toilet flush and see Hyojin come out of the bathroom, hair pinned up high with a rubber band she had in her mouth earlier. Standing at the foot of the bed, she pulls off her socks, rolls them up and throws them aside, and pulls off her T-shirt. My hands, still holding the bag, shake violently. Gritting my teeth to keep quiet, I watch her walk past me in her underwear, fumbling with her bra, and go back into the bathroom. A moment later, I hear the sound of water gushing from inside.

I count slowly to ten, cautiously set the bag down, still trembling, and open the closet door. Through the closed bathroom door, I can hear the water running. I fumble under the bed, grab my slippers, and creep to the door. As I gingerly turn the knob, a bead of sweat trickles down my forehead and onto the floorboards.

Luckily, no one is in the living room. I quickly slip out and quietly close the door behind me. After a quick look around, I run toward the stairs to the second floor.

The short distance between the closet and the stairs feels like the length of a decade. Completely drained, I feel like I'll collapse at any moment. I'm so desperate for the pills. I should have left one pill. Just one.

I need to take a breather and process everything I found in that room.

But as I climb the stairs, I realize something unnerving.

I don't remember if I zipped that duffel bag back up before I walked out of the closet or not.

CHAPTER

· 4 7 ·

I'll be working late because it's the last day of the month—
these reports! Oh, how I hate my job! Enjoy your lunch,
and see you later!

Even Soohyun's text, which would have normally made me stare, smiling, at my phone for a while, fails to brighten me up. After a quick glance, I throw my phone away. No time to dwell on a text message. My chewed-down fingertips are now bleeding, but I feel no pain.

I can't believe I made such a stupid mistake!

However hard I try to remember if I zipped up the bag, I can't, as if that one moment has been erased from my memory. Did I zip it before I set it down, or did I just drop it and shoot out like a bullet after I grabbed my slippers? How can I not remember?

But what's done is done.

Even if I did leave it open, would she even notice?

We all make human mistakes, like forgetting to turn off the gas when we leave the house. She can't be an exception. When she sees her open bag, she probably won't even realize she left it there in the first place. No, something inside me rejects that. But what about the contents? The camcorder, her wallet, her old cell phone, her personal stuff.

Won't she find it weird that they're sticking out of the bag, the bundle of socks and underwear in disarray? Wouldn't *I* be suspicious?

No, a different voice inside me replies. It's the voice that's always promised me that everything will be okay, that we will make it out alive and well and everything will end up perfectly fine.

After all, nothing's missing. Even if Hyojin feels something's amiss, the cash and cards are still there. Could she link me to the open bag and suspect me? Maybe since it's cleaning day, the maids will be the prime suspects.

Then it dawns on me.

The maid who used to work here got caught stealing and got kicked out, and there was a suspicious death. That's why they hire new maids every two years. So if Hyojin starts getting suspicious of the maids, there'll be another bloodbath, all because of me.

But I've got to look after myself first, so I push that worry to the back of my mind.

Oh, how I wish I'd left just one pill. If I could just swallow one pill, even without water, it would make everything so much easier. *Just one.*

There's a knock on the door.

I spit out the new bits of flesh I've chewed off my fingers and cough. "Yes?" My voice comes out in a ridiculous twang.

"I've brought Seung-Joon, ma'am."

It's her—Hyojin!

I'm so startled by the voice that I bite my tongue.

How dare she come all the way up here? With Seung-Joon? Does she know everything?

I want to turn around and jump out the open window.

I look down to find that at some point I flung my hastily rescued house slippers halfway across the floor.

I walk barefoot to the door.

"You shouldn't just jump in at the deep end, you should be observant. If you step back and look at what's going on, you'll find your enemy's weaknesses."

I open the door just a crack and take a peek to find Hyojin standing in the doorway with Seung-Joon in her arms.

Her face as blank as ever, her freshly damp hair smells faintly of shampoo.

"Mrs. Suwon said she was done feeding him, so I brought him here." She looks at me with a smile on her face.

When I reach out to take him, all of a sudden, she pries the door open and bursts into the room. I take a step back. It's finally just the three of us in the room, just like the first time we met. But none of us look like we did months ago.

I'm wearing a luxury-brand summer knit in a soft gold fabric, she's wearing a practical short-sleeved T-shirt and pants, and Seung-Joon is sucking his thumb in his mother's arms, wrapped in an imported French baby suit instead of a swaddle.

"I'll put him in his crib for you. He's a good boy, and he eats well." She walks across the room and carefully places him in the crib. Her voice betrays no hint of emotion.

"A good sleeper, isn't he?" I start in a shaky voice, studying her expression to see if she reacts in any way to parts of our exchange from the train. But this heartless wench doesn't even blink an eye; she simply lays Seung-Joon down and, after soothing him a bit, turns to leave.

I look straight into the eyes of this incomprehensible woman as she turns away with such ease. I'm trembling terribly, but now is the time. I'm fully prepared to get my ass kicked, ready to hear her yell, "You stole my life!"

But she just looks me in the eye, smiles slightly, and whisks out of the room. When I bump into her shoulder, I catch a whiff of shampoo. I reach out and grab her arm, leaving red handprints on the soft bare skin peeking under her short sleeves.

"What the hell do you think you're doing? What the hell do you want!"

Hyojin stops, her light brown eyes looking straight at me. I see a sneer lingering there. I'm positive she's laughing at me internally now. As if to say, "Oh, I've figured you out." As if to say, "Patience. It wouldn't be any fun if I showed you my hand yet." She flashes me a smile, the kind of smile a kid might have on her face when she's tearing off the wings of a dragonfly caught in a net.

That's when my hand on the woman's arm begins to shake.

"I'm home!" I hear Soohyun's breathy voice downstairs.

"Ah! Mr. Soohyun, are you back?" Hyojin shakes me off and walks past me, her voice rising as if pleased to see him home. Long after she leaves my room, my empty hands are still shaking.

CHAPTER
·48·

I stay holed up in my room until it's time for dinner.

You can't win if you don't know your enemy, and I'm unsure who my enemies really are to begin with or what they're trying to do. I have a sinking dread that they're going to fight back, that they already have plans they're putting into motion. I need to strike first, but I don't know how.

My mind lingers on the video—the part when someone new walks in, at which point I was forced to stop watching.

Just thinking about it makes me want to jump up and down and rip my hair out. If I'd watched a little longer, I would have seen whose head had just appeared on the screen.

But if I kept watching, I wouldn't have been able to hide in the closet in time. I wonder what Hyojin would have done had I confronted her right then and there? I don't even want to think about what would have happened had I given her that kind of push, seeing how completely unpredictable she is even now. I can't fight back when I have no idea what to expect.

What would she have done, even just now, had Soohyun not shown up in time?

I'm so deep in thought that I nearly jump out of my skin when I hear a knock on the door.

"Let's go eat." Soohyun's voice is filled with laughter.

It's like he's the pill I'm dearly missing right now.

I quickly scramble out of bed to open the door.

The moment I see his smiling face, I throw my arms around his neck. It's the first time we've been able to look each other in the eye properly since all the drama last night.

"Oops!" Soohyun, knocked back slightly, reaches over to pat me on the back in embarrassment.

"You've been busy all day?"

"Yeah, well, doing this and that. I see they've been cleaning all day. If I'd known it'd go on so long, I would have taken you and Seung-Joon for dinner somewhere nice."

"Oh." I click my tongue wistfully. "That would have been nice."

"We've got plenty of time, what do you say we go tomorrow? How about lunch? Greek food?" he asks, offering me his arm.

"I've never had that before."

I quickly take his arm.

"Perfect. Let's sleep in tomorrow and hit the road without break-fast, maybe around eleven in the morning."

"Sir?"

We're halfway down the stairs when I hear a sullen, hoarse voice from the front door. I quickly withdraw my arm. After all, I'm the daughter-in-law in the family, and my husband has run away from home, not heard from since, dead or alive. It wouldn't look too good if I have my arms around my brother-in-law at all times, looking too intimate.

"Yes?" Soohyun clears his throat and descends the stairs in quick steps.

Mr. Kim stands in the doorway, his bloodshot eyes staring through shaggy hair that hangs across his face.

"Your Audi's been taken care of for now. It'll start, but the high-pressure pump will need to be replaced. Park said you had some car troubles on your way to Seoul earlier, it broke down?"

"Yeah, I was going to find a mechanic in the city, but somehow it started right up, and I was in a hurry, so I just drove it home. But it's acting up again."

"Yeah, well, I'm off tomorrow, so I'll look into which part I'd need and order it later."

"Yes, please do. Get some rest, and it'd be great if you can get the car fixed yourself," Soohyun says in a cheerful voice, then he turns and walks into the dining room.

Mr. Kim gives him a curt bow and makes a point to throw a glance at me before turning away. Ever since my first day here, he's always been looking at me with a strange, piercing gaze that sets me on edge. As if to say, "You shouldn't be here."

Am I mistaken? Everything in this house, whether objects or people, seems to be screaming at me to get the hell out.

I follow Soohyun into the dining room, staring at his back. Seoul? Wasn't he busy with the company's monthly closing today? What business did he have that would have required him to travel all the way to Seoul, instead of taking care of business at the corporate-owned building right here in Juyoung-si? Since I came to this house, has he ever traveled to Seoul for company business or anything else?

"Come on, sister. I'm hungry!"

At the entrance to the dining room, he looks my way and waves me over, smiling brightly. I quickly force my face into a smile and hurry to fall in step with him. Changing my facial expression is as easy as flipping my hands now.

But when I walk in, I stop dead in my tracks, my face stiff again. Hyojin is sitting next to the old man, waiting on him.

"Sorry I'm late, Father," I offer as a swift greeting and take my seat, avoiding Hyojin's gaze.

"He was feeling a little under the weather, so I was helping him eat first," Hyojin says, looking back and forth between me and Soohyun.

"That's perfectly fine. Dad, how are you feeling today?"

"He's feeling a little weak," Hyojin answers instead.

The old man doesn't even look up, focused on his meal. What Soohyun said echoes through my head:

"My dad always loved my brother, not me. Had you not shown up in time, he would have donated everything he had."

Why hate his younger son, whom he had at such a late age, so much that he doesn't plan to leave him a penny? And why dote on the eldest son, who's basically abandoned his aging father? The old man showers *me* with gifts, like my pure platinum bracelet, so why be so hard on his own flesh and blood, the son who's stood by his side all this time?

I think about that 130 billion won. That ridiculous number is tempting me, just out of reach, like a cloud shimmering in the distance. If Seung-Joon and I got even a fraction of that money, even just 10 percent, I could save Soohyun. I don't know if there's a future for us, but if I make it out of this house alive, the only person I want to be with is Soohyun.

"Oh, this squid salad's delicious. It's been a while since I had Mrs. Suwon's specialty cooking."

Soohyun smiles, trying to change the awkward atmosphere at the table. He doesn't look in my direction in particular. We both know we shouldn't be too friendly in front of other people.

"I was craving something spicy. Can't wait to taste it."

As I pick up my chopsticks, Soohyun gently pushes the side dish toward me. I try to look nonchalant and speak casually.

"By the way, Soohyun, did you happen to go to Seoul earlier today? Why were you there?"

Clang!

"Chairman!"

"Father!" Soohyun cries.

When I turn around, the old man is face-down on the table. His water glass and rice bowl have fallen to the floor and shattered. A few strands of the old man's long gray hair are soaking wet in the soup bowl. But his face, slumped over the table, is looking up, his eyes shining. The muscles in his distorted face twitch. Our eyes meet. It's as if those eyes are trying to tell me something.

"Father?" I ask. "Father?"

"Quick! Call an ambulance! Quick!" Soohyun jumps to his feet and runs out of the room screaming. The chair he's been sitting in until just now wobbles and flips over a moment after.

CHAPTER
·49·

HYOJIN

THEN

With my due date just around the corner, the mere act of walking took such a toll on me. My due date was December 11, but by the middle of November, I already felt like my legs were giving out under my growing weight. But the passengers on the express bus were usually happy to offer their seats when they spotted me and would start small talk.

"What's your husband up to, letting you go about on your own in the cold?" an old lady across the aisle on a bus asked one day, pretending to be considerate but apparently wanting to pry.

I cleared my throat and told her what she wanted to hear. "He's working late again today. He'll join me at my parents' later."

"Ugh, yeah, it's good for a young person to keep busy. When you have kids, there are so many things you want to do for them. You better start saving."

After a fleeting smile, I took my earbuds out of my pocket and put them in my ears. That cut off all communication with her.

But I kept pondering what she'd said. Would I really want to do everything in my power for my child? Even a mom like me, who still doesn't feel anything for the little mishmash in my belly? Even if it was just a mistake from a one-night stand? If I could go back in time, would I let it happen again? I mean, honestly. I can't find a way to describe it, but when I look back, I can tell I was half out of my mind that night.

When my day began, I had a perfectly clear head. In fact, I took a carefully planned, very deliberate approach to my agenda. I had to be meticulous, of course, so he wouldn't suspect that I was living nearby or had been spying on him and his girlfriend.

Both of them had odd jobs, but they had relatively regular hours at the moment. She worked morning and evening shifts at a barbecue place, five days a week, and he drove a forklift at a construction site. I followed them in a taxi a few times when he left the house, but his work hours were inconsistent. When a construction site opened up, he would jump at the chance to work there for a few weeks, and when it was finished, he would move on to another one, but he rarely traveled far. At most, he'd go to a neighboring town an hour or two away.

That's how I picked out a place for our reunion: another city near the one where they lived. Sometimes he would have dinner with his coworkers, but otherwise he would just grab a quick bite to eat alone at a convenience store before heading home.

That day, I made sure I ran into him at the convenience store he frequented near the construction site. I bought milk and salad and stood behind him while he paid for a triangular kimbap, some hot bars, and a pack of soju. I deliberately stood so close to him that when he finished paying, I bumped into his chest as he turned around.

"Oops!" he yelled, with no apology to follow.

"Oh, I'm sorry!" I pretended to bow my head, then glanced quickly up at his face and boldly reached out to grab his arm.

"Huh?" I furrowed my brow, pretending to have been caught off guard for a moment.

"Hyun-Wook," I said.

His eyes widened as his brow furrowed, his hat pressed tightly to his head. For about ten seconds, he seemed to try to remember who I was. I had carefully blow-dried my hair, applied makeup, and even pulled out a floral dress I hadn't worn in a long time. Was it so hard to recognize me? Had I really changed so much in ten years?

"Oh . . ." A hint of recognition flashed across his face, although he didn't seem to remember my name.

So I offered, "It's me, Hyojin! Wow, you're still the same!" I dragged him outside and sat him down at a table in front of the stall. "It's been a long time!"

Unlike me, who pretended to be happy to see him, he just looked around with his legs twitching and refused to meet my eyes.

I'd been watching him for so long at the half-basement, but when we finally came face-to-face, it wasn't exactly how I'd expected it to go. When I saw him up close, I could see the damage time had done to him. Instead of the true Prince Charming he used to be, the man in front of me was roughened up and sun-kissed like Heathcliff.

Of course, this 2.0 version of Hyun-Wook wasn't all that bad because it built on an exceptional original. Before, he'd seemed like the kind of guy who would take me to a fancy restaurant, get down on one knee, and put a diamond ring on my finger, but now he seemed like the kind of guy who would push me down on the bed, rip off my stockings, and grab my breasts with his rough, rough hands. Both had their own arousing charms.

What had happened to him? Even I hadn't changed quite the way he had. He must have had a harder life than I did. But did that make everything fair for me? I couldn't think of him as the victim here.

"Do you live nearby?" he asked, his legs shaking, a nervous tic.

"Oh, I live a little farther away, and I was just thirsty after visiting a friend today."

I held up the milk. He took the plastic bag with the pack of soju in it and stealthily placed it on the chair next to him.

"What are you doing in a place like this? By the way, how's every-one? How's Chairman doing? And Soohyun?"

He winced and shuddered at the second name.

"Oh, I don't live there anymore, I'm too old for that."

For the first time since we met, he smiled. It was a faint smile, on the verge of a sigh, but a smile nonetheless.

"Oh my God, are you married?"

"No."

The answer was quick, which was nice, but just as quickly followed by an unwelcome explanation.

"We're just living together, for the time being."

"For the time being?"

There was an audible disappointment in my voice. I could hear my voice dripping with wishful thinking.

"That's just the way it is. We need to get our lives together, so we're not ready to take the next big step."

He kept looking around as if he couldn't wait to get out of there.

"Well then, it's only a matter of time. Sounds like you've made up your mind already! Wow! I wonder what kind of girl changed you so much that you want to get married now. Tell me all about it! Come on—why don't we go have a drink right now? You have time?"

I stood up, but he was still hesitant.

"What, you thought I'd say goodbye after meeting you like this? We've got a lot of catching up to do!"

I pulled him to his feet by the arm. Where I remembered his boyish, slender arms, there were now a man's arms with solid muscle. With those big hands, he could slap her slender body just once and she'd fly off and hit her head on the wall like in a cartoon.

I told myself not to forget that. Even though I was torn between longing to crush his lips to mine and wanting to smash his face with a glass bottle, I couldn't possibly forget why I was there to meet him in the first place. So I put my arm around him, boldly pressed my chest against his, and dragged him to a nearby bar.

It was that night that Seung-Joon was conceived. This child who, after all this time, still doesn't feel like he belongs to me.

When I left the bar a while later, I was in despair and wanted to throw myself out a window. So, I don't remember who made the first move that night. Just recounting the drunken stories we shared in the bar was enough to make us both tremble with want.

"She's a good girl, or should I say a decent girl. In love? I don't know. Maybe love? I don't know what love is, but I feel good with her, and sometimes I

miss her when I'm away. Home? My old family house? No, I never go there. I don't even remember when I left. Yeah, yeah. I just remember feeling like I was being tortured all the time there. I don't want to set foot in that house ever again. I didn't feel like myself there, and I acted all crazy. I went to therapists and counselors and whatnots and they were all telling me bullshit that didn't work. Trauma, right? Yeah, they always sugarcoat the truth. It's all bullshit. I just like things as they are now. Life is so different from what it used to be, but it's so much better now. You know what's really funny about life, Hyojin? It's that you're so much happier when you have nothing than when you have everything."

I can't tell you how many times I stared at the fork set on the bar table and imagined stabbing his eyeballs with it and crushing them like grapes.

How dare you talk about happiness? You've ruined other people's lives, their families, and you have the right to use the word *trauma*? How many people did he have to ruin, to find his happiness?

After I left the bar, I had to get myself drunk somewhere else, just to digest all that he'd said. Already hammered, I still needed more drinks in me to vent all the complex, overwhelming feelings.

Not sure that he was in love? Happier now? Never wanted to go back home because he was just feeling tortured all the time there?

As I pondered his words between drinks, I could smell the alcohol on my breath and feel the anger exploding out of me. I was taken over by that anger as much as the frustration and sudden madness of my drinking buddy, who was getting more and more upset as I told him all about it. It was new to me—him getting so upset and drunk—which both stunned and excited me at the same time, and that's why I made such a stupid mistake that night.

We were drunk, the world was spinning, and we wanted to tear up everything we could get our hands on. Both of us.

Buttons popping, clothes flying. The kind of sex with your butt slammed against the wall, panties ripped off, and breasts viciously grabbed. It was the kind of sex that filled me with a grotesque desire, the kind of sex that conjured up images of *him*, all distorted, my desires satisfied in the wrong place, everything wrong.

It was that day that Seung-Joon was conceived.

And it was that day when I realized what must have gone wrong all those years ago, what had really happened on that fateful day that changed our lives forever. Who had been the bad guy, who had been wronged, and who had really been the victim in this twisted story of ours. The hidden truth.

It wasn't until I heard the cursing, the screaming, and his name echoing through the night that I realized all this. But by then, it was too late.

This stop is Jaeil Hospital, Jaeil Hospital.

While I was lost in thought, the bus finally arrived at my destination. I barely made it off, dodging an old woman dozing on the other side.

The last time I'd been here was late last year, so the receptionist seemed surprised to see my belly full.

"It must have been a difficult trip."

I smiled wordlessly at the greeting and followed her through the familiar corridor.

"He's doing much better, and is very self-motivated. We think he'll be ready to be out in the next month or so. He should be able to go home by then."

"Would that be okay?"

"I mean, as you know, with diseases with no cure, self-discipline and determination are the most important things. Once he's out, he should go on living as if alcohol doesn't even exist in the world, and he's going to have to be very disciplined. It's not easy, but every once in a while you get somebody who actually starts anew and becomes a completely new person."

She opened the door to the break room, reassuring me. Rubbing my cold hands, I shuffled inside and greeted the man sitting at the head of the table.

"Hi, Dad."

CHAPTER

·50·

"Do you think a daughter-in-law in a rich family gets to sleep on a bed of roses all the time?"

Jisun, who worked with me at the barbecue place, was very savvy about the ways of the world.

She'd insisted on educating me: The super-rich refuse to die easily because they're sitting on billions and billions of won, and they live long, long lives, making a lot of money, holding on to it so their children will wait on them hand and foot. She said no one truly wants to take care of their old, ailing parents if not for money. That's why the daughters-in-law of the rich don't even hire caregivers, they drive their foreign cars to pay a visit to their old in-laws, and do all the work themselves with their own gold-beringed hands just so they can get a line or more in the will.

Truth be told, I'd never thought I'd be one of those daughters-in-law wearing fancy clothes and a platinum bracelet, and sleeping in a hospital room that costs over a million won a night.

But look at me now—I'm sitting next to an old man lying in bed with all sorts of machines attached to him. Soohyun and Hyojin are talking to the doctor outside. I'm horrified to watch over the scrawny man with his eyes helplessly closed. I will never forget how he looked at me through the overturned dishes on the table, those wide eyes paralyzed with a look of surprise.

What was he trying to tell me? Is this the end for everyone? He's not going to give all that money away like Soohyun said, because the eldest son didn't return home? He'd even called Attorney Kim the other day. So was the note in Chairman's room what I thought it was? How do you even amend the will of a semiconscious old man like this? Is it possible to do it without having a lawyer come to the house?

My head feels like it's spinning out of control with all these questions.

Without my meds, my vision's blurry and my hands are shaking, now that I'm left alone with the old man in a darkened room, listening to the beeps and whirs of the machine. As I watch the old man's IV go in, drop by drop, I think to myself, dizzy, "I wish that was for me." Am I turning into a junkie now?

"Since there are so many sensitive people in the family, we make sure to keep them in the house. . . . My father hasn't been feeling quite like himself since he fell ill, so he often takes them, too."

Their mother died in a food allergy accident of all things. Died because they couldn't get the medication she needed in time.

After such a strange and horrific experience, it's understandable that the entire family would be dependent on meds, even prescription ones. When you really think about it, everything that's happened in this house is suspicious. When you take each event separate from the whole history, it's a bunch of stuff that doesn't make much sense. I want to gather all those pieces together, spread them out, and look at them carefully, one by one, but my head hurts too much to focus. The big picture of the truth seems to lie far beyond my grasp.

You'd better stop being presumptuous and just figure out how to get out of here alive, my gut tells me.

Even if the old man dies this instant, even if he hasn't gotten to revise his will, I'll still manage somehow. I'm supposed to be the mother of this family's only grandchild, so even if everything goes to the eldest son, I have his blood. I don't know the law all too well, but if something goes wrong, the next of kin and spouse get everything, right?

And Seung-Joon is his grandson, 100 percent, right?

I'm sure of it. Soohyun asked the lab to do paternity testing.

It's unlikely that Soohyun would have called me "sister" if he wasn't sure that the child was related to him, so I shouldn't start doubting everything. All I need to figure out is how to use Seung-Joon to protect myself.

But I'm still curious about Hyojin's photo, where the brothers sat side by side, one with a wide smile, one with a serious expression. Now that I think of it—

The door to the hospital room creaks open and Soohyun walks in alone, looking very tired.

I jump to my feet.

"What did the doctor say?"

"They want to run some more tests. My dad had a cerebrovascular stent procedure a few years ago, and it sounds like he's having similar symptoms this time. He's been bedridden for a long time, and they say he's too weak to do anything right now. He'll need to get stronger before they can do anything."

"What about Hyojin?"

It's awkward to say her name out loud.

"Oh, she wanted to stay here, but I told her to go back home and get some rest and come back early tomorrow, because tomorrow is going to be a real push. Oh, I'll be here as well, so you should go home and get some rest. We'll take our shifts in turns from tomorrow onwards."

"No, I want to stay here with you."

"You don't need to. I think we've put out the fire for now, and you have Seung-Joon to worry about."

That's right.

When I left the house in the ambulance, Mrs. Suwon was looking over him.

So, that means Hyojin is with Seung-Joon at home now.

"Well, then I'll go check on Seung-Joon and come back early tomorrow." I hastily grab my bag. "Call me if anything happens!"

"Sure." Soohyun reaches out, and I take his warm, soft hand in mine.

We walk with our fingers locked, not wanting to let go, and only reluctantly release each other when we reach the door.

Before walking out, I glance back as if I had a sudden thought. "Oh yeah, I almost forgot."

"Yes?" Soohyun's just about to sit down in the chair next to the bed, but he stops and looks at me.

"It's about Seung-Joon."

His eyes narrow.

"The first day I came to this house, you did a paternity test."

"Yes."

"And you said they did the testing with your brother's hair? You had his old comb."

He nods.

"So do we still have all his old stuff at home?"

Soohyun looks at me questioningly.

"Oh, it's just that Father said something when I talked to him yesterday."

"My dad?"

"He was talking about him for a minute."

"About my brother?" His voice sharpens slightly.

"Oh, it's nothing, it seems he's still waiting for him. Father misses him, because Seung-Joon reminds him of your brother a lot. I thought Father might like it if I brought him an old picture or something, but I don't have any of his stuff with me. So I was wondering if you had any left around the house."

"Oh."

It's a clumsy, lame excuse, but Soohyun's eyes soften.

He laughs the clear laugh I know all too well by now. "I'm not sure, but it's probably in the basement. We're not big on throwing things away, but it'd just be old notes, old clothes, that sort of thing down there. I'll find them for you later."

I smile back before leaving the room. But strangely, his smile fails to calm my nerves this time.

CHAPTER

·51·

If my story were a horror movie, I'd say things are about to get real. Raindrops whip across the cab's windshield as it speeds up the winding driveway in the dark of the night. The magnificent iron gates, which usually remind me of the entrance to the Secret Garden, eerily mirror the front gates of a Western-style cemetery.

"Wow, that's a nice house hiding back here." The cab driver, who told me that he's on his way to Seoul after just getting his plate number, glances at the gate in wonder. After the car's lights fade into the distance, I punch in the passcode on the keypad and step inside. Gone is the woman who, a few months earlier, stumbled through the doorway in an old, raggedy hoodie, with someone else's child in her bruised arms.

The moment I step through the beautiful Western-style garden, I'm greeted by branches swaying wildly like a witch's hair shaken loose. The outbuilding where Mr. Kim resides is shrouded in darkness, as its resident is away on his rare day off.

All the lights in the mansion are also out. Only a faint orange glow leaks out from somewhere inside. I walk past the pool and across the lawn, and I slowly ascend the stairs.

This is going to be a long night.

No one else in the house.

Just me and the woman here.

No, I guess there's also Seung-Joon.

I punch in the number on the front door keypad and step inside. The house is eerily quiet, darkness flooding both the parlor and the foyer.

I slip off my shoes, which I leave at the front door.

Whatever Hyojin's up to, I plan to sneak up on her. Or maybe that's exactly what she's planning to do as well.

It strikes me that it's so unusually quiet here. I can't even hear Seung-Joon—did he already fall asleep?

Once I begin to explore the house, I quickly identify the source of the orange glow. It's not coming from the living room as I first assumed. An unfamiliar door to my right is open, from which the light's seeping out.

It's a door I rarely see open, except on cleaning days. The door to the basement. Wide open, as if to invite me down. It beckons to me like a lantern attracting flying insects, but I have no intention of acting like a supporting character in a horror movie, who steps into a place she shouldn't, only to face some unexpected terror. But my gut's telling me that the answers I desperately seek wait for me down there.

So, dragging my socked feet, I stand in front of the open door. I see a staircase leading down, with some lights on at the bottom, but I don't hear anything. Whatever waits for me down there might be ready to ambush me with some sneaky, clever moves.

I fumble in my pants pocket, find my cell phone, and cautiously descend the stairs. Halfway down, I'm already regretting not bringing a stick or a rock with me, but I can't go back up now. When I reach the bottom of the stairs, the cold air rising from the concrete floor makes my toes curl. Even in the thick of summer, this place is as cold as the devil's heart. And very, very spacious.

I stand at the foot of the stairs and take a look around. It doesn't reveal much at a glance, but I'm quite sure there's no one here. I wonder if someone has come down here and been rummaging around before deciding to leave without turning off the lights. Why? What were they searching for?

That's when—*bang!*—I hear the door shut behind me.

I whirl around.

The door at the top of the stairs is slammed shut.

Just my luck. I feel as though I'm in a bad horror movie.

I frantically run up the stairs, taking two steps at a time. I clutch the doorknob and shake it, but of course, it doesn't budge. It's locked.

"Open the door, are you crazy? I'm calling the police, I'm calling the police right now, open the door, you crazy bitch!"

There's no answer. I pull out my cell phone. Predictably, there's no Wi-Fi down here. I switch it to emergency call mode. My hands tremble as I punch in the numbers, but then I pause. I can't call the police, can I? Hyojin must have thought about that. I imagine what might happen if I call the police:

"Help! I'm trapped in the basement of my house!"

"What happened?"

"Someone slammed the door shut behind me and locked me in!"

"Who?"

"She's my father-in-law's caregiver."

"Why would she do that?"

"She's trying to frame me!"

"And can you think of any reason why she would?"

"Because I stole her identity."

Then they'll follow up with more questions: "Are you sure she's the one who locked it? Do you have proof?"

Maybe it's better to just call 911 and tell them I accidentally locked myself in. Otherwise I'd just be treated like I was delusional.

This thought calms my racing heart a bit. And clearly, reality is different from horror movies anyway. In the twenty-first century, we have cell phones that we can use to call people anytime as long as they're charged, and I can have a rescue team dispatched at a moment's notice if I absolutely need to. And let's not forget, there's also Soohyun. If he can't reach me, he'll come running to find me. No, I don't even need to go there, either. Tomorrow morning, the maids will come back to work. Hyojin won't be able to lock me up forever just because there's no one else in the house tonight.

I stop my frantic pounding on the door.

Hyojin knows all this, too, so she *isn't* trying to trap me here forever. That can't have been her goal.

Then, this isn't a horror movie but something else.

I try to steady my breathing. I can always call for help and get out of here. This place is bigger than my old half-basement, and I can hear the ventilation fans whirring, so I don't have to worry about air shortage, at least. I just need to stay calm until help arrives.

I turn around and slowly make my way back down the stairs. I peer into the orange-lit basement. My eyelids are slightly droopy, my hands shaking, but I try to stay focused.

Shelves run along one wall of the basement, whose opposite side is littered with shovels, hammers, pickaxes, and other seemingly murderous tools lined up in rows. Then, rows and rows of unidentifiable extension cords. The place is crowded with heaps of groceries, large sacks of rice and potatoes, and piles of soil, compost, and plant nutrients for gardening.

Farther back, in a dark corner where the light can't quite reach, is a large box that looks like a safe, with a few paper boxes stacked around it. The boxes are roughly taped shut but not perfectly sealed, contents jutting out as if the boxes are about to explode. They're as big as the boxes moving companies provide, and each one is numbered with a marker.

I wipe a sweaty hand across my face and drag the nearest box over, determined to go through them one after another.

The first one's full of plates and cups, extra utensils for guests. I set it aside and open another, which is filled with plaques of appreciation from some kind of alumni association, a certificate of achievement, and group photos. Some old, some seemingly newer. Probably the old man's.

Then there's a bundle of newsletters from the same year, twelve years ago. I take a look at one of them.

Eun-Sook Kang, the wife of Chairman Han-Soo Jung, a hardworking member of our association, passed away in an unfortunate accident. The funeral service will be held on March 15 at

Juyoung Hospital Funeral Home, and condolences and flowers are respectfully declined.

"An unfortunate accident," I murmur.

I close the box and move on to a lengthy checklist of some kind.

It seems to be a manual for the hired help. It's a neatly coated sheet of paper covering details of Chairman's wake-up time, mealtimes, favorite side dishes and allergies, cleaning frequency and method, and other precautions.

This must be the maids' handover sheet. The house staff are supposed to be replaced every two years, and you'd need this to train the new staff after the current ones leave. On the back is a meticulous list of all the items that are in the kitchen. At the bottom are the contact details of the previous staffers, such as Mrs. Zhu and Mrs. Shin. There are three contacts in total on the sheet itself, and one of them is crossed out with a marker. There are other contacts written on Post-it notes dating back to four years ago. The sheet itself looks straightforward, but something doesn't seem right, so I sit poring over it for a while.

Let me see . . .

The contacts on the coated sheet seem to belong to the very first staffers who worked in the house for a long time before the biannual turnover, and it seems the sheet's then been handed down at every turnover, with the contacts of new staff added in the form of notes this way.

Then this person who's been crossed out, Mrs. Kim, is probably the cause of all the commotion. The maid who got fired for stealing something and who was suspected of killing Chairman's wife out of spite.

I first take a picture of all the contacts in there and push the sheet aside. I then go through a few more boxes nearby, but they are all junk. After a quick glance around, I move farther in. Next to a box full of old books is a box full of personal items: old boys' clothes, old video games, drawings seemingly done by a young child, a middle school certificate with Soohyun's name on it, skates, and hockey sticks. It looks like they have crammed both brothers' stuff in one box.

One by one, I pull out the usual schoolboy items and soon get to the bottom of the box, but there is nothing special. The rest of the box is full of odd parts and what look like letter envelopes. At first glance, the parts look like they belong to a child's remote-controlled car, but they're much cruder than that. There are wires, screws, bulbs, and other things sticking out of them. When I turn the largest part over, I see that the bottom says, "Soohyun Jung, junior high, second year, class four." It must have been some kind of assignment. I don't know if he forgot about it and kept even this useless thing boxed up because he didn't care all that much or because he was nostalgic, like the Soohyun I know.

I pull out a letter envelope stuck on the back of the toy and open it to find a piece of paper folded twice. A medical report? A document used for insurance claims and the like?

A surgical fracture at the left ankle as the result of a staircase fall. A torn left ankle lateral ligament. A torn left ankle triangular ligament. A dislocated shoulder. A contusion of the knee. Required to be hospitalized for several weeks & bed rest for a considerable period of time.

I remember what Soohyun said: "Oh, my brother's ankle. He fell down the stairs in the house and broke it, and that's why he had to stop playing ice hockey." It was the event that stopped Hyun-Wook from studying abroad, not too long after the traumatizing death of his mother. This is how it all unraveled. I'm sure his desire to go abroad was more a spoiled rich kid's escape than anything, but he must have actually suffered a pretty serious injury.

The young man who'd tried to escape this house had his wings clipped just like that. The thought of him lying in bed, as helpless and immobile as the old man in the wheelchair, sends shivers down my spine, made worse by the chill in the basement.

———

One bright night in March, my boyfriend and I sat at a table outside a convenience store, drinking a pack of soju. He said, "If only I got to go abroad right then, I wouldn't be in the shape I'm in now."

We chatted as we picked at dried squid.

"Where were you going?"

"Canada."

"Wow, I guess you did well in school?"

"You don't go abroad to study. Smart students can study well enough here."

"Shit, then why do you go?"

"Traveling is for the people who don't think they can make it here but want to try to make it elsewhere." He chuckled to himself.

"Oh, really? Then why are you here instead of running away?"

"I *tried* to run away. I couldn't."

"I mean, why? Oh, because of your English? Or because of the entrance exam or something? Did you fail?"

He didn't answer, just tilted his head back and downed the rest of his soju in one gulp.

"I got injured."

"Injured? Where? How?"

"Let's just say I was caught off guard. I didn't know what was happening. I didn't think things would get that bad."

"What? What does that mean? What did you not know?"

He didn't answer. Instead, he just ruffled my hair and laughed. And he said he had no regrets. He said, "Never mind. Being with you is enough escape."

I ruminate on the phrase that he added, *"I was caught off guard."* Was he saying he got distracted and fell down the stairs and hurt himself?

What could he possibly mean?

None of that matters now.

I shake my head and shove the rest of the stuff back into the box.

As I'm putting things back in, I notice a familiar name on a thick notebook: "Law Firm Se-Yool." It looks like one of those gifts sometimes given out for promotion, but it's a pretty thick one. The entire notebook is mostly blank pages, but as I flip through it, something falls to the floor.

I pick it up to see it's a worn old Polaroid. The date, September 7, is scrawled in pen, slightly smudged. Twelve years ago.

And there they are.

Three people, side by side.

A young man and a woman standing shoulder to shoulder, smiling broadly, and a boy leaning against the man from the other side, staring expressionlessly into the camera.

This must be the same photo that I saw in Hyojin's room. The facial expressions and postures of the people in the photo are identical, as if the two photos were taken just seconds apart. The only difference I can tell is that this one's intact, with the cropped part still attached.

The person who has her arm around his shoulders is a girl in a school uniform with her hair pulled up in a high ponytail. A familiar face. It's her—Hyojin. She's smiling at him, her eyes more innocent than they are now.

So my boyfriend and that woman have known each other since they were very young.

It's clear that the three of them have a relationship that started a long, long time ago.

But Soohyun's never mentioned anything about all this to me, not even once.

CHAPTER

· 5 2 ·

"Ms. Hyojin used to work for my dad as a caregiver. I hired her back because I couldn't find anyone else. You know I was desperately looking for a replacement, then out of nowhere, she called me."

I stand in the middle of the cold basement, trying to recall. Did he ever mention that he'd known Hyojin since childhood? Was it mentioned in passing and I didn't catch it?

No, he did not. He'd called her "Ms. Hyojin." He never mentioned Hyojin was close with his brother. Is it possible that he didn't recognize her?

No. That's impossible. I'd recognized her right away, although I barely knew her. It doesn't make sense. A hand on her shoulder, a shy, wide smile on her face. Whether my boyfriend and Hyojin were in a relationship or not back then, the photo clearly shows how close they were. And yet Soohyun pretends to remember nothing.

I chew on my already tattered fingernails, mulling it over.

I can't jump to conclusions. Suspicion can lead to harm. I've been falsely accused before myself.

I need to try and see things from Soohyun's perspective. Maybe he didn't want me to get the wrong idea. Perhaps he felt uncomfortable having a girl in the house that his brother was close with, and he didn't want to explain how he'd known her for a while. It was all too complicated, perhaps, to explain all this to me, when I've obviously got a crush on him, and I'm supposed to be his brother's woman anyway.

The more I think about it, the weaker the buzzing in my ears gets.

I stretch my stiff back and take out my phone again. I've been stuck down here for over an hour now. I haven't realized the time because I've been frantically looking around. I can't hear anything from outside, just penetrating silence.

I suddenly remember Seung-Joon. What if Hyojin abducts him and runs away? I need to get out of here.

I scramble through the stacks of boxes, but when I try to make my way back to the staircase, I trip over a large black box lying on the floor. I hit my knee on the concrete with an audible thud, and the air is knocked out of my lungs. But soon, I manage to pick myself up and sit on the ground. Breathing heavily, I prop my aching knee up while I rest. The other leg, stretched out in front of me, feels cold. Down here, it feels like I'm sitting in front of an open refrigerator. I look around and spot the empty box that I tripped over. It's almost icy to the touch, with a few droplets of water collecting on it.

A freezer?

It's as big as one you'd find in a restaurant. The lid is slightly ajar. A mansion of this size would have a freezer, sure, but why leave it on 24/7? And why would someone leave the lid off a working freezer? The contents would melt.

I slip my hand through the crack and slide the lid of the freezer open.

At first, I can't see anything. As the dizzying chill hits my nostrils, I sneeze hard. Even as I take another look in, all I see is a large, whitish block of ice with a thin layer of frost forming on the surface. It seems the freezer hasn't been open long, as the block of ice is just beginning to melt, with a trickle of water along the edges.

I peer closer, and there it is on the floor—a camcorder wrapped in plastic! The same one from her room!

That's the moment I realize. All of this has been staged just for me.

The way I'm locked down here, with all these old things from the past, the photograph, and now this freezer.

I peel back the plastic slowly, afraid of what I will find. Whatever is in there, can I handle it? Wouldn't it be better to close it up, call 911, and leave while I have the chance?

But I can't stop myself. I sit there, watching the entire footage from start to end.

There's the argument, the physical altercation, the frying pan, the strike, my escape.

I don't fast-forward the video, but instead, I stare blankly at the screen as time passes. Five minutes and thirteen seconds after my exit, I watch everything that unfolded that night without blinking an eye. I'm frozen in place, unable to move.

That's how I find out the whole truth.

Now I know what happened to my ex, what happened to me, why I'm here, and why it all unraveled this way.

The whole story. I realize how a single choice can uproot a person's life. And how very ironic it all is.

Meanwhile, the frost inside the freezer turns into droplets. What was once a blurry block of ice is now melting and losing its shape. I bend down to take a closer look. When I wipe at its cool, damp surface with a swift swipe of my hand, I let out a scream. I scream and scream until the veins in my head feel like they're going to burst.

I don't know how to process what I just saw.

All I know is, I'm not alone in this claustrophobic place.

There he is, stuck in that block of ice.

The man I hit with the frying pan, the man I've been wondering about this whole time, the man I thought might still be alive and texting me.

The eldest son of the family has finally returned home, his face as cold as ice, his eyes closed forever.

I throw down the camcorder, run up the stairs, and pound on the door. I scream and pound until my hands threaten to rip. There's no response, but I keep screaming and pounding until I lose my voice. Just when I feel my head's about to explode, the door swings open and I fall forward.

A figure with its back to the bright light stands staring down at me, and everything plunges into darkness.

CHAPTER

·53·

Someone gently touches my forehead. A hand pushes my sweaty hair out of my face and takes mine in a warm and soft caress. I don't know if this is hell or heaven. I can't open my eyes. I don't want to. I hope this is all a dream. I can't stand what happened, what is about to happen.

Maybe it *was* all just a dream.

The night that felt endless, the scream bursting out of my mouth against my will.

The terrible stories whispered to me.

Truths I'd rather not know.

So many unbelievable realizations that ran through my head like an ongoing nightmare last night.

I remember everything. It all comes flooding back.

"Aaaahhhhh!"

I wake up screaming, a loud, earsplitting scream that continues to erupt despite myself.

"Shh, it's okay, it's okay. It's me, sister. It's okay, it's all over."

"Soohyun?"

There he is, sitting by my bed, smiling sweetly as always. He looks unfamiliar for some reason, and then I realize he's grown stubbly overnight.

A bright light is peeking through the curtains of the window across from me. It's a bright day.

"The basement! In the basement!"

"Yes, yes. I know, I know. I came over as soon as I heard from Hyo-jin. Here, have some water."

He hands me a cup of water and some pills from the nightstand.

"But I was down in the basement! I have to go back there right now! I have to go there! I have to go there!" I stutter, out of breath. Wheezing, as if there are fingers tightly wrapped around my neck.

"First, take this. Then take a deep breath."

I take the pill, pop it in my mouth, and drink some water.

"I need to use the restroom for a minute."

"Do you need me to help you up? Are you okay?" Soohyun asks, holding out his hand.

He gently takes my arm and walks me over to the bathroom door and politely closes it behind me.

When I emerge from the bathroom a few minutes later, I'm much calmer. But I'm still nervously rolling my eyes and tugging on his arm.

"The basement! It was there! It was there! We have to go now! It was her! It was her, I was suspicious from the beginning!"

Just then, the door opens and Hyojin walks in with a bowl on a tray. "Ma'am. I brought you some porridge."

"Soohyun, please! That woman! It's all her doing!"

"Sister, calm down!"

Soohyun hugs me tightly around the waist to hold me in place.

All the while, Hyojin stands in the doorway, looking startled. Her eyes are bulging like an actress in a play.

"She locked me up down there! And I saw everything!"

"What? What did you see?"

"It was him, Hyun-Wook!"

"My brother?"

He looks at me as if he's been punched in the face. "My brother was there?"

"Ma'am?" Hyojin looks at me in disbelief.

"He was really there! Please come with me! We need to call the police, come on!"

"Sister, what do you mean? That can't be true."

"Soohyun, please!" I stamp my feet, screaming his name.

I clutch my disheveled hair and scream hysterically, spittle splattering into the air.

"Sister, please!" Soohyun grabs my hand and pleads, but I shake him off.

"You crazy bitch, you showed up here to mess up my life from the beginning. You *killed* him and you locked me in the basement!" I force myself out of Soohyun's grip and lunge at Hyojin with full force, but she quickly steps back.

She even calmly explains, "She's been talking nonsense and sweating all night, ever since she got out of the basement last night. I should have let her out sooner. But I was too busy packing."

The woman cries crocodile tears, faking a look of concern.

"Shut up! It's all lies! What? You can't go down right now because you're afraid of Soohyun finding out about you? Then I'll go and see for myself. I'll report you right now, you bitch!"

I swat Soohyun's hand away and run out of the room, screaming.

"Sister!" he calls out from behind me and follows me as I run downstairs barefoot.

The maids in the kitchen come running out and stare at me as if they've seen a ghost. I don't give them a glance, nor do I have a mind to care about my rumpled clothes or disheveled hair.

I stand in front of the basement door and tug on the handle, but it doesn't budge.

"Open it, open! Don't do anything stupid, open it now!"

"Sister!" Soohyun sighs and tugs on my arm from behind.

"Come on, open it!"

My throat is already choking, refusing to let out an intelligible sound. "Ms. Heesun! Mrs. Suwon! Where's the key?"

"Here you are." At Soohyun's beckoning, Heesun rushes over to offer the key.

She holds it at a distance as if I had some kind of plague. I take a step back, leaving the key in Soohyun's hand. Hyojin's standing right behind us, looking impossibly calm, as if all this commotion is ridiculous.

Soohyun unlocks the door and takes the lead.

He explains, "The basement door is so old it sometimes locks on its own, so when we go in and out, we put something in the door to hold it open. You didn't know that, of course. I'm not sure why you came down here at night to begin with. Why did you come down here in the middle of the night, again?"

Without responding, I push past him and stomp down the stairs. The orange glow of the light fixture illuminates every corner of the basement just like last night.

But that's the only thing that's the same as yesterday.

Everything else is different.

The jumbled stack of boxes I'd opened and rummaged through is now lined up neatly in the back of the basement, every one of them sealed.

And the freezer!

I run to the freezer and find that its lid is wide open, but completely empty. No ice, no frost, not even a drop of water. Dry and clean, inside and out.

"Sister!" Soohyun has caught up and looks down into the open freezer. "What did you see in here?"

"Hyun-Wook."

I drop to the floor, my arms slumping helplessly.

"You saw him? In here?"

"He was here! He was in there! He was really here. . . . That woman must have . . ."

I point my index finger at Hyojin, who stands halfway down the stairs, looking my way. I can feel the house staffers crowding the entrance to the basement, looking down at me like I'm crazy.

"He was here! Lying there, frozen!" I scream, throwing myself over the freezer. "Are you all messing with me? He's dead! But I'm the only one who doesn't know. Right?"

I'm about to lose my mind, going back and forth between screaming and crying and gasping.

"You're just freaking out. You must be seeing things. This place has been empty the whole time. My brother can't be here, because he's not dead. He's going to be fine. Please calm down."

Soohyun slips his hands under my arms and pulls me to my feet.
"No, no, he's dead, he was dead."

I lean against his shoulder and sob, unable to form words. Soohyun pats me on the back, but even as he does so, I can sense that he's worried about the stares of the maids watching from the stairs.

Just then, his phone rings.

Patting me on the back with one hand, he reaches into his pocket with the other and pulls out his cell phone.

"Yes," he replies in a businesslike tone. I've never heard him answer someone so coldly before. I hug him tightly around the neck, not caring if the maids are watching or not. I feel Hyojin staring down at me. Our eyes meet. My whole body trembles. And I can't stop the trembling.

"What? What did you say?"

Suddenly, Soohyun pushes me off his shoulder and grabs the phone with both hands, a serious look on his face.

"What's that again? Yes, I get it, I'm on my way!"

As I cover my mouth with one hand and continue to sob, shuddering, Soohyun speaks with a stern look.

"It's the hospital, my dad has died."

Hyojin looks at me. Our eyes meet again.

CHAPTER

· 5 4 ·

It's over.

All over.

The old man is gone.

He never got to see his eldest son, for whom he yearned so much, and he left behind a myriad of questions.

I can't even fulfill my role as the daughter-in-law because I am completely drained. I can't even get up and get dressed to greet the guests with a clean face. My hands shake, and I run to the bathroom every few hours to throw up.

There are no close relatives among the mourners who visit us. The old man was a self-made man who was lucky enough to marry the only daughter of a wealthy family, and since she has been long dead, there is no one to come and cry for him. So it's just a few employees who manage his buildings, his tenants, people he does business with, and people from the law firm. The rest are just beggars in search of scraps.

"You should come to the clinic when you get a chance. I've been responsible for the mental health of this family, and I'd like to talk with you. I know things are hard, and in a time of crisis, you need someone to talk to."

At the funeral home, the high point is meeting a man named Dr. Kwon. He is the one who can give me the meds that I flushed down the toilet. He tells me he runs a high-end clinic that caters to people with money in one of the old man's buildings downtown. Probably most of the clinic's start-up costs came out of the old man's pocket, and that's why his entire family—his dead wife, his distraught eldest son, and occasionally even Soohyun—could at one point rely on him for help.

"Sooner or later, when everything is sorted out, you should visit the clinic. We've always been able to get the medications we need at Dr. Kwon's discretion," Soohyun finds a moment to tell me affectionately, even though he's busy acting as the head of the family in place of his brother. He looks like a little boy, but once he takes over the reins of the Jung family, he handles everything with remarkable aplomb. I can't believe how driven he is. I don't even have to worry about the funeral arrangements.

"This is my responsibility, so don't worry about all this. Please go in and get some rest, and don't forget to take your meds."

So I go back to bed and stay there, head in hands, in agony.

On the first afternoon after Chairman Jung's death, I spent a little time at the funeral home, greeting guests and making small talk, but ever since, I've been staying at home, waiting for the day of cremation. I haven't had enough time to recover and feel normal, but it's been enough time to gather all the information I need.

"Where? Sanghyeon-dong? Ah, Chairman Jung's house?"

When I dial one of the numbers from the turnover sheet I'd taken photos of, the voice on the other end of the line hesitates, but I don't back down. The other person on the note has changed her number, so Mrs. Zhu is my last hope. I try to disarm her by babbling as much as I can. I ramble on, as if I'm high on the meds Soohyun got me more of.

Finally, she opens up a bit, and the story starts to come out. She says she hasn't forgotten what happened, in fact, she remembers everything, and that it's as fresh as yesterday even though it was twelve years ago.

"People like us, no matter how many houses we work in, we remember every single one of them, because we get to know the owners really well. All the ugly and dark sides. And Chairman Jung's house was a unique case. So it's unforgettable, of course."

The pay was good, but she felt like she was always treading on thin ice while working there.

"Chairman's wife had a fiery temper. She was already sensitive, but as she aged and became more suspicious, she became more difficult to handle. Not to mention, she always drove her husband—Chairman—and son crazy, always throwing tantrums. Yes, the eldest, the wife's biological son. Then the younger son came to live with them at the age of nine or ten, and strangely enough, while most kids would hate siblings their fathers had with other women, that wasn't true in this case. The brothers got along very well. I guess they comforted each other. I found it quite heartwarming."

I hear the woman sigh on the other end of the line.

"Chairman and his wife got into a big fight not long after Soohyun came to live with them. I think the reason was Soohyun, although they wouldn't openly discuss it. Then one day, the wife ran into Soohyun in the garden, and she slapped him across the face, although he didn't do anything wrong. She was shouting something about ruining the flowers. I remember her hand swung, making a whiplike sound. Soohyun's cheek turned red. I saw it all, but he didn't even cry. Just stared. Soohyun just stood there looking at her."

I listen without responding, engrossed in the story to the point of almost forgetting to breathe.

"But you know, there was something about Soohyun that unnerved people. Even when he was a little kid, no one would dare underestimate him. Chairman's wife must have really hated that, because she hit him really hard that day. I mean, really, really hard. But he didn't even shed a tear, just took it in silence. Then the eldest son stepped in to save him."

"Save him?"

"The wife had Hyun-Wook under her thumb, too, so I don't know where the courage came from, but Hyun-Wook stopped her, took Soohyun's hand, and ran out of the house. They came back late at night and had to go back to their rooms without having dinner. From then on, Soohyun followed his brother around like a dog. When Hyun-Wook was supposed to go abroad, he cried his eyes out, day and night. And when Hyun-Wook hurt his ankle, Soohyun also blamed himself a lot."

"Really?"

"Hyun-Wook was going to study abroad, you know? Doing some kind of sport. But he got injured, so he never got to leave."

"Oh, you mean ice hockey?"

"Yeah, I think so. He slipped and broke his ankle coming down the stairs."

"Why did Soohyun blame himself?"

"Well, he made something for a science project, left it somewhere on the stairs, and Hyun-Wook stepped on it and fell. He was so badly injured that he couldn't even think about studying abroad. He was hospitalized for a while."

She remembers the incident in detail.

"The three of us, me, Mrs. Shin, and Hyojin's mom, had worked in that house for over five years by that point. We were almost like family. But theft? That's absurd. Why would she do something like that, when it's obvious she'd be the prime suspect? But the wife wouldn't calm down, screaming that she took everything valuable she had—a pearl necklace, a gold ring, some bracelets, and other items. But it doesn't make sense because the wife didn't even wear them. Maybe she was too careful with the jewels, I don't know."

Once she began talking, she hadn't held back, but at this point, she starts to tread carefully again.

"Hey, by the way, you're a reporter from where? You're not revealing my name, are you?"

"No worries, I'm just researching old cases for reference. Since Chairman passed away, I thought I'd look into it."

"Oh my God! Is Chairman dead? What's the use of all that money; it didn't save him. Was he ill? I heard he had a stroke and collapsed."

"Yes, that's all true. He had a heart attack in his sleep not too long ago."

And how unfortunate, indeed. A man receiving all the top-notch care he could in a million-won-a-night private room drops dead with no one by his side. Even his son staying by his sickbed wasn't present because he just briefly dropped by the house to check on me. Some say the expensive machine malfunctioned or got turned off, but I don't know whom to blame. They should be grateful that we decided not to sue the hospital.

"I hope I'm not out of line," the woman continues, "but it seems like it was a good death, at least. He enjoyed his life and had everything a man could hope for. By the way, where were we?"

"We were talking about what was stolen—pearl necklaces, gold rings, and some bracelets. So they found the missing items?"

"Oh, yeah, they were in the inside pocket of Hyojin's mom's coat. Chairman's wife stepped on a broken pearl. Some of them must have fallen on the floor. She slipped and fell, got back up all annoyed, and found the pearl. So she got suspicious and looked in the coat pockets since it was hanging right there on the rack, and that's when she found all the missing items."

"So, that was enough evidence."

"But it's kind of funny, isn't it? Who would steal them and put them where anyone could find them? Had I been the thief, I would have wrapped them up really tight and hidden them in my underwear or something. But I guess Hyojin's mom wasn't in her right mind with everything going on in her own home. And that's actually why everyone got suspicious."

"What do you mean?"

"Hyojin's dad was a heavy drinker. He was usually a very gentle man when he was sober, but when he got drunk, he'd turn into a dog. He beat his only daughter, his wife, and would go on a rampage, threatening to set the house on fire."

I can imagine the woman shaking her head on the other end of the receiver.

"All that drinking and the meds he needed cost a small fortune. He also went to the alcohol recovery clinic every now and then, and with all that, she had to scrape by trying to make ends meet. It took all she had, trying to keep the family afloat. Of course, the Jung family knew about it, and that's why they got so suspicious of her when those items went missing. Chairman's wife even paid her salaries in advance a couple of times. But you know how people can get. They can lose their minds when money's involved."

Yeah, money really does make people lose their minds sometimes; I sure know that.

"I would have called the cops and questioned her, maybe had her taken into custody on the spot," I say.

"Families like theirs don't act that way. They're not exactly law-abiding themselves, you know. Tax evasion and some other sketchy stuff. So they don't want to attract too much attention. If a reporter like you sniffs something out and makes a big deal out of it, it's going to be quite a headache for them. So they didn't even fire her right away, with a big holiday coming up and being so shorthanded, but they threatened her and humiliated her, apparently. The wife screamed at her to work her ass off during the holidays if she wanted to get her last month's paycheck before getting kicked out, but I don't think they knew what was going to happen."

"What happened?"

She sighs. Then follows a moment of sudden silence.

"That was the first time I'd ever seen someone die."

I remember the thin layer of frost inside the freezer. And the whitish shape that slowly revealed itself, melting away from the edges.

"You mean the allergic reaction?"

"That's the crazy thing about that accident. We're really good at keeping track of that stuff, and for people like us, it's really important, because you can live or die by it. And we'd been working in that house for, like, five years, and we didn't even need to think about it. It was like muscle memory. We wouldn't even go near the ingredients they were allergic to, because we were so used to cooking without those things. Naturally, we'd never used nuts, let alone peanuts. I don't know what the hell happened. Alas, my heart still skips a beat when I think of it. They were just the usual side dishes, but the chairman's wife took one bite and started rolling all over the floor, clutching at her throat."

"Didn't you have any meds on hand at home? Usually, people with severe allergies always have them nearby."

"She always had her medicines and EpiPens with her, and she always took them with her when she went out to eat. Very rarely, I've seen her inject herself. But I guess things happen, however well prepared you are."

She hesitates for a while.

"I ran to get the EpiPen, and it was usually in the mirrored cabinet in the master bathroom. She always kept it there with her meds and syringes. I saw it all the time whenever I was cleaning, but I couldn't find it anywhere that day. Meanwhile, she was gagging and gasping. Her face was all swollen and she couldn't open her eyes, her throat all bloody because she was just scratching and tugging at it. Her eyes were bloodshot and practically popping out of her head."

I can almost hear her flinching just at the thought.

"We ended up calling an ambulance and she was taken away, but she was already dead by that point. I rode with her, but her heart had already stopped."

"Oh my God, did you ever find the medicine?"

"Later, Mrs. Shin found them lying behind the toilet, and none of us had any idea why they were there."

"So that's why you were suspicious of that woman, Hyojin's mom."

"Well, yes, whenever something like that happens, the house staff will be suspected before anyone else. But think about this. Even if she was accused of stealing some things, could she really want to kill the wife out of spite? I mean, she'd be the prime suspect. In the end, they never found any compelling evidence, they never found the culprit, so everyone just assumed that some of the ingredients came from a factory that handled nuts or dairy products the wife was allergic to. So they concluded it to be an accident. But people don't let things go that easily. There was gossip, a lot of rumors."

"Rumors?"

"After the accident, everyone got fired, and the family hired new staff altogether. We all found new jobs after a while, but Hyojin's mom couldn't."

She lets out a long sigh.

"Rumors are rumors, but there was even talk of someone tipping off the personnel office. Even if it was just an accident, it was fatal, after all. She got caught stealing; someone died because of the food she made. . . . That's why she couldn't find a job afterward. I mean, would you hire her? People like us, we can only clean houses or clean buildings. We have no special skills, nowhere to go. I mean, Hyojin's mom really was the breadwinner and head of her family, so the family fell apart, especially with her husband drinking away all they had left. That's why she decided to end everything. Even left behind her daughter. Poor Hyojin."

"End everything?"

"She hanged herself in her house, and Hyojin found her."

"Because of the accident?"

"Well, that, I'm sure. It was about two weeks after the accident. She must have been devastated. Her husband was in and out of rehab for his drinking, with no money coming in. She was trying to make ends meet with the kid, but no one would hire her."

For a moment, all I can hear is the sniffling on the other end of the line.

"I mean, poor Hyojin! I think she's three years younger than their eldest son, and she was always following him around like he was her big brother. I think she secretly had a crush on him. She was a good-natured girl who just laughed it off when my mom would scold her for having her head in the clouds and chasing after a guy who would never think twice about her. And her family fell apart overnight because of the accident."

"You haven't heard from them since? Do you know what happened to them?"

"I don't know, Hyojin's dad probably has a bad case of alcoholism. I think he died in a nursing home or something, and Hyojin couldn't afford college, so she worked at a supermarket or something, and somebody saw her going to some kind of medical assistant or nursing home caretaker school. I heard her face looked like she was dead inside."

The phone is hot against my ear. A long call like this would have been too much to handle had I been groggy on the meds. I don't know when Soohyun might call. I've gotten everything I needed to get out of this, so I'd better go now. After some pleasantries to wrap it all up, I'm about to hang up when I hear the woman's voice on the other end of the line one more time.

"Hey, by the way, this is just my opinion, but I think that house is kind of creepy. And so are the people there. I just think it's best to stay away."

CHAPTER

·55·

I sit down on a bench, my legs stretched out before me.

What a beautiful, balmy summer night. I take deep breaths, gazing over at the blue water of the pool, the air potent with the faint hint of earth and flowers in bloom.

Even when I was a mere guest, I fell in love with this house at first sight, but now that it's actually mine, it's hard to contain myself. Each terra-cotta tile of the floor beneath me, every scoop of soil in the garden, every little twig and blade of grass, every brick that makes up the mansion belongs to me now.

The old man's will dictated to leave me the house and 30 percent of all his assets—me, his daughter-in-law, Jae-Young Yoon. None other than good-for-nothing me.

Five percent was donated to some charitable causes in his eldest son's name, another 5 percent went to Soohyun, but the remaining 60 percent was left to my son, Seung-Joon Jung, who is sound asleep in the room on the second floor overlooking this bench.

We've made it, haven't we? Just the two of us, the baby and I, who barged into this house out of nowhere one day, we've done it. This is an achievement beyond my wildest dreams, something I could never have anticipated when I was living in that cramped, dirty half-basement room that I didn't even own. But all of it feels like a different life now.

"He was going to leave everything to his eldest son, but it seems he lost all hope of his return," the attorney told me when he stopped by to pay respects, explaining that the last time Chairman amended his will was just a week prior. He told me that they'd been going back and forth via video call with his caregiver present to double-check and confirm all the details and changes. The attorney gathered up his papers and rose to leave.

"Who knows," he said, "but he probably felt like the end was near. Sometimes old people foresee their own deaths," he added. "I don't know which came first: the old man's premonition or the desire to revise his will. Maybe, just maybe, after getting everything in order, he simply lost the will to live."

But lost it so much that, just a couple days after revising his will, he would have a stroke in the dead of night?

"Anyways, I'm just a phone call away. When you feel like yourself again and have any business in Seoul, you should drop by."

"Seoul?"

"Yes, our office is in Seoul."

To prove his invitation was genuine, the attorney handed me a business card with the name and address of his law firm, Se-Yool.

"Mr. Soohyun sometimes stops by for tea whenever he's in the city. He came by just last week, in fact."

The attorney smiled in Soohyun's direction before letting himself out the front door. And I was left to digest what he'd said: just last week. Soohyun and I stood side by side to see him off. We both still wore our black suits from the funeral. In one arm, I held Seung-Joon, who was also immaculately dressed in new clothes. We must have looked like a handsome young family, with a stunning mansion to complement us.

The attorney also informed me before taking leave: "Seung-Joon will have his share to manage at his own discretion as soon as he turns twenty-five. Until then, it will be held in trust. The guardian, of course, is designated as you, his mother. Until Seung-Joon turns twenty-five, you'll receive dividends each year."

By which he meant that the list of fringe benefits went on and on: land, buildings, a vacation home, paid parking, cash, bonds, and stocks. But the bottom line was, I had to my name 30 percent of the estate and the whole mansion, with the other 60 percent my son's. Until he was of age, I'd be the guardian and continue to receive a hefty dividend every year in the form of child support.

So here I sit alone, living in a sweet, dreamy world. A world of pure gold. All that was once a bleak blur seems to suddenly turn aglow. I turn with a beaming smile when someone breaks the silence.

"Miss, may I sit with you for a moment?"

"Anytime."

Soohyun plops down next to me, sending my way a waft of fresh aftershave.

"Peace at long last."

Stretching, he looks up at the night sky.

"Here's what I've been thinking—" I start to speak, but he cuts me short.

"I know what you're about to say."

"But—"

"It's perfectly fine. I knew this was how things would turn out."

"But—!"

"Seriously, I'm good. He always chose my brother." Soohyun shakes his head and laughs. "That's the way it's been since forever, so I'm just glad the money stayed in the family."

"I doubt he was really planning to throw it all away."

"Either way, my dad never considered me the rightful heir, even if it meant giving it all up. Luckily, he accepted you and Seung-Joon, so he didn't leave everything to complete strangers."

"Still, that's not fair; you're his son, too. Why was he so partial to Hyun-Wook?"

"Can't really say. He was the son of my father's dreams, at least at first. A strong physique, a quick wit. The kind of man he would have aspired to be when he had nothing. A guy with money, good looks, and brains. My father was just a motivated country boy until he met his wife. He built a factory from the ground up, and yes, he was a self-made man. But he couldn't have climbed up the ladder without his wife, so he had high expectations for my brother. He wanted my brother to be the dashing tycoon he dreamed of, to take over the business and everything. As you can see, I'm not that kind of man."

A bitter smile flashes across Soohyun's face. "I'm not masculine and strong like my brother. A little bit of a sissy, as they say. More of a wimp when I was younger, getting beat up all the time."

I recall the Polaroid picture. A pale, skinny, handsome boy leaning against his older brother.

"My real mom, even if she hadn't died, would never have set foot in this house."

"Oh, come to think of it, I didn't even get to ask properly. How did she pass away? You mentioned that it was an accident?"

"Yes, a gas leak."

"Gas?"

He stares off into the distance, lost in thought. A faint, sad smile hovers at the corners of his mouth.

"We lived in a small apartment. I can't be sure, but I think my father paid for that apartment. Before I was born, my mom used to work part-time at my father's parking garage downtown. Obviously, it wasn't a serious relationship, and my dad didn't want to throw away his life for her or abandon his rich wife who helped him build everything he had. Then I came along, and my mom quit her job and raised me on the allowances he gave her. Maybe we were meant to stay in that apartment and stay out of his life, I don't know. Then the accident happened. One day, I came back from school and found her."

"Oh my!"

"We had a gas fireplace in the apartment, and it must have leaked because my mom was taking a nap. She wouldn't wake up when I shook her."

He slowly shakes his head, then casts me a look, a big smile on his face.

"Well, that's how it happened, and that's why I came to this house at the age of ten. If not for that accident, I would still be living in a cramped apartment with my mom and I might be using my mom's last name."

"Oh, Soohyun."

"So it goes—one door closes in life, another one opens. So nothing takes me by surprise. Whatever happens can be a blessing in disguise, or the very opposite. Same with this inheritance."

His eyes grow dreamy for a moment.

"No matter how you put it, Soohyun, it's really—"

"Oh, it's not so bad. I get to keep my job, even if it's a sham. And a piece of real estate, albeit in a rural area, so that's more than I could ever hope for."

"It's no laughing matter. And by the way, shouldn't we talk about that other clause?"

"Oh, that."

The smile fades from his face.

"Sneaking toxic clauses into contracts is my father's specialty. He always does. Sulking like he can't stand seeing anyone happy."

"I don't know what to say."

"It's just—he thinks ahead, thinks of everything. The family register and birth certificate issues with Seung-Joon will have to be sorted out first, but it's not like you and my brother were legally married. I bet my father couldn't bear the thought of you marrying someone other than my brother. Still, even just the language of that clause—if you legally remarry, you have to give up your share of the property. . . . It's a bit cruel. You're so young, and he's asking you to stay single for the rest of your life. I guess he was worried that some gold digger might try to ensnare you."

"But then you and I would have to—"

"A lot of 'what ifs' and 'might bes,' you know?" He clears his throat. "My father must have had a lot on his mind if he felt so inclined to include that clause even when we have no idea where my brother is."

I grab his arm, desperate for support, but he refuses to face me, his eyes fixed on the distant pool water.

He finally looks at me to ask, "You don't think my brother's in the basement of my house anymore, right? Do you?" His bloodshot right eye stands out against his otherwise pale face. "We all checked to make sure there was nothing in the basement, didn't we? Are you still unsure?"

I shake my head no.

"And still taking your meds, right?"

I nod.

"Good, because quitting right now will make your symptoms worse. Keep consulting the doctor on the dosage decrease. But the way I see it, you need all the help you can get right now, especially for Seung-Joon's sake."

He pats my arm gently with one hand, as if soothing an unruly child.

"Hey, about that clause," I say, "do you think your father might have noticed something off about us?"

"Can't say."

"The clause isn't our punishment, right? To keep us from being together? Either that or—"

"No way."

"The more I think, the more I feel it was all your father's master plan. Don't you find all of it too weird?"

"Don't overthink it, at least not right now. It'll give you a headache. Come on."

I can tell he's losing interest. He even yawns a little, clearly bored.

"Okay, let's say you and I have nothing to worry about, but what about Hyojin? Father left a billion won to a random woman like that out of nowhere. How does that make sense?"

"She'd waited on him hand and foot, and she did it twice. I'm sure he appreciated that."

"But he didn't leave anything to Mr. Choi or any of the other caregivers!"

"I'm sure she was somewhat special. He favored her since she did such a great job, so I'm sure he wanted to make sure she got a little something."

"Like what, a billion won? It's like winning the lottery."

"Well, after all, she was the caregiver who looked after him while he was on his final journey."

He doesn't seem to want to let the conversation drag on, but I push. "It's not like he knew she was going to be his last caregiver!"

"Maybe he had a gut feeling." Soohyun shrugs. "Speaking of Hyojin, now that my father has passed away, it's only right for her to leave now, but I'd like her to stay here a little longer so she can help with some of the housework."

"Excuse me?" My voice rises. "With the funeral done and the estate settled, she's got no reason to stay."

"Well, it's been almost two years now, and we're going to have to switch out the staff, and then we're going to have to worry about training and transition. And you're having a hard time right now."

"Me? No, I'm fine. I've been taking all my meds. I'm doing great."

"Are you sure you're okay?"

Soohyun pulls me closer by the arms and gazes into my eyes. I bring myself face-to-face with him to show him I'm okay. But before I know it, I find myself rolling my eyes nervously, shuffling my feet, and avoiding his gaze.

"See?" Soohyun pats my arm affectionately.

"No, I'm fine!" My grumpy voice sounds anxious.

"How have you been sleeping?"

"Fine."

"Any nightmares?"

I shake my head.

"Do you still dream about the basement?"

I shake my head again.

"What about my brother being down there?"

"That was all in my head."

"Are you sure?" He moves closer, his face right above me as I stare up at him, and he looks into my eyes.

"Sometimes, I do have dreams like that, but I'm fine. I take the meds and it all goes away," I say.

"If you ever go to Dr. Kwon's clinic, be sure to tell him about that."

"Really? Can I tell him something like that, like the basement story?"

"Sure. He's a professional, you should be honest and tell him everything." Soohyun lifts his hand and brings it down to affectionately stroke my cheek. Such a show of affection was unheard of when the old man was breathing.

"Any visions or nightmares, about my brother lying in the basement or anything like that—all of it. Dr. Kwon will give you a prescription that can help you. All you have to think about now is Seung-Joon and your health. And I'll be here for you."

"But, Soohyun, what happens with us now? What should we do?"

He avoids my intense gaze, gently taking my hand off his, and looks away. "Things are different now."

"Different?" I raise my voice again. "Does that mean . . . you've changed your mind about us?"

"You know it's not that."

I grab hold of Soohyun as he makes a move to stand up. "So what is it? Is it that toxic 'no remarriage' clause, or is it because you think I'm unstable?"

"It's not like that." He flashes me a sad smile. "You know my feelings haven't changed, but so much more is at stake now."

"Oh, that's it, isn't it? It's that stupid clause."

"All it takes is for me to get greedy and you could lose everything."

My voice grows louder. "You think I liked you for the money? Huh?"

"Sister."

"I don't need any of that, I don't care. I could blow up this house and throw away everything I have, all I need is one person who likes me!"

"Shhh! Please—"

"Are you worried about your brother? That he's going to show up one day?"

I jump up from the bench we've been sitting on side by side.

I'm like this all the time these days, my emotions running wild, as if I'm on a seesaw of feelings—I'll break out in a cold sweat, get anxious and cry, and the next moment, I'll suddenly snap and scream.

"Should I tell you what's really on my mind? Huh? Do you really want to know?"

"Sister." Soohyun stands, too, and grabs my arm, trying to soothe me.

"If he shows up, I'm going to ask for a divorce. No, we're not even legally married, so I'm going to ask him to break up with me, and I'm not doing it for the inheritance money. I've been beaten up all my life, and I can't live like that again. I'm going to tell him I'm choosing someone else."

"You can't make such a rash decision—"

"It's not rash at all. You're the one who let Seung-Joon and me into your life, who was on our side. I need that kind of love and support. Stable love. That's all I need, I don't need anything else. I want to raise Seung-Joon properly, not with someone who's going to beat his mom. It doesn't matter if his uncle will be his dad, all that matters is that he grows up in a happy family."

"Let's think this through later, but not like this."

I bat away Soohyun's hand trying to grab my arm. The more I yell, the more my words come out slurred, as if I'm drugged. It's quite a fit of drama, even for me.

"I don't care if I lose everything. I'll write a will! So I can prove it, right?"

"Come on."

"No! It's not like I'm going to live forever!"

"What are you talking about?"

"No, really! If something were to go wrong with me, who would take care of Seung-Joon? You're the only one who can take care of him."

"Sister!"

I lower my voice and grab both of his arms. I stare into his tired, bloodshot eyes.

"I'm not kidding. If I have to give up my rights so we can be together, I'm willing to do it. At least I want to prove how true I am. If anything happens to me, you get my share of the property, my rights, all of them, Soohyun, that's just the way it should be."

He wordlessly pulls me in for a tight hug.

Resting my cheek on his chest, I add, "But please let Hyojin go, because I never want to see her again."

CHAPTER

·56·

Mrs. Suwon knocks on the door, speaking without entering the room. "Ma'am, Hyojin wants to say goodbye."

The house staff know who the new boss is now. With the old man gone, word quickly spread about who holds the keys to this place.

"I'll be right out," I answer without opening the door, my voice carrying just the right amount of dignity and authority.

I scoop up Seung-Joon, who's sucking on his thumb. I have to show Hyojin his face one last time before she leaves for good. For a billion won, it wouldn't be so hard to say goodbye to her son, would it? I would have killed for that kind of money before.

When I walk downstairs, Soohyun and Hyojin stand waiting in the doorway. A familiar suitcase and some duffel bags lie at their feet.

"I just did my job, yet I'm leaving with a gift I don't even deserve," Hyojin says, not once looking in my direction, staring directly at Soohyun's face instead. I think about something else the woman on the phone said to me before we hung up.

"The three of them used to hang out together a lot, and I remember Soohyun running around crying and begging to join the two of them, Hyojin and Hyun-Wook. Hyojin was a teenager, and she wanted to be alone with her crush, of course, but his little brother always interrupted, so we thought Soohyun had a crush on Hyojin."

"Oh, please don't say that. You do deserve it, right, sister?" Soohyun quickly glances in my direction. "I know how demanding my dad can be. You did a great job when it was beyond all of us. We can't thank you enough."

"Chairman's wife didn't like it, either, so whenever the three of them got together, she'd cause a scene and make the kids cry. She got more and more hysterical, and at some point, I was even afraid the eldest son would commit suicide. He was so tortured by his mother that everyone could tell he withered. Between you and me, if Chairman's wife hadn't died, Hyun-Wook would have died first. It was a toxic relationship that would only have ended with one of them dying."

"Yeah, well, you've done a lot." I force out a compliment.

Only then does Hyojin look at me. First at my face, then at her child in my arms.

"And you know, thank you, for that day," I say. The woman's gaze returns to me. I continue, "When the basement door was locked that day—"

"That's no big deal. I should have gone down there sooner. You could have gotten in trouble. I'm glad you're okay." The woman smiles and picks up her bag before adding, "I really should get going, then. No news is good news with a house staffer like me once she leaves, I hope."

She brushes it off as a joke and glances back over her shoulder at Soohyun with a smile.

We follow her out the front door. Soohyun carries her suitcase down the stairs. Mr. Kim is watering the flower bed by the pool with a hose.

"Didn't you plant those new chrysanthemum seedlings on the day of Chairman's passing? So beautiful." Hyojin gestures with her chin. "They're my dad's favorite. They'll be so pretty when they're in full bloom. What a shame I won't get to see them."

Soohyun smiles and says, "Well, you're welcome to come by anytime."

"And Soohyun would be crying and looking for Hyojin and Hyun-Wook whenever they were out of sight."

I put one hand to my forehead.

"Are you okay, sister?"

"It's the sunlight. Just a little dizzy. Oh, come to think of it, the meds—"

"You skipped?" Soohyun looks at my face with concern.

"No, I took them in the morning, but I don't think they're working. I'll have to increase the dose. I haven't gotten much sleep lately. I think I'll try Dr. Kwon's clinic."

"Please do," Soohyun says happily. "Speaking of which, do you want me to schedule an appointment for next week?"

"Yes. Maybe Thursday?"

"Sure. I'm sure you'll feel better after the appointment." Soohyun pats the back of my hand comfortingly.

In the meantime, Hyojin mumbles a quick goodbye, turns around, and walks across the flower bed, pulling her wheeled suitcase along. Mr. Kim, just emptying a bag of soil, glances back at Hyojin before returning to his work in silence.

I climb the stairs with Seung-Joon in my arms without looking back. This garden, this house, and everything that comes with it are all mine, and there's no one I need to answer to now.

From now on, I can do whatever I want.

CHAPTER

·57·

HYOJIN

THEN

I didn't feel too bad about going through the whole duration of the pregnancy on my own, from birth to postpartum care.

I was no exception to the hormonal fickleness that strikes everyone during pregnancy, so sometimes I'd cry my eyes out all day, and it's not like I'd never looked down from my apartment window in the middle of the night and thought, *What would it be like to be done with all this?* But for the most part, I'd gotten through it well enough.

I gained about 18 kilograms and wobbled around, but I gave birth without any complications, a day after my due date.

I was also able to laugh off a nurse's insensitive joke: "Born on 12/12."

Because I didn't really feel anything for my child. It's not like I hadn't been trying. I held the tiny, bright red creature in my arms and stared hard, trying to see if I could feel anything stirring in myself. I waited for the slightest hint of maternal love, the faintest stirrings of sadness or joy, or even pity in the form of a resigned "Why did you come into this world?" but no, absolutely nothing. I wondered if that void was what a monk who had meditated and trained for her whole life would feel once she reached the state of enlightenment.

His thin, monolid eyes seemed to be the telling sign of the Jung family blood. And that alone could convince me that it was the right decision for me to have given birth to this child.

He brought to mind the house, the very house that I'd yearned for for so long and so sincerely, that made me want to live with them, eat the same food as them, use the same bathroom as them, and touch everything they touched. Only to feel, later, that I wanted to destroy everything and everyone in it beyond recognition, to burn it down to the ground. With the blood running in that family, I'd created in this child a living mass of burden, but a masterpiece born out of my own knot of compressed feelings, all my longing and all my hatred.

I left the postnatal care center earlier than planned and didn't register the child's birth. With his future still up in the air, there was no rush to seal anything. And I had too much on my plate. In the meantime, I kept up a steady stream of texts to the people who entrusted me with their secret missions. There was a lot to prepare, a lot to ponder.

Only one person came by while I was in the postnatal care center—my dad.

He visited me not too long after being released from rehab, and I felt an unfamiliar twinge. Who would have thought we'd see each other again under these circumstances? Both of us probably should have turned our backs on the world long ago, him a drunk, me beaten by his hands, both of us filled with pent-up anger. But both of us had survived through it all to see each other again, one as the mother of a fatherless child, one as a sinner seeking redemption.

He talked about his withdrawal symptoms—hand tremors—and how they had gotten a lot better. He was trying to get his old mechanic job back. He didn't ask to hold the child. He seemed to realize that he wasn't in a position to ask for that anyway, and that he'd better not get attached.

My heart still sank every time I looked at the man in front of me; even though the bad memories had faded, their emotions still lingered. I had worked so hard at putting those memories away into the farthest corner of my mind. All those memories of seeing stars after being hit by him, and feeling as if I was going to faint, the memories of him throwing all my important schoolwork down the bathroom drain, the memories of him cursing at me and throwing pennies in my face to go buy him a drink, the memories of him grabbing my mom by the hair and dragging her around the tiny house, screaming at her to do something about money, or at least go borrow some from the Jung family—I swallowed it all, and I asked him to help me out.

I asked him to help me if he truly felt remorseful over the past. If he thought it wasn't all his fault that my mom died a horrible death and our family was torn apart. If he felt that the tragedy that befell our family was even remotely unfair, unjust.

Dad nodded, much more enthusiastically than I'd expected. He said he'd even be willing to learn how to garden and landscape. He would earn a decent living, get room and board, get revenge, and help his daughter. He said it'd be like ditchdigging and crawfish catching all at once, as the Korean saying goes. He said that he could also prove his identity and clear any background check through someone he got to know at rehab, that he hadn't had a drop of alcohol since the release, and that he was tired of living the way he used to, always drunk. And he confessed, now that he was sober, he was thinking a lot about my mom, who died so unjustly. I promised him that I would find him a good job, one where he could help me.

I needed all the help I could get. To return evil for evil, you must join forces with your enemies.

If you find yourself down in the ditch, you have to crawl out, even if it means taking your enemy's hand. That's how revenge works.

And that's how life works.

CHAPTER

·58·

Shopping is the best morale booster.

I take down all the heavy curtains on the windows and replace them with lightweight ones in bright colors.

"Velvet's too fancy and grandma—who uses that these days? Leather is too old. I like linen."

I've also replaced all the couches in the parlor and furnished the room with a new plush white fabric sofa.

"The furniture's so outdated, too. It belongs in the basement, or I can sell everything."

The antique table and console with delicate wood carvings have been replaced with minimalist modern pieces from designer brands. When Soohyun comes back from work in the evening, his jaw drops.

"What is all this?" he asks.

"What do you think?" I ask, blatantly clinging to him. Heesun, just stepping through the living room with a load of laundry, flinches when she sees us and quickly disappears. Conscious of her stare, Soohyun slips away from me.

"This looks like a completely different house." He looks around with a stony face.

"That's exactly what I want. To make it a different house alto-gether."

"Excuse me?"

"Now that we're the owners of this house, we want to freshen it up. Brighten it up with youthful colors and designs. This place hasn't gotten to shine for too long."

"It's a little too soon for this," he says.

"Leave it to me, I'll make it look great! I went to the department store today, and I'll probably get a few more items next week."

"More coming?"

"Oh yeah, and while I'm at it, I got myself a department store card. Oh, and by the way!" I hold my hand up in front of his eyes. "Bam! How about this?"

"This is . . ." he starts, eyes wide. "It's an emerald, isn't it?"

"It's a little too big for a ring, but it's a gift for myself."

"Sister, you seem to be in a good mood today?"

"Really?" I smile broadly and put my arm around him. The stares of the maids seem to get on Soohyun's nerves, but I tighten my grip and don't let him slip away.

"I guess the meds from Dr. Kwon are working. It's good that you recommended him. I get to vent, I'm sleeping better, and I feel much better on the new meds."

"That sounds good," Soohyun says, sounding relieved.

"It does make me a little groggy and weak, but I definitely sleep better. And I seem to feel better after a good night's rest."

"If you're happy, then I am, too," he chirps.

"Isn't that right? Peace at home depends on a happy housewife," I say with a giggle, and Soohyun smiles reassuringly. "Go ahead, wash up and come back downstairs for dinner. Mrs. Suwon made a big bowl of eel rice. It's late summer and we need some hearty meals to survive the heat waves to come."

"That sounds good!"

"Yeah, I'll explain my next plan while we eat."

"Next plan?"

"I'm going to completely renovate my room on the second floor."

Walking toward the stairs, Soohyun stops dead in his tracks. "Your room, you said?"

"Yes, the room me and Seung-Joon are using now."

"You're going to . . . you're going to renovate it?" His facial expression changes.

"Yes, the whole thing. The flooring, the bed, everything is so old. I was thinking of combining it with the room right next door. To make a bigger room."

He doesn't answer.

I ramble on excitedly. "I was thinking I could make it really fancy, like a hotel suite. Rip off the floor and the windows and put in a big door that opens both ways. I'd have to get rid of that bed first. It's so old and creaks every time I turn. Would Mr. Kim want it, or is it too big to fit in the outbuilding? It's a shame to throw it away, but I can donate it, I guess."

"Shut up."

At first I think I've misheard him, the voice is so cold and unfamiliar.

When I look up at Soohyun, I see a pale face floating in the dark room like a mask.

"Soohyun?"

"Don't you dare change a thing in that room. If you do, I swear—" His voice is so low I can't make out his words.

"Soohyun!"

He peels my fingers from his arm, one by one, as if they are dirty things to be thrown away.

He flinches away from my outstretched hand, as if he can't bear the idea of me touching him, and stomps upstairs. The door to his bedroom slams shut, its sound echoing hollowly in the darkened living room. At the bottom of the stairs, in a daze, I slowly turn around.

A pair of eyes peers through one of the curtained windows. I blink as my eyes meet the sullen, dark gaze of Mr. Kim, who's hosing down the flower bed just below the window.

CHAPTER
·59·

When I wake up in the morning, I lie tossing and turning in bed for a while. Finally, I reluctantly throw on a robe over my pajamas and make my way down to the dining room. Now that the old man is gone, I don't know what is expected of me at home. In short, I'm free. I can enjoy my privilege to wake up at this hour and eat a late breakfast in unkempt clothes, now that there's no father-in-law to frown upon me.

Soohyun, neatly dressed, is taking a sip of his drink. When he sees me, he stops. I sit down across from him, avoiding his eyes. My hair in a loose bun and eyes bloodshot, I try to stifle a yawn.

"Hey, I'm sorry about yesterday." Soohyun speaks first. A sweet, gentle voice, as usual.

I don't respond right away. Heesun brings me a plate of omelet, bread, salad, and a cup of coffee and sets it down.

"I'm a little overwhelmed," Soohyun says. "So much has changed, and so suddenly. It's a lot."

He explains, "I'm still reeling from my dad's passing, and all of a sudden you're changing things up. It's just too soon."

"I thought you'd also like the change," I say, pouting. "You've been living in a dingy house with a sick father for so long. You're so young to have gone through so much, and you haven't really gotten to enjoy yourself. So I wanted to pamper you and give you everything that you deserve."

"I know," Soohyun says soothingly. "But—this house is like a chest of memories, and sure, there are bad ones, but also some good ones I'd like to keep, especially since that room used to be my brother's."

"What's the point? He's not coming back."

"Don't you miss him?" Soohyun's voice is rigid.

"I'm sorry to say this, but not anymore." My voice grows forceful.

Soohyun lifts his head at this, his gaze boring into my face.

"You probably miss him, but I don't. All I remember is being beaten half to death, and I can't even remember the good times anymore."

He puts down his fork.

My voice rises.

"Didn't you see for yourself—our old half-basement room? I worked my ass off to provide for my boyfriend and to pay for that cramped, filthy place, and you know what I got in return? Stalking, abusive words, and suspicion. He'd always find a reason to get upset and beat the shit out of me, and that was my life. Sometimes things were good, when he acted nice because he felt bad for having beaten me so bad. You said it was all because of his mom's accident, right? But it's just an excuse, don't you think? Hadn't he been violent, even before the accident? Did he ever hit you?" I see Soohyun bite his bottom lip, so hard that first it looks drained of blood, and then a prickle of blood actually appears.

"My brother wasn't that kind of person." It's that unfamiliar voice I heard last night: low, muffled, and thick. "It's that woman, I mean, his mother, that changed him. She never did him any good."

His eyes look right through me to search the far wall, as if I am invisible.

"She had such a temper. Whenever she was upset with my dad or the maids, she would take it out on my brother. On me, too, but I could handle it. But he was her blood, and he had to grow up with her. My brother was probably already broken before I got here."

"That's why it's even harder to understand." I yawn again and stab at my omelet with my fork. "Wouldn't he have felt relieved, in secret, when the woman torturing him so much was gone? I guess he was probably traumatized by it; she was his mother after all. But him turning violent over the accident? That doesn't add up."

I gobble up the omelet, rambling on. Soohyun has stopped eating and is looking at me blankly, but I no longer care, going on.

"It doesn't make sense that he'd become a violent man overnight because of his mother. Once she was gone, he didn't just get on with his life; he started beating up his girlfriend. Who the hell did he think he was? I wasn't his punching bag."

I greedily gulp down my coffee, muttering to myself. "He always said it's because he loved me too much. Can you believe it? He loved me so much that he wanted me all to himself. That was the reason."

Soohyun's unfocused eyes are now glued to mine, mouth ajar in shock.

"He said he's never loved anyone in his life the way he loved me and that's why he couldn't leave me alone. He couldn't stand me laughing or even just talking with other people. He said he didn't need a family or money if he just had me. And I believed him."

I click my tongue, take a sip of coffee, and speak again.

"I thought it made sense at the time, but the more he loved me, the more violent he became—how does that work? I couldn't take it anymore. Do you know why I like you, Soohyun?"

As I go on talking at Soohyun, I catch his hands trembling slightly.

"Because you're so different. You're the same inside and out, no dark side lurking deep down. You don't just beat people up or bully them because of love. That's why I like you. That's what a real man is. Oh, come to think of it!" I stop babbling excitedly and look at him. "I've been wondering—do you think there's any chance . . . that your brother staged the whole thing? You know, his mother's accident?"

Soohyun sits, utterly speechless. The edges of his eyes begin to turn bright red.

"If he was so tortured by his mom, he must have wanted to kill her sometimes. I mean, he would have been infuriated."

The fork in Soohyun's hand trembles.

"I know how he must have felt." Looking away from Soohyun's trembling hands, I keep going as I butter a slice of bread. "When you're cornered, you can explode all of a sudden. When your brother beat the shit out of me, sometimes I really wanted to kill *him*. I can't tell you how many times I thought, *I will kill this guy!*"

Clang!

His fork falls to the ground.

"Oh my God, what am I saying? I'm sorry, Soohyun!"

Without a word, he pushes his chair away, stands up, and storms out of the dining room.

I put down the bread I've been eating and rub my forehead. I need some fresh air. No, I need a lot of it.

Everything starts to feel overwhelming again.

CHAPTER

· 6 0 ·

Soohyun doesn't come home until late that night.

I eat dinner alone in the empty dining room. The sumptuous meal, prepared just for me, is tasteless without company. All the empty seats at the table seem occupied by the apparitions of those who died because of this house. No matter how hard I try, I can't seem to shoo away all the ghosts, even with new furniture and other cosmetic changes.

After dinner, I take Seung-Joon in my arms and take a stroll in the garden. The lights on in the outbuilding are a telling sign that Mr. Kim might still be awake. I sit on the bench, watching the water lapping at the edge of the pool near my feet and gazing up at the bright moon. We smell the rich scent of newly planted seedlings in the flower beds.

Seung-Joon, now a big boy and on solids, occasionally babbles. I wonder if he'll be able to say "mommy" in a little while. When I look into his eyes, he stretches out his tiny palms and smiles broadly, so irresistibly cute.

And I whisper: "I don't know if it was a good idea to bring you here, sweetheart, but don't worry. We'll be the last ones standing."

At that moment, I hear the sound of a password being pressed on the keypad, and the gate hisses open, followed by the sound of footsteps on the gravel driveway.

Soohyun emerges from the overhanging vines, bangs disheveled and shirtsleeves roughly rolled up. I have never seen him so unkempt.

He struggles up the stairs, past the pool, the garden, and the newly planted flower beds. He stumbles, about to lose his balance, but recovers.

I wait at the top of the stairs with Seung-Joon in my arms.

"Huh? This little guy!" As Soohyun comes closer, I can smell the alcohol on him. "You weren't asleep, were you?"

He pokes at Seung-Joon's cheek roughly with his index finger.

"Have you had much to drink?" There's an edge to my voice.

"A little." He tries to walk right past me.

"Soohyun." I tug on the sleeve of his shirt to stop him. "I woke up feeling so horrible this morning. I was losing patience. I forgot that, however I feel about him, he's still your older brother."

I can feel him flinch at the word "brother."

"I'll watch what I say and won't change things up so much, I promise. And when I said I wanted to kill him, I didn't mean it, so . . ."

He brushes my hand away before I can finish and staggers into the house.

The slam of the front door being shut echoes through the tranquil garden. The lights in the outbuildings also snap off, plunging everything into darkness. I scoop Seung-Joon up in my arms and follow him into the mansion.

It takes me a while to really gather up the courage to put my plan in motion, even though I am ready. Even after I put Seung-Joon to sleep, I pace around the room and hesitate for a long time. But I've come this far, and there's no point in stopping now. I need to see this through to the end.

I have on a white cotton nightgown trimmed with lace, the kind you can see through even in the dimmest moonlight. Such a befitting costume for this large mansion, with all its ghosts and skeletons in the closet, empty but for one man asleep on the other side of the hall, a baby sleeping soundly, and me.

Listening to Seung-Joon's stable breaths, I finally muster up the courage to step into the hallway.

Barefoot, I tread on the old floor. One step after another, down the long hallway with wainscoted walls and built-in cabinets, I round a corner and arrive at two doors.

Soohyun's room is on the left. It's always locked during the day.

"He doesn't like people going in there," the maids had told me.

It's the only room they always leave out on cleaning day.

But what about when he sleeps?

I stand in front of the door and listen for a while, then carefully grab the handle and turn it. The door opens without a sound, to my relief.

I stand still in the doorway for a moment. When my eyes adjust to the darkness, I can see there are a few old movie posters on the walls, and by the window, a desk cluttered with books and papers. It looks more like a boy's room, frozen in time, than a man's.

Soohyun's sprawled out on the bed, lost to the world. He's lying on his side, wearing only a pair of roomy boxer shorts, a corner of the blanket tucked between his legs. One cheek on the pillow and mouth slightly open, he looks exactly like the child I left in my room.

I can hear him snoring faintly. I step inside and close the door behind me, leaving it open halfway. Then I walk over to the bed and stand looking down at his sleeping face, before gently taking his arm to shake him awake. He doesn't stir at first, but when I shake him a little harder, his eyes flutter open.

"What's going on?"

His face remains blank for a moment, before a look of confusion appears. His darting eyes gradually come into focus. When he finally realizes it's me, his eyes grow wide.

I press my lips to his. They still reek of alcohol. When he tries to sit up, I push his shoulders back down and climb onto the bed. Hiking the hem of my white nightgown up to my thighs, I spread my legs and climb on top of him.

"What are you doing?"

"Shhh!"

I tenderly stroke his cheek with one hand and kiss him harder.

I think of Seung-Joon asleep in the other room. I've come this far, and I can't stop now.

"I know I made some mistakes, but we'll be fine. Nothing has to change, and this will work out, right?" I whisper, clinging to him in the darkness. "Please don't push me away. I can't do this without your love. I really can't."

I bury my lips in the nape of his neck and call his name as if to cast a spell. I wrap my arms around his head and mumble into his hair.

"It's just the two of us now. Nothing in this house to stop us. We've got all the money we need, and we're young, the whole world is ours. We can be happy. Let's forget about your brother. We have no idea when or if he's coming back. Who cares where he went or if he died. The living get to live, so let's just—"

I feel Soohyun's body, limp in my arms, stiffen right away. Like a robot that's been cut off from its power source, ceasing all its functions at once. Soohyun doesn't even respond to the light kisses I place all over him between words, and then he suddenly pushes me away and sits up.

Pushed back, I lie unseemly on the bed. In the moonlight pouring in through the window, I can see his bloodshot eyes glaring at me. For what feels like an eternity, I stare back, my blood cold.

Finally, Soohyun scrambles to his feet, grabs his clothes off the chair, and exits the room, leaving me in a heap on the bed. Just a moment later, the stairs creak and the front door slams shut. As if startled by the momentum, a picture frame somewhere in the house rattles and then falls with a thud.

CHAPTER

·61·

> Don't leave me hanging like this,
> at least send me a text to check in.

As I walk out of the parking lot to the elevator, I send Soohyun yet another text. The screen of my phone pops up with all the texts I've sent.

> Where are you?

> Have you eaten?

> Soohyun?

> You're not coming home today?

> You know I haven't slept in days,
> so answer me, please.

> Soohyun.

> You're alive, right?

> This is killing me.

Later, I realize he probably blocked me, because he's left me on read for a while now.

"Five days and still no response?"

Dr. Kwon sets down his teacup and asks affectionately. It's been three weeks since I started seeing him twice a week.

"He's not texting back at all. I even called his work, and they said he's still showing up there, at least. Otherwise, I would have called the police to report him missing." I let out a deep sigh.

"Well, he's a grown man, so let's give him a bit of space. He's a sensitive young man, and with his brother moving out so suddenly all those years ago, and now his father passing away, he's probably still reeling a little. He needs some time to himself."

"Right—so nothing's terribly wrong, right?"

"He's still got a little boy inside him. It's understandable because he was born into a dysfunctional family; it's the only kind of family he's known since birth. And his life had been eventful with a lot of accidents, big and small, while he was growing up. He doesn't seem to know how to process his feelings. He's smart, I'll give him that, but not disciplined or motivated. He's got an IQ of 148, right?"

"Does he? I had no idea."

"I remember Chairman bragging about it when Soohyun was just starting elementary school."

"That's impressive. Father must have liked him when he was little, then?"

"Well, I guess Chairman did, but . . ." Dr. Kwon's face clouds slightly.

"Things probably went downhill fast once Soohyun moved into that house. He could have even resented Soohyun for not taking advantage of such a sharp brain. Or . . ."

"Or?"

"Well . . ." Dr. Kwon laughs, hesitant.

"Some kids are just so smart that they overwhelm and scare their parents. I'm sure you know what it's like to raise a child."

"I'm not sure if I do yet."

"It's exciting to know that your child is so much smarter than you, but it's also frightening. You might fear them seeing right through you. I wonder if Chairman felt the same way? But Soohyun was his son, regardless. I'm sure he was fond of Soohyun, even if he didn't show it too much."

Dr. Kwon shakes his head.

"Anyway, let's not focus on Soohyun. He'll be fine. Maybe he's thinking of moving out. That's not necessarily a bad thing, and it's better for you as well than having to worry after your grown-up brother-in-law, isn't it?"

The doctor beams at me, an unusually gentle and affectionate gesture. Of course, the businesses in the building must have already heard the news and learned who the new owner was.

"He's a big boy. Let's leave him alone and focus on your issues. How's your insomnia?"

I answer that I still have trouble sleeping. Even when I take my meds, I sleep like a log for a while, only to startle awake in a few hours, after which I won't be able to sleep through the night.

Even when I manage to fall back asleep, I immediately sink into a nightmare.

"The same nightmare?"

"Yes."

"Is Hyun-Wook lying in the basement in this nightmare?"

"Yes, frozen solid as ice."

"And there's a camcorder next to him?"

"Yes."

"And the same video every time?"

"Yes, the same, the one showing me killing him."

"Does it unfold exactly the same way each time?"

"Always the same. We get into a tussle, and then he hits me, and then I fight back, and then I push him, and then I stab him with a knife, and then there's blood everywhere."

"And?"

"And then I wake up at that point, thinking my hands are still full of blood, but of course, when I look down at my hands, I see there's nothing there. I'll be in a cold sweat, so I take another pill and try to get some sleep."

"You actually went down to the basement, didn't you?"

"Yes."

"You couldn't find anything, right?"

"Nothing. I checked every nook and cranny with the maids and Soohyun, and it turned up nothing."

"Didn't you say you also went back to your old house?"

"Yes, with Soohyun. And nothing there."

"And you've also received those texts that you suspect are from Hyun-Wook?"

"Yes. It was just the phrasing—'how's it going?' It was from a number I didn't recognize. But I feel it must have been him."

"Well, then that means he's alive. He's probably just avoiding you because he wants to be free. The reason you keep having these dreams is because you're so worried."

"What if I really did kill him, and I just don't remember?"

Dr. Kwon looks puzzled.

"That's impossible."

"How are you so sure?"

He chuckles.

"I can assure you the Jae-Young I know is not a murderer. Common sense tells us that it's virtually impossible for a woman to kill a big man like Hyun-Wook by herself and then hide the body. Anyone can have nightmares about killing people, especially loved ones, family members, even parents. Don't you worry. Try to keep your mind off of that nightmare and don't go down that rabbit hole."

"That's what Soohyun said, too. But when I'm tossing and turning at night, I can't stop thinking about it."

"When that happens, use the breathing technique I taught you last time, remember?"

"Yes."

"Maybe try a warm bath. Or listening to music."

"I've tried them all. Sometimes one or the other works, but sometimes nothing does."

"And?"

"If this continues—"

"If it does?"

"If this nightmare doesn't go away soon, it will really suck life out of me and might leave me dead."

"Now, isn't that a bit dramatic? What about the last meds I prescribed? Was the dose okay?"

"I'd really like to get more sleep. I don't even remember the last time I slept well. A deep sleep. Do you think you could prescribe me stronger sleeping pills?"

"Well—actually, the current one is pretty strong."

"I'll never abuse it. Just want to use a little bit on really sleepless nights. Please?" I smile at the hesitant Dr. Kwon. "By the way, I noticed when I came in today that the massage parlor next door had moved out. Wouldn't it be great if you opened up your space and your clinic took up all of that dead space instead of someone new filling it? What do you say?"

"Well, we're good as is."

"Oh, too many stores in this building will be a hassle. Why don't you take the space as an extension of your clinic? Don't worry about the rent for that extra space, you've been so good to me."

Dr. Kwon laughs heartily and writes me a prescription with the caveat that I should only use it on the worst of my sleepless nights. As I walk to my silver foreign car parked in the corner of the lot, my cell phone finally rings.

> See you at home.

I smile.
The crisp autumn air suddenly feels so pleasantly cooler.

CHAPTER

·62·

As soon as I walk through the front door, I spot Mr. Kim raking leaves out of the pool. Upon sighting me, he gives me a short nod.

"There are some shopping bags in my car," I say.

"Sure, I'll go get them," he replies.

Gingerly walking up the stairs in my dizzying nine-centimeter stilettos, I stop to look back and say, "Oh, did he—"

"Yes, Mr. Soohyun just came in," Mr. Kim answers, as if he's read my mind, glancing toward the mansion. The house is fully lit.

I hurry up the rest of the stairs, kick off my shoes at the front door, and take a peek inside.

"Hello?"

Heesun, just coming out of the parlor with a mop, greets me.

"Is Soohyun home?"

"Yes, ma'am. In the dining room. Your meal's ready, so please go ahead and wash up. Seung-Joon has been fed and just fell asleep. His crib is also in the dining room."

"Okay. Thank you."

Instead of going straight to the dining room, I go upstairs and take a long, slow shower and wash my hair thoroughly, slip on a knit dress that shows a little of my body, my half-damp hair falling down my back.

When I get to the dining room, only my share of food is on the table. Soohyun has finished eating, and although the table in front of him is cleared, he's still sitting there, looking at the crib next to him. I sit down across from him, but he doesn't show any gesture to acknowledge me.

"How was your day?" I ask.

My awkward greeting is met with silence. Soohyun keeps staring down at the crib for another minute or so before finally and reluctantly looking over my way.

"Where have you—"

"I'm so tired. I'll go to bed first." He pushes his chair back with a loud screech, stands up, and leaves the dining room in long strides. Mrs. Suwon, carrying a water bottle, takes a step aside in surprise as he moves past her.

"Mr. Soohyun's just come in," Mrs. Suwon says, nervously looking my way.

"That's good. Did he eat properly, at least?"

"Yes, ma'am, he finished his meal."

"Good."

I eat my rice as if nothing has happened, savoring the soup and fussing about how it's faultless, even to the last grain of salt. I chew and swallow my share of food in slow, tiny bites, pacing myself as best I can.

"You left a lot. Wouldn't you like some more?"

"I'm full, thanks."

Dabbing at my mouth with a napkin, I wave to Mrs. Suwon as she clears the table.

"I steamed some sweet potatoes during the day, so help yourself to them if you're hungry later tonight."

"Thank you, Mrs. Suwon, you're the best."

And I stop her as she is about to walk out with the empty bowls.

"By the way, what's the length of your contract? Also Heesun's? I didn't keep track of that."

"Oh, us." A puzzled look crosses Suwon's face.

"It'll be two years at the end of the month."

"Less than two weeks to go?"

"That's right."

Although, to be fair, I now make the rules. The old man is gone, so I don't need to honor the two-year rotation clause if I don't want to. How refreshing to be in full control of everything in this house.

Glancing at Seung-Joon sleeping in his cradle for a while, I pick him up and slowly make my way upstairs. I can't just turn a blind eye to the harsh and uncomfortable reality forever, since I'll have to face it sooner or later. I put Seung-Joon down in his crib and cross the hallway again.

I stand in front of Soohyun's door, where five days ago I was standing in a nightgown in the dark, alone. But there's no sound whatsoever. No movement I can make out. Not even a flicker of light around the frame.

I cautiously knock on the door.

"It's me. Can we talk for a minute?"

There's no need to whisper. With the maids busy cleaning up downstairs anyway, there's no need to be secretive at this hour.

"I'd love to talk." I raise my voice a little, but still no answer.

"Hey, I went to see Dr. Kwon today."

Still silence.

"I haven't been able to sleep since you left, so I've been taking more meds, and Dr. Kwon gave me such good advice. I'm going to take my meds every day and sleep well. I just don't feel like myself these days."

I lower my voice a little. "Dr. Kwon said the nightmares are just a sign of my mind and body getting weak, so that's how I'm going to look at them now."

I continue with a slight tremor in my voice. "I just wanted to tell you what a great help you've been. If it's any consolation, when I think of you, I feel like I can get through anything, fight off any bad thoughts. That's what I wanted you to know."

Still the same silence.

"Well, that's it. Good night."

After waiting for a moment, I turn and walk quietly down the hall. As I descend the creaky staircase, there's no movement or sound from his room.

"Is Mr. Soohyun okay?" Mrs. Suwon, who is just getting ready to leave for the day, asks me with a worried look on her face as I walk into the kitchen.

"He's been pretty depressed since Father's passing. He's like a stranger now."

She's never shown any indication of noticing what's going on in the house, but my voice must have sounded so desperate that even she feels prompted to say something. I smile bitterly. "Maybe he just needs a little time. Dr. Kwon said that Soohyun is a very sensitive person with some anxiety issues. That he has some things to work through."

"Yes, I'm sure he'll feel better in time. Well then, we should probably get going."

Heesun seems as if she has more to say, but Mrs. Suwon stops her and hurriedly pulls her along. A prudent move, indeed.

With Mrs. Suwon's back turned, I speak up. "Oh, by the way?"

They've just crossed the threshold into the kitchen when they look back.

"It's only a few weeks until your last day here. Until then, please take good care of everything just as you have."

The corners of their mouths visibly twitch in disappointment at the prospect. I can see them sagging. They must have been hoping I'd extend their contract.

"When will the newcomers start coming to work?" Mrs. Suwon asks in a somber voice.

"Well, that's going to take some time."

"Even if it's just for a little while, with the house so big, it's going to be hard on you if there's a gap before the new staff arrive. When we first started, we had to work one day with the old staff present, because otherwise the workload would have been too much."

"It'll be fine, just let me know if there's anything else you want to add to the handover table we have. I'll also take a look and let you know."

"Oh, but—" Mrs. Suwon drags on this time. "You wouldn't be so comfortable staying in this big house even for a while. If you'd like us to extend our contract even for a few more days—"

"Oh, we'll be fine." I smile encouragingly. "We'll be perfectly fine on our own."

CHAPTER

·63·

Again, I wake up when the sun is high in the sky, and I am late for breakfast. Yawning, I hand Seung-Joon over to Mrs. Suwon. I'm still in my robe, hair disheveled.

"I tossed and turned so much last night. So hard to get up in the morning. I'm sorry for making you prepare two meals."

"No problem at all."

But I can see the undeniable irritation and worry on her face.

"What about Soohyun?"

"I'm here." His voice is too bright. "Getting a little lazy, aren't you?"

Rubbing his wet hair with a towel, Soohyun walks in, and unlike yesterday, he is full of life.

"Soohyun!" I call out to him, but without even throwing a look in my direction, he plops down on the other side of the table.

"It's going to get cooler in a week or two, so I'm going to use the pool a lot, morning and night."

"What about breakfast?"

"He got up at the crack of dawn and already ate," Heesun says, placing my share of food in front of me.

"Already? Are you feeling well today? Maybe we can go shopping together—"

Before I can finish my sentence, a cold reply comes back. "I have an appointment."

"What appointment?"

"I'm meeting some old college buddies for a quick drink. Oh, by the way, I'd like a cup of strong coffee."

"College buddies?"

"Yeah, I still haven't said proper thanks to the guys who came to my dad's funeral, so I'm going to buy them drinks."

"Dinner, then. We can go shopping together beforehand. No, you know what, do you want me to join you? Introduce me to your friends. I didn't get to say hello at the funeral, so maybe—"

"Oh, I'm sorry, they like it light and breezy, you know. They can't stand anything uncomfortable."

"Uncomfortable?"

The tone of my voice makes Heesun flinch as she steps back from putting down Soohyun's coffee.

But Soohyun doesn't even bat an eyelid.

"Of course. It's uncomfortable. You're older than us and my sister-in-law. I doubt any of us will be able to have a drink with you present."

"I'm what, just an older sister-in-law now?" I stare at him, not even touching the meal set before me.

"You'll always be my sister-in-law. It's not like you're exactly my friend. I need to respect that."

Soohyun finally looks straight at me. There is nothing in his eyes, no glimpse of emotion—be it joy, hatred, or anger. Just a pair of big, jet-black eyes staring back at me impassively.

"Why are you acting this way? Are you still mad?" I ask, lowering my voice.

"Why would I be upset?" Soohyun calmly picks up his cup and drinks his coffee.

"No, you're angry. Be honest. This isn't who you are."

"What kind of person am I?" He looks straight at me, a snide smile pasted on his face.

"Someone sweet and reassuring, just like the first day I came to this house. You were the only person in this whole house I felt I could trust and fall back on."

"I'm the same person I've always been. Nothing has changed."

"So this is who you really are?"

"What can you possibly mean?"

"Cold, distant, and disingenuous!" I raise my voice, but barely over the clattering in the kitchen.

"Well, I'm sorry if you feel that way. But I haven't changed much."

"You've been pointedly cold ever since I tried to renovate your brother's old room. Isn't that right?" My voice rings sharply in the high-ceilinged dining room.

"Don't blow this out of proportion."

He is so calm, in fact, that it's like watching a well-programmed robot. Even every single strand of his wet hair seems to rest on his forehead at a perfectly calculated angle.

"Then what's the matter? Is this about the inheritance? Because Father left me and Seung-Joon everything?"

"You're the one who's changed."

"Come again?"

"You're the one on edge. The one getting upset over things that don't matter. You walk around in a daze. You no longer seem like the person I knew. It's like the inheritance has poisoned you. You need to get a grip."

"What?" I jump to my feet.

A shrill, screeching sound comes from the chair as it drags on the floor. The clatter in the kitchen also comes to a screeching halt.

"I'm not sure what's wrong with you. The staff will only be here for a few more weeks, but you're making everyone nervous by acting this way. Take it easy. Are you off your meds? You seem especially on edge today."

As I stand shaking all over, Soohyun nonchalantly finishes the rest of his coffee.

"I'll be late, so don't wait for me. Ms. Heesun, Mrs. Suwon, I'm going out! I won't be eating dinner at home!"

Soohyun speaks in the direction of the kitchen, then walks breezily out. Droplets of water from his wet hair stain the light gray towel around his neck.

I sit back down at the table, knowing full well that the kitchen staff are sneaking glances at me. I spoon some food into my mouth and sit chewing slowly and thoroughly. I sit there until I hear the front door slam shut.

CHAPTER
· 6 4 ·

I'm leaning back in bed, patting Seung-Joon, moonlight streaming in through the open window.

As the clock on the nightstand strikes 1 A.M., I hear the front door downstairs creak open. The old mansion creaks at the slightest movement. When you listen closely, it comes alive with the littlest noises.

After a moment of silence, I hear footsteps ascending the stairs to the second floor, and now I can tell by the sound of them where the person might be. I hold my breath and stay still for a moment, wondering if the sound, echoing off the old floorboards, will stop at my doorstep. I can see the peach fuzz on my arms standing up in the moonlight. Maybe the person's waiting at the doorway, ear to the ground, listening. I imagine the door opening quietly, and a pale, icy figure sliding through the open door.

But after a while, I hear a door close quietly on the other side of the hall.

Then it falls silent.

One, two, three . . .

I count to exactly one hundred, waiting.

So much has changed, but I still have a lot of work to do. There's so much more to go.

No going back now.

I put my phone down and grab my meds from the bedside table.

CHAPTER

· 6 5 ·

"Ma'am? Oh my! Ma'am! Ma'am!"

Someone shakes me like an old ragdoll.

I feel as if I'm treading on a road of dark clouds. Or more like float-ing.

Now someone's slapping me across the face. But it doesn't even hurt.

"Oh my God, ma'am!"

"Sister!"

A loud bang, and I feel the mattress underneath me give as if someone has climbed onto my bed. I hear a child wailing.

"Oh no! I came in for Seung-Joon, and found the pills spilled next to her. What's going on?" I hear Mrs. Suwon weeping miserably. I blink, trying to clear my heavy head.

"Get the kid out of here."

"Do you want me to call an ambulance?"

"I—I'm okay—Soohyun?" I manage to work my stiff, twisted tongue.

"Are you waking up? I'm calling an ambulance!"

"Don't. Please don't. I—"

"Sister! Are you okay? Go get some milk! We need to do first aid, and call 911!"

"Yes, yes. Heesun, Heesun!" Mrs. Suwon hurries out of the room, bellowing like a thunderbolt.

"Ouch, my head." I grab my head with both hands and writhe on the bed.

"Sister, how many pills did you take?"

I grope for him with both hands, and once they find him, I wrap my arms tightly around his neck and pull him to my chest, even when he flinches and resists.

"Don't do this, I don't have anyone left, please." My vision still blurry and my head feeling as if full of gravel, I manage to spit out words that come out slurred, refusing to let go of him.

"Now, now, you rest first, okay?" Soohyun tries to peel me away, but I keep clinging to his neck and clutching the hem of his shirt as if it were my lifeline.

Mrs. Suwon and Heesun pull me away from Soohyun and force me to drink the milk they brought. With loud gurgles, I gulp it down, half of it dripping down my shirt, before sitting up.

Mrs. Suwon and Heesun help me to the bathroom, and I throw up, holding on to the toilet seat. I hear Soohyun call the paramedics. In spite of my protest, I still end up on an embarrassing ambulance ride to the emergency room, where I get a diagnosis that thankfully doesn't require a gastric lavage.

"I'm glad she didn't take a fatal amount. But if she ever does something like this again, it could be dangerous. We'll have to keep an eye on her," I can hear the doctor warning Soohyun as I lie there receiving fluids.

I lie with my eyes closed the whole time, even as I sense Soohyun walk over to the bed to look down at me. I know it was a reckless and risky thing to do, but I feel no regret. I've gone through so much to make things that didn't belong to me unquestionably mine.

So there's no reason for me to hesitate going forward.

There's no stopping me.

If I wasn't so sure, I wouldn't even have gotten started.

CHAPTER

·66·

Before I return home from the hospital, I have to put up with the doctor's lecturing.

Instead of finding and seeing a different psychiatrist, I agree to go to Dr. Kwon's clinic and schedule a consultation with him as soon as I feel better. Still, everyone treats me like a patient the entire time.

The house staffers lock me in a bedroom on the second floor and fuss at me whenever I take so much as a step out of my bed. They move Seung-Joon's crib out of my room and downstairs so that Mrs. Suwon can take care of him full-time during the day, as I'm ordered to rest and eat in bed. Soohyun stays at home and comes in for a few minutes every day, but he refuses to approach the bed or offer comforting words.

He just sticks his head in briefly and says, "Do you need anything?" If I hold out my hands and ask him to come in for a little chat, he says, "You know, maybe not right now. You need to rest," and he hurries away.

So I spend the next few days pretty relaxed. I occasionally sit on the garden bench and enjoy the breeze, but I never get to talk to Soohyun alone.

Mrs. Suwon and Heesun are just finishing up work when they notice the upheaved soil in the garden.

"Huh? We just planted that sapling there," the maid says. "Are you already planting something else?"

"It's pretty, but out of place. I'm thinking of moving it over there, by the bench. Mr. Kim said it will get much more sunlight there," I say.

"I suppose so."

They nod and turn to face each other.

"Mr. Soohyun planted it the night Chairman was over at the hospital. He said he wanted to show it to him. I wish Chairman had seen it," Heesun murmurs wistfully.

Concerned, Mrs. Suwon asks, "Will you be okay, ma'am? You're not fully recovered yet."

They seem to think this transplantation is another whim of mine. By now, they must have gotten used to my fickleness—one moment crying, the next laughing, then screaming again. They look at me, concerned, as if I might go out of my mind any moment.

Just this morning, I even heard Heesun tell Mrs. Suwon, "Now I feel it was best that I didn't get a contract extension."

When I overheard this, I stopped descending the stairs so I could listen. Their loud, casual conversation made it clear that Soohyun went out early in the morning. Their conversation continued, their remarks growing increasingly personal and pointed.

"I think so. When Chairman passed away, I was hoping for an extension. But now I can't wait to get out of here these days," Mrs. Suwon said.

"Every day is a slippery slope. It's hard to know where to stand."

"The other day, I thought my heart would stop."

"I know, I was dreading the worst, too."

"When she first came to this house, I thought she was no ordinary person, looking as fierce as a wild cat."

Heesun lowered her voice. "But her mind is actually like tofu."

"Tofu?"

"It's very soft! Weak!"

Mrs. Suwon, understanding a moment later, let out a laugh. "But money is truly powerful. In just one or two months, a person can completely change. She's gained weight, brightened up. For a while, I thought she was really thriving. But it seems she can also wilt like a plant in a greenhouse."

"She must be the type that can't live without a man."

"What?"

"No, it's true. Shamelessly moving in after having a baby unmarried, now clinging to the younger son of the family."

"Do you really think there's something between her and Mr. Soohyun?"

"Of course! Isn't it obvious? Even before Chairman passed away, something was off between them. Now she's got money, and she's young, still in her prime. Her husband abandoned her, her father-in-law was on his sickbed, and the rest of us were busy working around the house. A perfect situation for a love affair, isn't it? With Chairman gone, I thought they would openly enjoy themselves, but it seems like Mr. Soohyun has come to his senses, and she's completely flipped out."

"Shush! The walls have ears!"

"What does it matter? I'll be quitting soon anyway."

"That's even more reason to be careful! People like us can't just say whatever we want, even if it's a house we're about to leave! We still have to find work elsewhere!"

"Okay, okay."

And they laughed again.

I'd listened until I could no longer bear it, then I stomped down the stairs, my footsteps heavy and purposeful.

"Well then, we'll be on our way, ma'am. I can't wait to see the garden tomorrow—"

"What is going on?"

A hoarse voice startles Heesun and causes her to stagger.

"You're home?" I greet Soohyun cheerfully, but he doesn't seem to register my voice.

Instead, he rushes toward Mr. Kim, who's holding a shovel, and yells to his face, "I said, what are you doing?"

Mr. Kim, confused, looks between me and Soohyun.

Mrs. Suwon, supporting Heesun, turns to gawk at his tone.

"What the hell are you doing? I asked you what's going on!" Soohyun's face looks drained of blood.

"I'm going to move the sapling over there and plant the boxwood here," I explain.

"Are you out of your mind?" he screams in my face.

Everyone flinches at his unfamiliar, coarse voice.

"Has everyone lost their minds? Stop it! Stop it now!" Soohyun roars, snatching the shovel from Kim's hand.

"I'm just trying to redecorate the house for a fresh look," I try to explain.

Soohyun rushes up to me with the shovel in his hand and yells, his eyes bloodshot. "You've completely lost your mind. Haven't you?"

"Oh my! Oh my gosh!" Heesun cries out, seeing the way Soohyun threatens me with the shovel, at which Soohyun looks around.

It's then that he seems to realize where he is and recognizes the people surrounding him.

"I said stop. I mean—it hasn't been that long since we planted this."

"This is my house now. I can change it however I want," I say.

Heesun and Mrs. Suwon gasp, sucking in their breaths.

"It's just a plant, Soohyun." I try to soothe him, gently stroking his arm and speaking in the sweetest voice possible. "And not a special plant at that. I just wanted to make this area better, prettier, because you use the pool often."

Soohyun swats away my hand, looking defiant.

The look in his bloodshot eyes is too familiar, even the way he bites his lip and looks down at me. Those are the eyes of someone wanting to strike me, show who's the real boss, make me taste blood. The gaze of his brother.

I back away and rush over to hide beside Mr. Kim.

"Father passed away! Your brother left, too! I'm now the owner of this house! So let's start fresh!"

I point to the hole and shout in a voice mixed with tears.

"Look here. Is there some treasure buried here? It's all just dirt. Nothing down there. It's all good. This is all our land! So we plant whatever we want, we garden however we want, and we can live the way we want!"

"Wait, what?"

His already pale face is drained completely of blood.

"Look, Soohyun. I'll plant a boxwood here—"

Before I can even finish my sentence, Soohyun shoves me out of the way, almost making me fall in the hole, and rushes over to look down the hole. He leaves me stumbling and dives into the dirt hole, kneels down there, and begins to furiously dig, as if to find something buried deep underground.

Soohyun's hands suddenly stop as we stand watching with our mouths hanging open. A vacant expression appears on his face. It's the expression of someone who thought he had a winning lottery ticket, only to realize it's worthless.

From the stunned Mrs. Suwon and Heesun still frozen on the spot, to the sweaty Mr. Kim and the tearful me, all of us stand dumbfounded around the gaping hole with the dazed Soohyun down inside, all of us looking like actors on a stage.

CHAPTER

· 67 ·

Once again, I turn out to be the only one at the dinner table.

Just like the first time I was here, a thick steak sits on my plate stained with swirls of juice and blood.

"Do you want me to warm it up again?" Heesun asks anxiously.

"No, you've already heated it up twice. I'll just eat it." I reassure her with a smile and pick up my fork and knife. I eat everything laid out for me, from bite-sized pieces of meat to mashed potatoes and salad. I even take sips of the wine from my glass, savoring every drop.

Meanwhile, there's not a sound upstairs.

I haven't seen Soohyun all day, but he must be exhausted after yesterday's commotion. Today, after looking at the boxwoods I planted in the new pit, I'd taken Seung-Joon out to sunbathe in the garden for a while.

I showed up in good shape, just in time for dinner. Mrs. Suwon and Heesun looked extremely relieved. It must have been nice to know that at least one person in this house had come to her senses.

At the end of the meal, Mrs. Suwon brings out a plate of pears and hovers nearby as I eat.

"This is such a feast! You're really the best chef."

I offer these kind words, at which Mrs. Suwon starts, "Ma'am—"

"Would you like to sit down and have a cup of coffee? Or maybe some pears?" I suggest.

"Oh, no, I'm good," Mrs. Suwon declines, but she still pulls out the chair next to me and sits down awkwardly. "Tomorrow's our last day here."

"Yes, I'm aware," I say calmly and flash her a smile.

"It's been a busy day, and I thought you might have forgotten."

"Of course I didn't, and your last paycheck will be transferred without a hitch. I'll put a little extra on top of your severance package."

"Oh! You don't have to do that."

"No problem. We've had a lot of people here because we renew contracts every two years, but I know you two have been particularly hardworking. We had so much going on, and I'm sure you were surprised to have a guest like me show up out of the blue."

"Oh, no."

Mrs. Suwon throws up her hands. After seeing me running around like crazy with my hair unkempt for so long, she's probably both relieved and surprised to find me in good health and in one piece. And to top it off with some extra money—what more could she ask for?

"But, well—"

Mrs. Suwon doesn't show any sign of leaving the table, though. She looks uneasy.

"Is there anything else?"

"Are you sure you don't mind having us go?"

"Hmm?"

"Now it'll be just the two of you in this big house without us. We're . . . concerned."

I bow my head and laugh in silence.

"I'm just worried about you, really."

"Well, I'm going to cut back on my meds, so don't worry too much."

"Yes, by all means, don't take those pills," Mrs. Suwon says with a serious face. "You also have Seung-Joon to think about. My married daughter is about your age, and she's having her second child next month. I'm telling you all this because you remind me of her a lot. I know you might find this presumptuous of me, but—"

Mrs. Suwon looks me straight in the eye and continues, "I've seen a lot, working for rich families like yours. When you first came here, I knew things weren't easy. But I thought you were so resilient. Nowadays, you look really precarious. Mr. Soohyun is not the same as he used to be, either, and I'm worried for you two. You have money, and you two young people can live happily ever after. All you need is some healthy balance, and the whole world can be yours."

"Yes, I will look after myself, thank you."

I swallow the words *"This is the best advice I've heard in a long time."* I don't tell her that I really needed this loving criticism right now, or how very grateful I am. I swallow a hot lump creeping up in my throat and nod.

"I'd be happy to keep silent usually, but I couldn't help myself because something's so off about this house."

"This house?"

"Yes—" Mrs. Suwon shows me an uncomfortable smile, wringing her hands. "It's a big house. And it's kind of scary when you think about all the incidents that took place here. Even though some of it I didn't get to see myself. And that caregiver was sketchy, for sure."

"You mean Hyojin?"

"Yes."

"But she took care of Father until he passed away, so she did her job well before she left."

"I'm not denying that." Mrs. Suwon hesitates for a moment before adding, "I hear Chairman paid her quite a bit of money."

"Oh, that."

"Well, I'm sure she had a hard time taking care of the elderly, and she used to work here before, but I'm pretty sure she was—"

"What?"

"I think she was running some sketchy errands for Chairman or something."

"Something fishy?"

"I'm not entirely sure, but Heesun said—"

"Yes?"

"Hyojin was spying on some of the house staff."

"Um, how?"

"When you weren't around, she spied on Seung-Joon on the second floor, and sometimes she went to Mr. Kim's outbuilding."

"Really?"

"When you told me you got locked down in the basement while we were away, I knew something was wrong."

"But she's the one who got me out. I sure didn't like her, but she's gone now. What's done is done." I try to keep my tone light.

"I don't know what happened in the past, but I had a feeling she might be holding some kind of grudge, and that she might want more money now that she's gotten a taste. She could approach Mr. Soohyun. Maybe that's why he's been acting a little sensitive and weird lately."

I slide the empty bowl away and stand up before she can add anything else.

Mrs. Suwon notices the change in my behavior and jumps to her feet. "Oh my God, look at me. I'm rambling on and on. I'm so sorry, I didn't mean to be so presumptuous."

"No, thank you so much for your concern. I'm going to get my act together and do a better job taking care of myself and Soohyun."

Mrs. Suwon goes back into the kitchen, scratching her head, probably wondering if she's said too much.

I stroll out of the dining room, down the dimly lit golden hall, and stop in front of the stairs. I pass the now-empty room that once belonged to the old man, then the caretaker's room, thinking of the other empty rooms in this house. This house that's breathing silently like a giant monster lurking in the darkness.

This mansion is now mine, not that shabby half-basement room.

So it's going to be okay, everything will work out just fine.

I take my time climbing the stairs, running my hands over the old, scuffed railing.

CHAPTER
·68·

I wake up to a crackling noise.

It isn't until my eyes pop open that I realize it is just the rain pounding on the window. The rainwater running down the window-panes is casting eerie shadows on the walls of the dark room.

I shut my eyes, only to open them again quickly. There's another, more unsettling sound—something that's drowning out the rain.

That must be—

Careful not to wake Seung-Joon, I slip out of bed. When I look out the window, I see the garden's golden lights illuminating Soohyun standing by the pool. He stands soaking wet in the rain without an umbrella, staring down at the ground. I check on the sleeping Seung-Joon once more and run downstairs in my pajamas. I throw open the front door, and run into the cool breeze whipping through the wet leaves. Within a step or two, my thin pajamas are drenched and cling-ing to me.

I rush down the front steps and grab Soohyun's arm. His arms are trembling and ice-cold to my touch. I don't know how long he's been out here, but it must have been a while. The lights are off in the out-building where Mr. Kim lives.

"Are you out of your mind?" I yell to his face.

He swats my arm away. I lose my balance and stumble for a mo-ment, but then I regain my composure and hug him around the waist.

"Soohyun, come on, wake up! What's going on?"

He doesn't answer.

I can barely keep my eyes open or speak because of the rainwater rushing down the whole of my face.

"What's here to see? There's nothing. That's enough."

"That can't be right! Surely . . ." Soohyun trails off.

"What? Surely what?" I yell back.

We scream at each other in the dark, braving the gusts of wind and increasingly heavy rain.

Soohyun finally turns to look at me. Soaked all over, looking utterly hopeless.

"Are you looking for something? What was in there? Huh? Tell me!"

Just then, a light flickers on in the outbuilding. Mr. Kim must have heard our screaming back and forth. Soon, I see him rushing out of the outbuilding, pulling on a raincoat.

"Is everything okay, ma'am?"

"Help Mr. Soohyun!"

I can sense the tension leaving Soohyun's body, his strength draining. When Mr. Kim slips his arms under Soohyun's arms to support him, Soohyun leans back as if he has given up on everything.

"Come on in," I say.

We pick him up and hurry into the house.

There is a frantic howl from the rainstorm behind the front door as we quickly slam it shut.

It is a long, tiring night. I stay by Soohyun's side, dozing in and out of sleep. Soohyun leans against my shoulder, sometimes crying, other times seemingly lost in thought. I tuck him into bed and watch him slowly drift off to sleep. Asleep, Soohyun looks like a defenseless little boy. Harmless enough to shake my resolve.

I spend the night in a daze, listening to the rain pound against the windowpanes. At dawn, when the rain has stopped and it's fallen quiet, I startle awake at the sound of the front door opening. The foyer's covered in leaves, dirt, and rainwater. Mrs. Suwon and Heesun seem to have stumbled upon the mess, judging from the sound.

"Oh, my God, what's going on!" they exclaim upon seeing me head downstairs.

"Shh!" I signal for them to be quiet. I tell them in a low voice, "Something happened last night."

"What happened, ma'am?" Mrs. Suwon asks, her expression turning serious.

"I think Soohyun's a bit overwhelmed right now. He just got a little emotional and went off the rails, but he's calmed down now."

"Are you okay?"

I nod. "Now that he's got it all out, he'll feel much better."

"Shall we prepare some porridge?" Mrs. Suwon suggests cautiously.

"That'd be great. I'm going to go to Dr. Kwon's clinic, because if Soohyun keeps acting like this, I'm definitely going to need some more meds."

I see Mrs. Suwon frown slightly and turn away.

CHAPTER

·69·

Upon my return, the house arrests me with a renewed impression of its strange beauty.

It's a clear, mild late summer night that belies the commotion of the night before. The fragrant smell of flowers wafts through the air, light jazz playing from the pool's speakers. The sound of lapping water nearby. It's like a scene from a movie where something romantic is about to happen.

I stroll inside. The outbuilding and mansion are shrouded in the dark, all the lights off save for the ones around the pool that remain dimly lit.

And in the middle of the pool is Soohyun floating lazily. The light blue swimsuit he has on makes a refreshing impression against the turquoise tiles of the pool.

When I stride over and stand looking down, he smiles up at me. It's the brightest smile I've seen in weeks.

"Hi," he greets me, bobbing up and down in the water.

"Hi," I reply with a smile on my face. I want to ask, "Are we okay now? Are you feeling better now, starting fresh? How come you feel like a new person today?"

Soohyun wades through the water and moves over to me. "Where's everyone?"

I look back toward the unlit outbuilding. "It's their last day, so I let everyone leave early. They said they were sorry they missed you and couldn't say goodbye. Seung-Joon ate earlier and is already asleep. And Mr. Kim isn't in today."

"Where did he go?"

"Well, he's got a life outside this house. He had to get out of town on some errands, so I gave him a day off."

"That's generous."

He smiles back when I smile at him. "I wanted to be alone with you." Soohyun looks me in the eye and holds out one hand.

I set my bag down at the edge of the pool and walk over, smiling, to take the hand he offers me.

As I tug with both hands to pull him out of the pool, Soohyun, who is halfway up, suddenly yanks my hand back and I lose my balance and fall into the water.

"Ouch! Soohyun, what are you doing, you got water in my ear!"

I scoop up the water with both hands and send splashes his way, as I once did.

I'm teetering on one foot, and trying to shake the water out of my ear. That's when a hand reaches out and grabs my head. I'm under the water in the blink of an eye.

It's so sudden that I don't even have time to take a breath. The next moment, I'm submerged and struggling. I open my mouth and water floods in. My lungs feel like they're going to burst.

I flail desperately, only for my fingertips to brush against Soohyun's smooth, bare body. My lungs burning, I'm suddenly pulled out of the water by a hand yanking on my hair.

"Soohyun!"

Both my hands claw at the air. The next moment, the same hand that grabbed my hair plunges me back into the water.

Thud!

I open my eyes and flail my arms underwater, but all I can see are bubbles of air and splashes.

Soohyun's putting his whole weight on me to keep me under. If I can't get air in my lungs soon, it'll be over. Stars flash before my eyes.

No way, not like this!

Then my head is pulled up again, my face rising above the water's surface.

"Hmph!" I gasp for air, spewing water from my mouth, and the next moment, Soohyun's lips come up to mine and whisper sweetly.

"How long were you going to fake it, bitch?"

CHAPTER
·70·

HYOJIN

THEN

I don't know whom he took after, but the child was very gentle.

I didn't even do any sleep training and he slept through the night. There wasn't much crying or fussing.

Even when he woke up before I did or his diaper was wet, no matter how hungry he was, he never just broke into a full-blown wail like most infants. He always looked up at me first, his jet-black eyes wide open. He had a pronounced nose bridge for a baby, big eyes with unusually dark irises, and a small mouth with one corner that turned up slightly when he yawned—unmistakably Jung family traits.

Often, I'd forget what I was about to do and get sucked into those eyes with him in my arms, trying to feed him. I didn't like the way he unblinkingly stared at me. He felt like an old man in a baby's form. I still couldn't believe that I gave birth to this child who belonged in the family I had once longed desperately to be part of. I did end up being part of the family in the most unexpected way. I'd sigh, feeling horrible for thinking this way about such a small, innocent creature, and feeling sorry for his life, for having a mother like me.

At the same time, it was nice to have a baby so docile that his presence didn't interfere with my job too much. I'd put him to bed, take a bus over to spy on Hyun-Wook and his girlfriend, come back in an hour or two, and he'd still be sleeping soundly, so everyone could be at peace and kept in the dark, even in the midst of this world-shattering change. I continued to watch the couple and report back to the people.

Needless to say, the old man was eager to learn more about his grandchild. He grew more and more impatient and started demanding pictures. The man who had been so indifferent to what was going on at home in his prime seemed to have grown old and had completely changed near the end of his life. He wanted to know what the baby looked like, how much he grew up, and other details. He even got so frustrated that he'd say his son couldn't possibly raise a child properly in such a place. He'd asked me if I'd tried to talk his son into coming back home, and even suggested that I tell him he could bring his woman and child with him. He seemed to think money could make any problem go away.

The old man really intended to take her in. It was clear to me that he didn't want to be isolated in this house, alone with Soohyun. Just a year ago, I wouldn't have understood his obsession with his eldest son. I mean, in this age and time, why be so attached to the eldest son he had with a wife he didn't even love, just because he's the legitimate son and that's the way of Korean culture?

But now I am fully aware of the nature of his fear.

The fear that choked the old man, the fear that drove away those who used to live in the house, one by one. That secret source of evil that had finally cornered the old man.

So, if I managed to send his eldest son and his girlfriend home, the old man would be thrilled. I'd get a nice fat paycheck, the woman's life would completely change, and my old crush would go back to being a rich guy leading a comfortable life.

Maybe it would have been a happy ending for everyone.

But then what about justice? Someone had to pay for everything that happened, and whose responsibility would it be? At night these thoughts rattled around in my head. I often couldn't sleep until dawn.

One night, I was thinking those thoughts as usual, looking over my infant child, his mouth hanging half open like a rosebud dripping with milk. That is, until the phone rang.

The moment I saw the name on the screen, I picked up right away. It meant only one thing: emergency. As if that weren't enough, the moment I put the phone to my ear, I heard an eardrum-tearing scream.

"Where are you? Get the fuck out of there! And come over right this second!"

Soohyun was almost out of breath.

"I'm home, the kid's falling asleep."

"Cut the crap and get the fuck out! What the fuck does it matter?" His dad, the proud daddy who had no more affection than I did for this child, screamed away on the other end of the receiver.

"What's going on, where are you?"

"Fuck! That bitch!"

On the other end of the line, Soohyun was half crying and half laughing.

"Hey, what do you mean, are you at the half-basement?"

"She killed my brother! She just hit him in the head and ran away! Can you believe it? Can you fucking believe? That fucking bitch killed my brother!"

I could feel his hot breaths even through the phone. I felt dizzy.

"What do you mean? He's dead?"

Soohyun didn't answer the question, mumbled something to himself, and then shouted again. I thought my ears were going to fall off.

"I'll take care of this, but you go after her. She can't have gotten far because she just ran out. Take a taxi, take whatever you want, search the express bus terminal, the train station. Just find her, don't let her get away, catch her now and send her to me."

Soohyun's last words were eerily low and calm, burrowing into my ears.

"I'll skin that bitch. Send her to me at all costs."

CHAPTER
·71·

The sagging hem of my soaked clothes is deadweight on me.

The pressure from above crushes me, my head shoved downward. I whip my hands around to claw at his bare chest, but he's safely out of my reach. I'm on the verge of losing consciousness.

No!

My hand desperately fumbles in my pants pocket. My phone must have fallen out earlier, but it's probably broken anyway, leaving me utterly on my own and with no way to call for help.

Soohyun's now pushing me harder down and my head feels like a ball of lead.

I go through my other pocket. Not a thing that can help. No one to save me. No one.

But then, I feel something snagging at the lining of my pocket. A lifeline. I let the tension in my body go. On my last bit of air, eyes shut tightly, I press myself against Soohyun as close as I can, still underwater, then fling my ring-bearing right hand out of the water and swing hard.

"Aaaahhhhh!"

A good freaking scratch—how do you like that!

The moment his hand lifts, I push my head out of the water and gulp in a breath. My blurry vision clears ever so slightly. All the blood in my body begins to boil.

"You bitch!"

Soohyun clutches his face with both hands, blood dripping down his jaw into the pool water, where it swirls like bright red ink. I fumble around and swim away as fast as I can. I don't even have time to catch my breath, even though my lungs are on fire. One thing possesses my mind: *Get out of here. Get the hell out now.*

I've barely begun to push myself up over the edge of the pool when a hand yanks me back down.

"You bitch!"

Even as I slide back down, I don't even feel my arms scraping against the pool wall. The moment I end up back in the water, that pool will be my grave.

I latch on to the slippery edge of the pool and refuse to let go. He might have gotten ahold of one leg, but the other is still free. Soon, my shoes slide off as my legs struggle underwater, leaving me entirely barefoot. The moment I feel something touching my free leg, I give it the hardest kick I can manage.

"Aaaack!"

A sharp snap like dry firewood breaking. I don't need to look back to confirm the damage done. As Soohyun's pained scream tears through the jazz still blasting out of the audio system, I haul myself out of the pool. Teetering only for a moment, I turn and run for my life. Even when my knees buckle and I fall flat on my face, I scramble right back to my feet.

I'm on my own here, no one to help me, left to my own devices.

I still can barely breathe. My soaked pants clinging to my legs, I lug myself up the stone stairs. I manage to punch in a passcode on the keypad with my trembling hand. I can't help looking back over my shoulder, dreading that Soohyun's hands might shoot out to grab me at any moment. It takes two tries before the door creaks open. I rush inside and lock the door behind me. If nothing else, the locked door will buy me some time.

When I reach for the light switch, it clicks with that familiar sound. It clicks, clicks, and clicks.

But nothing happens.

Feeling faint, I flip the switch once more, but the house is shrouded in darkness. With the curtains drawn over all the windows, blocking out any hint of light, the mansion is as dark as the devil's gut. No, there's a faint orange glow. Coming from a single source, accompanied by a faint sound.

"Seung-Joon?"

It's coming from down in the basement. But truth be told, while the orange glow might be the only source of light in this dark house, I would have ignored it entirely if not for that sound. I would have run to the kitchen, grabbed a knife, and waited in the doorway.

But that sound? The moment I hear it, I can't think straight: Seung-Joon's breathless sobs coming from the basement. Who knows what that lunatic outside might have done to Seung-Joon.

I run down the stairs, determined to get him out of there and hide him somewhere.

Whatever original plan we had made is thrown out the window. Now I'll have to trust my instincts—

I frantically look around for Seung-Joon.

"Seung-Joon, where are you?"

As I stand in the immaculately cleaned basement, looking everywhere for him, I hear the door slam shut behind me.

Fuck.

I'm dead.

CHAPTER

·72·

I find a tiny speaker hidden in the corner of a stack of oil drums and sacks of rice.

There it is, alternating between babbling, crying, and whimpering. I hurl the speaker to the floor. After an angry glimpse at the shattered pieces scattered everywhere, I run back up the stairs.

"Open the door! Open the door, you son of a bitch! Don't you lay a finger on him! What are you going to do with Seung-Joon? He's yours! I know you used your hair to pass the paternity test! What are you going to do with your baby! Open the door, you crazy motherfucker! Come on!"

Still no answer.

A violent shiver runs through me. I've forgotten how cold it is down here. Would it be better if I strip off my drenched clothes? I wrap my arms around myself and look around the basement. At this rate, I'm going to freeze to death before anything else happens.

I rummage through the neatly stacked boxes, only to find there's nothing but one item of any use, which I shove into my pocket. I also toss aside the bundle of rope I'd packed earlier; it's now useless. Because my cover got blown too early, my initial plan is dead in the water.

Look at me. Barefoot on the cold concrete floor. Breaths coming out in gasps and teeth chattering. I rub my arms vigorously and hop around, trying to warm myself up somehow.

Then it hits me. The last time I was down here, there was a box containing something I can definitely use now.

After going through a few boxes, I finally locate the old clothes I was looking for. I quickly shuck off my drenched blouse and pull on a ridiculously oversized sweatshirt. It smells faintly familiar, albeit stale, reminiscent of mustiness and dust. The same scent has always lingered at the tip of my nose even in my dreams.

"I only use this stuff. Even if I became destitute, I couldn't give this up. The smell of this body lotion. And see how well it works? You go running around in circles, and eventually, you're here again, right next to me. I don't care if you leave me every now and then. Who else loves you as much as I do?"

The confident voice echoes in my head, but no, I'm not falling for him twice! I'm the only one who really loves me! And then I snap back to reality. I run barefoot up the stairs and pound on the door again.

"Open the door, Soohyun Jung, you son of a bitch! I know what you did, so stop playing games and open the door!"

I keep pounding until my fists ache, but there's no answer.

He might as well just leave me here alone until I starve to death. My cell phone is at the bottom of the pool, so there's no way for me to call for help. Even if some people eventually became suspicious and came to check on me when they're unable to reach me, they'd also be in danger the moment they set foot in this house.

Because now, Soohyun's baring his teeth.

He must have seen through all the games I've been playing.

He has no reason to restrain himself now.

The bastard out there has always been a psycho to begin with, but now he's gone berserk.

CHAPTER

·73·

I find two more old T-shirts in the box and layer them under my sweatshirt, but it isn't enough to keep the chill from creeping into my bones. I sit down halfway up the stairs, curled up in a tight ball, dozing off. I keep waking up with a start and rubbing my arms furiously before dozing off again.

I am still in a semi-dazed stupor, my head foggy, when suddenly I'm knocked off my feet and sent tumbling down a flight of stairs. I hit my head hard on the concrete floor and stagger to my feet, my vision blurry for a moment.

In front of me stands the bastard. Or not? If it's not him, maybe I'm—

A fist flies, and with a *bang!*—

Everything goes black.

CHAPTER

· 74 ·

"You're a ratty, nutty, unworthy bitch, that's what you are," a cheerful voice says.

It sort of rhymes, I think to myself. I'm barely conscious, unable to lift a finger. The very ropes I hid in the cellar with my own hands are now tied tightly around my wrists and ankles. Soohyun keeps working at a knot that binds my ankles.

"It'll leave marks all over me. . . . Even an idiot would see what happened." I probably got a concussion when I landed on my head, as I can't seem to make my tongue work properly. My stomach rumbles, the back of my head throbbing.

By the way, what's this other feeling?

A quick look down and I realize the neck of my sweatshirt is soaked through with a wetness that runs down my face—which isn't water, but blood.

"Don't you worry, it'll be over soon," he whispers with a sinister glee. "Isn't it neat how the bitch who used to get high and flirt with me every day ends up hanging herself in the basement? You've tried the suicide trick once before. Oh, and that *was* an act, wasn't it?"

He tugs hard on the rope. "You should win an Oscar for your performance. Well, good for me. The maids will all testify that you were a junkie, and Dr. Kwon will tell the police about your unstable state of mind. That's what I was hoping for, but I didn't think you'd actually pretend to go out of your mind without even touching the meds."

I don't reward him with an answer. Instead, I try to wrap my throbbing head around what must have happened.

"How long did you think you could fool me, huh? Did you enjoy performing?"

Soohyun thrusts his face close to mine once he secures my ankles.

I let out an audible gasp at the horrible sight of his face.

The pretty face I'd once adored is gone now.

My thick emerald ring has done its job, leaving a deep mark on his flesh. A jagged, elongated line tears across him at an angle, straight from his right eyebrow, past the corner of his eye, all the way down to the corner of his mouth. His nose has also begun to swell and bruise from my kick earlier at the pool, and it looks broken. His face now looks nightmarish and unfamiliar, more like a roll of dough than a person. The only familiar thing is his voice, which is filled with nothing but a bizarre cheerfulness.

"The acting was top-notch!" He spits out blood. "I was fooled at first by the way you clung to me, the way you acted high."

His puffy face twists into a smirk. "I bet you're wondering how I found out, and how long I've known?" Soohyun says, snipping the rope off with a large electric clipper.

"I found the pills you flushed down the toilet. Normally they would have dissolved in the water and disappeared without a trace, but last week I found them before they did, and I've been watching you ever since. I guess you've been pretending to take your meds, acting all this time!"

He stands up, looks down at me for a moment, and then suddenly kicks me hard in the stomach.

I gasp in excruciating pain, air sucked out of me at once.

I spit out the words: "Did you sneak into the next room to spy on me, like you used to with your brother?"

I'm in so much pain that every word shatters me, but it definitely works. Soohyun stops dead in his tracks in the middle of walking toward the door with the bundle of rope. One swollen eye's only half closed, and he looks horrible when he stares back.

"You bitch—"

"What? Was that an old wound?"

And here's the kicking again.

This time, the foot kicks me squarely in the pubic bone, and I can't breathe for a few seconds. But I'm not done yet! I push through the pain and taunt him again.

"You've been doing that—haven't you? Peeping through the hole in the wall in your old room, the one behind the framed painting in my room. You've been watching all along, you pervert."

Another merciless kick, this time to the ribs. It's nauseating to be punched in a stomach full of water. Still, I can't stop. I will not stop.

"You wanted to find your way into a rich family, so you got rid of your own mother, didn't you? A gas leak? Hah! That must have been an easy way out. You were born a monster. You joined this family that way, but because your brother was so nice to you, you idolized him, didn't you? You became obsessed and wanted to keep him to yourself, but you couldn't measure up."

"Shut the fuck up!"

He kicks me once more in the stomach and spits blood in my face. I can feel the disgusting liquid running down my neck as I struggle to breathe.

Soohyun grabs the remaining bundle of rope and goes back behind me. Now I'm really running out of time.

"So you killed your brother's mom, too, right? Did you think he'd appreciate it?"

I muster up some strength to laugh out loud.

"But no, your brother freaked out, didn't he? That's why he ran away from home—to get away from you! That's the only way he *could* have gotten away from you. He couldn't even study abroad because you broke his ankle. You were never going to let go. You drove him crazy. And if not for the money he had, the old man would've died at your hands a long time ago, and that's exactly what happened to him a few weeks ago. Once the old man found out who you really were, he was shaking in his boots! He would've given anything for your brother to come home."

"Shut up, bitch, shut up!"

This time, he kicks me in the ass from behind and continues shouting.

"I saved him! You don't know *anything*. That old bitch tormented him, nagging, nagging, nagging, nagging, nagging! She just wouldn't *shut up*, driving him up the wall until his ears bled! He couldn't breathe, couldn't do a thing, was always afraid! I *saved* my brother! Even that old fucker would have thanked me had he known! It was in everyone's best interest!"

Then there's a kick to my head, which leaves me dizzy and light-headed. But I press on.

"Is that why you framed the house staffer? Because your brother liked her daughter, because they clicked?"

My vision is blurry and I see things in double, but I have to go on.

"You got between them and made everyone believe you had a crush on Hyojin, like you did with me, but she didn't feel for you easily. So you get off on getting rid of everyone in your way? In one fell swoop, no less! Framing the staffer, killing your brother's mother, getting rid of your competitor? And then you expected your brother to thank you, you moron!"

Thwack!

Suddenly, a hand shoots out from behind me and puts a snare around my neck.

No!

"But what can I say—your plan was destined to fail, because here I am." I feel the hands tightening the knot flinch. "Sorry to say this, but your brother really loved me. And you know what?"

"You're bullshitting."

"That's what you want to believe. But it's true. He was sick of you. Why else would he leave home and stick around in a shithole of a half-basement with me? All because of you. It's because you repulsed him!"

My breath catches in my throat as the snare tightens around my neck.

"Say whatever you like. You're about to die."

But I can hear the quiver sneak into his voice. He struggles behind me as his hands keep slipping. I go on, trying to sound nonchalant.

"Sure, he beat the shit out of me, but I took pity on him and kept him because he begged me not to leave him!"

I choke as the rope tightens. I don't have much time left.

"All because of you! You made him feel like he was constantly being watched in his own house, in his own room, by his little brother. Because you stopped him from studying abroad, killing or chasing away all the people who got in your way! That's why your brother turned into such a freak, too, you bastard!"

"My brother was a freak? How dare you, bitch! If not for bitches like you and Hyojin, we would have been just fine! We could have had a good life! We did, until you dared to lay that dirty hand on my brother!"

He begins to stutter, and I hear something from behind me, as if he's dragging something across the floor. My stomach, head, and pubic bone throb from the kicks earlier. Even without turning around, I can tell what's about to happen.

This madman is trying to carry out my own plan. He wants to hang me with the same rope I intended to hang him with, and make it look like I committed suicide in this underground chamber. He's going to make it look as if I, heartbroken, hanged myself over his rejection.

That's the exact story I've painstakingly crafted for him while pretending to be as drugged as he wanted me to be. If everything went according to my plan, I would have kept him on his toes and on edge, and made him look so unstable that, when he was found dead, the maids would think they'd all seen it coming, based on the changes he'd gone through the past few weeks. I've been hanging around, buying useless things, digging up the garden, and trying to fix up his brother's room, all to agitate him enough that I could rip the mask off his face and reveal the maniacal psychopath underneath. If only I hadn't gotten caught too soon.

The puffy-faced monster slips his hands under my armpits and yanks me to my feet. I try to fight him off, but he doesn't let go of me even as he tumbles to the ground. I slam my head back into the concrete and my jaw rattles, a wave of excruciating pain jolting through me.

Then, from somewhere beyond the open basement door, I hear the faint sound of a child crying. It's a real cry this time. At first it is a small feline purr, then it grows louder and louder. Soohyun must have left Seung-Joon somewhere in the living room on the first floor. Soon, the baby starts wailing at full volume.

Terrified he might choke, I crawl on the floor, squirming like a caterpillar, hog-tied, but I don't make it far.

Soohyun now tries to attach a rope to the noose around my neck so he can hang me from an exposed beam overhead. I feel his hands shifting and knotting the cord behind me.

"So . . . you killed your brother with your own hands?"

It takes every ounce of strength I have left to spit out those words.

The twitchy fingers take a brief pause, then move again. The rope begins to tighten around my neck. The moment he slips his hands under my armpits and drags me up, I have no choice but to plant my feet firmly on the ground. Otherwise the rope above me will strangle me.

He lifts me up and stands me on a footstool he's brought out. It would have been a very romantic position if not for the circumstances. We're standing face-to-face, me in his arms.

But now I'm horrified to even look at that swollen face. I deserve a prize for having spent the last few weeks pretending to flirt with him, cling to him, and be in love with him just to survive. It's too unfair for me to die like this after all that I went through.

He steps up on the scaffold and hooks the end of the noose around my neck. My end is near. All he has to do is kick this footstool from beneath me and I'll be done. So it's only now that I can make my voice heard.

"Is that why you killed your brother, because he was too important?"

"What?" A dumbfounded look crosses Soohyun's doughy face.

"I watched the whole video. You really didn't know? It was all in there."

"What are you talking about, bitch?" He looks genuinely puzzled.

"If you didn't know like me, you should. Your fucking precious brother had a surveillance camera set up at the entrance to spy on me! That's how much you fucked him up, you fucking creep, and it caught everything you did in gory detail!"

"Shut up, don't give me that crap!" Soohyun takes a step back. "Because I don't have a clue what you're talking about." There's a genuine gleam of disbelief in his other, more intact eye.

"Are you sure you don't remember, or was it so horrible that you just wiped it out of your head, you asshole?" I scream, even as I choke, the rope digging into my neck. "That night, after I hit your brother in the head and ran out, you ran in a few minutes later, I saw it, I saw it, I saw it!"

Soohyun shakes his head. "Don't lie, bitch, you killed my brother, he died because of *you*!" The corners of his mouth, distorted by his swollen nose, twist into a crooked smile, making him look like a Halloween mask made of flour dough. "You killed him! If not for you, he would be alive and well."

"Get a grip, asshole, you ran in a few minutes after I left!"

"No, absolutely not, that can't be right." Soohyun shakes his head desperately, tears streaming down his face. Blood drips everywhere.

"He was still alive! He was just disoriented, and you stopped his breathing by plugging his nose and mouth with your own hands! Then you kept him in a freezer the whole time, and then you buried him in the garden and planted a sapling! Don't you remember? Killing me won't help! That video is in a safe place, and if anything happens to me, I'll have it sent to the police! Why did you do it? Why did you kill your brother, the one you loved so much, with your own hands? To punish him for running away from home and falling in love with me? To have him all to yourself forever?"

I scream until the rope squeezes the breath out of me. "Is that why you killed him, you son of a bitch?"

"Shut up!" Soohyun yells, and kicks the stool from under me.

Boom!

In an instant, there is no longer any foothold. The last thing I see before the blood rushes to my face and my vision blurs is that doughy, swollen face of his.

He whispers sweetly in my ear.

"Shut the fuck up, please."

CHAPTER
·75·

Suspended in midair hanging on nothing but a rope is the worst sensation.

There's nothing to support me, nothing to lean or step on, just a rope holding my body up.

My own weight keeps pulling me down and choking me.

I'm slowly losing consciousness, not to mention any hope that I'll survive. Weakly flailing and gasping like an earthworm on a bed of salt, I gasp for air in vain.

"This is for my brother," Soohyun whispers, looking into my eyes as they probably turn more lifeless by the second.

"For my poor brother who's gone because of you. Someone who was my whole world. Don't you dare think I'm doing this for money. I've been dying to do this since the very first day you set your dirty little feet in this house."

"Seung . . . Joon." I'm too out of breath to even utter the two syllables.

"No worries. His uncle is next of kin to take over, and I promise we'll thrive just as well without you." Soohyun thrusts his swollen face to sneer at me. "And you know what? In this cursed house where everyone drops dead, it wouldn't be too weird for that little brat to get into an accident, either. If that happens, of course, all the money goes to—"

His horrifying words threaten to take away the last ounce of strength left in my body.

But I manage to rasp out, "Where's . . . his body?"

"What?" His grin changes to something else, a flutter of unease in his eyes.

"Not found—" I want to let out a cynical laugh just as he did, but I can't.

"What did you say?"

"Nowhe—"

"Bitch!"

Suddenly, I can breathe precious air again. Soohyun's arms are wrapped around me tightly to lift me up and keep me from choking.

"Tell me! Where the hell is he? Where did you hide him? You dug him up! You stole him! Tell me where he is!"

I clam up.

"Where is he, where is he?"

He forces me around so we come face-to-face, each of us seething with hatred. His arms lock me in this bizarre, hateful embrace—my exact intention—drilling a hole in my face with his glare.

Too preoccupied with me, he doesn't notice someone sneaking through the open door.

He doesn't notice the person putting down a knife and instead retrieving the rope I abandoned on the floor before sneaking up behind him.

"Start talking, bitch!"

As he spews, splashing my face with bloody spittle, hands shoot out from behind him and wrap a rope around his neck tightly.

He lets go of me, the rope around my neck tightening once more.

"Dad! Dad, I'm down here!" Hyojin yells as she pulls the rope tighter.

The moment I spot Mr. Kim on the stairs, my vision goes black. The last of the air has been choked out of me.

CHAPTER

·76·

His nose might be broken and his face battered, but Soohyun isn't easily subdued by just one woman, and Hyojin definitely needs some di-
vine intervention to defeat a man blind with rage all by herself.

Soohyun struggles to break free and elbows Hyojin in the side,
causing her to lose her grip on the rope and grunt in pain. At that moment, he manages to kick Hyojin in the gut.

As Mr. Kim seems unable to decide whether to help me or Hyojin
first, the ropes binding my wrists finally snap. All this time, I've been
working at the rope with the small knife I'd found in one of the boxes
and pocketed earlier. I drop the knife and squeeze my fingers through
the snare around my neck to allow myself to take short, essential
breaths.

"Footstool! Footstool! I plead through gritted teeth, and Kim hurries over to push the footstool under me before cutting the rope with
one swift flick of his wrist. The moment the cord is cut, I burst out
coughing, gasping for a rush of air.

I urge him away. "I'm good, go help her, now!"

I can still hear Seung-Joon wailing at full volume somewhere upstairs.

Soohyun and Hyojin are wrestling on the floor—Soohyun clutching her hair, and Hyojin unable to move her head, almost on her knees
as he shakes and shakes her.

I catch a glimpse of Mr. Kim picking up a can of motor oil and smacking Soohyun in the head with a loud *thwack*. The familiar sound of impact on a skull rings through the basement, and when Soohyun whirls around on him for a counterattack, Mr. Kim smacks him squarely in the face.

"Agh!"

A pathetic groan. Soohyun's nose must be broken, again.

"Here! Over here!" Hyojin screams at the top of her lungs, throwing the rope in my direction.

I grasp and wrestle it around Soohyun's neck as he thrashes around frantically.

Hyojin comes running to my aid, breathless. The two of us struggle with the rope around his neck, but we're no match for the angry Soohyun fighting for his life. He swings his arms around, and I'm now too exhausted to even hold on to the rope for much longer.

"Dad! Dad!"

Hyojin screams for Mr. Kim.

As Mr. Kim runs over to help, Soohyun stops struggling all of a sudden. Even before Mr. Kim reaches us or lays a finger on Soohyun, strength drains from his body.

Hyojin and I cast each other a short, baffled look. But no time to ponder—the next moment, we're exerting the last of our strength and pulling on the rope harder and harder.

Finally, the last trace of light in Soohyun's half-open eyes disappears.

CHAPTER

·77·

People prove to be generous to those who have suffered too much misfortune at once. Especially to a young woman who's received a large inheritance, especially when they learn that she has been a victim of domestic violence and that her estranged husband, not heard from since the death of her father-in-law, has been found dead in her front yard. The sheer absurdity of it is enough to raise eyebrows. They whisper among themselves, I'm sure: "What's the use of all that money? I'd rather have a normal life. Do you think she might have killed her husband to keep the inheritance to herself?"

But all evidence points otherwise. I have a video of my brother-in-law, who lived in the same house as I did and whom I visibly trusted and was fond of, murdering my husband.

"I found the camcorder while cleaning out the basement, and I was so shocked that I confronted my brother-in-law, who was swimming in the pool at the time."

The story goes: The entitled younger son was never loved by his father. When his older brother ran away from home after getting fed up with his strict parents, he felt a brief glimmer of hope, but even so, his father always favored the eldest son. So the younger son made sure to keep tabs on his brother. He had been ordered by his father to watch him and bring him back home, so he had been watching and following his brother—and his brother's live-in girlfriend—

everywhere. One day, when the couple argued and violence erupted, the sister-in-law hit his brother over the head in self-defense and fled. Soohyun entered his house and killed his stunned brother in the heat of the moment. Soohyun thought he could pin all the blame on his sister-in-law, but when she fled to his family's house with their child in her arms, he decided to put on an act for the time being.

"I dropped by the babysitter's and took my child to my husband's in-laws. I'm an orphan, and I had nowhere else to turn for help. Fortunately, my father-in-law welcomed me into his house."

The house aides also give supportive testimonies. They tell the police how the daughter-in-law and grandson appeared on the doorstep one day.

The youngest son in the family was sweet but always had a bit of a dangerous edge to him.

He seemed to be getting along with the sister-in-law at first, but after his father died, he was no longer his friendly former self, which deeply troubled the sister-in-law.

They remember how he was livid with his sister-in-law for wanting to remodel the house, and one rainy day, he even started doing strange things, like digging all over the garden, screaming like a madman. Maybe he lost his mind over jealousy because his sister-in-law inherited almost everything?

Hyojin also provides a supportive statement.

"I'm so grateful to the family because they took me in as a caregiver twice, and they gave my dad a job when he was trying to start a new life after getting out of rehab. Jae-Young called to tell me to come pick up some things I'd left behind, so I went over to the mansion. By the time my dad and I got there, she was on the floor, not even breathing, and Mr. Soohyun was dead next to her. They got into a really bad hand-to-hand fight, and she would have been the one who was dead if he hadn't slipped and fallen trying to choke her. I don't know how a woman could fight off a man all by herself. I think he was trying to kill her when no one was home. He was probably trying to force-feed her the pills she was taking and make it look like suicide.

The pills were scattered all over the basement floor. I mean, how horrifying! I think that's why the chairman used to tell me he was scared of Soohyun. That's why he gave all the inheritance to his older son's wife and baby. I bet Soohyun went to the Seoul law firm and checked the revised will and lost his temper. The circumstances of the chairman's death were also suspicious."

My husband's body is found by the pool, in a vacant plot beneath a fresh flower bed. The police believe Soohyun buried the body there, close to home, out of guilt. I'm told Soohyun probably got confused and couldn't remember where he'd buried the body, and panic must have set in as he started digging up the beds that day.

Investigations large and small ensue, dragging on for a while, but the expensive lawyers covering my back prove their worth. They make all the suspicious narratives scatter into thin air.

The dead can't talk, and there's no one left in this whole house to tell a different side of the story.

Speaking of which, now it's just the three of us.

The three of us, who deserve a hefty reward for what we had to go through at the hands of these people—the three of us, whose lives are forever changed.

EPILOGUE

HYOJIN
NOW

"It's time we talked about Seung-Joon," the woman starts off.

Even after everything that has happened between us, I still can't bring myself to address her by her name.

I cut her short and offer a smirk. "What is there to talk about? You're already a more real mom than I've ever been to him. It's not a matter of birth, it's about how much you care. I guess I actually believe in the love of the caretaker now."

We're sitting on a bench in the garden, lazily watching the flowers sway in the breeze. The pool has been drained, cleaned, and covered. As the season gives in to the cold, we won't have much use for it for a while, and even then, I doubt we'll be in the mood to so much as look in its direction for some time, after what took place there.

"Seriously, I promise I won't show up when he's all grown up to announce, *I'm your birth mom.*"

The woman casts me a subtle, pointed look.

"I don't know if he deserves me," I insist. "Of course, I know he's innocent, but I don't seem to feel anything for him. I can't stop thinking about that crazy night I slept with Soohyun after being rejected by your ex. Needless to say, I can't get over whose kid he is, so there's that. When I saw you on the train that day, I made my decision on the spot.

I guess I was just so overwhelmed by the whole 'kid' thing. I just wanted to hand him over to someone and let it go."

"Oddly enough, I never think about whose child Seung-Joon is." This time, the woman smirks. "Maybe it's because he sort of fell into my arms out of nowhere, and we had this instant connection. It's weird, isn't it? I've never felt this way about anyone else."

"You must have a weakness for the Jungs."

We share a hearty laugh for a moment.

"Well, both of us are guilty as charged," I say. "We got carried away and ended up screwing up our lives."

"Thanks, though." The woman shoots me an arresting gaze and blurts out, "Thank you for that day—when I came home from the hospital and locked myself in the basement and we had a real talk. If you hadn't told me the whole truth, I would have kept suspecting you and walked right into his trap."

"To be fair, I went a little overboard with the shock therapy. Locking you in the basement with a corpse was a bit too much. Part of me probably wanted to torture you a little. I had already made up my mind to team up with you to take revenge on this family, but I did hold some grudges. I'm not exactly the forgiving type, you see, and I couldn't stop thinking about all the what-ifs, how I wanted to spend time with Hyun-Wook, and everything else I so desperately wanted."

"Well, I did have some good moments with him, but . . ."

"I know, they're not the good kind of memories; they're the kind that bring you nothing but pain. Still, I was foolish enough to hope something might happen between us, and I wanted to believe I could be happy with him. I know what it's like to be abused by the people you love, but the heart wants what it wants."

Our eyes lock for a lingering moment.

"Still, I can't thank you enough for siding with me. You could have just stuck with Soohyun and taken it all out on me, and God knows I wouldn't have seen it coming. And to think I thought the absolute worst of you until I realized what was really going on—"

I shrug. "At first, I was just as fooled. Can you believe I thought

Soohyun had a crush on me? I couldn't do anything about him because of the way he was—looking all innocent and sweet. He kept coming between me and his brother but I couldn't push him away. I never suspected it was because of Hyun-Wook, not me. I didn't even realize he was framing my mom."

"Then when the hell did you realize all that?"

"The day I slept with Soohyun. Funny, huh?" I giggle to myself. The woman just stares at me blankly, not finding it funny at all.

"At first, I was a pretty decent double agent, because that jerk and the old man each paid me separately to spy on you. I didn't realize what kind of person Soohyun was, so I wasn't suspicious at all. But it was a good deal for me; I got double paychecks and satisfied my curiosity at the same time. But then I thought I should talk to Hyun-Wook so I wouldn't have any regrets. I wanted to give him one last chance."

"Last chance?"

"I'd always thought it was Hyun-Wook who framed my mom. Soohyun, that freak, told me so, and I believed him. He said Hyun-Wook must have gotten so tired of being pestered by his abusive mom that he wanted to kill her, so he staged the whole thing."

"That nutcase framed his brother, too."

"I know how out of touch this sounds, but I still couldn't help my feelings for Hyun-Wook. I thought he tore my family apart and ruined my life, but he still gave me those old flutterings when I saw him again. So there I was, wanting to give him one last chance. I thought I'd forgive him if he only reciprocated my feelings."

My laughter is tinged with wistfulness.

"I saw you getting beaten up every day, and it reminded me of myself when my dad was drunk and hitting me. And yet, there I was, still wanting your boyfriend all the same. So I decided to seduce him that day. I pretended to run into him at the convenience store near where he was working. But he wouldn't budge. He said he liked you, that you made him feel at ease, and that he wanted to marry you. I drank a lot and came home crying, and Soohyun and I had a few more drinks, and we talked about his brother, and I cried some more, and I guess he was getting a bit emotional, too, because that night, the two of us spent the night together. But in the middle of it all, he started whispering his brother's name, over and over and over again, like a chant. He kept mumbling it, and his eyes were rolling back in his skull. That wasn't the Soohyun I always knew and that's when I realized the truth. I was like, *Oh, maybe the stories he's told me aren't exactly true.* So I started digging. I looked into everything that happened since Soohyun came into this family."

I glance down at my shaking hands. Even now that everything's over, this story still has the power to send me into a fit of tremors.

"And finally, I discovered that he was behind everything that went wrong with them."

"You didn't know any of this when you first got the caregiver offer, did you?"

I shake my head no.

"Not an inkling. I still thought Soohyun was this sunny little brother who had a crush on me. After my mom committed suicide, my dad went into rehab, and I was left alone attending an academy to become a nurse's aide. A few years later, I ran into him by chance. He brazenly asked me if I would consider working for him as a caregiver. He said his brother had moved out of the house and that his father had a stroke shortly after. At first, I thought he still had feelings for me, and that's why he offered me this job. Honestly, I was sick and tired of the place, but I needed the money. I also wanted to see this place again, since I still had feelings for Hyun-Wook. But then while I was working here, Soohyun brought up my mom's theft. He told me how his brother framed her, because he had been bullied by his mom and lost his patience. Then he gave me your address, told me his brother moved out of the house and was living with a woman. He asked me to spy on you. He knew I still had feelings for Hyun-Wook, and he used that to his advantage. The old man asked me to spy on you, too, so the timing was perfect."

"Yes, that's too perfect."

We smirk at each other.

"That jerk had been playing me from the beginning, and he'd been using me to get back at you."

"Still, had I just brought Seung-Joon here and left right away—"
The woman lets out a deep sigh.

"No, even if you hadn't stayed, he would have forced you back into
this house somehow. By God, he wouldn't have let you go. We plotted
to send you a series of strange texts to keep you on edge, get you
drugged, and later, send you to a mental hospital or drive you over the
edge and make you kill yourself so we could split the inheritance with
the kid. The old man had no intention of giving Soohyun a dime of his
money. He saw his younger son's real nature very early on. It freaked
him out."

"Right."

"I don't know how he found out, but he seemed to have been the
first of us to know. Soohyun didn't dare touch the old man because of
the inheritance, but I think the old man knew something was fishy
with his wife's death, the death of Soohyun's birth mother, Hyun-
Wook's accident, and some other little incidents. That's why he was
terrified of being left alone with Soohyun, and why he was so obsessed
with Hyun-Wook and wanted to bring him back home."

"So both his sons were monsters, after all."

We keep silent for a moment, each thinking about the old man.
The old man stood idly by while this whole tragedy unfolded, and he
can't escape his part in it, but maybe he's the most pitiful of all, because
in the end, the blood of the monster he feared so much took everything he'd accumulated in life. That's probably the punishment befitting his crime.

"Had I been kept in the dark and not found out about Soohyun's
true colors, I would have gone along with his plan. I'd be out there
creeping you out and then showing up as a caregiver and making you
lose your mind, and he'd be pretending to be a nice guy and stabbing
you in the back. But once I found out who he really was, I got a mind
of my own. I kept pretending to be on his side, buying time, but I was
waiting for the right moment to join forces with you and stab *him* in
the back. The whole 'siding with the enemies of your enemies' thing is
kind of funny."

But despite my giggles, the woman's face remains serious.

"So, Mr. Kim, no, your father, is—"

"He came back from the brink of death in rehab, so I decided to make up with him." I shrug, yet again. "Of course, the bitterness is still there, but I feel like he did his time. So I strategically partnered with him to get our revenge. I asked him to help me, and I arranged for him to get a job in this house under someone else's identity—as Mr. Kim. You can say I've been working with the enemy to get even with my worst enemy."

"It was a big help. If not for your father—" The woman frowns, fiddling with the scarf around her neck. I can still see the bloody bruises the rope left.

"No need to fret. Thanks to you, he got a house, a car, and money. Thanks for taking care of all that. But I'm gonna keep a close eye on him, and if he starts drinking again, I'm gonna take it all away from him."

We hang our heads and chuckle.

"So what are you going to do with this house? Are you going to sell it? I mean, with all the rumors, who's going to buy it?"

She shakes her head at my words. "Yes, what a shame. This place has really grown on me. I'm thinking about ripping it all down and just starting from scratch. Speaking of which, it would be nice if your father could supervise the construction. I'll pay him a lot. It's not about the money, it's about having someone I can trust. I've got no one, you know."

Yeah, just like me. That's how we both have gotten ourselves into this mess in the first place. Thing is, I could have just as easily sided with Soohyun. For me, it was a question of which one of them I'd enjoy watching suffer more. The woman who stole my first love, or the man who ruined my first love. But she sees me. I see her. I wanted to be stronger, I wanted to be different, I wanted to start over. Alone, it was impossible, but together, we could make it happen. We both felt we could start over, together.

"Okay, I'm all for it, as long as we can keep my dad from going out and having drinks with the crew."

"I want the house completely modern, clean, and pretty."

334 · SE-AH JANG

"With an elevator and everything?"

"That would be great. Tear open the whole floor and make the kitchen a big open space."

"I'm sick of those creaky wooden stairs."

"How do you feel about those cool metal floating staircases that look like they're suspended in the air?"

"And all new furniture, I assume?"

"Absolutely. I'm not a fan of tacky Victorian furniture. Why not go clean and modern, just with a flair of subtle vintage here and there?"

"Oh my, aren't we kindred spirits? And all that money definitely bought you some class, I see."

"You have no idea—I've always been a snob. I've just never had the money to throw away."

"Good for you, good for you."

We laugh again, careful not to hurt our sides, which are still sore from Soohyun's kicks. It's nice to be able to sit here in the sun and talk, smiling. So life does offer days like this, too.

"About Seung-Joon—"

"Huh?"

"Are you sure you're okay with me raising him?"

"Well, on top of the fortune he's going to inherit—I'd be grateful if you could raise him well." I smile, feigning nonchalance and ignoring a pang in my chest.

Of course, it would work out fine. I didn't even like the idea of having a child, and I really shouldn't be feeling this modicum of bitterness. I'll just watch from a distance sometimes. Now, now. Everything's alright now.

"You know, I'm terrible with kids." The woman shakes her head. "It's been so hard to pretend to know what I'm doing."

"You can get a sitter, or a new maid. What are you going to do with all the money you have?" I deliberately play it cool to hide the slight tremor in my voice.

"I think it would be really helpful to have someone living with me and helping me out."

"Like an expert?"

She smiles. "Yeah, someone with parenting experience, someone with professional qualifications. Someone like a caregiver. Someone who will love and care for him like he's their own."

I quickly avert my gaze from the woman's, whose eyes burned into mine. My eyes well up with unwelcome tears.

I clear my throat. "What about the pay? That kind of expert would surely cost a lot?"

"Oh, sure, if you're that kind of person, I'll give you the best pay in the business. What do you say?"

"You sure can talk."

I feel a slow wave of warmth spreading through my chest. Maybe—yes, maybe it's time I harbor something like this in a heart that has only ever cultivated hate, even with my own child in my arms. Seung-Joon and me, maybe we can start over, too.

After a long pause, the woman speaks again. "Hey, since when, do you think?"

"What?"

"Him. How do you think he became such a monster?"

"Well, I'm sure it wasn't like that from the start, it was maybe just envy or something. He must have heard his dad's family was rich and wormed his way in at the expense of his mother. But even the most brilliant sociopath was a kid once, and he must have had a hard time getting used to his new life for a while. When the older brother who was six years his senior looked out for him, it must have been nice. For someone who has no one to turn to, that's something irresistible—to have someone, a real family, on your side—we both know that."

The woman nods.

"But it wasn't just love he felt for his brother," I say. "I don't know if it was love, devotion, obsession, lust, or something entirely different, something darker. I'm sure he wanted to get rid of the mother who was bullying his brother, and I'm sure he wanted to get rid of me, the girl who was chasing his beloved around. And I bet he was seething with jealousy the whole time as he watched his brother start a new family with someone. In the end, it was that damn love and jealousy that drove him to end his brother's life. It may have been a momentary lapse, but in the end, in that moment, when he killed his beloved brother with his own hands, he must have been already dead inside. At least I think so."

"Did you also see that look he had at the last moment?"

"You mean that night in the basement?"

I confess I do remember. Yes, I remember the moment when the two of us were strangling him with all our might, one of us on the verge of collapsing and barely able to help, both of us so desperate. I still don't understand how we could finish him off all on our own. He could have easily thrown us off himself, couldn't he? But instead, he let his hands fall in a quiet surrender, as if the will to live was leaving the body. Even before my dad ran over to help, a lamblike, helpless look went over his face, and he just gave in. Just like that.

Maybe in that moment, he wanted to reset his life. Maybe he also wanted to return to the very beginning, before everything had gone so horribly, irrevocably wrong.

Jae-Young and I get up from the bench.

Neither of us looks back as we walk side by side toward the house. Still not fully trusting each other, still a lot to put behind us. But one thing is clear. Neither of us will ever be the same. Some of us, after all, get to start over—to be reborn.

AUTHOR'S NOTE

"A woman studies her tired face in the bathroom mirror on a train at the crack of dawn." Everything started from that single image.

One sleepless night, this image drowned out all the other fleeting thoughts in my head and stayed with me as this vivid impression. This woman was terrified for some reason, and splashed her face with tap water after taking a long look at herself in the mirror, washing her hands. She was on the run, and couldn't wait to escape whatever was chasing her.

The more I tossed and turned in bed, thinking, the more this pale, fragile woman transformed from that first impression, getting stronger and ready to fight, in the story I was brewing. Ironically, she got herself into a lot of trouble thanks to that resilient streak she had, her desire to survive at all costs.

And she grew on me. Because she was no "good girl." Because she was so realistically desperate and seemed to sink in the quicksand of reality as she tried to save herself.

I believe many of us, including myself, must have also experienced a point in life when things seemed to only get worse, no matter how hard we tried. So I wanted to write a cathartic story in which twisted, realistic characters went beyond the ethically acceptable measures to solve the problems they faced.

Then I injected the story with some gothic elements I've always been partial to—a dark, eerie mansion, a family with dark secrets, and two ordinary women who find themselves in a strange place—and that's how *A Twist of Fate* was born.

A Twist of Fate revolves around the two main female characters, Jae-Young and Hyojin, but everyone in this story is a victim and simultaneously at fault to some extent. I'm a big believer that "No one's entirely innocent or evil," so I wanted to explore that evil side of our human nature, our instinct to strike, whatever the consequence, when we're provoked enough. Of course, that's why I believe in living as mindfully as we can so we do not become someone's trauma in one way or another.

In that sense, *A Twist of Fate* might be a novel about desire. Everyone in this book—Jae-Young, Hyojin, Hyun-Wook, Soohyun, and Chairman—all wanted something out of their reach, and ended up hurting a lot of people, trying to get their hands on what they desired.

Koreans say every finger aches the same when you bite it, but I'd say I have a weak spot for Soohyun, if I have to pick one character of all.

A beautiful young man with a sensitive side.

He's no heartless psychopath, but a deeply troubled individual who came to develop an unhealthy obsession with his loved one because of his deep-rooted attachment issues (and this is not to say any of his actions can be justified by any means).

I didn't dwell on this question while working on the rest of the book, but I cannot forget the night when I wrote the part where Soohyun dies. After finishing up that part, I couldn't stop pacing around my room for a while, ruminating on the incomprehensible pang of pain and sadness I felt for Soohyun.

That was a first for me, because I usually don't get so emotionally attached to fictional characters I create. I still can't be sure if Soohyun loathed Jae-Young from start to end with the same unwavering intensity, or if even for a moment, he found in himself a flicker of some gentler emotion for her, just as he did for his brother.

Now it's really time to send these characters on their way, out into the world, and finish this story.

ACKNOWLEDGMENTS

I'd love to thank everyone who lent me such strength as I labored to bring this book into the world:

Producer Jung-Eun Kwon on the Kyobo IP team, who saw this book's potential and pushed me—with just the perfect amount of carrot and stick—to polish the book. How happy I was to find out we have just the same tastes in thrillers!

President Jadeok Joo at Aphros Media, who helped me add some warmth to this book that could have gone in a very different direction, and who gifted me an amazing cover for the Korean edition.

President Moon-Hee Yang and lovely Joo-Hye Choi, who always showered me with comforting words and indispensable advice.

The incredible Jenny Chen, who had an eye for the raw potential of this book before its refinement and helped make *A Twist of Fate* become the best version of itself. The amazing team at Bantam, thank you for joining me on this tough journey with this book.

S. L. Park, who brought this hefty book to such vivid life in another language.

Barbara, my agent, who paved the path for *A Twist of Fate* in an entirely new world beyond my home country. Mi-Kyung Kim, the coolest essayist I know. (I love you, auntie!)

My beloved family: Dad, sister Sung-Lee Jang, my furry muse Snow White (Baekseolgi), and especially my mom, who always wondered what the hell was going on in her rebellious daughter's head, thank you for always being there for me.

Last, you, my reader. I had such fun writing this story—if my readers have as much fun reading the book, what more could I possibly hope for? From the bottom of my heart—thank you for picking up this book. I hope that you had as much fun reading *A Twist of Fate* as I had writing it, and that, in the end, I managed to make you believe that anyone gets a chance to be born again—to start anew.